ONCE UPON A MIDNIGHT DESERT

A SHANNON SERIES (4)

JOHN EVANS

In memory of my sister, Cherie. To Lee and Barbara.

CHAPTER 1

Near Kabul, Afghanistan

The U.S. Army platoon slowly topped a small rise on the well-worn dirt road they had been following since before daylight. Some 400 meters off the main road, nestled in green pastures with trees surrounding it stood a cluster of three buildings. An important Taliban leader and his entourage were reported to be held up inside them. The soldiers orders were to capture or eliminate the terrorists.

In the early morning quiet the soldiers were commanded to spread out and wait for orders to proceed. Captain Colbert quietly spoke into the radio headset while looking at the buildings through his optics. Off to his right another team was getting into position to lead the assault.

The soldiers hunkered down and studied the buildings for forty-five minutes while waiting for word to proceed. Several soldiers had crawled out onto natural berms, watching for signs of enemy movement. All of the troops had either binoculars or scopes. To the back and to the left of their staging position were steep rocky hills. For the moment the morning feels peaceful.

Colbert put down his binoculars and looked around. In a low shout he called out, "Sergeant Lee!" Motioning for him to come to his position. Sergeant First Class Dawson Lee gave him a nod and slid down from the small berm. Tall and lanky, he ran, hunkered down, to his commander.

"Yes Sir?"

The captain put his hand on Dawson's shoulder and grinned.

"Sergeant Lee, I hate to do this to you but I want you to babysit the lady correspondent and her cameraman. Keep them back out of harm's way. If things get hot, don't let them get in the way. Move them back here if you have to."

Dawson gave him a questioning look.

"Why me Sir?"

Colbert laughed.

"I think that lady reporter is sweet on you, Lee. She's always watching every move you make. I think she will listen to you if things get sticky. Just keep her out of our hair. We cannot afford any screw ups or interference while we do this thing."

"Okay Sir. Will do!" Dawson said with some resignation.

Sergeant Lee started his way down the line of soldiers hiding behind the rocks and berms alongside the roadway. He stopped and instructed his men to follow Sergeant Blevins when the call came to move out.

"Sergeant Lee. How come we gotta follow Blevins?" asked Corporal Stafford, a stocky built kid from Minnesota.

"I have to see to the reporters Stafford. You'll be okay. Just stick with Blevins."

"Something doesn't feel right Sarge. I'm getting bad vibes," he said, his face filled with anguish.

Dawson squatted down and looked at Stafford. He patted his shoulder and gave him a small smile.

"Come on Stafford. We've been through this before. Be careful. Watch yourself. Stay focused."

"Okay Sarge. I'll do my best," he said with a sigh.

Before moving on, Dawson scanned across the field to the small group of buildings. Other than smoke rising from a chimney, no other movement or signs of life were evident. A shiver of dread coursed through his veins when he looked at the distance of open ground they had to cross. It reminded him of Pickett's Charge in the Battle of Gettysburg in 1863. Three fourths of his troops were lost trying to cross the long stretch of open ground before reaching the enemy. The Southern troops were totally exposed and vulnerable to whatever the North could throw at them. Dawson said a quick prayer and moved on to where the correspondent and her cameraman were positioned.

Hunched down behind a berm covered with a stubby growth of scrub brush, Lianne Palmer, CNN Correspondent, was giving a report as her cameraman sat on the ground while filming her. She spied Dawson working his way toward her. Careful to stay concealed, he scurried low to the ground to her position.

Smiling, Lianne had the cameraman tracked Dawson's arrival. She was giving a spiel about who he was and where he was from. Lianne admired his six-foot two inch slender frame. He had dark blond hair and that sweet altar boy looks.

"Sergeant Lee. Tell us what is going on and when the assault will begin."

Slightly taken aback, Dawson motioned for her to cut the interview.

"Listen, Miss Palmer. We will be moving out at any moment. Things can get dicey and dangerous real fast. You two will stay behind me. If we come under fire you are to immediately drop to the ground. Lay low and wait for my instructions. You and your cameraman are taking a big chance. Don't do anything stupid to jeopardize yourself or this operation."

Lianne stuck out her bottom lip and gave a faux pout. Her short black hair and bright blue eyes glistened in the rising sun.

"Awe shucks Sergeant Lee. We will be careful. You don't worry about us. You won't even know we're behind you. You just do your thing. We're not new at this."

Dawson looked at her with a slight air of irritation. He worried his bottom lip with his teeth for a moment.

"I know you have a job to do like I do, but this is a very dangerous situation. Once we step off, we are sitting ducks if we come under fire. I just don't want you guys to get hurt."

Lianne gave a little laugh.

"Are you concerned because I am a woman, Sergeant Lee?"

She straightened up and stuck out her chest, such as it was. Lianne was short and stocky built and wearing the bullet proof vest, she had little shape to her. In spite of that, she was still an attractive woman.

"To be honest Miss Palmer, yes. Yes I am uneasy with you out here. I could not handle you getting hurt in my care. My conscious would not be able to handle it."

"Well Sergeant. I'll take that as a chivalrous compliment. I thank you for your concern. I will be careful and I will follow your instructions."

CHAPTER 2

The word came down the line to move out. In unison the platoon rose up and cautiously stepped out onto the grassy field and headed toward their objective. The other platoon to Dawson's right were already half way to the buildings.

Captain Colbert and the men spread out as they slowly moved forward. Once all of the platoon was fifteen meters ahead, Dawson led the correspondent and her cameraman along behind them. Dawson, as well as most of the other soldiers were experiencing a sense of time distortion in which everything seemed to be going in slow motion. The building seemed to be further away and they felt they were walking on an ocean of soft sand rather than foot-high grass.

Sheer terror grabbed at their lungs. Every man was acutely aware of their vulnerability as they moved across the wide open expanse of ground. Glancing back, Dawson noticed Lianne and her cameraman were just off to his right. Lianne's face appeared serene in the midst of the dangerous moment. He wondered how she could be so calm. Does she have any idea of how precarious the situation is right now? He shook his head in amazement.

Cautiously watching all around him, Dawson continued on. He felt like his body was trying to shrink up into the relative safety of the bullet proof vest he was wearing. He hunched forward as he gingerly crept, praying that there were no mines in the area. Other than a few tactical commands, there had been little voice traffic on the headset.

In an instant the air began to crackle with sounds of small arms fire. The soldiers dropped immediately to the ground. They began firing upon the cluster of buildings. A bullet snapped by Dawson's helmet as he turned his head to check on the reporters. To his shock, Lianne was up on her knees giving a narrative before the camera.

"Get down now!" shouted Dawson.

She either did not hear or was ignoring him. More shots spat into the ground near him as he watched her. Dawson turned and began to return fire. He then noticed several of the men around him were firing off to their left toward the hills rather than at the buildings. Confirmation came over the headset that they were taking fire from both directions.

"Bravo platoon. Direct your fire toward the high ground," came the command over the headset.

Alpha platoon was closest to the buildings and were laying down withering fire upon them. To his surprise, Dawson suddenly found a man in his gun sights. Standing on the hillside, the man was pointing a RPG tube in their direction. Dawson let go two three-round bursts. The man dropped his weapon and flew backwards at the same time.

AK rifle rounds rained down all around Dawson. He and his fellow teammates continued to pour rounds into the hillside. A soldier near Dawson screamed out in pain. A bullet had found its mark. Calls for the medic began to filter through the din of battle noises.

Firing round after round, Dawson's M16 rifle's chamber locked open, signaling it was empty. He released the empty magazine and let it drop to the ground. Quickly, he slammed in another magazine and chambered the first round. Before resuming fire he stole a glance back at Lianne. In disbelief he saw that she had gotten down on the ground as he had instructed, but she was busy giving a narrative report. The cameraman was lying prone with the camera pointed at her; both appeared oblivious to the bullets plopping into the ground around them.

"Unbelievable!" bellowed Dawson.

Shaking his head, he turned back and resumed fire. Doc Thompson, the medic, crawled by Dawson and began to help a wounded man. The amount of incoming fire seemed to suddenly increase.

"Bravo platoon! Pull back to the road!" came the urgent command over Dawson's headset.

Letting loose a volley of fire, Dawson crawled back through the foot high grass to where the reporters were.

"You two. Get ready to run back to the road. Stay low. Run fast. I'll be right behind you!"

"Okay!" yelled Lianne, who now appeared wild-eyed and frightened.

Snapping in a fresh twenty-round magazine, Dawson fired another long string of rounds.

"Now. Go, go, go!" he yelled, then fired a burst toward the hills.

Lianne and her cameraman started running with Dawson right on their tails. His weapon was empty again. Blood pulsed through his fingers as a burst of hot wind blew past his face from a close round.

As the trio ran, they were surrounded by retreating soldiers who took turns stopping and laying down cover fire. Several men had reached the roadside berms and were set up and pouring rounds up into the hillside. Puffs of white smoke from enemy rifles rose in dozens of places along the hills. Dawson stopped to reload and return fire. He could plainly see the enemy scurrying around taking shots and ducking out of sight.

He emptied another magazine and began to run again. Suddenly he was knocked down by a nearby explosion. Recovering quickly, he gathered himself back up and made for the road. He saw Lianne as she topped a berm and dropped off out of sight. Continuing on through the smoke and haze, Dawson finally made it over the small berm and down beside Lianne.

"You okay Miss Palmer?" he yelled.

"Yeah, I'm okay but I lost Jim. I don't see him anywhere."

Dawson climbed up the berm and scanned the field. Most of the soldiers had made it to the safety of the road and were laying on a blanket of fire for the few strugglers. Two helicopters came roaring over and let loose a barrage of rockets, turning the hillside into a black and white cloud. The explosions were deafening.

It was then that Dawson spotted the cameraman. Splayed out on the ground some thirty meters away, he was not moving, his shattered camera by his side. Lianne had crawled up beside Dawson. She started screaming when she saw her assistant lying on the ground.

"Get him, please!" she screamed.

"Stay right here!" Dawson ordered, and then leapt from the safety of cover.

CHAPTER 3

For Dawson, everything went into slow motion as he ran across the open field, firing blindly as he went. In short order he reached the fallen cameraman. Dropping down by his side, he checked for signs of life and found he was still breathing. Blood was oozing from his chest.

Taking fire all around him, there was no time to waste. Dawson shouldered his weapon, grabbed the wounded man and threw him up onto his shoulder. Like a drunken sailor, he staggered back for the safety of the roadway with his heavy burden. Bullets whizzed and popped all around him, both incoming and outgoing. Still, high on adrenaline he kept shuffling.

An AK round slammed into the back of Dawson's bullet proof vest. He and his charge were thrown to the ground. The wind knocked out of him, Dawson struggled to breathe again, then picked up his wounded man and started for safety only a few yards away.

Kaboom!

Suddenly the air around Dawson seemed to burst into flames. Searing heat burned his lungs. He felt himself being lifted into the air. Moments later he crashed to the ground. A curling plume of gray smoke obscured his vision. Lying on his back, Dawson fought to suck in air. It wasn't working well. He began to panic. Darkness began to surround him.

When the smoke and black fog began to clear, Dawson could see blue sky above but could hear no sounds. Far above he saw a helicopter rotoring into position just off to his left. The mechanical dragonfly wig-waged and let loose a volley of rockets. Then the copter recoiled to the left and began to pitch wildly. A billowing plume of gray smoke scorpioned the back rotor. The smoke changed from gray to black.

Watching the scene on his back, Dawson saw the wounded machine yaw and heave. It then plummeted downward and disappeared from his field of vision. The ground shook. Dawson was pitched upward again. While floating through the air he saw the helicopter blowing apart; black smoke mushrooming from it. He hit the ground again; this time feeling nothing. Another explosion catapulted Dawson into the air and once again he slammed onto bare ground. When he regained consciousness, Doc Thompson was dragging him back to safety.

"My legs!" screamed Dawson, feeling a wave of excruciating pain.

"They're broken," someone said.

The wounded sergeant was covered with blooded clots of dirt. One leg was broken so badly that the femur protruded from his thigh. Tourniquets had stopped the arterial bleeding. Both arms were fractured and riddled with shrapnel wounds.

It was difficult for Dawson to focus on anything. All he could recall were orange flashes and the buzz of a million insects. An unbearable wave of pain engulfed him like a tidal wave. He screamed then passed out again.

When he came around again, Dawson felt his lips first before anything. Strange, he thought. It was as if they were caked with mud. Experimentally, he tried to move them and felt them crack apart, breaking into plates of dry skin. There was no moisture in his mouth.

Strangely, he heard the drip-drip-drip of something. He could not move. His body was hardly there. Searching with his eyes, he finally noticed a plasma bag and an IV line snaking down on him. He saw another bag dripping fluid on the other side somewhere. He then discerned that he was swaddled in bandages.

"Dawson, can you hear me?" came a sweet female voice.

It sounded like Amydee, his fiancé. How could it be? She was back home, not here in this forsaken land. Struggling to stay focused, Dawson tried to bring the face before him into clear view.

"Amydee?" he croaked.

"No Dawson, it's me, Lianne, your friendly neighborhood news reporter."

"Um-hmm," he moaned, feeling another round of pain.

"Listen, Dawson. Look at me. You are going to be okay. You're going home. They are going to fix you up like new."

Her face finally came into focus and Dawson recognized her. She smiled at him. Her lips were trembling. Tears were in her eyes. She then leaned forward and kissed him on the forehead.

"You will forever be my hero, Sergeant Dawson Lee. I will never forget what you did for Jim. You saved his life. You have a friend and a fan for life. I will see you again one day."

Somewhat confused, he looked at her curiously. Nothing she was saying made any sense in his rattled state. Lianne saw his confusion.

"Dawson, do you remember what happened?"

"Nooo," he moaned out with a rush of air as a spasm of pain grabbed him.

She explained to him that a mortar or RPG round had exploded beside him, and then a helicopter crashed near him. He began to understand and piece things together.

"What about the cameraman?"

"Jim's in bad shape. But they think he will pull him through. He's right over here beside you. You two will be on the same medivac together.

"It's due any moment."

"Mm-hmm."

She took his face in her hands.

"Dawson, listen to me. When I get back to the states I am going to look you up. I want to see how you are doing. If I can, I would like to take you and your fiancé to dinner."

She paused and kissed his forehead again.

"I want to see you well again. I want to tell your Amydee how brave you are."

"O-okay," he whispered.

Her eyebrows puckered. Tears flowed freely down her cheeks.

"Thank you Dawson. You saved Jim's life. I really appreciate it. I really care for you. Your kindness will never be forgotten."

He nodded jerkily and passed out.

CHAPTER 4

By the time Sergeant Dawson Lee reached Walter Reed Army Medical Center in Washington, D.C., three weeks had passed since he had been wounded. He had spent those weeks in a hospital at Ramstein Air Base, Germany. There he had undergone surgeries to repair the ligament and bone damage in his left and right legs. He had surgeries to repair damage to his arms and remove shrapnel embedded in his limbs.

Dawson had been lucky. He had almost bled to death from the arterial bleeding. Both arms had been fractured and pitted from shrapnel wounds. A neurologist had performed a delicate surgery at the base of his skull to remove shrapnel there. For most of the last three weeks he had been heavily drugged and slept a lot.

Stabilized, Dawson was transported by bus and loaded onto a C-141 Starlifter. He was placed on a littler, a rack where soldiers were stacked four-high in the center of the aircraft. Everyone onboard were issued earplugs to muffle the industrial roar of the four huge turbo fan engines. The stench of urine and blood permeated the cabin. The fully-equipped airborne ICU went from steamy to frigid once in the air.

Immediately after reaching Walter Reed, Dawson underwent additional surgeries on his left leg and one more on his right arm. He would walk again but expansive rehabilitation lay ahead of him. The medical personnel had explained to him that he might not regain full use of his legs again and could possibly be left with notable limp. He might even have to use a cane or crutch for assistance. His injured arms would also involve expansive physical and occupational therapy as well. His hands and fingers seemed to have a life of their own. Often they would not respond correctly to the signals his brain would send to them.

As the days began to pass, the doctors reduced his pain medications and he was forced to face the pain head-on. Bouts of spasmodic pains depleted his energy reserves causing Dawson to slump into episodes of depression. He began to have nightmares. Sleep medications were administered to get him through the nights. Each day was trying for him to face. The intensive physical and occupational therapies were frustrating for he could see little progress in regaining control of his legs and hands.

His parents came and stayed for several days, visiting him each day. It was through them that he learned that Amydee, his fiancé, was having second thoughts about their relationship since he had been injured. Dawson's parents had given him a cell phone so he could stay in contact daily. He had called Amydee several times but could not get through to her. She had sent him a get well card with the message that she would see him soon. He was unsure as to what that meant since she would not answer or return his calls.

Hurt and lonely, Dawson began to feel sorry for himself. There were times that he wished he had not survived his injuries. Amydee had been his entire reason for being. Now, lying in a ward of badly mangled men, Dawson questioned his existence. It was then that he discovered he had a new power. He could simply not do anything he did not want to do. He had always been strong and independent, always carrying his fair share of the load. Now, he set about to rebel with reckless abandon against any and everything.

The medical staff and rehabilitation crew told him that he must begin learning to live his life anew. He must exercise his arms and legs to develop strength and endurance again. But, Dawson only wanted to not hurt. As soon as he felt the pain, he would let go. Finally, he decided to lie in bed and do nothing. He would become an invalid and crawl into a world of nothingness. He had lost the desire to live, to engage in life itself. To make matters worse, Amydee walked into the ward unexpectedly and toppled his last reserves of hope.

Dawson had just had a falling out with the occupational therapist. He lambasted him until he walked out of the session. Shortly after the therapist left, his attending physician came by to try to talk some sense into him. Dawson in turn, unloaded on him.

"I'm a useless cripple Doc. Face it. I'm no good anymore. I'm not a man. I have not one but my mom and dad. I'll be a burden to them and they don't need it. No woman will ever want me. I'm used up. Why didn't I die when I was wounded?"

"Sergeant Lee."

Dawson threw his arms up.

"Awe, cut the Sergeant crap. I'm no longer a soldier. Those days are gone. I'm a spent bullet. A discarded shell. Why don't you go ahead and put me in a home for cripples and let me rot my days away?"

Doctor Turner looked at Dawson for a long moment.

"Son, you have a right to be angry. That I cannot deny. But, I will tell you this. You can overcome this adversity and build another life. Perhaps an even a better life than before. The only thing standing in your way is your pride and desire. You have got to want to get better in order to do so."

He took a deep breath and pointed his finger at Dawson.

"I will not tolerate you treating my staff with your petty insolence. I plan to order a psychiatric evaluation and consult. I will turn you over to mental health if you are not willing to cooperate. You think about it soldier."

With that said, Doctor Turner walked out of the ward.

CHAPTER 5

Sullen after being chastened by Dr. Turner, Dawson lay in his bed stewing in his misery. Anger and hatred directed at no one in particular spewed forth from his soul. He hated the world. He could care less if he lived another day.

"Death would be a blessing," he muttered, gazing out of the nearby window.

Tears stung his eyes but he refused to let himself cry. He felt worthless. He would not cry, he said to himself. He was one of those staunch believers that real men don't cry.

"Real Man!" He bemoaned. "Not anymore."

Continuing to stare out the window, he would not allow the serene blue sky to sooth his wounded pride. His heart felt ugly and blackened.

In his state of anger, the buzzing in his ears prevented him from hearing someone walk up and stand by his bed. Only the familiar smell of a perfume made him aware that she was there. He slowly turned his head and lifted his eyes to find Amydee standing there.

Dawson let out a gut wrenching sough when the reality of her being there hit him. She was as beautiful as ever. Her blond hair, her big liquid brown eyes, her precisely applied makeup, were as familiar as they had always been. She wore a peach colored dress and was beaming her breath-taking smile that had always melted his heart.

The two stared at one another for a long moment. Dawson had prayed for a chance to confront Amydee. Now, he was at a loss for words.

She stared a moment longer then looked down at his arms and legs. Her lips quivered and tears pooled in her eyes and began to drip down her cheeks.

"Hey Dawson," she said, softly.

He nodded, unable to speak.

"Mind if I sit down?" she asked.

"Of course not," he whispered.

Amydee slid a chair close by the hospital bed and sat down. She got some tissue from the box on his night stand and wiped her eyes, careful to not ruin her mascara.

"How are you feeling?"

"The pain is rough but I'm making it."

"Can you walk?"

"Not yet."

Her eyes widened as she looked at him.

"Will you be able to?"

"I don't know. Maybe. They say I can."

Which is it Dawson?" she asked, looking at him curiously.

He let out a sigh.

"They say I can learn to walk again, but I haven't been able to so far. It had been six weeks now.

"Oh," she said quietly.

Silence.

Dawson looked at her until she locked eyes with him.

"Amydee, why are you here?"

Her eyes fluttered. Her face tightened from the blunt question, cheeks reddened with shame.

"What do you mean Dawson?" she asked, trying to recover from the embarrassment.

"You would not answer my calls. You wouldn't call me back and you have been avoiding my parents."

She folded her hands in her lap and stared down at them.

"I'm sorry. This has been too much for me. I wasn't prepared to have you hurt and messed up."

"Well I am," he said with a touch of anger.

She looked up and blinked her eyes.

"Sorry, I think that didn't come out right."

Amydee leaned forward and took his hand and held it. She laid her forehead against his side. Dawson closed his eyes and fought back tears. He reached out with his other hand and caressed her neck and cheek.

"I have missed you so much Amydee. I have wondered if I would ever see you again."

"I'm here now," she said softly.

"How long can you stay?"

"I have a flight out day after tomorrow. I plan to spend all day with you tomorrow."

"That's nice. Thank you," he said, and meant it.

His defenses began to melt away. It felt good having her by his side. His pain and troubles seemed to ease away.

Still holding his hand, Amydee began telling him about how she was doing and what was going on in her family. She eased up and sat on the side of the bed and rubbed his chest while she talked. After a time she slid off the bed and looked around.

"Whew! I'm famished. I flew in this morning and checked into the hotel just down the street. I haven't had anything to eat since early this morning. Where can I get a bite to eat?"

"There is a cafeteria here somewhere. If you will help me get in that wheelchair over there I'll go with you."

"Great."

Amydee wheeled the chair over and Dawson worked his way off the bed and into it. She pushed him down to the nurse's station and asked for directions. The nurse on duty was surprised to see Dawson up and congratulated him. She praised Amydee for motivating him.

"He has been a real butt of a bear to deal with Miss Carter. We are sure happy to see you here. This is the best we've seen him."

Dawson shook his head and smiled sheepishly. The nurse laughed and patted him on the cheek then told them how to get to the cafeteria.

"You two have a nice time," she said as Amydee wheeled him toward the elevators.

CHAPTER 6

The smell of hamburgers and fries reached Dawson and Amydee long before they found the cafeteria. She pushed him to a table then went to the counter and ordered for both of them. Dawson watched her as she placed the order and paid the bill. She was a vision of beauty. She had been his inspiration each day that he was in Afghanistan. They had planned to marry upon his return. However, his return was not what either had expected.

Dawson wondered now if they would ever marry. He did notice that she was not wearing the engagement ring he had given her over two years ago. Not sure what to say or do, he decided that he would let her lead this visit. He would do his best not to push for anything at this point if he could help it.

Amydee picked up their order and walked back to where Dawson was waiting. She set his cheeseburger, fries, and coke down in front of him then arranged her food and sat down.

"I saw you staring at me while I was waiting for our food. You okay?"

"Yeah, I was enjoying the view. It has been a long time since I've seen you. Seems ages ago that I left to go overseas. You look good, Amydee. Beautiful!"

"Why thank you Dawson. You look better than I thought you would. What about all those cut places on your arms and legs, will they heal without scars?"

"I'm afraid not. There will be plenty of scars. That's the least of my worries though. Walking and trying to get my hands to function properly again are my primary concerns."

"Oh, okay."

She was silent for a moment.

"I understand Dawson. You have a good point. Maybe your arms and legs won't look so bad when you fully heal."

Her statement disturbed Dawson but he shook it off rather than let it bother him. He picked up the ketchup package and tried to open it. His hands would not cooperate and he kept dropping it.

"I'm sorry to ask Amydee but would you put the ketchup and mustard on for me? I still can't do the fine motor stuff."

"Sure honey, no problem."

She opened the condiment packs and spread them on his cheeseburger and fries. Then she put a straw in his soft drink cup for him. It was awkward but Dawson managed to feed himself without too much difficulty or embarrassment. He dropped a few of the fries in the process but they both ignored his clumsiness.

It was time for Dawson's afternoon therapy session when they finished eating. Amydee excused herself to go back to the hotel to rest a while. She promised to return later in the afternoon and visit for a time. She kissed him on the cheek when she left him at the physical therapy department. He went about his therapy with a renewed spirit.

"My, my. This is the first time you have put forth an effort with your therapy," commented Sharon, Dawson's therapist. "A little bird told me your fiancé is here. I would like to meet her and express my appreciation for getting you out of your rotten mood."

Dawson smiled.

"Sorry Sharon. I kind of lost sight of things. This has been harder than I could have ever imagined."

"Well, if you will keep your head up like this, we could have you walking out of here real soon. You were seriously injured but you still have both your arms and legs. You will walk again if you wish. You may have to use a cane some. It is better than most of the guys that come through here."

She worked with him on his leg exercises, then on strengthening his arms. Sharon then gave Dawson a pair of gloves and began instructing him on getting around in the wheelchair. It was difficult to propel himself with weak and hurting arms. However, it did feel good to be able to do it on his own. He had not gotten used to being pushed around by others.

Amydee came back that evening. She brought Dawson a milkshake and a chicken sandwich. As she talked about her life at home, Dawson felt a strange sensation inside. He sensed that she was avoiding something. She had yet to talk about the two of them and how things would be when he came home.

Dawson also noticed that Amydee had yet to show any intimacy other than a kiss on the forehead or cheek. He wondered if she was repulsed by his damaged limbs. He did have to admit that the extensive scars and stitches were ugly to look at. Several times he started to ask where the two stood but was fearful that she would express second thoughts about their relationship and pending marriage.

Just before dark she said goodbye and that she would return in the morning. After saying goodnight and kissing him on the forehead, Dawson reached out and took hold of her arms before she could get away.

"Amydee, I love you."

She appeared embarrassed for a moment, then looked down at the floor.

"I love you too Dawson," she said quietly, then walked out of the ward.

CHAPTER 7

After Amydee left, Dawson could not shake the uneasy feeling gnawing at his gut. Something was amiss with her. He would need to clear the air with her before she went back to Georgia. If their marriage plans had changed, he wanted to know now, not at the last moment.

Restless, still early, Dawson wanted to get out of bed for the first time without being prompted. With the wheelchair parked on one side of his bed, he slid off and into it. With a struggle he put his slippers on his feet. With even more of an effort he slipped into his housecoat.

Collecting his billfold, Dawson put on the gloves that Sharon had given him. He slowly wheeled out of the ward to the nurse's station. Getting directions to the PX, he set out for the elevators.

To his surprise, Dawson rode down the elevator and wondered along several hallways and no one questioned him as to what he was doing. A few times passersby would offer to push him. Determined to do it on his own, he politely declined their help.

It was a long arduous trek but he made it to the PX. He picked out some snacks consisting of two boxes of caramel coated popcorn, a package of chocolate covered peanuts, and a bag of fireballs. After paying for his purchases, he renegotiated his way back to his ward. He was thoroughly exhausted and did not have the strength to lift himself back onto the bed. A nurse happened to be nearby and gave him a boost to make it out of the wheelchair and up onto the bed.

Too tired to enjoy his treats, Dawson fell fast asleep. He did not wake up until early the next morning. After the breakfast trays had arrived and he had eaten, an orderly helped him bathe and change into a clean sweat suit. He had expected Amydee early that morning but she did not arrive until he returned from his physical and occupational therapy sessions. It was almost 11:00 A.M.

I'm sorry I didn't come earlier. I slept late, then had breakfast and did a little shopping," she said apologetically.

"Oh, that's okay. I'm just glad you're here. How long can you stay?"

"Hmm. You've got me the rest of the day. I'll stay until dinner, then I'll go pack and get ready to leave tomorrow. My flight leaves at ten out of Dulles. I will need to leave by eight in order to get there in plenty of time."

"I wish you didn't have to go back so soon, Amydee. I've missed you so much."

"Me too," she said with a sad smile. "I have to get back to work. Got bills to pay ya know."

"Yeah, I understand. I am thankful for the time I do have with you."

At lunch time before Dawson's tray arrived, Amydee went downstairs to the cafeteria and picked up a sandwich and brought it back up and sat with him while he ate. She then went with him to his therapy sessions. By the time he got back to the ward, he was exhausted and in pain. A nurse brought him a pain pill.

Amydee sat beside the bed and held his hand while he waited for the painful spasms to subside. She looked uncomfortable sitting there as his body shook from the pain.

"How often do you get like this?" she asked with a look of concern.

"Mainly when I exert myself too much. Sometimes the pain just comes over me without warning."

"Will that go away?"

"I don't know Amydee. They should over time. I sure hope they will."

"You can't live like this, can you?"

He lay there, unsure what to say. His fears and concerns lay just below the surface. What should he say? What should he share about his own fears?

Dawson looked up at Amydee. Her eyes drifted away and would not meet his.

"Amydee?"

"Yes."

"What's going on? Are you having second thoughts about us?"

Her face reddened and tears began to fill her eyes. She grabbed some tissue and blotted her eyes.

"Oh Dawson. I want you back whole. I want you like you used to be. I want my strong jock, the quarterback I fell in love with."

Dawson swallowed a lump that had formed in his throat. His lips began to quiver, yea he did too.

"I'm afraid that Dawson's gone. All I can offer is slightly damaged goods. My heart is still strong and it is still devoted to you."

Amydee stood up, then sat on the edge of the bed. She leaned over and gently kissed his lips. It felt good to Dawson. It was the first kiss she had given him except for the friendly pecks on the forehead and cheek.

She held the kiss for a long moment then drew back a short distance. He found his eyes looking at her breasts bulging out from the top of her blouse. His heart skipped a beat when he caught the scent of a man's cologne on her. It was an unmistakable fragrance; one he had worn himself in the past.

Catching the look on his face, Amydee was taken aback. She stood up and looked around a moment.

"I'll be right back," she said, and quickly started out of the ward.

"What's wrong Amydee?" called Dawson.

"I don't know, need air," she replied, nonsensically as she hurried out of sight.

Dawson wished he had the strength and ability to run after her. A wave of pain almost doubled him over as he looked forlornly at the entrance to the ward.

CHAPTER 8

A half hour passed before Amydee returned to Dawson's bedside. The wait had been excruciating for him. When she sat back down beside the bed, he could see that her eyes were red from crying. She clutched a hand full of tissue and had wiped most of her mascara off. Forcing a smile, she looked at him sympathetically.

"I'm sorry Dawson. This is all hard for me. I can't get used to seeing you messed up like you are. It was not supposed to be like this. You were supposed to come home in one piece, you know, just like you left."

He fought to hold back his wounded anger that flashed through his brain.

"Sorry to disappoint you."

"Oh Dawson, I didn't mean it that way. You were to come home a hero. We would marry and live happily ever after."

"Well, I'm no hero, Amydee. I am coming home soon. Just had to make a pit stop at the body repair shop. I won't be good as new but I can still deliver. I will spend the rest of my life giving you all I can."

Tears came to her eyes as she pasted on a trembling smile.

"That is so sweet. You have always been a charmer."

Dawson looked at her intently for a long moment.

"Amydee, you are holding something back."

She looked surprised. Her breath caught.

"No Dawson, I'm just me. I am just confused by all of this. I'm scared that you won't be whole again."

"I am whole, Amydee. I'm just beaten up a bit. I have just got to work the wrinkles out and I'll be okay again. This won't stop me from taking care of you.

"I wish I could believe that," she said, looking at him with doleful eyes.

Dawson's heart slammed against his chest. He quickly recovered and forged on to assure Amydee that he was going to be okay.

"Believe it. I promise. I will be on my feet very soon. I will be walking out of here and into your arms. You'll see."

"I hope so," she said softly, wiping her eyes with the wad of tissue.

"What is going on Amydee? I feel a wedge between us. You are not the girl I left behind when I went to Afghanistan."

Her face saddened.

"Things are different now. This..." she held her hands out, palms up. "This is just too much."

"I am truly sorry Amydee. I did not plan this. It just happened."

"I know Dawson. I'm not blaming you. I just feel uneasy about all of this."

He looked at her a long moment.

"What about us?" he asked in a soft voice.

She pinned him with her eyes.

"What do you mean?"

"Are we still together?"

"I'm here, aren't I," she said with a bit of sarcasm.

Startled, Dawson took a deep breath. He let out a soft sigh.

"Yes, you are here in body, but your mind and your heart are somewhere else."

He paused and took another deep breath.

"Amydee, is there someone else?"

Her eyes widened. She blinked several times in disbelief of his question.

"Of course not Dawson. What makes you think that?"

"Things just don't feel right between us. Do you want us to still get married when I get home?"

"Well... Yeah. Um. Eventually."

"What about June like we planned?"

"Hmm. I'd like to wait for a while."

Dawson sat quietly looking at her.

"I see," he said softly.

Neither spoke for a time. Finally Amydee reached over and took his hand.

"Don't read anything into it Dawson. I have just got to get used to seeing you this way."

"Yeah," he said flatly.

"I'm sorry," she whispered.

"Me too, Amydee."

Silence.

An orderly came with Dawson's dinner tray and sat it down. Dawson looked at it and then pushed it to the side.

"Aren't you going to eat?" asked Amydee.

"No. I'm not really hungry right now."

"You need to eat. Please don't be upset with me. Eat for me, please."

"Okay."

He took the tray and picked at the roast beef and potatoes. Amydee sat quietly watching him clumsily work with the knife and fork. When he ate all that he could, he put the plastic cover back on the tray.

Amydee eased up onto the side of the bed. She brushed his hair with her hand and gently kissed him.

"I love you Dawson. I always have and I always will. I'm going to go back to the hotel and get ready to leave in the morning. If I can get up early enough I might come back by for a few minutes. If not, I will call you tomorrow night from home."

He nodded but could not speak. His throat swelled with sadness. Amydee took his face in her hands and looked at him.

"If you don't come home soon I will try to come back up again. If I do, I will stay longer."

"Okay. That would be nice."

She kissed him again and said goodbye. He watched her disappear through the doorway. His heart sank and loneliness engulfed him.

CHAPTER 9

After Amydee said goodbye and left, Dawson dropped into a sour mood. The pain from physical therapy had abated but now he was restless and frustrated. He tossed and turned, unable to find a comfortable position.

It was still light outside, too early to try to go to sleep. Irritated, he finally got up and eased off into the wheelchair. Still wearing his sweat suit, Dawson decided to go to the PX just to burn off some restless energy. Stopping at the nurses' station, he let them know where he was going and rolled off. His progress was slow but he was steady this time. His arm muscles seemed to cooperate better.

At the PX Dawson wheeled along the aisles looking for something to purchase. He ended up with just a soft drink from the cooler. While at the register he saw the cigarette display and picked out a pack of Marlboro Lights and a disposable lighter. He had smoked in the past but had been quit for two years now.

Leaving the PX, he headed for the front entrance so he could go outside and smoke. He had no problem with staff or security when he wheeled out the front and parked off a ways and lit up.

"Why am I doing this?" he muttered to himself as he took another deep draw.

Blowing out the smoke, he shook his head. Even though he knew better than to go back to smoking, it was a relief and it calmed his frayed nerves. Taking a long deep pull, he looked up at the sky. It would soon be dark. He could smell rain in the air.

Finishing the cigarette, Dawson lit another one off the butt. He leaned to one side and propped his elbow on the arm of the wheelchair. He watched an older man and woman get out of a taxi and hurry into the hospital.

"Guess they are coming to see someone who has been through the meat grinder and spit out the other end," he mumbled.

Taking in the surroundings, Dawson looked down the street and noticed the hotel that Amydee was staying at. It did not appear to be all that far away. He wondered what she was doing at the moment. It would be great if he could walk down and visit her. It would be even better if he could march into her room, sweep her off of her feet and make love to her like old times.

"Huh!" he snorted, and shook his head.

With him being a cripple, would they ever be together again? He still had an uneasy feeling about her and their future together.

"Hmm. What if?" he said, and put his gloves on.

His mind began to play out a scheme. He looked around, put the cigarette in his mouth and wheeled out to the sidewalk by the street. After rolling along the sidewalk for a short distance, he stopped. He turned around and looked back at the hospital. It was set back from the street by a hundred yards of grass and short trees.

People were still coming and going but no one paid any attention to him. What would happen if I rolled on down the street to the hotel? Would I be missed? It was still two and a half hours before they turned out the lights and passed out the night meds.

A smile spread across Dawson's face. He felt giddy with anticipation. He turned the wheelchair around and looked longingly toward the hotel. He could surprise Amydee. If he showed up at her door she would see that he was not helpless. Earlier at therapy he had stood on his own for a few seconds. Determination began to set in.

"I am going to stand up and knock on her door. She will see that I am still a man. Yes sir! That's the plan Dawson. Let's do it!" He said with authority, and started rolling along toward his destination.

The distance was much further and harder than anticipated. Dawson had to stop several times to rest. It was dark now but he continued on, determined. Upon reaching the hotel, Dawson rolled in as if he belonged there. He headed for the bank of elevators without looking in the direction of the registration counter. As soon as he pressed the third floor button, the elevator door popped open and he wheeled on in.

"Whew! So far so good," he said, with relief.

A ding alerted him he had reached Amydee's floor. When it opened, he rolled out into the hallway. Orienting himself, Dawson read the sign indicating which direction room 349 was located.

"Okay, here goes," he said and rolled along the carpeted hallway until he found her door.

Parking the wheelchair just to the right of the door, he locked the brakes and eased his feet to the floor and slid forward in the seat. He took a deep breath, grabbed the door frame and pulled himself up.

Letting out a whoosh of air, Dawson took another full draught of air. On wobbly legs he positioned himself in front of the door. Holding on to the door facing with his left hand, he composed himself and knocked on the door.

Nothing, silence.

He knocked again.

Noises. Then, the door locks clicked.

A haggard looking Amydee opened the door. She was wearing a housecoat, her hand clasping it closed at her throat. Her eyes flew open wide with shock. Her mouth dropped open. She let out a scream of surprise and jumped back.

CHAPTER 10

"Dawson! What are you doing here?" screamed Amydee, a look of sheer terror on her face.

"What do you mean? I came to see you Amydee."

His legs began to tremble from weakness. Dawson grabbed the opposite door frame with his right hand. He struggled to remain on his feet.

It was then that he looked over Amydee's shoulder and saw a man standing by the bed. He was fastening his pants. He had no shirt on. His hair was mussed. The bed covers were all askew.

Understanding hit Dawson like a brick. His legs buckled and he sat down like a drunk in the doorway of the hotel room.

"Oh, Dawson," Amydee said in a sough.

She backed up and sat down on the edge of the bed and put her hands over her face and began to cry. Not knowing what to do, the man behind her grabbed his shirt and retreated into the bathroom and quietly closed the door.

Dawson did not know what to do or say either. Overcome with grief, he half crawled through the doorway and up into the wheelchair. Two couples walked by throwing awkward glances at the scene and quickly moved on.

Once in the wheelchair, Dawson released the brakes, spun around and rolled himself to the elevator and pressed the down button. With hot tears pooling in his eyes, he fought not to look back toward her room. The wait was excruciatingly slow. Mercifully the door to the elevator finally opened and he boarded it for the short ride to the lobby.

He wheeled out of the lobby as quickly as he could. With eyes blurry from the outpouring of tears; he did not realize it was raining until he was well on the way of being soaked.

Only a short distance from the hotel, Dawson emotionally imploded. He shuddered and heaved as he sobbed in utter disbelief and grief. Amydee had been in his life for so long. He had never considered life without her. They and everyone who knew them had accepted the two as being mates for life. Dawson had been building their dream home and had almost had it completed when his reserve unit was activated and sent to Afghanistan.

He sat slumped in the wheelchair, his head hung down. Soaked, he shivered from the cold. The rain was steady, stinging like cold ice picks.

Sucking down a sob, Dawson began to head back to the hospital. He had difficulty wheeling himself. The leather gloves were soaked and his grip slipped each time he grabbed the metal rim of the wheels.

The rain came harder. He had to stop again to rest. Exhausted both mentally and physically, Dawson felt at the end of his ability to cope.

"Dawson!" Came Amydee's voice tumbling through the rain. She was running toward him, half attempting to keep an umbrella over her head. She was wearing jeans and a jacket that were already soaked. Her hair was wet and plastered to her head.

"Wait Dawson!" she called as she ran up to him.

Amydee stopped in front of him, her chest heaving as she tried to catch her breath. Gaining some semblance of composure, she attempted to shelter the two of them from the rain. Dawson looked up at her. Her eyes telegraphed despair. Her face broke into places of grief and tears rolled down her cheeks mixing with the raindrops beaded on her face. She was achingly beautiful. Dawson's breath caught in the back of his throat.

"Oh Dawson. I'm so sorry. I was going to tell you but I couldn't figure out how."

"Why, Amydee?" he asked, pleading.

"It just happened. You were on the other side of the world and I met Jimmy. It just happened. I don't know how else to explain it."

Dawson stared at her a long moment. He nodded jerkily and blinked away fresh tears.

"I see. Couldn't wait for me to get back home from the war?"

"Oh, Dawson. It wasn't like that at all. I was not looking for anyone. I just happened to run into him. It was instant love."

Dawson's body trembled as he looked at her.

"Um-huh. Well..."

He reached down and gripped the wheels. He backed the wheelchair out from under the umbrella into the pouring rain. Slowly and with difficulty, he turned it toward the hospital and moved away.

"Take care Amydee. Have a good life with him."

She stood watching him struggle to roll away.

"What about you Dawson?"

He stopped and looked back at her.

"What do you care?" he quipped. "This charade was heartless of you, Amydee."

"I'm sorry," she said softly.

He looked at her a moment.

"So am I Amydee. So am I."

Fueled on wounded anger, Dawson set out at a steady clip and did not stop until he reached the hospital.

CHAPTER 11

The encounter with Amydee devastated Dawson, sending him emotionally into a downward spiral. His appetite waned, so he lost weight. Losing interest in his rehabilitation, Dawson slowly disengaged from life in general. His parents came to see him and could not motivate him. A chaplain visited him but could not inspire him to find his way out of the dark world he had slipped into. A psychiatrist loaded him up on psychotropic medications that only took him lower into a netherworld of nothingness. He talked little, did nothing much more each day than lie in bed and stare into space.

Because of his sullen mood, the nurses and staff avoided Dawson as much as possible. Many had given up on him and said little to him when they had to deal with him. His doctors and psychiatrist met with him concerning his treatment. He was warned that if he did not show signs of improvement soon that he would be transferred to a mental hospital. That revelation had little impact on Dawson. He was beyond caring. He wanted to die. He could see no future, nor did he care to have one. He honestly felt his life was over and did not want to continue. But, that self-made misery did not plan on an unexpected visitor who was not going to let him waste away and give up on life.

Lunch trays had just arrived. Dawson was lying there basking in his self-pity. The orderly tried to be pleasant and made a cheerful comment about how fresh the salad was. Dawson grunted and pushed the tray table away. When he did, the foam cup of iced tea fell off the table and on to the bed. Only a small amount leaked out around the lid before he could upright it. Frustrated and angry at the world, he threw the container across the room. It splatted against the wall, and tea shot everywhere as the foam cup skipped and bounced.

"Well now, that's a fine hello!" Came a soft feminine voice.

Dawson jerked around and looked at the woman standing there with droplets of tea on her immaculately tailored outfit. Staring at her in disbelief, he recognized her but could not place where he knew her from. She was short and sturdy built, but elegant appearing in her business suit. Her short black hair framed a pleasant face. Her bright blue eyes wide with surprise.

"Uh, sorry Ma'am," said Dawson, in a shameful apologetic tone.

"Sergeant Lee. I thought you were better than this. You look like death warmed over."

"I feel like it too," he replied, sarcastically, still unsure who she was.

He turned away from her and tried to ignore her. He figured she was one of the administrative stiffs who had come to give him a pep talk about his therapy program.

"Soldier, look at me!" she commanded.

Dawson slowly looked up at her and pinned her with his eyes.

"What do you want Ma'am?" he asked in a huff.

"Don't talk to me that way Sergeant Lee. I'm on your side here."

He glared at her.

"Who the hell are you?"

She shook her head and let out a chuckle.

"I guess I didn't make much of an impression on you. I was practically throwing myself on you and all you would talk about was your sweetheart back home."

Still confused, a rush of irritation flared in his voice as he spat out, "Well, she's gone now so whatever you want, say it and get…"

A light clicked on in his brain.

"Oh, my goodness," he said with a sigh.

She grinned at him.

"Yep, it's me in the flesh. Your friendly neighborhood news reporter, Lianne Palmer."

"I'm sorry Miss Palmer. You caught me at a bad time."

"It's Lianne, please. From what I hear you are being a 'bad time', all the time around here."

Dawson gave a small grimacing smile that quickly faded away.

"Not much left to live for. My life is over. Look at me now Miss Palmer…"

"Lianne!" she shot back.

"Lianne then. Just look at me. My arms and legs look like garbage. They don't work all that great either. There is nothing left to live for."

The ward grew quite. The other patients were listening to Dawson's tirade. Lianne looked around a moment then looked at Dawson.

"Is that your wheelchair?" she asked, pointing to the one near his bed.

"Yeah, it is."

"I'll be back in a moment. Get in it and be waiting for me," she said sternly.

"What for?"

"Because I said so, that's what for. Got it now!"

She spun around and walked out of the ward. Sullenly he made his way off of the bed and into the wheelchair.

CHAPTER 12

Several minutes passed before Lianne Palmer came back into the ward to where Dawson was sitting in his wheelchair. The ward got quiet again as the other patients watched to see what was going to happen next. Lianne stood there a moment and looked at Dawson sitting there with a scowl on his face. She looked around the room at all the other men who were staring at her expectantly. She smiled and gave a little wave.

"Hey guys. I'm not going to beat him. At least not yet. Anyway, sorry to disturb you."

There were a few murmurs and chuckles and the ward returned to the normal level of noise. Lianne looked back down at Dawson.

"Do you have a comb or a brush?"

"Yeah," he answered sarcastically.

"Use it then," she shot back sternly, crossing her arms across her chest and tapping one foot.

"What for?" he asked, staring at her with a smirk on his face.

"Never mind. Can you manage yourself or shall I push you Mister Helpless?"

"I can do it!" he snapped. "Lead on."

Lianne walked smartly out into the hallway with Dawson trailing behind. The nurses got quiet when they were passing the stations. A short distance down the hall an orderly was standing by a doorway. He held it open when Lianne reached him. She stepped inside nodding a thanks' as she went. Dawson followed her in. He looked around and realized they were in a utility room filled with cleaning supplies.

Dawson looked around again and started to ask what they were doing in there when the door closed behind him with a thud. He looked back, the orderly was gone. He looked at Lianne.

"What's this all about?"

Lianne glared at him. Her throat and neck had turned red. She was breathing heavy. Her hands began to tremble and she propped them on her hip to control them. She took a deep halting breath.

"Dawson Lee. I am very, very disappointed in you. I..."

"What do you care?" he interjected.

She held her hands up.

"Shut up. Don't say a word until I have had my say. You listen to me Dawson and listen good!"

She dropped her hands. He slumped back in the wheelchair and glowered.

"I have been checking on you from time to time. I have spoken with your doctors, the staff, and with your parents. I have been doing this not as a reporter, but as a concerned friend. An admirer. To me, you are a hero. I watched you under fire. I saw you save my cameraman. Because of you he is alive today. He made it back to his wife and two little kids. Thanks to you. I know you got hurt in the process, but you are alive. You are in one piece. You are battered and bruised but the doctors say you can be functional again if you will get your head out of your butt and work for it."

She was trembling all over. Dawson started to speak. She held up her hand for him to be quiet.

"When I met you and interviewed you I was impressed with your professionalism and sense of duty. To me you represented the quintessential American soldier. I was proud to know you. I admired you." She paused a minute.

"I understand your fiancé left you for someone else. But you know that does not give you the right to give up. You are too good. You have too much potential. You are a good man. So now, straighten up. Back up. Regroup. Get better. I will not allow you to quit on living."

She paused to catch her breath again.

"I live here in Georgetown. I'm not very far away. I will come back and kick your butt everyday if I have to. You will not be an ass anymore. You will clean up your act starting right now. You will work with your doctors and therapists. You will walk again. I expect you to take me to dinner and you will dance at least one dance with me... A slow dance, preferably," she added with a shy smile.

Dawson's anger bled off. He felt like a deflated tire. He looked at her curiously.

"Why?"

"Because I care, that's why."

"Oh."

He did not know what to say.

"I have an assignment in New York for a couple of days. When I get back and come see you, I want to see you looking better."

"What's wrong with the way I look?"

"You look like crap. I want you to get a haircut, shave and take a bath – and I mean daily at that. I want you to eat and put some meat back on your bones. I want you to get off your butt and walk out of here. If you do all of that I will be the best friend you ever had. And, even more if you want it."

She let out a whoosh of air.

Dawson looked at her and smiled.

"Are you through?" he asked.

"Yep."

"For you, I will do it."

"For you too," she shot back.

"O-o-kay! For me too."

CHAPTER 13

The lambasting from Lianne was just what Dawson needed to overcome his air of defeatism. He cleaned himself up, started eating and working his therapy with zeal. Wherever Lianne was, whether in town or out, she called him every night and had him give her a report on his progress. When she was in town she visited him as often as she could.

For the first time since Dawson had entered Walter Reed Hospital, he began to look forward to the day he would be released. He wanted to go home, to build a new life – doing what, he was not sure.

Because of his extensive injuries, the VA declared Dawson to be fully disabled. He would receive a decent VA disability income for the rest of his life. He would be able to live comfortably if he was careful with his money. Dawson had always worked in construction but he knew that form of hard work was no longer an option. Maybe he would go to college or trade school and find something else to do. He and Lianne tossed around some ideas. He felt no urgency to make a decision; that would work itself out in time.

In occupational therapy, Dawson was able to regain full use of his fingers and hands. He would occasionally have episodes of cramps and tremors. Other than that, he was pleased.

One of the activities in occupational therapy was basket weaving to promote fine motor control skills. Dawson's attempt to make a basket turned out surprisingly well. Lianne was so mesmerized by the intricate and delicate design that he gave it to her as a token of appreciation for her support and friendship.

It was amazing to Dawson as to how close he and Lianne had gotten. He felt they were becoming more than friends but was unsure as to what that meant. There was not much of a physical attraction on his part; at least he did not think so. There was something deeper than friendship developing between them. He could honestly say that he loved her, but exactly what kind of love was still a mystery. All he knew is that he enjoyed Lianne's attention and sought to please her with his rehabilitation efforts.

His therapy to learn to walk was frustratingly slow. After weeks and weeks of trying, he was still struggling to keep his balance. The commitment to Lianne for dinner and a dance was still dangling in front of him like a carrot on a string. It remained just out of reach but he was still filled with hope and determination.

Along with the great relationship he had built with Lianne, he had become well-liked by all of the nurses, therapists and staff at the hospital. They all marveled at his dramatic attitude change and lauded him. They knew that Lianne was the driving force behind it all and treated her like royalty whenever she came to visit.

Because of Dawson's vast improvement, the psychiatrist discontinued his psychotropic medications and released him from his care. Once off of these medicines, the lethargy he was experiencing abated and his energy level increased. He began to walk better. With some assistance he began to walk to and from therapy pushing his wheelchair. He would only use the chair when he was exhausted or in too much pain. His gait was still unsteady and he still had a notable limp but he was improving dramatically.

Dawson had just put in a hard day of therapy and was nursing a cup of postprandial coffee when Lianne walked in unexpectedly. His face lit up when he saw her.

"I thought you were still in Baltimore. I was waiting for your call."

She walked up and kissed him on the cheek.

"I just got in a little while ago. I wanted to come by and say hello in person and see how you day went."

"Great, Doctor Kishor says I will be ready to go home soon. I'm getting close to reaching my therapeutic goals."

"That's wonderful, Dawson. I will surely miss you when you do go home. I've gotten used to hanging out with you."

He smiled appreciatively.

"You know Lianne. I have gotten used to you too. You have been great for me. I hope our friendship does not end here."

"Squash that thought! I'm a phone call away and you can visit whenever you want. I'll even come visit you if you would like for me to."

He nodded and smiled.

"I would be honored to have you visit me and meet all of my family."

"I feel like I have known your mom and dad forever. I've talked to them enough on the phone. You know they love you dearly Dawson."

"Yep, that I know. "They are the greatest. They think a lot of you too."

An orderly came by with coffee refills and gave Lianne a cup. She sat on the edge of the bed and filled Dawson in on her assignment in Baltimore. For the first time ever, he felt the heat of her body next to him. It set off a tingling in the pit of his stomach. In his eyes, Lianne suddenly went from short and stocky to petit and sensuously sexy. She was wearing a well-tailored business outfit consisting of a navy skirt, matching jacket, a white silken blouse and navy heels. The hint of décolletage was tantalizing.

Sitting on the bed, her skirt had slid well above her knee. She noticed Dawson starring at her and grinned.

"What's on your mind soldier?"

He laughed.

"I plead the fifth!"

CHAPTER 14

The surprise visit by Lianne had been delightful for Dawson. He experienced feelings for her that he had not felt before. She had been really good for him and to him. He first thought she was seeing him because she felt she owed him for rescuing her cameraman. Also he had wondered if she just felt sorry for him.

It did not take him long to realize that she genuinely cared for him. How much? He was not sure but happy with what she was showing him. After the pleasant evening with her, he was sensing a spark of interest from her beyond friendship. Now, he was hoping for more. He smiled when he thought about how at first he had felt no physical attraction for her. Now, after tonight, he wanted to explore that possibility of being with her more.

"Sergeant Lee you have a smile on your face!" exclaimed Nurse Davis as she walked up to his bed.

Dawson jumped at the sound of her voice. Nurse Davis broke out in laughter.

"I bet you were thinking about that sweet little news lady that comes to see you all the time."

His face reddened with embarrassment. Dawson smiled and nodded.

"I thought so," she said, propping her hands on her hips. "Are you two officially a couple yet?"

"No not yet. I'm not sure how much she likes me."

"Oh, she likes you a lot. Any fool can see that. And just think Sergeant Lee. She has seen you at your worst, and still likes you. That's something to think about. If you had been mine a month ago, I would have flushed you down the toilet!"

She patted him on the shoulder.

"But my, my. Look at you now. You are a model patient, and a handsome one at that!"

Dawson laughed.

"I apologize for being such a jerk. I feel like I had crawled through the depths of hell and finally found my way back. I feel alive and human again. And you know what? These ugly scars don't bother me so much now. I guess I can thank Lianne for that."

"I think you are right about that. She sure turned you around."

"You know Miss Davis, when I came here my fiancé came to see me, then walked out of my life. She was the woman I had planned to marry and spend the rest of my life with. I had been going with her since high school. The sting of all that is still with me, but I believe I have found something much better."

Nurse Davis nodded sadly.

"Good to hear that. You will be leaving here soon. You need to keep that momentum going. Go find a nice new life and live happily ever after."

She kissed her finger and touched his lips.

"I'm proud of you Sergeant. We all are. Seeing the turnaround you did makes all out efforts worthwhile."

Nurse Davis said goodnight and left. The lights were turned down low. Dawson lay there in the dark. For the first time he began to look to the future in earnest. What would he do now? He certainly did not want to do nothing. When he drifted off to sleep, he had not made any progress toward formulating a plan.

His sleep was filled with bizarre, fragmented dreams. At times the dreams were particularly lurid in that a woman was yelling right in his face. Then she stepped away and into the arms of a stranger, a man he could not discern. Dawson twitched himself partially awake, and then drifted back into another strange dream.

He awoke the next morning feeling exhausted and slightly shaken. His pillow was soaked from drool and his head was pounding. Moving away from the wet spot on the pillow, Dawson tried to recall what he had been dreaming. However, it would not come forth from just below the surface of his conscious mind where it was teasing him with snippets of images. He did know that whatever the dreams were, certainly unpleasant. It took most of his energy reserves to shake off the knot in the pit of his stomach and focus on his physical therapy.

Dawson had set himself a personal goal to stop using the wheelchair and not rely on crutches or a cane. When he completed his morning session in physical therapy he announced to the therapists that he would no longer utilize the wheelchair or any other support device. They clapped and cheered as he walked out of the PT department.

"I will never use a wheelchair again," he said, reassuring himself.

And, he didn't. At times when walking he would have to stop and rest. He knew that in time his strength would return. When he tired, Dawson's foot would drag, causing him to limp notably. Still, he persevered.

After his afternoon therapy session, Dawson was totally spent. Rather than pile up in bed, he gathered clean bed clothes and went for a hot whirlpool bath. The hot swirling water felt great and relaxed his tense muscles. While sitting there enjoying the moment, he thought about the house he had almost finished building. It had a Jacuzzi hot tub and now he was certainly glad he had put one in. It actually had been Amydee's idea to do so.

"Thanks Amydee, I will enjoy it without you."

He flinched when he spoke her name, choking back an unexpected sob. Dawson had not realized how sensitive he still was to her leaving him for someone else. He knew the reality would not hit him fully until he went back home. A slight sense of dread rolled over him. He shook it off and got out of the tub. It would soon be time for the dinner trays.

CHAPTER 15

Dawson's parents flew back up the next week to visit. They attended his meeting with the treatment team and it was decided that he was reaching maximum medical improvement and that he would be discharged in two weeks. This was welcomed news.

While his parents were there he introduced them to Lianne. She had dinner with them before they left to fly back to Georgia. They had discussed plans to either drive or fly up and escort Dawson back home, but Lianne invited him to spend a few days with her before he left town. Dawson accepted her offer and planned to fly home after that. Intrigued by her invitation to show him the town and get to know each other better, he was duly excited and looking forward to it.

Lianne had to go out of town for a reporting assignment but promised to be back before Dawson's discharge date. The day before he was to be released, the physical therapy department threw a little ice cream and cake party for him. Most of the staff members in the various departments Dawson had worked with came by to wish him well. That evening Lianne made it back home and gave him a call.

"Hey soldier. Are you still getting out tomorrow?"

"I sure am. You still want me to spend the weekend with you?"

"I'm looking forward to it. Oh yes, before I forget, do you have clothes to wear besides gym suits?"

"I have a bag with a few things in it that Mom and Dad brought up for me. I may need to go shopping for something more appropriate to wear if we are going out for dinner and for the dance I owe you."

She laughed.

"You haven't forgotten your debt?"

"Nope. Sure haven't. Dinner will be no problem. Dancing, I'm still not sure. My knees are still a bit wobbly."

"I promise to be easy on you. I'm really wanting to slow dance with you anyway."

"Um hmm I see. A slow dance I can do. Heck, if that's what you like, I'd be happy to do two or three slow ones!"

"Hmm. Flattery will get you everywhere!"

"I sure hope so!" He said, and meant it.

Lianne broke into laughter.

"You sure are talking tough. Think you can handle things?"

"Oh, I'll sure give it the good old college try, my dear."

"Well, I do declare Rhett Butler, you southern boys sure know how to charm a lady!" she said in a thick southern drawl.

They talked for a few more minutes then said goodnight. Dawson asked for a sleeping pill so he would get a good night's rest. Tomorrow promised to be a big day. His anxiety was building. He had been at Walter Reed for four months now. His future was uncertain. He still had no clear cut plan as to what he was going to do with the rest of his life.

The sleeping pill kicked in and Dawson had an uneventful night of sleep. Rising early, he showered and put on a clean sweat suit before breakfast. Just after he ate Dawson began the process of discharging. He met with physical and occupational therapy for home workout instructions. He saw his attending physicians and was signed off for release. He was then given a stack of paperwork to take to the VA hospital near him. A nurse brought him more paperwork; prescriptions as well as a temporary supply of pain and sleep medications to take with him.

"Take these pills as prescribed. I will return in a few moments with a little more final paperwork. As soon as you have that you are free to go."

"Thank you, Ma'am."

"Do you have someone picking you up or do you need transportation to the airport?"

"Someone will be here to get me just any moment. Thank you anyway."

The nurse said goodbye and wished him well. Dawson retrieved his travel bag from the closet and laid it on the bed. Looking in it, he found something to wear for the day. He chose a button-down shirt, khaki pants and loafers. As he started for the restroom to get dressed Lianne walked in.

"Hi there Dawson, are you about ready to get out of here?"

"Yet. I just have to get my walking papers. I've signed everything and the discharge nurse will be back with them shortly. I was just going to change into street clothes."

"Great. Go ahead and get ready. I'll say goodbye to all of your ward mates here," she said looking around and waving at several of the patients.

CHAPTER 16

In the communal bathroom Dawson changed into the pants and shirt his parents had brought him. It felt good to be in form fitting clothes after months of pajamas and sweat suits. Dressed, he checked himself in the mirror and gathered his things.

"Well, for better or worse, this is it Dawson. The rest of your life starts now," he whispered.

When he walked back into the ward, he was surprised to see Lianne talking with three smartly dressed Army officers. One was a lieutenant general. They all turned and looked at Dawson when he approached.

"Sergeant Lee," greeted the general. "I am General J.G. Belt."

The general stuck his hand out and firmly shook Dawson's hand. After shaking the general's hand, Dawson stood at attention.

"At ease Sergeant. I understand that you are a civilian now."

"Yes Sir."

"We are sorry to lose you. That is why I'm here. I would like to present you with this award."

An officer beside him handed the general a small velvet case.

"I am honored to present you with the Purple Heart for injuries sustained while in action in Afghanistan."

Dawson almost let out a chuckle. The same general had presented him with the same award a few months earlier. Dawson nodded appreciatively to the general and thanked him. He thought it would be better to go along with the presentation and not create any embarrassment for the brass.

Another officer took a photograph of Dawson receiving the medal with Lianne standing by his side. She was clearly impressed and filled with pride for Dawson. At that moment, it was all that mattered to him.

After handshakes, "Atta boys", and farewells, the brass took their leave. The rest of his discharge papers were delivered and he was free to go. As he and Lianne left the ward and walked along the hallway to the elevators, they were met with cheers and applause. Dawson laughed at the good humored banter from the nursing staff about his earlier days of being a grouch. Lianne was warned to keep him fed, watered, and on a tight leash.

Outside the entrance to the hospital, the two stood in a pleasant spring morning for a taxi. As if on cue, a cab zipped in front of them and they piled in. Lianne gave the driver her address in

Georgetown. Moments later they were motoring along streets of row houses of finally crafted colonial American residential architecture. The taxi came to a stop in front of a red-brick two story house with black shutters. There were trees in full spring bloom spaced along the brick paved sidewalk.

"This is very nice." Dawson said as Lianne paid the fare and they got out of the taxi.

"It is pretty here."

"It must have cost a bundle," he added.

"I inherited this place from my grandmother. It has been in my family for ages."

As expected, Dawson was not surprised to discover how finely decorated the house was. The furniture appeared to be costly antiques. The entire home made one feel as though they had stepped back in time.

Lianne led Dawson into a nicely appointed bedroom on the first floor.

"Dawson, I'm not sure how well you can handle steep stairs so I thought we would make use of this guest bedroom because mine is upstairs."

He was unsure if she meant that she would join him or not. He hoped so. He was still unsure of where their friendship, relationship, or whatever it was called was heading. He had not really thought it through. Somehow, maybe they would find a way to discuss it before he left for home.

Lianne showed him around the first floor then they ventured up the stairs. She showed him her bedroom and her study. The trip back down the stairs was tricky for Dawson with his still unsteady legs.

"Whew! I sure know what you mean about the stairs. They are a tad steep. Good idea about the bedroom down here," he said as they stood in the living room.

"Are you hungry?" she asked.

"Yes I am. I didn't eat much for breakfast. Too excited."

"I bet. Well then let's go have a bite. You up to a short walk? I know where a nice little cafe is if you feel up to it."

"Certainly, anything is fine with me."

She smiled at him then put her arms around him. He reciprocated and pulled her close.

"I'm happy you are here Dawson" she said, looking up into his eyes.

"Me too Lianne. This part is like a dream."

"This is no dream. This is the real thing. I am all yours if you want me."

He raised his eyebrows and gave her a crooked smile.

"Meaning?" he queried.

"Take it anyway you want," she replied with a mischievous grin. "But first we both need food for energy."

"Show me the way!"

They started to disengaged but instead locked eyes, then lips. The kiss was deep and filled with emotion. When they broke, the two stared at one another a long moment.

"Okay Honey. Time to eat," he said hoarsely.

They walked out the door hand in hand. Walking along the tree shaded sidewalk, he gave her hand a little squeeze.

"I'm proud to be in your company Miss Palmer," he said, and meant it.

"You are infernally kind Mister Lee," she said sweetly.

CHAPTER 17

Less than two blocks from Lianne's a street lined with an assortment of shops, cafes, and restaurants. She and Dawson stopped into a small café specializing in deli-styled sandwiches. They both ate BLT sandwiches, salads, and iced tea. The café was relaxed and quiet, even with a steady flow of customers. The two took their time eating and enjoyed one another's company.

After their leisurely lunch, Lianne took him to a men's clothing shop and Dawson purchased three outfits for the weekend. On their way back to her place they stopped by a small grocery store and picked up some food items. Not wanting to tire Dawson his first day out of the hospital, she planned to cook dinner for him so he could rest up for Saturday. It was then she had in mind for their special dinner and dancing.

Back at her house, Dawson helped her put the few groceries up into the cabinets and fridge.

"How do you feel?"

"A little sore and weak, but the walk and lunch were wonderful. It feels great to be in the real world again. You live in a wonderful neighborhood. It looks like you have about everything you might need within walking distance. It sure saves on gas, I bet."

Lianne giggled as she led him into the den.

"I don't own an automobile. I don't even know how to drive. I'm a city girl through and through."

"Yikes! What about the country? Would you enjoy living there?"

She reached up and patted his cheek.

"Just know I'm adaptable. You could plant me anywhere and I could thrive."

"Sounds good to me."

As they sat on the sofa within inches of each other, Dawson paused a moment and looked at her seriously.

"What do you say about us having a heart-to-heart talk right now?"

Lianne pursed her lips and nodded thoughtfully.

"I think it would be a great idea. We have never really said anything about where we want to go, or if we want to go anywhere with our relationship. Do you want to go first or shall I?"

"Ladies first!" he said, wiggling his eyebrows, giving her a cheesy smile.

"Pig!" she quipped and socked him playfully on his shoulder then laughed nervously. She took a deep breath.

"Okay. Here goes." Her breath caught for a second. "Whew! This is not easy. I thought it would be."

Dawson reached over and took her hands in his.

"Take your time. Tell me what you would like to happen with us."

"All right." She paused. "You know I like you a lot. I liked you from the first time I met you in Kabul at the army base. But now I like you even more. It might be love. I'm not totally sure yet. I think maybe this weekend together will answer that. I have grown attached to you and would like for us to see each other as often as possible and see where it leads. If we decide for more, then we'll go from there. Like I said, I'm flexible and I can adapt to wherever this takes us."

He looked at her curiously.

"Why me Lianne?"

"What do you mean?" she countered, studying his face.

"Why do you want to be with me? I am a battered and bruised has been. I'm an ex-soldier without a job. I'm classified as disabled by the military. I have little to offer you. I don't have a college education. I don't have much money. I have a home, a truck, and a disability check. And, I don't know where to go from here."

"Hmm. Maybe I want you for your truck!" she said and giggled to break the tension.

"Seriously Lianne," he said solemnly. "Look at you. You have a wonderful job that takes you all over the world. You have a gorgeous home here and an interesting life. I like it here but I'm not sure I would want to live like this all of the time. I live in the slower paced Deep South. I love living in the country. I like the quiet, the solitude."

"Well, we could go back and forth until we decide which is more preferable. If things get serious between us, I could possibly transfer to Atlanta. How far are you from there?"

"About two hours' drive."

"Hmm, that would be a long commute, huh?"

"Yeah it would. Listen, I guess we are getting a little ahead of ourselves. I take it you want us to be together as a couple. That I would like, but again Lianne, I have little to offer you."

"Oh but you do."

"What?"

"You, yourself silly. I like you for you, not for what you have or don't have. I don't care about the scars and bruises. I was there when you got them. If anything, that brings me closer to you. You are a good man, the best. I watched you under fire. You saved Jim's life. You are a hero."

"No, not really. I was doing my job."

"Well, you are my hero, case closed!"

Before he could protest, Lianne was in his arms. Their embrace, their kiss, was long and with heartfelt passions.

CHAPTER 18

Dawson felt as if he were in a dream as he sat holding Lianne in his arms. They had come to an agreement to work on bridging a future of some kind together. For him it appeared to be a daunting task. Lianne was a high profile correspondent. She was well entrenched in her career and he knew that she would not want to give that up, nor would he expect her to. He envied her having such a wonderful career and future. There was a time when he had one, now it was all but gone. Amydee and the war took care of that.

He felt a surge of sadness engulf him but quickly recovered. Smiling at Lianne to mask his melancholy thoughts, Dawson admonished himself for not being appreciative of her acceptance of him. She had made no demands in their fledgling relationship. This he found surprisingly different from Amydee who had been very demanding in many respects.

"What are you thinking?" asked Lianne as she gazed deeply into his eyes.

"Well, to tell you the truth, I feel I am the luckiest man in the world to be the object of your desire."

She grinned and shook her head.

"That kind of talk almost makes me want to lose my inhibitions."

"I'm not sure if I could handle things if you did."

She giggled.

"We could probably work something out."

He laughed.

"This is going to be fun. I needed a good time after all that has happened and I think you are it."

"You better believe I am," said Lianne as she kissed him again.

The afternoon passed off quickly as the two sat in the den and got to know one another. Lianne had planned for their first night together that she would cook dinner.

"I need to go back to the market down the street to get a few more things for dinner. While I'm gone you lay back and rest. Watch television or take a nap if you would like. I want you rested up for later."

"What's going to happen later?"

"You're going to give me that dance you owe me!"

"Mm-hmm." He nodded. "You got it!"

Lianne picked up her purse and said goodbye as she headed out of the door.

"Make yourself at home!" she called out before closing the door.

"Will do, thanks!"

After flipping through the television channels, Dawson switched it off and walked around the house. Other than the front part of the first floor, he had not seen it all. He found her home office. It had a massive antique roll-top desk on one wall surrounded by large built-in bookshelves filled with books of all descriptions. He was surprised to find not one, but two computer stations. He surmised that one must be dedicated for her correspondence work.

Strolling through the kitchen, Dawson opened a door that he thought would lead out back but instead opened into a glassed in room with a hot tub.

"Wow! Nice," he said, thinking mischievous thoughts about being in it with Lianne.

Back in the kitchen he poured himself a cup of coffee, then walked out the front door and sat on the steps. It was pleasant watching people walking along the sidewalk. In the street, traffic was light. The noise level was not as bad as he thought it might be. It was hard to imagine that just a few blocks away was the White House and just beyond it was the U.S. Capital. Lianne's world here was truly incredible.

"What would it be like to live here with her?" he whispered.

He was staring off into nothing when a taxi pulled up and stopped. Lianne hopped out while the driver went around and opened the trunk. Dawson's heart fluttered when he saw her.

"Glad you're out here. Come grab some bags."

"Gladly."

He stepped over to the taxi and she loaded his arms with bags.

"Can you handle all of that?" she asked, concerned with his weakened arms.

"Always," he replied with a smile.

She smiled and nodded appreciatively.

"I like it when you talk like that."

In the kitchen he helped her sort out and put the groceries up in the cabinets and in the refrigerator. She kept out what she planned to prepare for dinner. She held up a bottle of wine.

"I bought this for dinner. Do you think it would be okay for you to have alcohol?"

"I don't see why I couldn't. The only medication I have taken lately is an occasional sleeping pill. I try not to take anything for pain."

"All right then. Do you feel up to helping me get everything ready to cook?"

Smiling, he walked over to the sink and washed and dried his hands.

"I love to cook myself so you will never get any complaints from me about kitchen duty."

"My, my. The love meter just went up a notch!"

"Hmm. Where am I at on the scale?"

She cupped her hand under her chin as though she was contemplating something serious. She tapped her nose with her index finger.

"Umm. On a scale of one to ten you are at a two or two and a half."

"Whoa! I got a lot of work to do."

"Yep. I'm counting on it!"

He held his hands up like a surgeon standing at the operating table.

"I'm up for the challenge."

CHAPTER 19

While Lianne prepared veal parmesan, fresh asparagus, and scalloped potatoes. Dawson made salads and set the table. With little else to do until the veal was ready, the two had a glass of wine and watched the world news.

They ate dinner by candlelight out on Lianne's small patio. It was surrounded by tall hedges, giving them complete privacy. The meal was superb, the company even better. Dawson sat back sipping on wine and enjoyed watching Lianne's animated facial features by the light of the candle. He felt as if he were in a dream and thought he should pinch himself for a reality check.

After dessert of fresh strawberries and cream, Dawson helped Lianne clear away the dishes and clean the kitchen. She had gotten the hot tub going earlier and proposed that they have a relaxing soak.

"Lianne, I don't have a pair of swim trunks with me."

She gave him a mischievous grin and said, "Just wear your boxers. The lights will be off. Meet you there in ten minutes. Open another bottle of wine and don't forget the glasses," she said, and then bounded upstairs.

Dawson slipped out of his clothes except for his boxer underwear and put on the housecoat he had worn at the hospital. Uncorking the wine and gathering a pair of glasses, he retired to the hot tub room and eased into the water while waiting for Lianne he filled the wine glasses.

The door opened, Lianne walked in wearing a silky housecoat. She turned the lights out and slipped out of her wrap. It took Dawson's eyes a moment to adjust to the darkness. The outside lights gave the room a soft amber glow. He could see her standing there in a bikini. Even though her body was compact, she was definitely all woman.

"Care to join me?" he asked softly.

"I was hoping you would invite me."

He laughed.

"That should have been my line but I'm already here."

Dawson stood up and held out his hands for her. She leaned forward and stepped down into the warm water and into his arms.

"This is nice" he said softly.

"Me or the water?"

"Both."

"Good."

Their lips melded together for a pleasantly lingering kiss. When they finally parted, the two sat down beside each other. Sipping wine, the two begin to talk and share about their childhood and young adult years.

Lianne refilled their wine glasses and turned to where she could see Dawson's face in the ambient light.

"You've never mentioned Amydee much. When I had dinner with your parents your mom told me about what happened. I am so sorry that you had to go through that, especially alone."

"Yeah. Well. Thanks...."

"Your mom showed me pictures of her. She is very beautiful. I see why she had your heart."

Silence. Dawson did not know what to say. Lianne reached out and put her hand on his shoulder.

"Dawson. I know I am not pretty like her. I'm plain faced and built like a troll. I know you are probably not all that physically attracted to me. I do hope in time that you can come to accept me. What you see is what you get. I'm all yours if you want it."

Dawson felt a lump form in his throat. He swallowed hard.

"I hope you don't have the impression that I am not attracted to you. I am very much so. I'm still trying to get over Amydee. We were together a long time. Please be patient with me on that."

"Her loss is my gain," she said softly.

Dawson took her hand in his.

"Lianne, you are beautiful. You are the first woman I've gotten to know who is just as beautiful on the inside as the outside."

She giggled.

"My, my. You have a silver tongue. I like it. I like it a lot."

"I must confess Lianne; it's hard to believe that you are interested in a nobody like me. Look at you, you are somebody special. You are famous. Your face is seen around the world. People recognize you when you're out, like today at lunch. And here I am with you. Me! A plain Joe from the South. Another thing, I am appreciative that you don't seem to mind the scars. Amydee was repulsed by them."

"Well, like I said, I saw you when you got them. They don't make you less of a man. They give you character. And, I really like your character."

Dawson leaned over and gently kissed her on the lips. She stood up and moved out in front of him. Slowly, she untied her bikini top and tossed it to the side. Then she wriggled out of the bottoms and stood looking at him. He stood up and slipped out of his boxers. The two stood gazing at one another for a long while.

"Well," she said.

"Well," he replied.

"Well?" she queried.

"Well?" he countered.

"Dawson Lee! If you don't take me to bed right now, you will have twice as many bruises by morning."

Smiling, but saying nothing, he climbed out of the tub and pulled her out. They dried each other off and he led her to the bedroom.

CHAPTER 20

Waking, Dawson looked around for a moment. The early morning light gave the room a rich blue hue as it filtered its way through the curtains. He smiled when he felt the weight and warmth of Lianne in bed beside him. He gently turned over and laid there admiring her. She was laying on her side, curled in a fetal position, her back to him. Her delicate spine was clearly visible pressed against the thin nightgown she wore. Such perfection, he thought to himself. Her compact build was becoming more and more appealing to him. She reminded him of an Olympic quality gymnast.

The night of love making had been wonderful. It started off shaky. For a time Dawson thought he would be unable to perform. With Lianne's patience and charm, he got past the anxiety that was hindering the moment.

For a while he watched her sleep then carefully eased off the bed. As quietly as he could, he took a shower and made a pot of coffee. When the house filled with the aroma of fresh coffee, Lianne stirred and came into the kitchen.

"Good morning. If you had gotten me up I would have made the coffee for you. You are my guest. But, I like this. I could get used to it."

"I could too. I was just thinking about surprising you with breakfast in bed."

"Hmm. Not a bad thought, but I'm taking you to breakfast. You like bagels?"

"Yep, sure do."

"Great. I'm getting in the shower. Pour me a cup and bring it up to me if you're up to climbing the stairs."

"Oh, I'm up for the challenge," he said with a cheesy grin.

She kissed him and went upstairs. He poured two cups of coffee and slowly negotiated the stairs, careful to not spill the hot liquid. It was easier this time than he thought it would be. He decided then that sex must be better than physical therapy. He snickered at himself as he made his way to the top of the stairs.

"I never thought I'd be thinking things like that again," he muttered.

The bathroom door was open and he went on in. Lianne was in the shower. It had a clear glass door so he could plainly see all of her. She looked at him and struck a pose.

"See anything you like?" she asked in a sultry voice.

"Yep."

"What?"

"All of it?"

"Care to join me?"

"What about the coffee?"

"We can get more later."

"Okay, sounds good to me."

He got undressed and joined her. An hour later they were sipping coffee while getting dressed. The two walked arm and arm to a nearby bagel shop and had breakfast.

"Are you up for a little sightseeing this morning?" she asked, finishing off the last of her bagel with cream cheese.

"Sure, what do you have in mind?"

"I thought I would take you over to the Mall area and let you see the monuments."

"I'd like that."

They walked a few blocks and came out beside the White House, then crossed Pennsylvania Avenue and strolled out on the Mall. Moments later they were standing in the shadow of the Washington Monument.

To the west of where they were standing was the Lincoln Memorial. Off behind it was Arlington Cemetery. To their east was the stately U.S. Capital building. All along both sides of the mall were the various Smithsonian Museums.

So as to not tire Dawson too much, they sat on the grass of the mall and took in the scenery. Lianne lay back against Dawson. He wrapped his arms around her.

"This is great Lianne. You know, its humbling sitting here with the White House and Capital in plain view. Just think, the President is right there," he said, pointing at the White House.

"It is magnificent. It's thrilling to live right here where all of the decisions and laws for our country are made."

After they rested, Lianne led Dawson over to the Smithsonian Museum of American History. The two took in the displays, and then ate lunch in the basement cafeteria. She then took him to the nearby underground metro station. They boarded a subway train and rode back to Georgetown.

Another leisurely soak in the hot tub and the two rested up for an evening on the town. Lianne reminded him of the dance he still owed her.

"I thought I was supposed to pay up last night," he said.

"Well, we kind of got distracted doing other things," she said coyly.

He laughed and said "You're right about that."

While Lianne was getting dressed for their outing, Dawson called his parents to let them know all was well and that he and Lianne were enjoying themselves. He then went over his flight schedule for the coming Monday and they promised to be waiting for him at the airport.

CHAPTER 21

Dawson was sitting out back on the patio when Lianne finished dressing. She walked out to let him know she was ready. He looked up and watched her come down the steps.

"My goodness Lianne. You look magnificent!"

She was wearing a simple lavender dress but she looked elegant in it. The matching hose and sandals accentuated her shapely legs. Dawson was amazed at how her attire transformed her into such a tantalizing beauty. He had already noticed that her face and hair appeared fresh and camera ready at all times. He assumed that went along with her job. On television her appearance was pleasing to the eye and her voice distinct and professional in quality. He knew well that she had a long prosperous future in broadcasting ahead of her. Dawson felt truly lucky to be in her company.

"You don't look so bad yourself Dawson."

She embraced him, and then pulled him up from his seat.

"Are you ready for dinner and a dance with me?"

"Show me the way sweet lady."

Walking, they headed east along the sidewalk. The sun was going down and the air was cool. Lianne had been watching for a taxi and caught one for them. Five minutes later they were at DuPont Circle and paying the cab fare. Climbing out of the taxi, they stepped into a nicely appointed restaurant. Lianne had made reservations and they were led to a table for two secreted away from the main dining area. The lighting was turned low; candles cast dancing shadows on the tables, emitting a romantic ambiance. Looking around at the other patrons, Dawson was thankful he had purchased the dinner jacket Lianne had suggested.

A waiter appeared, took their wine order and handed them menus. Dawson's eyes bulged when he saw the prices. Lianne gigged when she saw the expression on his face.

"Don't worry about the cost. It's on me."

Dawson raised his eyebrows and smiled.

"Perish the thought. I worked for this. Dinner and dancing is on me. If we are going to be together I think I had better get used to nice places like this verses Billy Bob's Barbeque."

Lianne laughed and shook her head.

"You have such a way with words. Tell me they have some decent restaurants where you come from."

59

He nodded appreciatively.

"That we do have. I think you would be pleased with some of the places I plan to take you."

The waiter returned with a bottle of merlot and filled their cut crystal glasses. Lianne ordered for both of them and within minutes their soups and salads arrived. The salads were comprised of Boston lettuce stacks with grilled peaches, feta cheese and pecans. Dawson found the pea-shoot soup delicious. Later their main course arrived. Both had tender thick cuts of beef along with a lobster tail, Portobello mushrooms and stuffed potatoes. For dessert the two had strawberries and rhubarb topped with whipped cream.

Dessert plates gone, Dawson and Lianne finished the wine then lingered in the moment. Dawson was relaxed from the wine and good food. He watched Lianne as she spoke to several people who recognized her and stopped to say hello. She was so gracious and nonchalant about her notoriety. It was nice to see that fame did not make her unapproachable or haughty.

The couple that had stopped to speak said goodnight and left. Lianne looked at Dawson and smiled.

"You look happy. It's nice to see you smile so much. I take it you are enjoying yourself."

"I certainly am Lianne. It is impressive to watch you handle your admirers. You have a way of putting them at ease in your presence. I can't see that your popularity has gone to your head."

"I hope it never does. I don't want to think I'm better than everyone else. I have interviewed far too many famous people who put themselves high above the world. That stuffy better than though attitude is shameful."

Dawson looked at her a long moment. He leaned forward holding his glass with the remaining dregs of wine. Lianne reciprocated and they clinked glasses.

"Lianne. Thank you for coming into my life. You make me feel whole again. You make me feel special."

"You have always been 'whole' Dawson. Your injuries did not make you less than whole. If you will take a good look at yourself, you will see that they have made you stronger. Dawson, you are a very special person. You have an aura that drew me to you. Your ex threw a good man away. I can imagine how much you loved her. I saw that in you in Afghanistan. I hope that in time I might be able to have the love you had for her."

For a long moment he looked at her. He held his hand out and she placed hers in his.

"You already have the love I had for her."

Her eyes pooled with tears. Her voice caught and she sucked in a breath of air.

"I'm selfish Dawson. I want all of it and more."

He nodded thoughtfully.

"I don't see a problem with that."

CHAPTER 22

It was well after eight o'clock when Dawson and Lianne left the restaurant. The streets were brightly lit and the night air crisp. Dawson took his jacket off and draped it over Lianne's shoulders. Though cool, they opted to walk the three blocks to the nightclub she wanted to take him to.

Lou's Place was a pleasant and inviting establishment. The small band played a mixture of jazz and blues that were stimulating and made for a lively atmosphere. Dawson and Lianne found a small table and ordered mixed drinks. When the band began a slow song, he motioned to Lianne and she acknowledged by holding out her hand. He led her out on to the small crowded dance floor and wrapped his arms around her.

Swaying to the music, it felt good holding Lianne in his arms and her arms felt wonderful around him. As short as she was, the top of her head rested against his chest.

"I feel like a giant dancing with you," he said, looking down.

"Get used to it. I'm not growing any taller."

"Oh, I'm not complaining. I would not change a thing about you my dear."

"Good, cause what you see is what you get!"

"Couldn't ask for anything more."

Having never been one for jazz, Dawson was surprised at how much he was enjoying the band and liked the music. He and Lianne danced through the evening.

It was midnight when they left the nightclub. With no taxi readily available, they opted to ride the subway back to Georgetown. There was a Metro entrance just down from Lou's. The two descended on the escalator and caught the Red Line.

Whisking their way underground, soon they were back across town and exited less than a block from Lianne's house. When they arrived home, Dawson got the hot tub ready while Lianne put together a tray of cheese, fruit, and crackers. She opened a bottle of wine and the two snacked and relaxed in the tub.

It had been a wonderful evening. Dawson had done well on the dance floor, though now paying the price. His back and legs were sore and he began limping notably on the trip from the club to Lianne's. The hot tub was a godsend. Within minutes the pain and spasms had eased up and he felt reasonably well again. He was pleased now that he had included a hot tub in the new house waiting for him back in Tanner.

Neither Dawson nor Lianne bothered to wear bathing suits in the hot tub. They sat in the soothing hot water in each other's arms as if they were old lovers. Indeed, Dawson had commented how comfortable he was with her. Lianne whole heartedly agreed with him. She kissed him on the cheek and ran her fingers through his hair.

"So, Dawson, your debt is paid. I told you that you had to do dinner and a dance with me. You are free and clear of any obligations now. Whatever happens now is on neutral ground. Neither one of us have any obligations pending."

Dawson laughed, and then looked at her with great affection.

"You know, that day you stormed into the ward and demanded that my sorry ass get better and take you to dinner and dancing, I had no intentions of getting better. I really believed my life was over. You gave me the kick start I needed. You are the reason I decided to get better. Then when I started making progress, I began to do it for myself too. And for all of that, I thank you."

"You are welcome Dawson."

She looked at him for several moments, and then took a deep breath.

"I have one more day and night with you. What happens after that?"

He closed his eyes and held a hand to his forehead.

"Mmm. I'm looking into my crystal ball at the future now. Oh! Wait. It's coming to me now. Umm. Mmm. Uh. Okay. Got it!"

Dawson stopped rubbing his forehead. He took his hands down and opened his eyes. Sitting back and relaxing, he picked up his wine glass and took a sip. Then he just sat there, stone faced and aloof as if nothing was going on.

Lianne looked at him incredulously and gave him a mock look of anger. She playfully grabbed him by the neck like she was going to strangle him.

"You better tell me what you see in that crystal ball Mister and it better be good."

"Okay, okay," he said laughing.

Composing himself, he looked up and held a thoughtful expression.

"Dawson the great fortune teller sees large long distance phone bills and lots of air miles in the future."

She reached up and put her arms around him.

"So, do you see any problem with that?"

"No ma'am. Not one. I will gladly answer your calls and pick you up at the airport."

She squealed and playfully beat him in the chest.

"You rat, you! You better come see me too. I was going to offer you a key to my home."

"Okay, okay! You win; I'll accept a key to your place only if you will accept a key to my place."

"Deal!" she said and kissed him passionately.

They cuddled for a while the Lianne led him to bed. Their love making was intense and their feelings for one another were growing by leaps and bounds.

CHAPTER 23

It was near dawn when the two lovers finally fell asleep. Late in the morning they rose and ate a light breakfast. Lianne planned for them to have a leisurely picnic later. Dawson helped her prepare sandwiches and refreshments and pack the picnic basket.

Near noon they walked to the Metro and rode the subway to Potomac Park. There they found a pleasant scenic spot between the Jefferson Memorial and the Franklin Delano Roosevelt Memorial overlooking the Tidal Basin. From their vantage point they could see the Washington Monument, the White House, the Lincoln Memorial and Arlington Cemetery.

Spreading a blanket on the grass and setting up the lunch, the two ate sandwiches, chips, and fruit and drank raspberry tea. They walked and talked their way around Potomac Park then lay back and relaxed on the blanket.

"I'm already dreading taking you to the airport tomorrow," Lianne said as she lay in the crook of Dawson's arm.

"Me too. Other than seeing my parents, I'm not all that enthused about going home. Everything has changed from what I left to what I am returning to."

"I hope that us being together will make it a little easier."

"It will, Lianne. Knowing that I have you makes it all worthwhile. You have given me more reasons to move on with my life instead of giving up."

"When will we see each other again?"

"I'm not sure. I've still got to settle in and figure out what to do now that I'm unemployed. My VA disability is good so I have no real money worries for the moment. I have just got to set a course and go for it."

"Make sure I am a part of it."

"Oh you are Sweetheart. You are very much a part of my life now."

They were silent for a time then Dawson turned to her.

"Lianne, what is your schedule like over the next few weeks?"

"I have a few out of town assignments to do, but mainly I'll be here at the D.C. office. I'm covering the Senate hearings for the next few weeks."

"Why don't you plan on flying down to see me one weekend soon?"

She nodded, thinking.

"Okay, I'll check my schedule and lock down a weekend. I have lots of leave time so I will take an extra day or two if you like."

"I would love that. I want to show you my world. It is simple compared to your life here. But, I think you will like it nonetheless."

"I'm sure I will. Like I have said, I am adaptable."

Dawson looked deeply into her soft eyes. He slowly leaned over and kissed her long and tenderly. For one stolen moment, all in the world seemed right and serene.

Late in the afternoon the two took the Metro and rode over to Chinatown. Lugging the picnic basket, they walked to an oriental restaurant and had an early dinner then caught a taxi for the ride back to Georgetown.

As the night wore on, both became subdued and struggled to stay upbeat about his going home. They were sitting on the sofa together watching a movie when Lianne suddenly broke down in tears.

"I'm sorry. Silly me. I know we are not going to be all that far from each other with phone and airlines readily available, but I have come to enjoy you being here too much, I guess."

"I know how you feel. I'm thinking the same thing. At least flight wise it's a short trip flying to Atlanta then on the Tanner. I can pick you up at either airport."

She tried to smile through her tears.

"It sounds good but it's still a long way off when my heart is lonely."

He pulled her close and wiped her tears.

"Call me if you get real lonely and I will come to you if you can't come to me."

"Fair enough."

Before they went to bed Dawson packed his bag. Lianne had washed and dried his clothes and helped him with his packing. While packing, he pulled out a small velvet box and handed it to Lianne. She looked at him quizzically.

"I want you to have this," he said softly.

"I know what it is. It's your Purple Heart medal. Dawson, I can't take this. It's too special."

She tried to hand it back to him. He blocked her hands.

"They gave me two. I guess the paperwork got crossed. Please Lianne. You were there when I got hurt. It would please me for you to have this as a token of my affection and my gratitude to you for caring about me."

Lianne did not know what to say. With tears in her eyes she fell into his arms.

CHAPTER 24

Lianne arose before Dawson. She dressed and started breakfast. He awoke to the smell of fresh coffee and bacon. Greeting her with a kiss, she then handed him a cup of coffee and had him sit at the table. Moments later she joined him with their food. He had butterflies in his stomach but ate as best he could. Both were struggling with the dread of saying goodbye. They talked little while eating.

When they finished eating breakfast, Dawson went to get dressed while Lianne cleaned the kitchen. Packed and ready, he sat his bag by the front door. He was standing in the middle of the living room feeling awkward when she came down the stairs. She looked at him and her eyes began to glisten. He took her in his arms and looked into her beautiful blue eyes, then kissed her slowly and with passion.

After their kiss he looked at her trembling face.

"I'm going to miss you terribly," he said, and meant it.

"Same here, I've gotten used to going to bed and waking up with you."

"That, I'll miss the most."

"Promise?" she asked with tears in her eyes.

"Promise."

Lianne pulled him tight to her and looked up into his moist eyes.

"What if I don't let go?"

Dawson's throat tightened and his body shook.

"Oh my," he croaked and kissed her again.

It was time to leave. It was all they could do to gather themselves and leave. Moments later the two were in a taxi on their way to National Airport. Lianne laid her head against Dawson's shoulder while they rode in silence. An air of sadness hung over them.

Dawson reported to the Delta reservations counter and checked his bag. Lianne used her press credentials and was allowed to walk with him to his departure gate. They held one another until time for him to board. A kiss goodbye and a promise to call that night, Dawson boarded the flight for Atlanta.

Finding his seat, Dawson sat down and buckled in. His eyes were glazed over and his heart felt like lead. In a short time his life had gone from the garbage heap to a complicated long distance affair with a most special woman. A woman he would have never dreamed of having. Dawson saw Lianne as a woman that would have normally been beyond his reach. She was a classy professional lady through the through. And, he also knew that if they were to stay together and one day make it permanent, that he would have to accept her profession. He would have to tolerate her being gone a lot. Could he do that? It would be difficult but from what he had seen so far, it would be worth every moment of it to be with her.

Airborne and speeding southward, Dawson sipped a coke and began to focus on going home. It had been eighteen months now since he had left to go to Afghanistan. His reserve unit had long since returned home. They had been met by a crowd of well-wishers, American flags, and yellow ribbons. Now, here he was, alone and returning in civilian clothes, disabled and lucky to be alive.

Instead of returning to the sweet arms of Amydee, a marriage ceremony, and a new home for two; here he was heading to an empty house and leaving behind an even sweeter love.

"Love," he whispered, liking the sound of it on his tongue.

As he rolled the thought of love around in his mind, Dawson admonished himself for not telling Lianne that he loved her. He had wanted to make sure but deep down he already knew the answer. He had long since fallen in love with Lianne before spending the weekend with her.

"I'll tell her tonight," he whispered.

A short time later the 757 descended and landed at Hartsfield airport in Atlanta. Dawson deplaned, walked up the jet way, stopped at the nearest restroom then headed for his departure gate for the flight to Tanner. A half hour later he boarded an ASA commuter plane for home.

The flight to Tanner was less than thirty minutes. Soon the plane was on the ground and rolled up to the terminal. When he reached baggage claim he was met by his mother and father.

"It's so nice to have you back home," said his mother as she hugged him. "You look great now. Once you get some weight back on you, then you'll be good as new!"

"I feel fine, Mom. I'm still a little weak but I'm getting stronger every day."

"Well, I hope you are hungry. We plan to take you to lunch before we take you home."

"Sounds good to me. I am hungry."

Mr. Lee drove them to a nearby catfish restaurant. Dawson stuffed himself with fried catfish, French fries, slaw, and hush puppies.

"This is the best meal I've had in ages. There is nothing better than good old southern styled cooking."

"I second that," added his father.

CHAPTER 25

The ride to Dawson's house was almost like a dream. To him it was bittersweet as he rode by familiar stores, restaurants, and places he had always known. He noticed that there were several new restaurants and service stations that had not been there when he left to go overseas.

Dawson's house was fifteen miles north of Tanner. It was country, but quickly being encroached with new subdivisions and individual homes. A new high school had opened just minutes from his place. The small community he lived in was mostly small farms and homes on a few acres of land or more. No one was crowded. It was over two hundred yards to his nearest neighbor.

His father turned off the highway onto Jones Road and two minutes later they pulled into Dawson's driveway. A rush of mixed emotions overwhelmed him when he saw his home. The 3,500 square-foot, four bedroom, three bath, brick home had a two-car garage, great room with a fireplace, and a pool in the backyard. The lawn was freshly cut and the flower beds were a riot of spring colors.

"Someone has been busy!" commented Dawson.

"Yeah Son, I've enjoyed taking care of it but it's all yours now. I've already gotten you a small vegetable garden planted out back near the pool."

"Wow Dad, thanks!"

"That's not all," piped in his mother."

"Now Rebecca!" admonished Mr. Lee. "Don't spoil the surprises."

"Surprises?" queried Dawson.

"Just two," conceded his father.

After parking and getting out, the Lee's went into the house. His father had finished out the inside of the house that Dawson had not gotten done before leaving for Afghanistan, as well as the entire house was now completely furnished too.

"This is absolutely beautiful! How much do I owe you two for all of this?"

"Nothing. It's all paid for. You know I had power of attorney over your military pay while you were gone. So, you paid for all of this and you still have a nice nest egg in the bank."

"This is great. I have been wondering whether or not I could manage a saw and a hammer."

"That's one less worry. We want you to relax and get your strength back. Don't worry about anything for a time. Just get your life back on track and in a positive direction."

"With you two and Lianne I should be able to do that without a problem. I feel like my future will be better than my past."

"I like the sound of that," said his mother. "We were so happy you two have gotten together, even if she has a job that keeps her on the road a great deal. She is good for you Dawson."

"That she is Mom. She sure has been a help in me getting through the rehabilitation part of my ordeal."

His father placed a hand on Dawson's shoulder.

"Rebecca and I both were heartbroken over the way things turned out with Amydee. Her parents are disappointed in her and told us to tell you to please not hold it against them. They truly love you and said you are welcome in their home anytime."

"That's nice of them. I will have to go visit them soon."

His mother and father smiled and nodded at each other.

"Okay Dawson. We have one more surprise for you. It's in the garage."

Mrs. Lee took him by the hand and led him through the kitchen and into the garage. Dawson stopped in his tracks and gasped. There was a brand new Ford F-150 truck sitting there.

"Oh my goodness. You didn't get this with my military pay."

He looked at them curiously.

"Well son, it's paid for. When you got hurt, donations started pouring in from well-wishers and many local businesses. The Carter's sent a check for five thousand. I bet Amydee had a duck!"

Dawson laughed. Tears pooling in his eyes from the thought of how caring the community had been.

"This really is something!" was all he could say.

"Anyway, we thought it would be a good idea to replace your old truck. This baby here is loaded. It has leather seats that heat and cool themselves for you. The color is called 'Golden Bronze Metalic'. I hope you like it. I picked it out."

"It's fantastic Dad. Just great. I am absolutely blown away by all of this. I had better get busy with thank you letters."

"Good idea Dawson," agreed his mother. "We sent thank you cards to everyone but it would be very nice for you to write them also. I will get you all the addresses and list of donors."

"I will Mom. I just can't believe all of this. I wished I had known this. I probably would not have been such a jerk for all of that time I first wasted at Walter Reed."

"Dawson, we told you. You would not listen. If I could have put you over my knee and gave you a thrashing, I would have," said his mother.

"You should have."

"Well, I think Lianne did a fine job straightening you out."

"Yep. She sure did Mom. She had really been good to me."

"And for you!"

CHAPTER 26

After Dawson's parents unloaded his travel bag from their car, they left so he could get reacquainted with his home and give him space to unwind. He promised to eat dinner with them that evening.

Walking around inside the house, he was amazed at how nice it looked now that it was finished out and fully furnished. It was familiar in one sense and foreign in another. He had built much of it with his own hands. But, it had been all done with Amydee in mind. Now, it was difficult to picture it without her. He had learned from his parents that she had removed all of the pieces of furniture and decorations she had put in it before he left for Afghanistan. He was actually relieved that she had done so. He wanted nothing of hers now.

With a soft drink from the fridge, he walked outside and looked over his property. In the backyard, the pool was still covered. He would need to get it ready for the summer soon. But would he swim in it now? It would be good therapeutic exercise for him, but it was not all that appealing at the moment. Maybe when Lianne came down he would be more interested. He and Amydee had planned on having children. In his mind's eye he could still see a couple of kids running around and playing in the pool and in the playhouse he had drawn up to build. He shook his head and walked around the pool.

Dawson let out a sigh when he noticed the spot on the concrete apron surrounding the pool. There Amydee had inscribed their initials inside a heart while the concrete was still wet. Blinking away tears, he swore that he would get some concrete patch and cover it over so he would not have to look at if forever.

Now his mind began to flood with thoughts of Amydee. She was here in Tanner, not too far away. What would it be like to run into her? He knew he would eventually and probably soon. What would he feel? What was there to say to each other now?

Back around front, Dawson walked into the garage and stared at the new truck. He opened the door and looked at the interior. He smiled as he breathed in that new car smell. Climbing in, he cranked the engine and listened to the powerful V8 purr. He checked out the satellite radio system and the GPS display. Shutting the engine off, he felt giddy with excitement as he patted the dash and got out.

Back in the house Dawson decided to take a hot shower and rid himself of the travel grime. Twenty minutes later he was putting on blue jeans and a pull-over shirt. It was then that he realized the amount of weight he had lost over the last months. His waist size had dropped a good four inches. Now that he was home, he reckoned he would pick it back up easily enough.

While getting dressed, Dawson went through his closet and dresser drawers. He found all of his old familiar clothing. He could tell that his mother had washed and pressed just about everything he owned. They all smelled fresh and clean.

It was now three o'clock in the afternoon. He was due at his parents at 5:30 pm. With nothing in particular to do he decided to ride around Tanner and take a look at the town he had been away from for so long. He would call Lianne at bedtime as promised and let her know how his day had gone.

Not far from the house he stopped at a convenience store and picked up a large mocha coffee to go, then rode to the river walk and parked. He got out and walked along the river, taking in the views he had not seen in a long time. The wet earthy smells assaulted his nostrils, bringing back many moments of better times.

He walked along the river for a half hour before turning around and heading back to his truck. On his walk he had discovered that several restaurants and shops had opened along the river. He made a mental note to check them out soon.

It was five o'clock when he made his way out of the parking area and started for his parents. On the way he stopped at a floral shop and picked up a bouquet of flowers for his mother and drove on to their house. He pulled into their driveway right on time. He had always prided himself on punctuality.

"Some things never change," he chuckled as he got out of the truck. "I might be a scarred up junkyard dog, but I'm still on time!"

CHAPTER 27

His parent's house looked much the same as it had when he left for Afghanistan eighteen months ago. Dawson pulled into the driveway and parked. When he walked up onto the porch, he noticed the door was already open. Calling out that he was there, his father answered from somewhere in the house.

"We're in the den. Come on in!"

Dawson walked on in and made his way down the hallway toward the den in the back far right. Something felt odd to him as he walked along the lifelong familiar way. He then heard soft tittering and suddenly a raucous round of "Surprise" from several directions.

Relatives and old friends come out of adjoining rooms into the den to greet Dawson. It was overwhelming at the expressions of love and gratitude to have him back home.

The evening flew by with all of the excitement and camaraderie. The kitchen was filled with all kinds of food and desserts. There were house warming gifts of all descriptions piled up for him. His head was spinning with all of the joyous festivities. It was after ten o'clock when he left for home with the truck loaded with gifts and containers of leftover food.

He had just gotten everything unloaded and was putting the food containers in the refrigerator when his phone rang.

"Hello?"

"Guess who this is?" asked a female voice, soft and sexy.

"Hmm. Let me think. Your voice sounds vaguely familiar. Umm. Is it Susie Mae?"

"Nooo!"

"Is it Lucy?"

"You're digging your own grave Buddy!" She shot back.

"Oh. Oh yeah. I remember now. You're that sexy weather girl on the Hispanic channel."

"You're dead Dawson Lee. Wait until I get my hands on you!" chided Lianne.

Dawson laughed.

"I'm so happy to hear your voice. I just got in from a surprise welcome home party at my parents' house."

"Wonderful! How did it go?"

"It was great. My aunts, uncles, and cousins were all there. A couple of my old buddies were there too."

He then told her about his house being finished and furnished by the labor and love of his parents. He told her about his new truck and all the gifts he had gotten at the party.

"So it sounds like you had a great homecoming."

"Yeah, it has been. The only thing missing is you."

"That's sweet. I have really missed you today, especially when I came home this evening. The house seems empty without you."

"Same here Lianne. I have a fine little house that is begging for you to grace it."

"I have thought of nothing else today, Dawson. I want to come see you soon if you would like."

"That would be fantastic! I want you to see where I live. I hope you will like it enough to want to come here often."

"I'm sure I will Dawson. I'm looking forward to it. I have to work this weekend but I am off the next one. How about that?"

"Excellent! I'll be ready and waiting. I will see that you have a good time."

"I am sure you will. I can't wait to see you again."

After he and Lianne finished talking and said goodnight, Dawson kicked off his shoes and put together a late night snack of leftovers. He filled a plate with chunks of honey baked ham, potato salad, and slaw.

Full from eating so much, Dawson took a shower and changed into shorts and a t-shirt. He turned the television on and flipped it through the channels. He broke into a big smile when it landed on CNN and he saw Lianne. She was interviewing a congressman on the steps of the Capital. It was amazing how sharp she appeared on television. What he saw on television and in real life were two totally different people. It just did not seem to compute that they were one in the same. A sense of pride washed over him that she had chosen him above all others to be with.

He walked around the rooms of his home taking in the completed features that were his now. It was still hard to believe how nicely finished and completely furnished the house was now. And, a new truck too! He had no idea how caring his family and the community had been. It was humbling.

Tired but not particularly sleepy, Dawson switched the lights off and crawled in bed. He lay there thinking of Lianne. Then, Amydee popped in his mind. He had thought about her off and on at the welcome back party. It seemed as though everyone mentioned how sorry they were about their breakup. Never in a million years did he think that they would have every gone their separate ways. Deep down inside he still felt love for her, but now he had Lianne. He would be all right. Life was going on for him. Even a better life he said to himself, not really believing it.

"Oh well," he sighed and closed his eyes for the night.

CHAPTER 28

The soft patter of rain brought Dawson out of his early morning slumber. He arose feeling pretty good to start his first full day at home. Within a short time he had showered, dressed, and made a pot of coffee.

Stepping out of the warm coffee-scented kitchen, Dawson stood on the patio under the portico and breathed in the wet woodsy smell. The rain had gone but the air hung heavy with moisture. The dark overcast was slowly giving way to lighter shades of gray.

Sipping the coffee, he stood there looking around at the greening yard as if seeing it for the first time. There was certain poignancy in the shadows of the hydrangeas bordering the fence behind the pool. He felt at home again, and it felt good. He hoped that Lianne would find it to her liking and not want to leave it or him.

Back in the kitchen, he refilled his cup and sat in the den. He turned the television to CNN, now out of habit, hoping to get a glimpse of Lianne. Sitting in an old early American rocking chair that had belonged to his grandparents, Dawson felt a soothing balm wash over him. It was wonderful sitting in the beamed, high-ceiling room, still with the smells of new wood. The golden heart-of-pine floors appeared unusually bright, radiant in spite of the light of the dull overcast sky filtering in the expansive glass windows.

The phone rang. It was his mother calling to say hello and asked how he was doing. She invited him to dinner again that evening and he accepted.

"No surprise party tonight Mom, okay?"

She laughed.

"No. Once is enough. That's a lot of work. But, it was worth it. You do have to admit though, it was nice!"

"Yes it was great seeing everyone. I want to thank you and Dad again for everything."

"Please Dawson, think nothing of it. We love you so much. We have missed you more than you can imagine. We are thankful to have you back home."

"I'm happy to be back home Mom."

He said goodbye and promised to be there for dinner. While talking to his mother, Dawson had been walking around the house. He noticed the mail carrier as he came by when he looked out the front window. He walked out to the mailbox and collected the mail.

Adding the new stack of mail to the pile that his father had left on his desk in the den, Dawson sat down and began organizing and reading through the bank statements, utility bills, and junk mail. He compiled a list of things he needed to do over the next week.

"Might as well get started today," he said.

Twenty minutes later he was headed into town. He pulled into the parking lot of the Main Street Café and parked. It was a nice feeling to sit and eat breakfast in a place he had gone so many times to over the years. He felt as though he had been away a lot longer than eighteen months.

Since the local newspaper office was just across the street, he walked over after breakfast and renewed his subscription for the newspaper to be delivered to the house.

Climbing back in the truck, he drove through town to his old reserve unit headquarters. Captain Colbert was pleased to see him. Dawson said hello to all of his old unit friends who were there working. The secretary gave him a set of forms to take out to the military base to have a new ID made since he was now classified as a disabled veteran.

After saying goodbye to everyone with promises to visit again, Dawson rode out to the army base and had his new ID card made. While there he stopped and walked through the huge PX Mall and the Commissary. The benefit of having access to the post amenities would save him a lot of money and help him stretch his VA disability check until he found a way to bring in more money.

It was well after noon when he made it back home. Tired and hungry, he made a sandwich and salad, and then ate while he watched television. As usual he watched CNN but did not see Lianne on any news reports. She was on his mind frequently now. He missed her. It was beginning to sink in that he loved her; really, loved her. The love he felt was different from the love he had once for Amydee. He could not explain the difference, but this one felt good and much more meaningful.

"Weekend after next!" he said, and smiled.

He was looking forward to her visit. Maybe then they could seriously talk about making their relationship a little more permanent. What would it be like to be married to her? He was surprised at himself for wanting to make a more formal commitment to Lianne. From the start, he knew that their relationship would not be an easy one. She would be gone a lot and they would be spread between two homes; here in Tanner and there in Georgetown. Could he live like that?

"You bet!" he said, and meant it.

Shaking his head and laughing at himself, Dawson could not believe how much he was in love with Lianne.

"And already thinking about marriage!" he exclaimed. "I got it bad."

CHAPTER 29

Dinner at his parents was pleasant and relaxed. It was just the opposite from the dinner party the night before. After dinner they sat in the den drinking coffee and enjoyed one another's company. His parents again expressed their gratitude for Lianne coming into his life and told him how much they hoped that things would work out between them.

"I know that she is a professional and truly devoted to her work. You know you must accept her career and stand behind her. She would be gone a lot and I can see you both bouncing back and forth between homes. All in all Dawson, I think she is worth it," said his mother.

"I really do think a lot of her. She has been there for me. I still have a hard time understanding why she has been so good to me and wants to be with me. She lives in a different world up there in Georgetown. I'm not sure she would be happy being here in the country all of the time. Hopefully after her visit next weekend I will have a better handle on where we stand."

"We want the best for you," said his father. "I think you have got a good woman there. Not like you know who."

Dawson let out a strained chuckle.

"You know, it's hard to believe that Amydee is gone from my life. I guess it is good that I found out how she really was before we got married and had kids."

"I agree," added his mother as she got up and walked to the kitchen.

Mrs. Lee came back into the den with the coffee carafe and refilled everyone's cups.

"Have you made any progress on deciding what you want to do for a vocation now since construction is out?" asked his father.

"No, not really Dad. I want to do something. I cannot see sitting around drawing a VA check and doing nothing."

"I have been doing some thinking myself. I'm kind of tired of being retired. I haven't worked in three years now. It's not that we need the money, I would just like to feel needed."

Mrs. Lee laughed.

"It would be good to get your father out of the house. He's watching too much television and gaining a little too much weight."

"You mean you don't like my love handles Rebecca?" asked Mr. Lee with mock surprise.

"Thomas, those are not love handles. Those are spare tires!" She quipped.

Dawson laughed and held up his hands.

"All right, why don't we open a business of some kind Dad?"

"Fine with me son. Do you have anything in mind?"

"Not really. I would like for it to be something that will be enjoyable and interesting."

"I think I have just the thing in mind. And, I know where an empty store front is that is begging for a new business."

"Sounds like you have been thinking about this for a while now."

"Yes I have. When we saw that you would not be able to go back into construction work anymore, I have been tossing ideas around. What I have in mind is an outdoor sports store. What do you think?"

"Hmm. I love backpacking and camping. But what about Tanner Outfitters? Could the town support two outdoor gear stores?"

"They went out of business last year. From what I understand Mister Greely wanted to retire. He couldn't find a buyer who would meet his price so he just went out of business."

"You know, he was not in a good location. Business traffic had died in that area of town anyway."

"Well, you're right Dawson. I know there is an empty store front at the Village Shopping Center. What do you think about there?"

"Wow! That would be a nice spot. What about the rent?"

"I think it's doable if we work it right."

"All right then, let's take a look into it Dad."

The two discussed ideas of the types of equipment and name brands that they might would want to carry. When Dawson left two hours later he was filled excitement about the idea of opening a sports shop. Later that night when he talked to Lianne, she too was excited about the idea.

"With my Dad and I doing this together I would be able to come and go more freely." He added.

"That sounds even better. You could still come up and see me often."

"Sure could."

"I'm looking forward to next weekend."

"Me too. I am hoping you will have a grand time. I want you to want to come down often."

"I'm sure I will Dawson. You did enjoy yourself here, didn't you?"

"You know I did. I plan to get back up there soon too."

"Promise?"

"Promise."

CHAPTER 30

Over the ensuing days, Dawson and his father began researching and organizing the setting up of their outdoor sports shop. While Mr. Lee worked on leasing the store and obtaining the necessary business licenses, Dawson contacted vendors and received catalogs and price lists. He worked up an inventory list that cost wise was growing quickly.

With the start-up cost analysis completed, Dawson and his father set about to get a small business loan. It went through surprisingly painless, much easier than either expected. On the day that Lianne was to arrive for her first visit, Dawson and his father signed the lease and received the keys to their new place of business. After the two left the real estate office, Dawson said goodbye to his father and drove to the airport.

At the airport, Dawson found that he had arrived almost an hour early. He located the airport café and ordered a cup of coffee. Just as he sat down at a table his cell phone rang. It was Lianne.

"Hi Dawson. I'm at the Atlanta airport. I'll be boarding my flight to Tanner shortly. I should arrive on time."

"Sounds good. I am already sitting here at the airport waiting on you."

"My, my. You missed me that much?"

"Yep. Can't wait to see you. You should be here in less than forty five minutes."

"They just called for us to board. Be there shortly." She said.

"Okay, I'm standing by."

Dawson drank his coffee, found the restroom, and then walked around the airport for a time. At 11:45 am Lianne's plane landed and rolled up to the jet way. Moments later she walked through security and into his waiting arms. Dressed in slacks and a knit pullover, Lianne appeared even more petit and prettier than before. She felt great in his arms. He felt his spirits rise.

"I have missed you so much Dawson," she said as she kissed him several times.

"Same here. I missed you more than I ever thought possible. It seems longer than a few weeks since we were together."

"It sure does."

"Hungry?"

"Yes I am."

"Let's get your luggage and have lunch."

The two made their way over to the bank of baggage carousels and waited for her luggage to arrive. How good it felt to be with Lianne again. They laughed and joked with each other easily. Dawson began to realize more and more that he wanted her and needed her in his life. He was still amazed at how thoughts of Lianne had quickly replaced Amydee. He still thought of her and still had some feelings for her, but Lianne was gaining ground in his heart. And, he liked it. She was definitely the real deal!

The bags arrived and soon they were climbing into Dawson's truck.

"Whew!" said Lianne. "This is one big truck. I have never been in one this nice. These leather seats are heavenly."

"This is more truck than I would have bought myself. I am very pleased to have it."

A short time later they pulled into the Village Shopping Center. Dawson parked in front of the empty store that would soon be the sports shop.

"This is where our store will be. After we eat at the restaurant just down the sidewalk, I'll give you a tour."

"All right. Lead on."

The Mediterranean Café was getting crowded for lunch. Lianne and Dawson were lucky to catch an open booth for two and soon they were dining on bake ziti.

"How was your flight down?"

"Very pleasant. It's a fairly quick trip. The wait in Atlanta was brief. I know the Atlanta airport well so I had no trouble finding my way around."

"Happy to hear that."

"It's astonishing how much greenery you see when you are flying into Atlanta."

"We are blessed with lots of pine forests and country. I hope you will enjoy yourself here."

"I already am Dawson. I think I could be happy anywhere with you," she said, looking at him with loving eyes.

Dawson gazed back at her appreciatively.

"Those were nice words," he said softly.

"They were meant to be Dawson. You know I am in love with you. I started to say 'falling' but I'm way passed that. I am deeply in love with you."

He smiled and reached across the table and took her hand.

"I once read that one does not fall into love; one grows into love, and love grows into you."

"And?" she asked expectantly.

"And, I've grown a lot!"

Oh Dawson," she blurted around a mouthful of food, realized the gaffe, and tried to cover her mouth with a napkin.

She giggled. He started laughing.

"Sorry," she said. "I am so happy. I feel like I have spent my whole life looking for you."

"I know the feeling Lianne. Who would ever think we would find love in a war torn country like Afghanistan."

CHAPTER 31

Lunch, proclaimed Lianne, was the best she ever had. The profession of love for one another bolstered the savory ziti meal even more. They left the café feeling rejuvenated in what only new unbridled love can do.

A short walk along the portico put them back in front of the future outdoor store. The windows and glass door were covered over with paper, blocking the view of the interior. Dawson unlocked the door and the two stepped inside.

"Oh Dawson, this is perfect!" She exclaimed, her voice echoed through the empty building.

In the afternoon sun, light filtered through the papered front windows, giving the sales area a soft glow like the color of churned butter. The diffused light cast the chestnut walls and hardwood floor a warm amber tone.

"This was a clothing store at one time. My dad and I think the rich wood finish would add a nice accent to the rugged outdoor equipment and clothing."

"My goodness Dawson. It will be charming. I don't think you could have picked a better setting."

"I agree. Dad is the one who discovered this place."

Though dusty, the sales floor was in great shape. Only minor repairs and a good waxing were needed. In the stockroom, an assortment of wooden counters, bins, and shelves were stacked against one wall. These would suffice for much of their display needs.

Back at the truck, Dawson helped Lianne up into the passenger seat. She giggled when she plopped up onto the seat.

"If it wasn't for you I would need a ladder to get in and out of this tank."

Dawson laughed and said, "You'll get used to it." He paused a moment to look at her. "At least I hope so."

"Oh I plan to Mister Lee. I don't scare off very easy."

"Glad to know that!"

In the truck he rode around and gave Lianne a quick tour of downtown Tanner and the river walk overlooking the Chattahoochee River, separating Georgia and Alabama.

"This would be a lovely place to come for a picnic and a walk," said Lianne, thoughtfully.

"It's doable, but this is only the beginning, you will see some very nice places for picnics and walks this weekend."

"Looking forward to it. Anywhere with you Dawson is a nice picnic," she said. The lightness of her voice touched him.

Dawson reached over and took her hand.

"I'm glad you're here," he said softly.

"Me too."

When Dawson turned off of Veteran's Parkway onto Jones Road, he began pointing out places of interest and the names of neighbors as he passed their homes.

"And this place is mine," he said, pointing.

Lianne squealed with delight and clapped lightly.

"This is gorgeous. I knew you had good tastes. This is absolutely perfect Dawson!"

He took great pleasure in the complement.

"Why thank you. I have been hoping that you would like it."

As he pulled into the driveway, Dawson punched a remote button on the truck's visor and the garage door opened up. He parked inside and walked around to the passenger side and helped Lianne down. He grabbed her bags from the back and led her in through the kitchen. He sat the bags down and showed her around the house.

"I am truly impressed Dawson. This is an absolute dream home. I love all of the yard space you have, and the pool and especially the hot tub!"

"We're on ten acres of land here so it's quite a walk to our nearest neighbor."

"I see why you have a vehicle here. Nothing is within walking distance."

"Yeah. You pretty much need wheels here in the South. It's too expensive for a taxi to come out this far and we don't have much of a transit system except in the downtown area. I'll be happy to teach you how to drive."

"Hmm. Might just take you up on that one day."

Dawson collected her bags up and led her back to the bedroom.

"Here is you very own dresser and half of the walk-in closet is yours."

"Mmm. Sounds like you might be making permanent plans for me," she said coyly.

"As a matter of fact, yes. I want you as permanent as we can work it out."

"I like the sound of that Dawson."

She stood there quietly a moment, looking up at him.

"Are you sure you want to try to make us permanent? It will be a crazy ride going back and forth from your place to mine."

"I am very serious Lianne. There is nothing I would like more than to see us succeed. I am ready and willing to do whatever it takes to win you forever."

"Well then, I guess we really need to talk more about how we will balance two careers and two homes."

"I'm ready when you are," he replied.

She grinned at him and put her arms around him.

"I had rather do something else besides talk right now. How does that sound?"

"I like that sound."

"I'm all yours."

"And I am all yours," he said softly.

Having Lianne in his arms and in his home gave Dawson a feeling of utter pleasure. He knew then that somehow, some way, that they had to find a way to be together forever.

CHAPTER 32

After spending a glorious afternoon getting reacquainted, Dawson and Lianne had dinner at his parent's house. Dawson was pleased to see how easily Lianne fell into a comfortable sync with his family. She graciously sat through Mrs. Lee's digging out and showing her photographs of Dawson while growing up. Lianne enthusiastically kept "oohing," and aahing," and "oh how precious!"

From the den where he and his father sat, Dawson could see the two women at the kitchen table. His mother beamed with pride and joy basking in Lianne's accolades for Mrs. Lee's baby boy!

It was nearly ten o'clock before Dawson and Lianne headed home. She laid her head against his shoulder while he drove.

"I really like your mom and dad. They sure made me feel welcome."

"They think a lot of you Lianne. They are all for us being together."

"Good. Now you will have to meet my parents."

"Think they will approve of me?"

She laughed.

"They will probably bow down and worship you," she said giggling then laughed again.

"Why's that?" Looking at her curiously.

"I haven't brought a guy home to meet them in so long that they are worried that something is wrong with me."

"Hmm. Sounds like I have a chance."

"They are going to love you Dawson. They already know all about you and are anxious to meet you."

"All right then, we will have to do that real soon."

When Dawson's house came into view, Lianne let out a gasp of delight. The outside lights had come on at dusk and the house was bathed in a warm amber glow.

"Oh how beautiful! Your place is even prettier at night."

"I am quite proud of it. But you know you have a gorgeous home too."

"We have the best of both worlds to share with each other. This just gets better and better, doesn't it?"

"Sure does."

As they walked into the darkened kitchen, Lianne looked out back and saw the pool lit up.

"My goodness. The pool is lovely. Could we go for a late night swim?"

"We could. The water is still mighty cool. But, I'm game if you are."

"Okay then..."

She stopped and put her hand to her mouth. A look of surprise on her face.

"Oh, wait. I don't have a bathing suit."

He gave her a cheesy grin.

"That's optional on the bathing suit. We can turn the outside lights off and swim under the moonlight."

"Let's do it!"

Before they stripped and went outside, Dawson filled the Jacuzzi tub and turned the heating unit on. He knew they would be chilled coming out of the pool and the hot tub would be a welcomed respite.

He switched the pool lights off, then the security lights. The two walked out wrapped in towels. After dropping their towels on the deck chairs, they held one another and kissed under the moonlight.

"Okay, should we go for a swim before we get carried away?" he asked when they separated.

"I'm ready."

"The water is chilly so I suggest you jump or dive in and get it all over with at one time. It will take a minute or two to get used to it."

"Okay, I'm with you. I'll follow your lead."

Dawson dove into the deep end and Lianne followed him moments later. She let out a scream when she reached the surface.

"Told you it was cold," he chided.

"Whoo hoo! I like it though."

They swam for several minutes until Dawson could hear Lianne's teeth chattering.

"Okay Lianne. It's time to hit the hot tub. I don't want you to catch a cold."

"Fine by me."

He helped her out and wrapped her in a towel, then got his. They hurried in and piled into the hot tub.

"Oh my gosh, this is wonderful. That pool water is freezing!"

"It's a lot better during the day when the sun is out. It will be just right in a few more weeks."

Lianne giggled as she snuggled into his arms.

"It was fun though. I've never been skinny dipping before. Always wanted to!"

"You are welcomed to anytime you would like. One nice thing about out here in the country is that the neighbors are too far away to see."

"I still need to get a bathing suit. I'm not sure if I would be comfortable in the daylight."

"We'll get you one tomorrow."

CHAPTER 33

It was early, just after dawn when Dawson opened his eyes. He rolled over to curl up close to Lianne, but she was gone. Looking around, he saw no sign of her except for her nightgown draped across a chair.

Sitting up, he caught a whiff of fresh brewed coffee. He listened but heard no signs of movement in the house. Getting out of bed, Dawson went into the bathroom, brushed his teeth and combed his hair. Slipping into a sweat suit, he padded into the kitchen. There he found the coffee had been ready for some time and a third of the pot already gone. He looked around for Lianne then noticed through the window that she was curled up on a deck chair by the pool. The sun was just edging above the line of pine trees off to the east.

He poured himself a cup of coffee, then added creamer and sugar. Opening the back door, he called out to Lianne and asked if she needed a refill.

"No thanks. I just got one. Come out and watch the sunrise with me."

"Sure."

Dawson walked out and slid a deck chair over beside her and sat down.

"Have you been out here long?"

"A while now. I woke up early and was restless. I didn't want to disturb you so I came out here to enjoy your beautiful yard and view. It is so peaceful here Dawson. I can understand why all of this means so much to you."

"I do love it Lianne. I'm glad that you do too. I wanted you to like it as much as I do."

She looked at him a long moment.

"Are you asking me to go steady with you?"

"Un-huh. I don't want to ever not have you in my life since I've found you."

"I'm feeling the same way Dawson. But, I would like to ask you a couple of things."

"Ask away."

"Are you over Amydee?"

He was taken aback by the blunt question and faltered for a moment. Lianne patted his arm and smiled.

"You still have feelings for her. That's okay I understand. I would be disappointed if you didn't."

"We were together a long time," he said softly.

"Let me ask you this. If she were to come to you and want you back, what would you do?"

He sat there a moment then said, "As much as I cared for her I could not do it. If she would leave me when I needed her the most, then that tells me right there that I could never count on her in the long run."

Lianne listened intently and nodded her head.

"I believe you and I agree with your thinking. Okay now, I need to tell you something about me before we proceed any further."

"Okay, I'm all ears."

She laughed and said, "I like your ears."

Lianne took a deep breath.

"Now. Seriously. I noticed that you have those extra bedrooms. Those were to be for kids, right?"

"Yeah, they were."

She cleared her throat. Tears pooled in her eyes.

"Dawson. I can't have kids. I had cervical cancer a few years back and I had to have a hysterectomy."

He sat there in silence, lost for words. Tears began to trickle down Lianne's cheeks. She tried to wipe them away with her hands.

"I'm sorry Dawson. I feel like a fool. I should have told you before we got so far into this. I meant to. I just couldn't find the right time."

Dawson reached over and pulled her to him. They held each other in silence. She sobbed softly. He held her until she stopped crying.

"Lianne, I love you. Nothing can change that. If it takes not having kids to have you, then so be it. With the way we are heading in our relationship, kids would pose a hardship. You have your work, your life in D.C., and I have mine here. We'll be jetting back and forth until one of us retires and decides to live up there or here. So, what I am saying is that I want you and I want to be with you always. Let's keep going and see if we are happy with one another to make it legal and permanent."

They kissed and held on to each other until long after the sun had risen, then went inside and back to bed. Later in the morning, Dawson cooked breakfast and the two dressed for the day.

"Is there anything special you would like to do today?" asked Dawson.

"Not particularly. I would like to find a bathing suit somewhere. I would like for you to show me more of your world here."

"Umm. I've got that covered. Let's go for a ride."

CHAPTER 34

The sky was bright robin egg blue as they drove along the highway. Within minutes they passed through the little town of Hamilton in Harris County and reached Pine Mountain. There, Dawson pulled into the entrance to Callaway Gardens. After paying the admissions fee they wound around beautifully maintained forests of rhododendron, azaleas, dogwoods, and stands of fragrant honeysuckles.

Their first stop was at the horticulture center where they walked through both indoor and outdoor gardens of lovely flowers of all colors and descriptions. Next, Dawson took Lianne to the Sibley Butterfly Center. There they walked into a huge glassed in building with a jungle filled with colorful butterflies of all sizes and types. Lianne was enchanted with the ability to observe them close up. She was captivated when one landed on her hand. Her smile was priceless as she studied the iridescent colors of its wings.

Leaving the butterfly center, the two of them rode throughout the gardens. Dawson took Lianne by the golf course, Robin Lake where people could swim and water ski. He told her about the big national Master's Water Ski Tournament held there each year.

Dawson then headed back down a road that Lianne noted that they had already been on.

"I have one more place to show you that I have always enjoyed stopping and visiting."

After turning onto a narrow road, they came out by a lovely lake nestled in the woods.

"Oh my goodness, Dawson. That is so beautiful!" exclaimed Lianne, looking across the lake.

In the corner of the lake sat a small stone chapel with ornate stained-glassed windows. The smooth surface of the lake mirrored the reflection of the gorgeous chapel. The scene had the appearance one would find on a picture perfect puzzle.

Dawson pulled into a parking lot overlooking the chapel. The two got out and walked down the steps and across a small stone bridge to reach it. Inside the chapel the light took on the appearance of a rainbow as it shown through the stained-glass. The slate flooring lent to a cool peaceful ambiance.

"Oh Dawson, this is absolutely lovely. Could you imagine what it would be like to hold a wedding here?"

He smiled and nodded appreciatively.

"That's a thought to tuck away for the future," he said thoughtfully.

She grinned and threw her arms around him.

"You have a romantic soul my dear Dawson!"

He held her close and shamefully thought about when he and Amydee looked into the possibility of being married there. However, Amydee did not want to because she complained that the chapel was too small for all of her family and friends she wanted to attend.

Piling back into the truck, Dawson and Lianne drove out of Calloway Gardens and stopped at the Country Store and Restaurant just across from the entrance to Roosevelt State Park. Enjoying a late lunch, Dawson was pleased listening to Lianne bubbling with excitement about how much she had enjoyed the gardens they had just left.

With ice cream cones for dessert, the two got back in the truck and rode along the scenic ridge road that traversed the Roosevelt State Park over Pine Mountain to Warm Springs. Warm Springs is where President Franklin Delano Roosevelt's, Little White House and the hot springs are located. Roosevelt bought the 1,700-acre farm surrounding the springs in 1927. He founded the Institute after hearing about a boy who had regained the use of his legs, through a treatment known as hydrotherapy, which involves the use of water for soothing pains and treating diseases. Suffering from polio himself, Roosevelt traveled to the area frequently, including sixteen times while he was President of the United States, and he died in 1945 at his Little White House, which he had built in 1932.

Dawson took Lianne to downtown Warm Springs. The small square was lined with quaint shops filled with collectables, arts, and crafts, and antiques. After a quick walk through the Little White House, the two tired lovers drove back to Dawson's place.

Worn out, they took a shower together and lay down for a nap. Dawson had plans to take her out to dinner later.

At five o'clock they got up and dressed; he in coat and tie, she in a silk dress, the colors of raspberries n cream. Downtown Tanner, Dawson found a parking spot just down from the Broadway Restaurant where he wanted to take Lianne for a special dinner. When they got out of the truck Lianne spied a woman's boutique two doors down.

"Hey, look over there. Could we get me a bathing suit before they close?"

"Sure thing."

They hurried into the shop. Ten minutes later they were coming back out the door. Dawson was surprised at how quickly Lianne chose a swimsuit and paid for it. Outside the store Lianne grinned at Dawson.

"I'm not that hard to please, sometimes."

He shook his head and smiled.

Dinner at the Broadway was wonderful. They dined on prime rib and baked potatoes. Sharing a fine bottle of wine, the two toasted to their future.

CHAPTER 35

The ride back home after dinner was pleasant. Neither spoke much. Lianne lay against Dawson's shoulder and rubbed his chest. When they neared his house she sat up and smiled.

"The house is stunning lit up like that. It's so inviting. Makes me want to stay."

"That would be okay with me. You can stay as long as often as you want."

"Same with my place."

"You got it."

He parked the truck in the garage then walked around to the passenger side and opened the door. Lianne slid down into his arms and kissed him fervently.

"Mmm. What did I do to deserve this?" he asked hoarsely.

"Oh, everything." She said in a soft sultry voice.

They made their way into the house without turning on the interior lights.

"Are you tired?" Dawson asked.

"I'm a little too relaxed from the wine. I need a little pick up so I don't fall asleep."

"How about another late night swim?"

"Hoo-ee! That was a little too cold last night."

"Trust me, it will be nice tonight."

"How so?"

"I know so. It will be great tonight. I promise."

"Well, I might as well try my new bathing suit on."

"All right then. We can leave the lights on in the pool tonight."

"Okay. Make sure the hot tub's ready. I'll go change."

Dawson filled the tub and fired up the heater and turned the jets on. He got in his swim trunks. Lianne came out of the bedroom in her new two-piece peach colored bikini. Dawson smiled.

"Wow! You look terrific."

"Why thank you."

Hand in hand the two walked outside to the pool and laid their towels down. Dawson dove into the swimming pool and came up smiling. Lianne stood by the ladder with her arms wrapped around her chest.

"Come on in. The water's fine," coaxed Dawson.

"Oh well, might as well get it over with."

She dove in and came up squealing.

"This is great. How did you get it so warm?"

"A heater my dear. I turned the heater on this morning."

"You rat you! Why didn't you do that yesterday?"

He laughed and threw up his hands.

"I'm sorry. I didn't think about it ahead of time."

She swam over and wrapped her arms around him.

"I love you anyway. This is heavenly. Why don't we work our way over to the shallow end so we can stand on the bottom."

Lianne swam for the shallows. When Dawson got to where she was standing the water was only up to his chest. Lianne wrapped around him again and kissed him deeply. Their hands began to explore one another with urgency.

"Dawson?"

"Yeah," he said breathlessly.

"No one can see us, can they?"

"Nope."

Lianne reached up and untied her top, then slipped out of her bottom. Dawson stepped out of his swim trunks. Wrapped around him again, Lianne looked up into his eyes.

"I want you right here," she whispered.

"You got it."

By the time they made it to the hot tub an hour later, both were satisfactorily exhausted. They spent only a few minutes in the hot water, then took a quick shower and climbed into bed. Holding each other close, they were both filled with total commitment and enduring love.

"Dawson. This has been an absolutely wonderful weekend. I am so happy with you. I love it here. I love this house. I love your life here. I like mine too in D.C. but I like this just as much. If I had to choose one right now, I don't think I could do it."

"Don't you dare try to choose one over the other. Let's do both and see how it goes. I don't mind coming up there to your place to be with you some. I will be tied down a little while until the business gets up and running smoothly. I'll still be able to get away a few days at a time."

"Oh, I don't mind flying down here. I am for sure used to traveling often. It's second nature to me now. I will be down as often as my schedule allows."

"Same here."

They kissed for a long moment. Lianne then laid her head on his chest while he caressed her back.

"What's the plan for tomorrow?" she asked.

"I thought we would have a leisurely day together and not do too much except each other."

She giggled.

"I like that."

"When I take you to the airport tomorrow, I want you to be completely satisfied. In fact, I want you feeling so good that you will want to come back for more."

"Whoo-hoo cowboy! I like the sound of that!"

CHAPTER 36

Even though they had planned to sleep in, Dawson and Lianne both woke early, energized and feeling good. Instead of cooking breakfast, Dawson decided to take Lianne for a traditional southern breakfast.

A short time later they were pulling into the parking lot of Cracker Barrel Restaurant.

"I have seen these before but I have never been inside."

"Well, this will be a treat. It's a good representation of southern styled cooking."

The two walked into the restaurant and were soon having eggs over easy, country ham, grits, and huge biscuits along with steaming coffee.

"What do you think?" asked Dawson.

"Hmm, great. I think I feel my arteries clogging up though. I'm not real sure about those grits yet."

He smiled and said, "Give it time. They'll grow on you."

"I plan to," she replied, giving him her best smile.

"You really know how to make a guy happy Lianne."

"So do you. You really make me happy."

Finishing breakfast. Dawson paid the bill and the two climbed in the truck and rode over to the river walk. They walked holding hands along beside the river flowing lazily southward. The morning was quite, pleasant, and relaxing.

Hot and thirsty when they left the river walk, Dawson stopped at a convenience store and bought them both cokes. They then rode around the old historic district of Tanner. Dawson showed Lianne the restored pre and post-civil war homes that overlooked the river.

It was time for lunch when they made it back to the house. Dawson put together a light lunch and the two ate then went for a swim out back. After swimming for a while, Lianne lay out by the pool and enjoyed the sun. Dawson sat on a deck chair and enjoyed her company.

Lianne rolled over onto her stomach and looked over at Dawson.

"This weekend has really gone by quickly, hasn't it?"

"Yeah Lianne, it sure has. I'm already not looking forward to taking you to the airport this evening."

"I know. I will be back real soon. That, you can count on."

"I'll do my best to come up your way soon too. Dad and I will be mighty busy for a spell while we get the store running smoothly. As soon as we can get a good staff trained and able to handle things, then I see no problems getting away frequently."

"Don't worry if you can't get away. I will be happy to come down as often as I can get away. I really do like it here Dawson. I look forward to spending lots of time here with you."

He reached out and took her hand.

"Think of this as your home too. You gave me a key to your home so I am giving you keys to this place too."

"That is so sweet of you. I like the return gesture. You consider the Georgetown home as being yours too. You are welcome anytime."

Lianne got up and climbed on his lap. She gave him a lingering passionate kiss.

"Why don't we take a shower and lay down for a while," she suggested.

"I can't think of anything else I had rather do."

They took their time in the shower then spent the next few hours finding as many ways as they could to please one another. Late in the afternoon while Lianne dressed and packed, Dawson cooked dinner.

While they ate, it became difficult for them to keep from getting sad and down. Both tried their best with manufactured smiles and light-hearted banter. It was trying as they attempted to keep their spirits up.

After the early dinner, the two sat on the sofa and held each other. Both were amazed at how close they had become in such a short time.

"You know Dawson; usually goodbyes didn't really bother me. All of a sudden I'm not doing so well."

"I understand. I have never been good with them myself. Unfortunately we are going to have to get used to them until things change one day."

Lianne raised her eyebrows and pinned him with her luminous eyes.

"What will happen 'one day'?"

He gave her a shy smile.

"Well, one day I hope we will never have to say goodbye again. I could easily get used to waking up to you every day."

"Hmm. Me too," she nodded, appreciatively.

Time came to leave. Lianne took a walk around the yard one last time. Dawson loaded her bags in the truck, opened the garage door, then walked out and joined her. She leaned against his chest.

"I love this place Dawson. I do enjoy my life in D.C. It was all I ever knew until now. This has a strong pull. It feels like home too. I'm torn over which I like better."

Dawson held his fingers against her lips.

"Shh. Don't even try to make a choice yet. It's not time. We have lots of time to worry about something like that. Let's just enjoy both worlds. I'll be coming up there and you will be coming down here. We will talk every night. In my heart I feel this is going to work out great for both of us. Just know that I love you enough to live anywhere with you just to have you as my own."

CHAPTER 37

The ride to the airport went by all too fast. After finding a parking spot, Dawson helped Lianne down out the truck and kissed her before letting her go.

Checking in at the Delta counter for her ASA flight, Lianne found she had forty minutes before her departure. The terminal was crowded. There were many soldiers milling around waiting to fly out or for transportation to the nearby army base.

Dawson found a pair of vacant seats near the security entrance and the two sat down. Holding hands, the two made small talk and tried to remain upbeat and light hearted. Everything was going well until the announcement was made that Lianne's flight arrived. She needed to clear security and get to the boarding gate.

Lianne looked up at Dawson with doleful eyes. Her trembling lips gave way to a rush of tears and sobs.

"Oh Dawson. I'm sorry for being for being such a goof. I had such a good time. It just didn't last long enough."

They stood up and embraced each other.

"You have got to stop crying," said Dawson. "You are going to get me to blubbering too."

For a long moment they held one another. Then, Lianne smiled through the tears and said goodbye. Dawson watched her go through and cleared security. She waved one last time and disappeared. Feeling a mixture of joy and sadness, he walked back to the truck and drove home.

The house seemed empty and forlorn when he went inside. He could still smell the lotion Lianne liked to use. The scent was comforting. To break the spell of sadness, he got busy and cleaned the kitchen. After loading the dishwasher and turning it on then sorted the dirty laundry and began washing clothes.

Still restless, he went out and backwashed the swimming pool filter pump. He then connected the robotic pool cleaner and drops it in. It was almost dark when he went back in the house. Working around in the house, he noticed that it was almost 9:00 p.m. Lianne planned to call him at ten. He was already looking forward to hearing her voice.

He called his mother and talked to her a few minutes and then talked to his father. They planned to begin setting up the sports shop and would meet there early in the morning. Having a lot of work lined up was a comfort for him because he figured it would help him as he learned to adjust to having a long distance affair with Lianne.

With a cup of coffee, he sat at the kitchen table and spread out a pile of sporting goods catalogs. He began making out tentative orders for merchandise to go in the new store. At ten o'clock he was still filling out order forms when Lianne called.

"I miss you," she said sweetly when he answered the phone.

"I miss you too. Ready to come back?"

"Yep. Are you ready to come up here?"

"Uh-huh. As soon as we can get the store organized and going I will break away and come up."

"Oh, I'll come back down long before then, I'm sure."

"I hope so. I'm already looking forward to the next visit."

"It will happen before we know it," she confirmed.

"Good." He paused. "What does your work schedule look like?"

"For now I am staying close to D.C. I know of no travel assignments at this time. When I am in town working, I'm usually off on weekends. I thought I would maybe come back down in two weeks. How's that."

"Sounds good to me. Maybe by then the store will be taking shape and I will have a sense of my schedule."

"Maybe you will. If not, I will keep coming as often as I can."

"Listen Lianne, if you need me to help out on travel fare, let me know."

"I will Dawson. Financially I'm in good shape. I also have a lot of travel miles and I get discounts on travel as well."

"Excellent. Things are sounding better and better."

While they were talking Lianne was unpacking from the trip. She let out a squeal and dropped the phone.

"Lianne?" queried Dawson.

She picked the phone back up.

"Oh Dawson! I just found the card you put in my bag. It is so pretty. Thank You."

"I mean what the card says Lianne. You mean the world to me and I love you."

"I love you too."

They talked a few more minutes then said goodnight. Tired, Dawson decided to go to bed. He turned the kitchen light off and went into the bedroom. He took his clothes off and pulled open the dresser drawer to get out a pair of pajamas. He broke out into laughter. There on top of his pajamas was a card.

Still laughing, he picked up the phone and punched in the Lianne's number.

CHAPTER 38

At eight o'clock, Monday morning, Dawson pulled into the parking lot and parked in front of the soon to be Lee Outdoor Sports store. His father's truck was already there. When he opened the front door, Dawson could smell the aroma of fresh coffee mingled with the musty odors of the dusty sales floor and stockroom. Also, he could hear several voices.

In the stockroom he found his father and four Hispanic men. Standing around a little table, they were availing themselves of coffee from a new coffee maker his father had brought.

"Good morning Dawson," greeted his father.

"Hey Dad. Hello everyone."

"Good morning Senor Dawson," greeted the men.

"Dawson, I hired these fellows to help us clean and get the shelves, fixtures, and the sales counter out on the sales floor. This is Julio, Antonio, Garcia, and Roberto."

"Glad to meet all of you," Dawson said as he shook their hands.

After a cup of coffee and two donuts, Dawson got busy with his father and the work crew. They began by washing down the sales floor walls and windows. Next they scrubbed and mopped the sales floor. In the stockroom they wiped down all of the shelves and counters. Before they all broke for lunch, two men applied wax to the sales floor.

Dawson and his father took the four men to the nearby Kentucky Fried Chicken. Mr. Lee bought lunch for everyone. Dawson found himself having a good time working with and getting to know the Hispanic day laborers. He admired their work ethics and desire for a better life in America for them and their families.

During the afternoon the crew arranged the shelving units and counters out on to the sales floor. At five o'clock Mr. Lee paid the four workers and let them go. He then left for home but Dawson stayed long enough to lay another coat of wax on the hardwood floor. Tired and pleased with the day's results, he drove home.

Too tired to cook, Dawson filled the Jacuzzi tub and turned on the whirlpool jets. After popping a bag of microwave popcorn, he poured the contents into a bowl. With a cold beer and the popcorn, Dawson slid down in the hot bubbling water and relaxed. His arms and legs were so sore that he had begun to have muscle spasms while driving home. He was mildly frustrated with himself because he had expected to get past the weakness. Other than a multitude of scars resembling white lines like a road map on his arms and legs, they had returned to a decent shape and tone of normal musculature.

The hot relaxing bath did its magic and Dawson felt rejuvenated again. He began nodding off so he got out and dressed for bed. It was his turn to call Lianne at ten. He struggled to stay awake to make the call.

When time finally came to call her it lifted his spirits. He immediately felt better. Still, Lianne detected a strain in his voice.

"Are you okay? You sound as though you are in pain."

"I guess I worked a little too hard today. I am completely worn out. We did get the worst of the setting up out of the way. I think when it's all done it will be a fine looking business."

"I'm sure it will, Dawson. I would expect nothing less from you and your Dad. Do try not to overdo yourself. You need to stay in shape to take care of me."

"Hmm, I will. I promise. I will always be ready for you anywhere, anytime, anyplace."

"Is that a fact?"

"Yep, you can bank on it!"

"That I will. Speaking of which, next weekend is a holiday weekend. I have four days off. Care if I come down?"

"Mmm. Let me check my busy schedule and see if I can work you in."

"Dawson Lee, if I could get to you right now I would give you a thrashing!"

He laughed.

"You know you are welcome here anytime you can get away. You don't even have to ask, just come on home to me."

"Same here Honey. You know the way. You have your key. My home is your home."

"I like the sound of that," he said and meant it.

She was silent for a moment.

"Dawson, may I ask you a serious question and will you give me an honest answer?"

"Whoa! Is everything all right Lianne?"

"I hope so."

"Well then. Ask away."

"Have you seen Amydee since you have been home?"

"No I haven't. Why?"

"If she wanted you back, would you go?"

He let out a long sigh and collected his thoughts.

"Listen Lianne. That part of my life is gone. She is no longer any concern of mine. I wish the best for her. I have you now. I am happy with you and what we have."

"But Dawson, she's so perfect. She is about the most beautiful woman I have ever seen."

"And I think you are the most beautiful women in the world?"

"Be honest Dawson. I am a troll compared to her."

"Please don't talk like that. I love you Lianne. You are beautiful to me. I'm not alone. Your beautiful face is recognized everywhere we go. You are mine. I am yours. That's all that counts. Besides, look at me. I'm not a hunk. I'm a beat up, junkyard dog."

Silence.

"Dawson," she said softly. I just don't want to ever lose you."

"And I don't want to lose you Lianne. I am not even in your league. I'm the luckiest guy in the world to have you."

"Thank you for loving me," she said softly.

"Ditto. Please don't worry about Amydee. If I were to ever run into her, it will not change a thing between us. I am yours for as long as you want me."

"I want you for a long, long time."

"You got it!"

CHAPTER 39

Over the next few days the outdoor sports store began to take shape. A phone system was installed, a computerized cash register was put in place, and Dawson had furnished the store's office. Merchandise orders were beginning to arrive. On Thursday they received a shipment of kayaks, canoes, and paddle boards. A sign company hung a temporary store name banner outside while the permanent lighted one was being made.

Dawson arrived at the store on Friday morning to find a delivery truck already waiting. A large shipment of outdoor clothing and footwear had arrived. Later that morning two more good sized shipments of stock arrived.

Just before noon Dawson and his father were stacking boxes of merchandise in the general location of where they will be displayed when someone opened the front door and called out. They looked up to see a strikingly beautiful blond haired woman with bright blue eyes and a dazzling smile walking toward them.

"Hello, I am Cali Kinsley from Kinsley Accounting Services. You two must be Thomas and Dawson Lee."

Dawson and his father stood up.

"Yes we are. It's nice to meet you," greeted Dawson as he and his father shook hands with her.

"If you have some time, I'm here to go over what we need in order to handle your accounting."

"Sure thing," said Dawson. "If you would, follow me over to our office and we'll get started."

Mr. Lee said that he would keep sorting the merchandise while Dawson handled the setting up of the accounting procedures with Mrs. Kinsley.

"You have a lovely place here Mister. Lee."

"Thank you. I think we picked a great location and this store interior is perfect with the rustic woodsy look."

"I agree Mister. Lee. I don't think you could have chosen a better set up."

"Please call me Dawson."

"Call me Cali as well."

He offered her a cup of coffee and she accepted. After pouring them both cups, the two went to work. She gave him the materials and charts he needed to figure employee tax withholdings. Cali then installed the accounting package on the computer and went over it with him. They were still working on everything past one o'clock so they stopped for lunch. Cali, Dawson, and his father ate lunch at a small café a few doors down from the store then went back to work and finished setting everything up.

During the course of the time with Cali, Dawson learned that her husband was Peyton Kinsley, the famous outdoor photographer whose photographic artwork was widely known.

"He loves the outdoors. He spends a lot of time traveling and trekking in the wilderness. He will be thrilled with your store here. I'm sure you will get a lot of business from him," said Cali.

"I look forward to meeting him soon."

"If you would like, I'm sure Peyton would be happy to be here for your grand opening. He often does signings and meet-and-greets at events like that."

That would be wonderful. I haven't thought much about ideas for the grand opening yet."

"I'll talk to him about it. He's up at our cabin in Shannon, Tennessee. That's where all of his photo artwork is produced and distributed. In fact, I will see about getting you a couple of his works to go up on the walls here if you would like."

"Certainly. Just send me the bill."

"No, no. Our treat. We are pleased to have your business and hope to for a long time to come. Having some prints of his up here would be great advertising for Peyton too. So it's a win, win."

"You are so right about that!"

"I have another suggestion for the grand opening."

"Let's hear it."

"Why don't you have some attractive young women model some of your outdoor clothing and swimwear? It would be a great draw."

"I like that idea. You know where I could hire some young ladies for it?"

"I think I might be able to round up some for you."

She paused a moment and grinned.

"Your father tells me you are dating the famous reporter, Lianne Palmer. Wouldn't hurt to have her as one of the models."

Dawson laughed.

"I'll have to run that by her and see what she thinks. I like the idea."

Cali got Dawson talking about his relationship with Lianne. He told her how they met in Afghanistan and about her helping him through his recovery at Walter Reed. The two then compared thoughts about long distance romance. Peyton was gone often, just as Lianne was with her work. Cali encouraged Dawson, pointing out that their relationship could be even better because of it.

"One thing about it Dawson, Peyton and I don't get a chance to get tired of each other. He has offered several times to give up his work for me but I will not let him. Photography is his calling. It's in his blood. I wouldn't want to hold him back."

"I understand completely. I would not want Lianne to give up her career for me either. We'll somehow work through all the separations."

"I think the only regret Peyton has is our daughter, Lindsey. He would like to spend more time with her, but he more than makes up for it when they are together. I know that when our little girl gets older he plans to take her with him as much as he can."

"He sounds like a great guy."

"He is Dawson. I can't wait for you to meet him. You know, when he is in town and Lianne is here we will have you two over for dinner."

"That would be very nice. Thank you."

CHAPTER 40

Dawson felt good when he left the store that evening. It had been a productive week. The day had been wonderful, meeting Cali Kinsley. Not only had they gotten all of the accounting procedures organized but she had made several fantastic recommendations for promoting the business. Her ideas for the grand opening were especially great.

When he stepped up in his truck, Dawson looked back at the store. The temporary banner up on the roofline looked great with "Lee Outdoor Sports" in bold lettering. His chest swelled with pride. Dawson was thankful that his father had suggested opening the store. It was just what he needed. He felt good about himself now. It made him feel like a productive member of society. He felt a surge of happiness. Now he had a great business and a super love life with Lianne.

Rather than cook dinner when he got home, Dawson decided to stop and eat on the way. He did not have any place particular in mind as he rode along toward home. Near the turn off that led to the house he spied a seafood restaurant that he had always enjoyed eating at in the past.

"Seafood sounds good," he said, pulling into the parking lot.

There was a waiting list of customers for seating so Dawson opted to sit at the bar. Since he was at the bar he ordered a Bloody Mary to go along with his meal of fried shrimp and raw oysters. He downed it before his meal arrived. The bartender had just set another one down for him when someone tapped him on the shoulder.

"Dawson Lee. I thought that was you!" said an old friend.

"Well, hello Royce. Long time, no see," greeted Dawson as he shook hands. "Care to join me for dinner?"

"I would but I'm here with my wife and in-laws. I heard you were back in town. We were all pulling for you when we learned you had been injured. How are you doing now?"

"Great Royce. I got banged up a bit, but I'm fine now."

"Are you working anywhere yet?"

"Yeah, sort of. My Dad and I are opening up an outdoor sports store. We are setting it up now and should open in a few weeks."

"That's good to hear. Have you hired any employees yet?"

"No, I am going to start taking applications. We plan to hire four to begin with. Neither Dad nor I plan to be there all the time so we hope to find a staff that is dependable. I hope that it will eventually run itself and we can mainly float in and out."

"Do you have any leads on anyone in particular yet?"

"No, not yet. An ad will be in Sunday's paper. I do have two interviews in the morning of people that happened by the store this week."

"I have someone in mind that I think would be an excellent worker for you."

"Let's hear it."

"It's my daughter, Holly. Do you remember her?"

"Oh yes, I remember Holly. She married a soldier. Is he stationed here now?"

"No, not anymore. They are divorced. Holly and the baby have been staying with us until she can get a job and on her feet. She wants to get her own place and go to college at night. She's a good girl, Dawson. She would work hard for you. She's certainly dependable and trustworthy."

"If she's anything like you she will do fine. Could she come out to the store for an interview in the morning?"

"She will be there. I'll see to that. Give me your number and I will have her call you tonight and confirm a time with you."

"All right."

He gave Royce a card with the store's address and phone number and wrote his cell number on the back. They said goodbye. Dawson ate his dinner and made his way home.

Not long after he got there, Holly called and said she would be there in the morning to meet with him. He was pleased at how nice and professional she sounded on the phone. He liked the idea of knowing her parents. Unless something was terribly wrong, he knew he had his first employee.

At ten o'clock he and Lianne had their nightly talk. She filled him in on her busy day. He told her about his. She was excited to hear about him meeting Cali Kinsley and her suggestion of having Peyton at the grand opening.

"I have seen his work. He is awesome. That's a superb idea to have him at the grand opening. I can't wait to meet him. I plan to take a week's vacation and help out."

"Well, well! Excellent. You just made my day that much better."

"That's why you love me so much. Isn't it?" she queried, coyly.

"You got that right, love of my life."

Waking earlier than he had intended, Dawson got up and made breakfast. He had slept well and felt good this morning. Eager to get to the store, he quickly showered and dressed. It was still early, 7:00 a.m., when he reached the store. His first job applicant interview was not until 8:30, but he had plenty to do. There were still stacks of merchandise to price and put on display. Just before time for his first interview, Dawson made a fresh pot of coffee, and then poured himself a cup.

At precisely 8:30 a.m. the front door opened and a young man appeared. He introduced himself and Dawson sat down in the office with him. The interview went okay. The young man had no sales experience, nor any outdoor skills or hobbies. The only job he had ever had was as a dishwasher and he had gotten fired from it for being too slow.

The next interview was with a young woman just out of high school. Amber Wilson, revealed that she had worked since she was fifteen as a part time cashier at a local grocery store. Dawson was pleased to learn that she had been in the Girl Scouts for several years and had earned her silver and gold awards. She enjoyed camping and hiking and had spent some time on the Appalachian Trail. Amber was versed on the various types and brands of camping and hiking gear. He tentatively told her that she would be hired and promised to call her back the next week with his decision.

He had gone back to stocking the shelves when Holly arrived. It had been a long time since he had seen her. Dawson had forgotten how pretty she was. He smiled when he noticed that she was as short as Lianne. She had long blond hair that she wore tied in a ponytail. Her eyes were a lovely blue and her smile infectious.

"Good morning Mister. Lee," she greeted, sticking out her hand.

"Hello Holly. Please call me Dawson. It has been a long time. Good to see you again."

"Thank you."

He took her in the office and they got reacquainted. He learned that she had been divorced for six months and had a two year old son. While married she had worked at the PX at Fort Lewis, Washington. She also had experience working in a floral shop. She had no real outdoor experience, but on the plus side she had some college already and had just enrolled in night classes, studying business management. Dawson was also pleased to discover that she had a strong background in computers and was familiar with the accounting software that the store would be using.

"I know I don't have much outdoor recreational background. I do like to swim and I have been camping some with my parents. I've not been able to do much as a soldier's wife and a mother."

"I understand that Holly. No problem. I'm more interested in your business background. I think I would like to hire you on as my assistant manager. Would you be up to handling a little of everything in the business?"

"Oh yes, I would!"

CHAPTER 41

"Holly, what I have in mind is for you to learn to run the store completely. I plan to back out of it at some point in time and float in and out as needed. I don't want to be tied down all the time. Dad will be in and out as well. He's not interested in managing it but he will help anyway he can."

"That's fine with me. I would like a challenge. I want to build a good life for my son, Jason. I want to be independent. I don't want to be totally dependent on anyone else again."

"I take it your marriage was a little rough."

"Yeah. My husband was a jerk. He was a control freak and had to have everything his way. Anyway, he's gone and I'm ready to move on and make my way."

"Good for you!"

"When can I start to work?"

"When could you?"

"Now."

Dawson laughed and shook his head.

"How about Monday? You could help get the place ready to go. I have more interviews to do. I'm hiring three more people. I think we will be ready for business in about two weeks."

"All right then. Thank you for giving me a chance Dawson. I won't let you down. Mom and Dad are excited about this."

"I've known your Mom and Dad all of my life. We grew up and went to school together. I have no doubt you will do well."

After Holly left, Dawson poured another cup of coffee and sat back down at his desk. He sorted through invoices and looked over the ever growing pile of inventory items that needed to be entered into the computer.

The phone rang. It was his father wanting to know if he needed him to come down and work.

"No Dad. I'm just sorting out some paperwork and then I'm heading home."

His mother got on the phone and invited him to dinner and he accepted the invitation. He hung up and powered the computer down and put the files and invoices away. He cleaned the coffee maker and took all the trash in the stockroom out to the nearby dumpster and locked up the back.

Before leaving, Dawson stood in front of the store just inside the entrance. The partially stocked showroom looked good to him. Even the mixture of odors from the new supplies and equipment seemed nice.

"Can't wait to get it open and going."

CHAPTER 42

On Sunday Dawson fought the urge to go down to the store and put up stock. He knew he needed a break so he forced himself to stay home.

The swimming pool needed cleaning so he vacuumed the leaves from the bottom then added chemicals including an extra dose of algaecide. He had gotten hot and sweaty so he went in and changed into swim trucks and went for a swim. There were still a few leaves on the bottom of the deep end so he made a game of diving down and collecting them up.

While diving down for the last leaf he thought he heard a splashing sound. It was odd because he was already several feet underwater. Not wearing a mask, his vision underwater was blurry. He looked around as he as he made his way back to the surface but did not see anything unusual.

As he swam upward, Dawson angled his way to the surface at the safety rope that separated the shallow end from the deep end. He held onto the rope and looked toward the back of the house and saw nothing out of place.

Hanging there on the rope, he caught his breath and rested. He tossed the leaves he held in his hand up onto the grass beyond the pool's apron. At that moment he had a strange feeling that he was not alone. Before he could react someone grabbed him from behind. He let out a cry of shock as he tried to jerk away.

"Whassup?" yelled Amydee, with a huge grin.

"What the…. Oh my God!" cried Dawson.

Amydee was naked. She had slipped out of her clothes and dove in behind him. Breaking out in laughter, she moved closer to him.

"You should see your face. I surprised you good, didn't I?"

"What are you doing here?"

Treading water, she worked her way around beside him and grabbed the safety rope.

"What? No how ya doin', glad to see you, you look nice in your birthday suit?"

Shock began to give way to a bit of anger.

"Amydee, what's this all about? Why are you here?"

"Hoo-ee Dawson, calm down! I came by to say hello and see how you are doing. The water looked inviting so I thought I would join you. Don't like what you see?"

She stuck her chest toward him.

"You're naked!" he exclaimed.

"Well, duh! You've seen me naked before. You used to like it."

"Yes, but we were together then."

"So, here we are, you know, together again." Pushing herself against him.

"Oh, I don't think so. You left me for somebody else, remember?"

Dawson ducked under the rope and swam for the shallows, then began exiting the pool. Amydee followed behind him. He picked up his towel and dried off. Amydee got out and stood in front of him, arms folded under her breasts. She was achingly beautiful as she stared at him with seductive eyes.

"I need a towel Dawson. Don't you know how to treat a guest?"

"Sorry," he mumbled softly, handing her the towel.

She dried off then wrapped the towel around her bottom, leaving her breasts exposed. Dawson stood there, unsure what to do. She looked at him a long moment.

"My clothes are on the other end of the pool. Will you get them for me?"

"I guess so," he said with a sigh.

Uneasy and irritated, he walked around the pool and collected her dress, underwear, and sandals. When he started back she was going into the back door of the house.

"Dad gummit!"

By the time he got into the house, the shower was running and Amydee was stepping into it.

"Care to join me?" she asked in a sultry voice.

"No thanks," he said and laid her clothes on top of the counter by the sink.

"Mm,mm. Too bad," she said.

Dawson quickly put his shorts and a t-shirt on and sat in the den.

"How am I going to get her out of here?" he muttered.

A short time later, Amydee walked into the den, still naked. She stood there combing out her long blond hair.

"You want to take advantage of me while I'm naked?" she asked in a silky voice.

"No thanks."

She walked across the room and stood in front of him.

"Awe, come on Dawson. For old times' sake. Don't be mad at me. We can still get together for a friendly fling from time to time."

Dropping down on her knees in front of him, she spread his legs apart and slid up between them. She tried to kiss him but he turned his head.

"No, Amydee!"

"Yes, Dawson."

She then began to kiss his chest and ran her hands under his t-shirt.

"Stop please," he said with firmness.

"Oh Dawson, You know you want me."

"No I don't Amydee. That's over. You have someone else."

"Don't worry about Jimmy. We can still see each other."

"No Amydee. It's over."

She stopped fondling him, sat back on her haunches and looked at him. A look of disbelief on her face.

"You have someone else. Don't you?"

"What if I do." He shot back.

Her eyes opened wide and her mouth formed an 'O'.

"Whoo hoo! Dawson's got himself a new girlfriend! Who is she? Where is she at? Is she on her way here now? Wouldn't she be surprised to walk in right now?"

He shuddered at the thought but said nothing. To his surprise, she started crying. He just sat there. He wondered if she was really upset of just playing a game.

"Huh!" she huffed, wiping tears from her eyes.

"I see how it is," she said with asperity in her voice.

Amydee stood up and looked at him a moment, then walked back into the bathroom. She dressed and came back out brushing her hair again. She stood in front of him, looking at him with sad eyes.

"I still love you Dawson. I know you still love me. We have a special bond. We were each other's first. We'll be together again one day. I'll be waiting. You'll come back to me."

She leaned down, kissed him on the cheek, and then walked out the door. As he heard her drive off, Dawson broke down and wept.

CHAPTER 43

Two hours had passed since Amydee had left before Dawson could regain his composure. The encounter with her had shaken him to the core. He was still amazed that he had not given into her charms. Her beauty and sex appeal were bewitching. From the moment he had first met her he had been smitten with her magnetic sensuality and had always given into her wishes.

As the shock of what had happened began to subside, feelings of guilt started to eat at him. He felt as though he had somehow betrayed Lianne. Sure, he had no warning and was unable to prevent Amydee showing up, but he did stand his ground and resisted. Would Lianne understand? Would she believe him? Should he even tell her?

"I got to," he said with a sigh. "I can't live with this. I don't want to ever have any secrets from Lianne."

"Pacing the floor, he looked at the clock. It was 6:30 p.m. His and Lianne usual call time was at ten.

"I wonder if she's home?" Muttering.

Grabbing the phone, he punched in her number. It rang a couple of times and her voice mail answered. After Lianne gave her unable to answer right now spiel, there was a beep for him to leave a message. He almost lost his nerve before he could croak out a message.

"Lianne. This is Dawson. I really need to talk to you. Please call as soon as you can. It's about Amydee. I would like to discuss it with you. Please call soon."

As soon as he hung up he felt a small spurt of relief in that he had said it was about Amydee. Then he began to wonder if the message he had left made any sense.

"Oh well. I'll just have to wait and see."

Nervous, Dawson busied himself with doing laundry and cleaning the bathroom. At seven o'clock the phone rang. Dawson's heart slammed up into his throat when he heard it. Mustering up the courage to answer it, he felt a mixed rush of relief and anxiety when it turned out to be his father. He called to discuss the plans for the next work week. As soon as they hung up the phone rang again.

"Hello?"

"Dawson, I got your message."

As soon as he heard Lianne's voice he began to breakdown. He could hardly talk as he tried to tell her what happened.

"Whoa, Dawson. Slow down. Get a hold of yourself. Take a deep breath and tell me what happened.

Pulling himself together as best he could, Dawson told her all that had taken place. Lianne listened quietly. When he finished she said nothing.

"Lianne, you still there?" he asked worriedly.

"Yeah," she said softly.

"I'm sorry Lianne. It all happened so unexpectedly. I feel so bad about it. The last thing I ever want to do is to hurt you in anyway."

"You know Dawson, you could have not told me this and I would have probably never found out. Why didn't you?"

Somewhat taken aback, his eyes filled with tears and his mouth went dry.

"I don't understand."

"Why? Why did you choose to tell me?"

"Well, because I love you. I want to always be honest and up front with you. I could not live with myself if I didn't tell you."

Lianne broke down and began sobbing.

"Oh Lianne, I am so sorry about this. Please forgive me?"

"Dawson, I'm not mad. You have made me so happy."

"Huh?"

"I am so touched by your honesty. I knew you had a good heart when I met you. Now, I know that you are the one I would very much like to spend the rest of my life with."

Relief washed over him like a tidal wave. He felt so giddy that he was dizzy.

"Did you just propose to me?" he asked.

She let out a nervous giggle that was interrupted by a hiccup.

"I suppose I did, didn't I?"

"Isn't it my job to do the proposing?"

"Well, yeah. It just kind of came out of me," she replied in a voice like a caress.

"Did you mean it?"

"Yes."

"Well then, I would be willing to marry you if you are willing to marry me."

"Hmm. What a proposal. Is that the best you can do?" she quipped.

"Well, this is kind of short notice, but how about this one? Lianne Palmer, would you marry me?" he asked seriously, meaning it.

"When?"

"That's to be worked out post haste."

"Do I get an engagement ring?"

"That depends."

"On what?"

"The size."

"I wear a five."

"Hmm. I think it's doable."

"It better be!" she shot back playfully.

CHAPTER 44

"Wow!" was all Dawson could say when he hung up from talking to Lianne. He walked out into the backyard and stood on the patio. It was dark. The night security lights were on and the pool was lit up. The visual effect of the glowing water was somehow comforting.

It had been a surreal day. First an encounter with Amydee that could have spelled disaster if he had given in. Then the confession call to Lianne turned into a pivotal moment.

"I asked her to marry me!" he crowed. "And she said yes."

Though exultantly joyful, he was suddenly overcome with exhaustion. The emotional rollercoaster of events and having gone all day without eating much slammed his energy reserves. He had been running on pure adrenaline and it had run its course, leaving him trembling with weakness.

Not sure what his stomach could handle, Dawson heated a bowl of canned soup and ate it. That was enough to settle him down. He got undressed and climbed in bed. In no time he was fast asleep.

When he awoke on Monday morning he felt great and got an early start on the day. Instead of cooking breakfast, he stopped by the Waffle House for steak and eggs with hash browns. Even doing that, he beat his father to the store.

Mr. Lee and Holly arrived at the same time. Holly began entering inventory into the database program while Mr. Lee put up new stock. Dawson answered calls from job seekers and lined up interviews for the day.

A large shipment of outdoor gear arrived. Dawson, his father, and Holly unloaded the boxes of gear and stacked them on the showroom floor. From there they sorted through items and distributed them to the location in the store where they would go.

The day flew by for Dawson, and the next days as well. By Wednesday afternoon he had interviewed several people and finally decided he had enough applications. He made his choices for employees. His first choice was Amber Wilson, whom he had interviewed the same day he had hired Holly.

Since he had hired two women, Dawson decided to hire two men. The first was Paul Conklin, a retired businessman who enjoyed fishing, hunting, and camping. He had a full head of silver hair and luminous brown eyes. Slim and agile, he was quite affable and proved to be a great asset to the business.

To Dawson's surprise, Robert Garcia called and came in for an interview. He had been one of the day laborers that his father had hired to help clean and set up the store's shelving units. Other than having risked a long arduous trek across the border to get in the United States, he had no real outdoor sports interest. However, his positive demeanor and hunger for a chance at having a respectable job won Dawson over.

With a holiday weekend coming up, Lianne had planned to fly in on Thursday evening and back on Sunday night to avoid as much of the holiday air traffic as she could. Dawson had told all of his new employees, less Holly who was already working, to begin the following Tuesday. He got his father to cover the store most of Thursday while he met with Cali at her office, then went shopping. He went to a jewelry store and picked out a one and a half carat diamond solitaire engagement ring for Lianne. With that in his pocket, he headed for the airport in Tanner.

At two o'clock he was sitting in the Atlanta airport waiting to board a flight to Washington D.C. By four o'clock he touched down at National and was walking up the jet way. Lianne's flight to Atlanta would leave at five-thirty. He planned to surprise her by being on the same flight.

Near the departure gate for the Atlanta connection Dawson waited in a lounge. He was sipping on a Rolling Rock beer when he saw her checking in at the departure counter at the gate. His heart fluttered as he watched her, unaware of his presence. It was all he could do to not run to her and spoil the surprise he had planned.

Lianne checked in with the agent and sat down to wait for the boarding call. She pulled out her cell phone and called Dawson's number. Seconds later his cell phone vibrated in his pocket.

"Hello?"

"Hey Dawson. It's me. I'm at the airport here in D.C. My flight leaves at five-thirty and it is supposedly on time. I should be arriving in Tanner around eight if there is no delay in Atlanta."

"That's great. I'm looking forward to seeing you again."

"I sure have missed you this week."

"And I have missed you too."

Just then the boarding announcement came over the speaker system. Dawson tried to block the sound on the cell phone."

"What was that noise?" asked Lianne.

"Oh nothing. Somebody just being loud."

She paused.

"Mm-hmm. Where are you at?"

"Well, I just left the store a while ago and I stopped for a drink."

"Oh!"

"Oh what?"

"I'm just kind of surprised. That's all. Well, I need to board now. I'll call you when I get ready to leave Atlanta."

"All right then. I'll see you soon."

CHAPTER 45

Lianne gathered her carry-on bag and got in line for the gate. She handed the gate agent her pass and walked down the jet way. Boarding the plane, she made her way back to row twenty-three and found her seat. She slipped her laptop bag under the seat in front of her and settled in. In minutes the plane had filled with passengers and most were buckled in. She sensed the jet's door close and felt the pressurization begin.

"Miss Palmer?" asked the stewardess, looking down at her.

"Yes?"

"If you would please, we are moving you up to fist class seating. If you would, grab your things and follow me."

Lianne looked at her, a confused expression on her face.

"I don't have a first class ticket."

The stewardess smiled.

"Miss Palmer. Your ticket has been upgraded. You are our special guest this evening. It is a pleasure to have you abroad with us today!"

Still perplexed but flattered, Lianne got her carry-on bag and followed the stewardess to the front of the plane.

In first class there were only two other passengers. The stewardess pointed to a window seat and asked if she would like a glass of champagne.

"Sure, thanks."

Moments later the stewardess sat the glass of champagne down on Lianne's tray table. She took a few sips and relaxed. She stared out of the cabin window and watched as the big jet as rolled back from the gate.

Just before takeoff the stewardess took her glass and said she would pour her a fresh one after they were airborne. Lianne thanked her and settled back on the plush leather seat. She was wondering how her seat had gotten changed to first class. It was not something that was normally done for a news reporter that she knew of. Oh well, she said to herself, just enjoy the comfort Lianne.

The jet reached altitude and leveled off. The stewardess began serving champagne and snacks to the other two first class passengers. Lianne gazed out of the window at the landscape speeding by below her.

"Here we are," said the stewardess, setting another glass of champagne down along with a small tray of snacks.

"Thank you," Lianne said without looking.

She then turned her gaze from the window and looked to see what kind of snacks she had been given.

"Not too bad," she muttered.

Picking up the champagne, Lianne started to take a sip. She then noticed there was something in the bottom of the glass. She started to call out to the stewardess when she saw that it was a ring.

"What?" she said in astonishment.

The stewardess must have dropped her ring in the glass, Lianne thought. She looked around and saw the stewardess standing in the aisle with a big goofy grin on her face. Then, Dawson stepped into view.

A shock of surprise lit up her face, then quickly turned into a dazzling smile. She was speechless. Looking back down at the glass of champagne with the ring in it, droplets of happy tears dribbled down her cheeks.

Dawson slid onto the seat beside her. She was still holding the glass. He took it from her and fished out the ring and handed the glass to the stewardess. She quickly returned with two new glasses and set them down and backed away.

Lianne stared at Dawson, still unable to speak. Her body trembled and tears continued to slide down her cheeks. He took her by the hands.

"Well?" he asked.

"Well?" she countered, her voice quaking.

"Still want to marry me?"

"Sure do."

"You got it."

Slipping the ring on her finger, Dawson gently kissed her. They sat back in their seats and held hands. Lianne laid her head against the headrest and looked at him.

"You okay?" he asked softly.

"Couldn't be better," she replied.

They sat in silence for a while, both deep in the moment of unspoken exaltation and elation.

"I love you, Dawson."

"I love you, too."

She shook her head in amazement.

"You really out did yourself this time. Never in a million years would I have thought of this."

"I did good, didn't I?" Dawson said beaming with pride.

"Yep, you did!"

"I wanted this to be an unforgettable experience."

"It is that for sure. It's one for the books. You sure must have gone to a lot of trouble and expense."

"This is a once in a lifetime moment Lianne. I am forever with you."

"And I am with you forever."

CHAPTER 46

The rest of the flight to Atlanta was smooth and uneventful. Even when the ASA commuter plane's tires barked against the tarmac at Tanner airport, Lianne was still in a state of amazed shock. They gathered her luggage and piled into Dawson's truck. She lit up with a brilliant smile.

"This feels so good," she said as they drove out of the airport parking. "I feel like I'm coming home."

"You are home, Lianne. My home is your home. Get used to the word 'ours' in that regard."

She held up her hand and looked at the engagement ring. "It almost feels like we are married already Dawson."

"In my heart we are. Soon we will make it real, legal, and permanent."

"Maybe when I come down for the week of the grand opening we can decide on when."

"Sounds good to me."

When they arrived at the house, Lianne unpacked while Dawson warmed dinner. His mother had cooked and dropped off more than enough food for the two of them.

A short soak in the hot tub and they were in bed by eleven. It had been quite an adventurous day for both of them.

On Friday morning Dawson and Lianne had breakfast at Waffle House then drove to the store. Lianne was impressed at how nice the store was shaping up. She met Holly and was quite taken with her abilities and personable attitude.

More inventory had arrived the day before so Holly and Mr. Lee busied themselves with putting up the new stock. Later in the morning Cali and Peyton Kinsley came in. Dawson and Lianne were excited to meet Peyton. The two had a early lunch with the Kinsley's and discussed his participation in the grand opening.

The Kinsley's were charmed by Lianne and were thrilled to hear that she and Dawson had become engaged. While discussing the grand opening, Peyton suggested that Lianne pose in some of the outdoor gear and he would photograph her and have the pictures made into large framed prints to display in the store. Jokingly Lianne suggested that Cali would be a much better model. Dawson and Peyton conspired that both would be perfect models and planned a photo session for Saturday.

Back at the store the group picked out some outdoor clothing and gear for the ladies to wear. Peyton sketched out plans and wanted to do the photo shoot at Roosevelt State Park, just north of

Tanner. The Kinsley's said goodbye with plans to meet at Dawson's house early on Saturday morning for breakfast. Peyton wanted to do an early morning shoot for the best lighting.

When the Kinsley's were gone Lianne turned to Dawson and said, "I can't believe you guys think I would be a good model. I'm not blind. My face is fine but my body is not model material. Cali is one hundred percent prime for modeling. She has a fantastic face and body to match."

"And you don't?" asked Dawson with mock surprise on his face.

Lianne grabbed him around the neck and pulled his face to her and kissed him.

"That's why I love you so much. You know how to make a girl feel special."

"You are special Lianne. You are the best."

"Keep talking like that and I might jump you right here!"

From two aisles over Holly broke into squeals and laughter. Dawson's father guffawed from where he had been working. Lianne's face turned blood red with embarrassment. Dawson laughed and hugged her.

"Okay, you two behave now," chided Mr. Lee.

With intermittent smiles and giggles, the gang went back to work and put up all of the stock that had come in. They closed the store at three and broke for the holiday weekend.

Dawson and Lianne left the sports shop and dropped by Kroger's and shopped for groceries for the weekend. For Dawson, it was a pleasurable experience grocery shopping with Lianne. The more he thought about it, the more he wanted their wedding to happen soon. There was nothing more thrilling than the thought of having her forever.

They drove home and put up the groceries, took a shower and changed clothes. By six o'clock they were sitting in the Olive Garden having salads, wine, and waiting on their pasta dishes.

There was a stir in the restaurant when several people noticed Lianne. Some came over and asked for her autograph. Two even had their picture taken with her using their cell phone cameras. Dawson was again amazed at how humble and gracious Lianne was with the recognition. He proudly looked on with amazement as she made each person she met feel special and welcomed.

On the ride home Lianne leaned against his shoulder. Her closeness was something he never wanted to lose and something he vowed to always cherish every moment he could have with her.

CHAPTER 47

It was still dark the next morning when the Kinsley's arrived and had breakfast with Dawson and Lianne. A short time later, with camping gear, a paddle board, and a kayak, the quartet piled into Dawson's truck and motored north through Cataula, Hamilton and on to Pine Mountain and Roosevelt State Park.

They first stopped at one of the side trails that led to the twenty-three mile Pine Mountain Trail. The first vestiges of daylight on the eastern horizon were showing as they got out of the truck. All four donned backpacks with camping gear, outdoor clothing, and camera equipment and took the trail for the short trek to the site Peyton had in mind.

Fifteen minutes later they arrived at a picturesque campsite overlooking a lovely valley. Dawson quickly set up a tent while Lianne and Cali got ready for the shoot. Peyton set up his camera gear then helped Dawson ready a camp stove and get coffee going.

The first photographs of the women taken by Peyton were of them sitting by the tent sipping coffee and looking out over the valley. Lianne and Cali both were wearing hiking shorts, shirts, and boots. He took shots of them with backpacks on and standing on the trail on a high ridge with a scenic back drop of distant mountains, reminiscent of the great Smokies.

Once satisfied with the assortment of pictures he had taken, Peyton was ready for the next setting. They hiked back to the truck and drove into Roosevelt Park's campground and stopped next to the scenic little Delano Lake nestled in among a stark green forest of pines.

Cali and Lianne went to the nearby campground bath house and changed into swim suits while Dawson unloaded the props and arranged the camera gear. When the ladies returned, Dawson was astonished at how perfectly apportioned Cali was. He wondered why she was not a fashion model instead of an accountant. She laughed when Lianne said as much.

"I used to be a stripper."

"My goodness!" blurted Dawson. "I bet you were the best."

"Yep, she was," added Peyton. "Her performance would knock your socks off. And now, just look at her. She gave it all up to be the best accountant in Tanner, and the prettiest I may add."

"I enjoyed dancing but I really did it to pay my way through school and get the business going."

"Is that how you two met?" asked Lianne, looking at Cali then Peyton. "You know, while you were stripping."

"Not exactly. It's a wild story if you care to hear it."

"We would love to," agreed Lianne and Dawson.

Cali told them that she and Peyton had become neighbors after he had been exonerated and released from prison after serving eighteen years for a crime he did not commit. Peyton was struggling to make a new start and moved next door to Cali. They became fast friends. Cali was going to college full time and stripping at night to pay her way and save to open an accounting business after she graduated.

Peyton had gotten a job as a credit officer for a loan company. He worked as a vice president of a bank prior to his arrest. When Cali met him he had just moved out of a homeless shelter and had little in the way of furniture or personal effects. The loan company he worked for quickly found that he was a valuable asset and was quite pleased with his work. His boss even allowed him to take over the note on a repossessed car so he would not have to ride the bus to work and back.

Since the day he had been cleared and released, two local detectives who had originally brought the charges against him were not happy about his being free and set out to destroy him and send him back to prison. For a time, Peyton was able to maneuver around their threats and harassment.

Peyton and Cali fell in love and decided that when she graduated that they would marry and go into the accounting business together. Shortly before they were to marry, the detectives severely beat Peyton and ran him out of town with the threat that if he came back or tried to cause any problems for them that they would harm Cali.

Battered and barely able to walk, Peyton threw some things in a backpack and caught a freight train out of town. He eventually ended up in the foothills of the Smokies with no idea where to go or what to do. While looking in an outdoor store for camping supplies he hit on the idea to get on the two thousand plus-mile Appalachian Trail and head north until he found somewhere to settle down and start a new life again.

In northern Tennessee he happened on the small quaint town of Shannon nestled in a valley below the Appalachian Trail. He moved into a ramshackle shack and with the money he had and set about to find a way to make a living.

Shannon was known for its arts and craft shops. While walking around one day Peyton saw some outdoor and wildlife photographs for sale. He thought about and believed he could take better shots and bought a camera. His first photographs were immaculate. With the help of a local art shop owner his photographic art became a sensation that has blossomed into a fantastic career for him.

"How did you two ever get back together?" queried Lianne.

Dawson told her that the two corrupt detectives were finally exposed. The FBI tracked Peyton down and questioned him about what they had done to him. It was then that Cali was able to find him.

"As soon as I found out where he was, I went after him. We have been together since then," Cali said proudly.

"In spite of eighteen years in prison and the problems with the detectives, I have done well. I am one of the luckiest men in the world with what Cali and I share together. We have a lovely little girl that has made out lives even better."

"That is a beautiful love story," said Lianne.

"And I thought Dawson and I had a special one."

"We do," added Dawson.

"Tell us about it please," said Cali.

And they did.

CHAPTER 48

Sharing their stories of how each couple met formed a special bond that began a lifelong friendship between them. Each gained a new appreciation for the others character and abilities.

Cali mounted the paddle board and Peyton shot a series of stunning photographs of her on the lake. Her beauty and poise were beyond description.

Given Lianne's small size, Peyton took photos of her getting into the kayak and paddling around. Dawson's favorite picture was one of her standing in the water up to her thighs. She had one hand on the kayak and in the other she was holding the paddle. The bright colors of her bathing suit and the kayak against the bright blue of the lake and sky set off her blue eyes and shining hair to the extent that they were mesmerizing.

Finished with the photo shoot, the women changed back into shorts and t-shirts while Peyton and Dawson loaded the kayak and paddle board back on the truck. Peyton started to put his camera away, and then stopped.

"I would like to take a few more shots before we leave," said Peyton when Lianne and Cali returned from dressing.

"What do you have in mind?" asked Dawson.

"I would like to take one of you and the ladies together."

"Oh my goodness! Not me. I look like a train wreck," exclaimed Dawson, unconsciously reaching and trying to cover his scarred arms.

"Trust me Dawson," Peyton said gently. "I have a great idea. I think you will be pleased."

"Come on Dawson, please?" Begged Lianne. "You know how nervous I was about posing. Now I'm happy with the pictures he took. It will be great, okay?"

"Well, okay."

Peyton had Dawson sit on top of a picnic table with his feet propped on the bench. He had Lianne and Cali sit on either side of him. They sat sideways with their backs against him. With their knees up and feet on the table, the women laid their head against his shoulders and all looked at the camera. Peyton strategically placed three backpacks against the bench so it would look as though the trio were taking a break from hiking. He then had Dawson place his arms around each of the women's waist and they held onto his arms so that very little of his were exposed.

Shooting picture after picture, Peyton moved back and forth trying different angles to find the perfect one. Dawson struggled to not break out in a nervous sweat. He had never been photographed like that before and felt extremely camera shy.

Mercifully Peyton finished. He sat up his laptop and the group reviewed the pictures. Dawson was astonished with the ones of him, Lianne and Cali.

"I must say that being photographed with two beautiful women helped me to not look so bad," said Dawson with a nervous chuckle.

"Are you saying you are not handsome?" queried Lianne, her eyes wide open and eyebrows puckered.

"Well, face it Lianne. You are the beauty and I am the beast!"

Cali and Peyton broke out in laughter.

"That's what Peyton used to say!" chortled Cali.

"Yeah, but I finally realized that when I was by her side I couldn't help but look good."

Dawson laughed.

"You know, I guess you're right. I never thought of it that way. I think you are on to something there," nodding appreciatively.

Cali walked over to Dawson and put her arms around him. She kissed him on the cheek.

"Dawson, don't ever feel ashamed of your arms and legs. You earned those scars so that we can be a free people. Be proud. We are proud of you. Don't ever forget it!"

"Thank you," was all he could say. A small lump formed in his throat.

To break the emotional tension, Dawson suggested that they have lunch in Pine Mountain before they drive back to Tanner. They ate at Cricket's Restaurant, sharing a bottle of wine. It had been a wonderful outing for them all, in more ways than one.

When they arrived back at Dawson's house, Lianne talked the Kinsley's into joining them for a swim in the pool. Cali and Peyton stayed until five. They were invited to stay for dinner but bowed out. They needed to pick up Lindsey from the babysitter. Dawson and Lianne thanked them for their company. After a warm round of hugs, the Kinsley's left.

"I'm liking life here more and more," commented Lianne.

"Keep on liking it. It's yours for the taking."

CHAPTER 49

Becoming the norm, the weekend passed off too quickly. Lianne flew back to D.C. late Sunday to avoid the Monday holiday air traffic. The farewell was much easier for both this time. In two weeks Lianne would return for a week-long visit.

Over the next week the new employees, Dawson, and his father continued to get the store in order and prepare for the upcoming grand opening. Sales representatives for several of the outdoor gear companies came in and gave product demonstrations and offered sales tips for their various items of equipment. An MSR representative taught them how to use the different cooking outfits and expounded on the virtues of their new line of lightweight backpacking tents.

The various sales representatives provided the store with colorful displays and ad materials for their products. Lee Outdoor Sports would quietly open its doors on Monday. The grand opening would not be until that Saturday. Dawson wanted to operate for the week in order to iron out any problems that might occur with the computerized cash register and inventory system. It would also give all of the sales staff time to get adjusted to their duties.

On Friday Dawson and his father took the four employees to lunch then closed until opening day on Monday. With the weekend free, Dawson struck on an idea of surprising Lianne. He caught a three o'clock flight and landed in D.C. at five-thirty. Finding a taxi, he pulled up in front of Lianne's house in Georgetown at six o'clock. Outside her door he took out his cell phone and called her.

"Hello?"

"Hey Lianne. What are you doing?"

"Oh hey there. I'm glad you called. I just got in from work. What are you doing? You sound chipper."

"Missing you."

"I miss you too. I wish we were together."

"We could be together if we wanted."

"I know, but we can't afford to travel back and forth every weekend."

"I know, but wouldn't it be nice to be together this weekend?" he asked, baiting her.

"Don't get me depressed Dawson. I miss you bad enough all the time now."

"I'm sorry. Oh well, I got something to do right now. I'll talk to you later."

"Oh, you got to go?" she asked, surprised and taken aback.

"Yeah, for now. Later, okay?"

"Okay," she said, a touch of sadness in her voice.

Dawson hung up, and then rang her doorbell. He stood far to the side of her door so she could not see him through the peephole. A moment later he heard the security locks being unlatched. The door opened and she peered out. A look of surprise formed on her face that was priceless to Dawson.

"Care if I spend the weekend with you?"

She screamed and jumped into his arms.

"You rat you! I can't believe you tricked me like this. That's two weekends in a row you have gotten me."

"I know. Isn't it great?"

She squeezed him tightly.

"Yes it sure is!"

Inside, Dawson took his bag upstairs to Lianne's bedroom. He was pleased that he was strong enough now to handle the steep stairs.

"Have you eaten?" she asked.

"No."

"Hungry?"

"Yeah, I'm starving."

"That's too bad. You've got to make up for tricking me. Bed me now!"

"My pleasure Madame."

Their love making was intense and filled with sweetness. When they finished, the two went downstairs and cooked dinner together. Lianne broiled steaks and made salads while Dawson sautéed mushrooms and onions.

After dinner the two lovers were so charged with energy that they went out for drinks and to dance for a while. By the time they made it back home it was well after midnight.

In the bedroom Lianne showed Dawson where she had made space for his clothes. She had emptied several dresser drawers and a large space in the closet. She had already purchased him a full complement of toiletries, some socks, underwear, and pajamas.

Dawson asked her what plans she had for the weekend. She said she had planned to visit her parent's and have lunch with them on Saturday. Now she was excited that they would finally get to meet their future son-in-law.

"Do you think they will like me?"

"What's not to like?"

He had no answer. She finished putting up his clothes he had brought with him and turned to him.

"Dawson."

"Yes?"

"Shut up and kiss me," she said in a seductive voice.

"Yes Ma'am," and he did.

When they broke from the kiss, Dawson pulled her close to his chest again.

"What if I don't let go?"

"I could die happy in your arms right now."

He kissed her again, slowly and tenderly.

CHAPTER 50

Though in no hurry to get up early, Lianne and Dawson were up and dressed by 7:30 a.m. They walked over to the bagel shop and had a leisurely breakfast. Afterwards they stopped by a floral shop and purchased an arrangement of flowers to take to Lianne's parents. Back at the house Dawson read the paper and sipped on coffee while Lianne got ready to go.

Later in the morning the two caught a taxi for the ride to Falls Church, Virginia, just a short distance from Georgetown. The Palmer's lived in a three-story brick house in an upscale suburban neighborhood that was quiet and peaceful. Dawson found Lianne's mother and father to be congenial and they made him feel like family from the moment they met.

Lunch was served in a dining room large enough to seat ten. It was an enjoyable experience getting to know the Palmer family. There was light hearted banter between Lianne and her parents while they ate and shared a bottle of fine wine.

"Dawson, we are so pleased that you have come into Lianne's life. We were beginning to wonder if she would ever find someone and settle down," said her father, half-heartedly.

"We had about given up!" added her mother.

Lianne laughed.

"Now Mom. You know I was waiting for just the right one to come along."

Mister Palmer looked at Dawson.

"Son, what took you so long to come along? We were afraid we would have to make reservations at the retirement home for three instead of two."

"Daddy!" squealed Lianne.

Dawson broke out in laughter.

"Actually Mister Palmer, I didn't find Lianne. She found me."

Lianne grinned and said, "Yep, I did. He was banged up and couldn't run from me."

Dawson held up his glass.

"Well, I must say, I got caught by the best."

"Here, here," chimed Lianne's mother and father.

The afternoon passed quickly. Instead of taking a cab back to Georgetown, Mr. Palmer drove them home. Lianne and Dawson took a long romantic shower together and redressed. They rode the Metro subway to Bethesda to a special restaurant Lianne had chosen. The couple who owned the fine Italian restaurant knew Lianne well and were gracious hosts who treated them like royalty.

When they made it back to the house, the two spent a long while in the hot tub before calling it a night. Dawson had really enjoyed himself. He especially liked the time spent with Lianne's parents. He looked forward to his and her parents getting to know one another.

After they had made love and were nestled in one another's arms, Lianne reached up and caressed his face.

"Dawson, I know we have discussed this once but I would like to bring it up one more time since we have gotten serious."

"What's that?"

"About me not being able to conceive."

"Lianne, I am okay with that. I promise."

"I just want you to be sure. I would dearly love for us to have children, but I can't. I am concerned that you might decide you want kids and I can't fulfill my end."

"To be honest Lianne, it would be nice to have a family one day. If we want kids then we'll look into other options. We could always adopt or be foster parents."

"You mean you would be okay with that?"

"Why not. Kids are kids. I would not have a problem with being a father to a child who does not have one."

Lianne slowly eased up to where she was propped on his chest. She kissed him tenderly.

"I knew you were a special man. Each day I learn more of just how special you really are. I thank my lucky stars every day that we found one another. We can surely say we picked a unique way to meet. I guess pick is not quite right, but nevertheless, not many people now days can top that."

"You are right there. I never could have imagined that you and I would ever be together like this when I met you."

"You know that I know that you were not pleased to have been chosen to watch after us when the raid on that compound began."

"No Lianne, I wasn't. I was torn between watching after my squad and keeping you out of harm's way. But you know it all worked out for the best. I must admit though, it was a rough way to win you over."

She giggled.

"It was the other way around silly! You were the one playing hard to get."

He looked at her smugly.

"Am I worth it?"

"You bet!"

"Show me."

"My pleasure."

CHAPTER 51

Sleeping later than usual, Dawson and Lianne spent a quiet morning around the house. For lunch they ventured out to an Indian restaurant near DuPont Circle and enjoyed steaming dishes of Samosas and tea. From there they trekked over to the Smithsonian Air and Space Museum and then to the National Art Gallery.

Lianne cooked an early dinner and they ate before she rode with him to the airport to catch his flight back to Tanner. A warm embrace, a kiss goodbye, and soon he was airborne and southbound.

Arriving in Atlanta, Dawson went to the departure gate for his connection to Tanner. There he learned that the flight had been over booked and he had been bumped. The next available flight was three hours away. He started to call his father to come get him but it would take him an hour and forty-five minutes to get there. It was then that he remembered there was an airport shuttle service that had vans running to and from the airport and Tanner. He found the pickup point and within minutes was on his way.

He called his father who met him at the shuttle station which happened to be much closer to his home. His father took him from there to the Tanner airport to retrieve his truck. He was home well before the flight from Atlanta would have gotten in.

Late that night he called Lianne and told her about what had happened. They discussed her using the service as a backup it she ever had a flight connection problem in Atlanta.

"I'm looking forward to this coming weekend. Just think, I'll be with you an entire week!" exclaimed Lianne.

"Nine days actually" added Dawson. "But, who is counting anyway?"

"Think you will get tired of me?"

"Never!"

"Good answer."

"It will be a busy week with the store but we will still have the nights."

"Oh, I plan to work right along beside you Dawson. I am looking forward to learning the trade."

"It should be a piece of cake for you. Your smile will make the customers want to buy out the store!"

"Whoo hoo! You sure know how to charm the drawers off a girl!" She chortled in a mock southern drawl.

"Promises, promises."

"You got it lover boy!"

He went to sleep much easier than he thought when they hung up. The night was filled with pleasant dreams. He woke the next morning excited about the upcoming week and especially the grand opening to be held that Saturday.

Leaving early, he had his usual breakfast of steak and eggs at Waffle House, which had quickly become a habit. He then stopped by a pastry shop and picked out an assortment of treats for the store staff. When he got to the store, his father was already there making the coffee.

Dawson had set the store hours from nine to eight Monday through Friday and until six o'clock on Saturday. Except for short periods there would be two employees there at all times. Once the business was open for a while and running smooth, he and his father would mainly spend only a couple hours a day there in order to keep an eye on the operations and take care of any problems. However, Dawson knew that he would spend much more time there than he needed, especially when Lianne was away.

Holly Conyers and Roberto Garcia arrived and a short time later the doors of Lee Outdoor Sports opened. Word of mouth had gotten around that the store would open so several people came by and checked out the new store. Sales for the early week were slow, but that was to be expected. The advertising Dawson had placed on the radio, television, and in the paper was geared for the grand opening.

During the week more stock arrived and the crew efficiently put them either on the showroom shelves or in the stockroom. There were a few glitches with the computerized sales and inventory system but were corrected and by Thursday. No other difficulties occurred.

All of the employees had adjusted well and were confident and ready. Dawson was very impressed with how well Roberto fit in and performed his duties.

Dawson closed the store on Friday at noon so they could prepare for Saturday's grand opening sales event. Cali and Peyton came and brought a dozen beautifully done poster-sized framed photographs of Lianne and Cali, as well as two of Peyton's own famous works. Dawson was mesmerized and starred in disbelief with how well the one of him, Lianne, and Cali turned out. The shots of Lianne and Cali on the lake were superb. Dawson was surprised at how well the beauty in both Lianne and Cali complimented one another.

With the showroom stocked and dressed for Saturday, Dawson left the store at five to pick Lianne up at the airport. She was expected to arrive on the five-thirty flight.

CHAPTER 52

"Wake up sleepy head," called Dawson, gently as he sat on the side of the bed.

"Umm. What time is it?" asked Lianne, rubbing her eyes.

"It's five-thirty. I would like to be at the store by six-thirty. Lots to do for today."

"Five more minutes, please."

"I know you are tired. If you would like, I could get Mom to come by and pick you up when she gets ready to come to the store. That would be about eight."

"Sounds tempting, but I don't want to miss a minute of this day."

"Are you sure you wouldn't want to rest a while longer? It's going to be a long day."

"Oh no, I'm too excited about it."

"Okay then let's do it!"

While Lianne showered, Dawson brewed a pot of coffee and made a light breakfast. By the time he set the table she was dressed and ready to go. Soon they had eaten and were riding into town sipping on their second cup of coffee.

Mr. Lee pulled into the parking lot at the same time Lianne and Dawson did. Lianne was thrilled at how nice the showroom looked. She was astonished with the modeling pictures Peyton had made of her and Cali.

"Cali is one beautiful lady," commented Lianne.

"Yes, but so are you. I am very proud of these. You make an awesome model Lianne."

"Not really. Just by being beside Cali makes me look good. But, you know, my favorite poster is of you, Cali, and me together.

"I am overjoyed with how well it turned out too. Peyton is certainly a magician with a camera."

"Yep, I agree."

All four of the store's employees arrived and got ready for the big day. Tables were set up under the portico and on them they arranged special sale and promotional items. One table held a selection of special Lee Outdoor Sports logo t-shirts and hats. Each employee, including the Lee's and Lianne, all wore the t-shirts along with hiking pants or shorts, and boots.

At 8:00 a.m. the Kinsley's arrived. A special table had been set up for Peyton. He would sign and give away souvenir prints of Lianne and Cali's modeling pictures. One of the local radio stations arrived and set up a remote broadcast booth in the parking lot to promote the grand opening. Three of Cali's lovely girlfriends came in and changed into assorted outdoor outfits. They were to meet, greet, and show off their beauty as walking displays.

When 9:00 a.m. arrived the day was in full swing for the grand opening. A large crowd of customers were already milling around. Several outdoor gear representatives had arrived and were answering questions and showing off their merchandise.

The models that Cali had enlisted were quite a draw. Off and on during the day they would put on a runway style fashion show of outdoor clothing including swimsuits and wetsuits. Along with those were drawings for prizes, balloons for the children, and samples of trail foods. Sales were impressive. Dawson could not have been happier with the turn out for the event.

The local television station came by and filmed some of the festivities and did an interview for the noon and evening news. Dawson was pleased when Lianne stepped up and did the honors. The news reporter was stymied when she learned who Lianne was. Within minutes the television station's manager came out to meet Lianne. The manager invited her and Dawson for a tour of the station the next week while she was in town. She graciously accepted.

Dawson was also very pleased with Amber, Holly, Paul, and Roberto's participation during the grand opening. They tirelessly tended to customers and making sales. Dawson's mother kept busy keeping the shelves stocked and straightened. Mr. Lee spent most of the day assisting Peyton as he signed autographs and had his picture taken with customers.

Late in the afternoon things began to wind down. The models were paid and let go. Peyton and Cali had left. The radio station had long gone. When the store closed at six, everyone was tired but happy. It had been a fantastic day for Dawson.

Before letting everyone go, he called a meeting and thanked all of his employees. He reminded them of the cookout he had planned for them on Sunday afternoon. They all said they would be there as they said goodbye. Dawson had also invited Peyton and Cali who tentatively agreed to come.

Leaving the store, Dawson, Lianne, and his parents stopped and had dinner together at Applebee's. On the ride home, Lianne laid her head against Dawson's shoulder and fell asleep. He smiled to himself when he looked down at her beautiful face, so peaceful and relaxed. It was a good feeling knowing she would be with him for the next week.

CHAPTER 53

After breakfast on Sunday, Mr. and Mrs. Lee arrived at Dawson's home. He and his father set up two additional grills besides the one he already had on the back patio. They set up and arranged several tables and chairs for the cookout guests. Mrs. Lee and Lianne unloaded the large containers of food that were bought for the party and began preparing for the gathering.

The guests began arriving at noon. Dawson had invited all four employees, along with their family or significant others. Holly came bringing her two year-old son, Jason. Amber came alone. Paul brought his wife, Susan. Roberto brought his nearly grown daughter, Crucita. To Dawson's surprise, Peyton and Cali came and brought their four year-old Lindsey along.

While Dawson, his father, and Peyton manned the grills, Holly, her son, Amber, Crucita, Cali and Lindsey went swimming in the pool. Paul's wife joined in helping Lianne and Mrs. Lee. Roberto and Paul set the tables and organized and distributed the drinks.

Lunch ready, everyone got out of the pool and ate. The grilled items included barbecued chicken breasts, steaks, and hamburgers. The children had a choice of hotdogs or chicken nuggets and fries. There was plenty of food to go around and everyone ate their fill.

After eating, many of the guests went swimming. Lianne got into her swimsuit and joined in playing with the children. She appeared to be enthralled with Holly's and Cali's children. Dawson's heart ached for her, knowing that she could not conceive.

It ended up where all of the women were in the pool and all of the men were sitting around it enjoying one another's company. Everyone talked and acted as though they were old friends.

Dawson was happy that Peyton and Cali had come. He liked Peyton and admired his success. Peyton had suffered long and worked hard to get to where he was. More amazingly to Dawson, he was still a very personable and humble man in spite of his fame. Cali was a fantastically beautiful woman, and with a warm personality to match.

"Peyton. Your daughter looks like a miniature version of Cali. She's going to be a heart breaker when she comes of age," said Mr. Lee.

"She already is. But you know, I am so happy she got her mother's looks and not mine."

"Here, here!" Chirped the men, bringing a round of laughter.

Dawson turned to Roberto.

"Crucita is sure a lovely young lady. How old is she?" asked Dawson.

"She is seventeen, almost eighteen now. My heart hurts sometimes when I look at her. She looks so much like my dear wife before she passed."

"Is it just you two here in the states?" asked Peyton.

"Yes it is. We have been here two years now."

Peyton turned to Dawson.

"You know, if you ever want to do some more fashion shots of outdoor wear, we should use Crucita, Holly, and Amber. They are all so pretty."

"You are right about that. I have been tossing the idea of setting up a mail order website. Having model shots of the ladies might be a great asset. Excellent idea Peyton. Thanks!"

The afternoon wore on and the party broke up. Mrs. Lee and Amber stayed and helped clean up and clear away everything. When everyone finally left, Dawson and Lianne got in the hot tub with a bottle of wine and relaxed.

"This has been a wonderful weekend Dawson. I like the life you have here. I think somewhere down the line I would like to settle here versus Georgetown. I do love my home there, but this is home in more ways than one."

"It is a good life here Lianne. You have made this home an even better home now. I can't imagine now you not being a part of my life."

"I am committed to you now Dawson. The only thing missing is the legalities of it!"

"And now that you brought it up, when would you like to do the deed?"

"You have any suggestions?" she queried.

"Soon."

"All right. If we do it soon, where would you like to get married?"

"Here or D.C., it does not matter to me. What would your parents prefer?"

She giggled.

"I don't think it would matter to them. They are so happy about this that they would go to the moon if that was where it was going to be."

"That's a little far. I have a place in mind that I think would be awesome."

"Where?"

"The chapel at Callaway Gardens."

Lianne let out a squeal of delight.

"Yes, yes, yes! I love it. Let's do it!"

She fell into his arms.

"Now, let's pick a date and set it up while you have this week with me, that way we can get busy arranging everything," he suggested softly and kissed her.

CHAPTER 54

He watched her sleep settle into somnolence before easing out of bed. Dawson had awakened a half hour earlier. He started to get up then, but Lianne put her arms around him and wanted him to hold her for a while.

As quietly as he could, Dawson took a shower, dressed, and made a pot of coffee. When it was ready he took a cup and walked out to the pool and sat down by it. The sun had just risen about the tree line and it promised to be another nice day.

While at the pool he took the pH test kit and checked the pools water and added the necessary chemicals to put it back in the pool equipment shed.

Walking back into the kitchen, Dawson was pouring another cup of coffee when Lianne came in. She still had her nightgown on which caused Dawson's heart to rev up.

"Good morning," she said with a yawn

"Good morning to you pretty lady. I' was trying not to wake you so you could sleep as late as you wanted to."

"Oh, I've slept enough. I wanted to get on up and cook breakfast for you before you left."

"Why don't we both cook?"

"Fine with me. You do the bacon and I'll do the pancakes."

"Your call."

The two fell into an efficient lockstep that had seemed to come about naturally as they prepared breakfast together. In minutes they were at the table enjoying blueberry pancakes, bacon, orange juice, and coffee.

"Do you still want to spend the day here at the house?" asked Dawson.

"Yes I do. I would like to relax and get to know the place that will be 'our' place one day soon."

"It's 'our' place already Lianne."

"I know. I've just got to get used to the idea. It feels good here. I want to see what it feels like to be a housewife and wait for my man to come home from work. I want to have dinner ready for him when he gets in."

"Are you trying to get domestic on me?"

"Mmm. Just testing the waters. I want to see how the other half lives."

He laughed.

"Test all you want. Enjoy your day here. If you need anything, call me. If you decide you want to come down to the store, call me and I will come get you."

"I'm sure I will be fine here. You enjoy your work day. Think about what is waiting at home for you."

"Oh, I will for sure. It is a nice thought knowing you are here, and waiting on me."

"You go to work then. Have a good day and don't worry about me. I'll be just fine. This will be a special treat."

"Okay dear."

With a fresh cup of coffee in hand, Dawson walked into the garage and raised the door. Lianne kissed him goodbye and stood in the garage as he backed out of the drive and drove away.

Holly and Paul worked the morning shift. Much of the day was spent putting things back in order after Saturday's grand opening. Holly printed off inventory sheets and everyone checked the on hand stock against them. Orders were placed to replenish the sold merchandise.

Early in the afternoon a scout master and the treasurer of one of the local Boy Scout troops came in and wanted to negotiate a large order for camping equipment. Dawson gave them a nice discount and ordered for them twenty-five back packs, tents, and ground cloths.

Another customer came in and placed an order for expensive mountain bikes. Paul sold a canoe and a kayak. Business was looking good and Dawson was pleased at how well sales were going.

Mr. Lee came to work for the late afternoon and evening shift. Dawson left the store at 5:00 p.m. for home. He had called Lianne to check on her and she had been enjoying herself. He asked if she needed anything picked up on the way home. She requested a bottle of wine. He stopped at the liquor store and purchased a couple of bottles of assorted wine to have on hand, then headed on home.

CHAPTER 55

When the house came into view, Dawson could see Lianne sitting on the front steps. She was wearing shorts and a bikini top. The garage door was already opened for him. She followed him as he pulled in and parked. As soon as he stepped out of the truck she was in his arms.

"It has been a great day here, but I am happy you are home. I missed you!" she said, lavishing him with kisses.

"I missed you too; especially knowing you were here and not in D.C."

Walking into the kitchen, Dawson smelled dinner. It was a wonderful aroma. Lianne had made a pasta dish using Fusilli and special homemade sauce. Along with it she had steamed broccoli and baby carrots. Dawson uncorked a bottle of wine and the two ate and swapped tales about their day.

"I have had such a good day Dawson. It's like being on vacation. I checked my emails, paid a few bills online and made a list of things I want to buy for here. I want to buy a small wardrobe of clothes just for here. That way, I won't have to bring much with me when I come down."

"Good idea. Why don't you go to work with me tomorrow? There are several nice stores in the shopping center. I could take you over to the mall if you need to as well."

"That was my idea exactly. I'm sure that I can find what I need around the shopping center." She paused then slid the strap of her bikini top off of her shoulder. "Look, I laid out in the sun. I swam some too. It's really nice having your own pool."

"Yep it is."

"Oh yes, I talked to Peter Stanton, the general manager at Channel Ten. We are invited to tour the station and have dinner with him and the owner, Tom Wellborn. The invitation is for tomorrow night. I took a chance and accepted. I hope that's okay with you."

"Oh course. I've never been to the station nor had I ever met Mister Stanton until last Saturday. I don't know Mister Wellborn. I do know that he is very wealthy."

"I've done things like this before when I have been on location in some of the smaller cities. They are usually pleasant experiences. Lots of handshakes, pictures, and good food!"

After cleaning the kitchen, Lianne and Dawson went for an evening swim. Later they made popcorn and watched a movie. Lianne lay in his arms as they curled up on the sofa. During a lull in the movie she sat up and looked curious at Dawson.

"How come you don't have a dog or cat?"

"I like pets. I just haven't gotten around to getting anything yet."

"With all this space you have it would be great to have a pet."

"Well, perhaps we can look around while you are here. What would you like?"

"I don't know. Let's go to a pet store or better yet, how about the animal shelter? It would be great to rescue an animal."

"You got it."

Lianne kissed him, first playfully, then with passion. She then placed a delicate finger on his lips and gave him a cheesy grin.

"More?" she queried.

"More," he confirmed, giving her a lupine look.

"Here?" she asked.

"Here, there, everywhere."

She laughed huskily.

"Let's start in the pool. No swimsuits."

"I like the way you think," he said, and meant it.

Their romantic interlude in the pool was a mountain top experience for both, leaving them in a state of euphoria. After a short soak in the hot tub the two lovers climbed in bed. They talked for a time on the subject of the wedding. Lianne had several one and two week assignments scheduled for the summer. The best time they could come up with for a wedding was in July, with a little time for a honeymoon.

"That brings a question we haven't talked about, and that's where to go for a honeymoon," said Dawson.

"I would be happy to honeymoon anywhere or even here or at my place in Georgetown," she offered.

"Well, I would like to do something a little more memorable than that Lianne."

"What do you have in mind?"

"I don't know but let's plan on something to make it special. If we get married on that Saturday in July, how long could you get away?"

"I should be able to get the next week off."

"Hmm. That sounds great. No problem having the store covered."

"Let me look into it and come up with an idea for a trip or something," she suggested.

"Why don't you let me handle it and let it be a surprise?"

"Umm. I like your surprises. I'll leave it up to you."

CHAPTER 56

Getting up early, Dawson and Lianne cooked breakfast and ate before going to the store. Lianne had coffee there with Dawson before she left out to go shopping. She purchased several outfits and accessories to have on hand at Dawson's.

They left the store earlier than usual so that they could change clothes and drive to the television station. Lianne was treated like royalty as they were led around and introduced to everyone. She had her picture taken with several of the stations executives and the news room staff.

Lianne, Dawson, the manager, and the station owner then piled into a limousine and were taken to the country club for dinner. Dawson smiled and enjoyed the show of honor they bestowed on Lianne. The small talk they engaged in about the television industry was boring, but Dawson did not feel out of place nor left out. Both men congratulated Dawson on his engagement to Lianne and extolled her virtues as a fine reporter.

During after dinner drinks, Mr. Wellborn told Lianne that if she ever wanted to settle down in Tanner and leave CNN that she would be welcomed to join Channel 10. Flattered, Lianne thanked him and said she would keep that in mind.

It was late by the time they made it back to the television station, got their truck and drove home. It had been an interesting and uplifting evening for both. Dawson clearly saw that he was most definitely marrying up by taking Lianne. His soul soared with pride.

On Thursday Dawson got in touch with Callaway Gardens and rented the Chapel for their July wedding and reception at the nearby Gardens Inn. Also, he made reservations for Lianne's parents to stay there. He and Lianne began inviting family and friends. Dawson was not surprised at how few of her family and friends could make the trip. He questioned her about the possibility of having the wedding in D.C. instead of Callaway Gardens.

"No Dawson. I would really like to marry you at the chapel. It is such a beautiful and special place. Most of my relatives would not be able to make it to D.C. either. I really don't have a lot of close friends. I guess that comes with the type of work I do. I have cultivated few relationships until I met you."

"Okay then. We will stick with the plans we've started."

The rest of the week passed quickly. Lianne flew back to D.C. on Saturday so she could get organized for returning to work. She would fly out to California on Monday to do a report on the devastating forest fires that were currently raging there.

The weeks began to roll on for both Dawson and Lianne. Every other weekend either he would travel to D.C. or Lianne would fly to Tanner. She took one of the visiting weekends off and she and her mother traveled to New York City where she had a wedding dress made.

On one of Lianne's weekends in Tanner, Dawson took her to the animal shelter. They found and adopted a white Persian cat and named him Max. Dawson installed a pet door in the kitchen so the cat could go in and out of the house.

Max took right to living there and won the hearts of Lianne and Dawson in no time. He loved to be petted and could barely contain his delight with the attention he received. Dawson had bought Max a cat bed but he took to sleeping on top of the firewood bin by the hearth instead.

As time drew near for the wedding, Lianne's schedule began to get jumbled up. Their honeymoon time ended up being cut a few days short so she could go overseas on an assignment. They would still have four full days and for what Dawson had planned, it would be enough.

Lee Outdoors continued to prosper. The four employees turned out to be loyal and hardworking trustworthy people. They worked well together and the store ran smoothly. Dawson was able to give them all a raise sooner than he expected.

He continued to spend a majority of each day at the store though he did not have to. Holly had the accounting end down well which took a load off of Dawson. His father worked off and on with no set schedule. He mainly chose to work during the store's busiest times which were on Fridays and Saturdays.

Unable to keep the house work up and watch after the store, Dawson hired Roberto's daughter, Crucita. She started by working two days a week cleaning the house. On the days she worked. She even had dinner waiting on Dawson when he got home. She surprised him further when she took it on herself to cut the grass and clean the pool. He began letting her work more hours.

Having Crucita around made life a lot easier for him and for Lianne when she was down. She rapidly became indispensable around the house.

CHAPTER 57

It was near 5:00 p.m. Dawson was sitting in his office at the store. Amber and Paul were manning the sales floor. Dawson and Roberto were getting ready to leave. Stepping out of the office, Dawson called Roberto.

"Come in a moment, I would like to talk to you about something."

"Yes Sir," said Roberto as he walked in.

"Have a seat, Roberto."

He sat down and looked at Dawson expectantly.

"Roberto, I wanted to talk to you about Crucita."

"Sir?" he queried, giving Dawson a concerned look.

"Oh, it's nothing bad. In fact, Crucita is working out wonderfully. I wanted to talk to you first before I talked to her. I would like to increase her hours. Basically it would be full time."

"That would be nice Mister Dawson. She enjoys working for you and Miss Lianne. The money is very helpful."

"Great. Since the store is doing so well and I spend a lot of time here, I thought I would let her work at the house Monday through Friday. She has really been doing great. She goes above and beyond what I ask her to do. I can tell she is like her father."

He smiled and said, "I have done my best to teach her well. Honest work is good work."

"All right then. Instead of you picking her up this evening, I will bring her home after we talk. What I will propose to her are the full time hours and as part of the deal I have tabs on a little car for her. That way you won't have to drive her back and forth to my house."

"Mister Dawson, that is so kind of you. How can we pay for it?"

"I have a friend that has a nice little Toyota that is only a few years old. It is in great shape. I'll get it and I will subtract some out of each week's pay until it's paid. Crucita will need to get her own auto insurance. But, if she needs help with that then we will work something out. How is that?"

"That will be fine with me. We are very grateful. I know Crucita will be very happy."

"All right then. I'll have her eat dinner with me while we talk, then I will bring her home."

"Thank you Mister Dawson."

Roberto said goodnight and left. Dawson called the house and told Crucita he would be home shortly and that he had talked to her father about giving her more hours.

"We'll talk about it when I get there. I told your father I would give you a ride home."

"Very well Mister Dawson. Your dinner is almost ready. I will set the table for you."

"Crucita. If you would, set the table for two."

"Two? She queried, slightly confused for she knew Lianne was not due in town.

"Very well, Sir."

Dawson chuckled when he got off the phone. Crucita was always so formal. He knew that she had him a place set at the table. If she was still there when he ate, she would wait in the kitchen or den for her father to pick her up. If she ate any of the dinner she prepared, she always ate it in the kitchen.

After saying goodnight to Amber and Paul, Dawson drove home. When he pulled into the garage, Max met him at the truck.

"Meow."

"You smell good Max. Crucita gave you a bath today."

"Meow."

Dawson went into the kitchen and was greeted by Crucita standing at the stove.

"Good evening Mister Dawson."

"Hi there."

He put the cat down. Max walked over to his food bowl and looked back at him.

"Have you fed Max already?"

"Yes Sir. He thinks there should always be food in the bowl. I think you have spoiled him."

Dawson laughed.

"Yep, I have. And, tonight is special so I'll let him have a second helping," he said while refilling the dish with dry cat food.

Max watched Dawson pour the food in his dish. He sniffed it then looked at Crucita expectantly.

"Meow!"

"Go ahead fat cat. Chow down," she said.

Max dug in happily.

Dawson laughed again.

"He won't mind me. He sure knows who the boss is."

CHAPTER 58

While Dawson washed up for dinner, Crucita set the food on the table. He walked back into the dining room and she had just sat a pitcher of tea out.

"Mister Dawson, I have the table set for two as you instructed. Is someone arriving soon?"

"No Crucita, I want you to eat with me this evening. I thought we could talk business while we eat."

She appeared embarrassed and taken back by his request.

"But Mister Dawson, I am your employee."

"So, that does not mean you can't join me for dinner. You and your dad are wonderful people. I have the utmost respect for both of you. I would very much like for you to feel more like family than an employee. That sounds too formal. Relax, do your work and be comfortable here."

Still uneasy with his kindness, it was awkward for her to sit across the table from him. He worked to put her at ease then explained that he wanted her to work full time around the house. She began to relax as they talked and ate. He then explained the plan for her to get the car. Tears came to her eyes. She thanked him profusely."

"Please Crucita. You have been a wonderful help around here. Lianne and I both appreciate you and all you do. She's excited about the car idea and is anxious to hear how you feel about it."

"I feel very honored that you would do this Mister Dawson. You have been very good to my father and me. Since my mother died it has been very hard for us. You have been a great help. We thank you."

"My pleasure and I must say thank you as well."

They ate in silence for a few minutes.

I have one more issue to bring up with you Crucita. You know the wedding is coming up. Would you mind putting in some extra time while Lianne's family and friends are here? Two of Lianne's girlfriends will be staying here at the house and I could really use your help."

"Oh yes Sir. I will be happy to."

"Also, while we are on our honeymoon, I would like for you to look after the house and take care of Max," she nodded that she would.

"All right then. This is all working out just great for us."

Crucita smiled shyly and said, "For me and my father too."

Dawson drove Crucita home after they finished eating. He visited with her and Roberto a few minutes before saying goodnight. He told them that the car would be delivered to the store the next day. They thanked Dawson again before he left.

You guys are welcome. Now, after tonight no more Mister Dawson. It's just Dawson, okay?"

"Okay Sir, I mean… Okay Dawson," replied Crucita.

On the drive back home, Dawson felt good about his helping Roberto and Crucita. They were good, honest, hard-working people who deserved a break. Lianne had been pleased with the suggestion of helping them and really liked the idea of using Crucita more.

Lianne had told him that CNN was to air an hour long special in which she was the host. He and Max piled up on the sofa and began to watch it. Viewing her on television was oddly surreal to Dawson. She was so professional and charming as she interviewed the famous aging actor. "So lovely," Dawson said and shook his head in amazement that she would soon be his wife.

"There is your mommy on television, Max."

"Meow."

Max purred and butted his head against Dawson's hand, wanting him to scratch his head. As Dawson scratched, max rolled over onto his back in ecstasy.

Toward the end of the television special, the phone rang.

"Hello?"

"Hi there. Are you watching me?"

"Sure am. Max is too!"

"What do you think?"

"You have nice legs."

"Dawson!" she screamed.

He laughed.

"Seriously, Lianne, it is great. It is so hard to believe that the woman I see on television is going to be my wife in a few weeks."

"Get used to it!"

"Oh, I intend to."

CHAPTER 59

It was one of those weekends alone. Lianne was on an assignment somewhere. Dawson had worked most of the day on Saturday. On the drive home he felt an overwhelming sense of loneliness. He always did when he and Lianne were apart for more than a few weeks. She had worked the last four weekends so she could take off for the wedding and honeymoon.

As he pulled into the driveway, Dawson saw Max loping out of the woods and heading for the garage toward the opening door. When he opened the trucks door, Max was looking up at him meowing.

"Hello Max. Looks like you're lonesome too."

"Meow, meow, meow."

Max followed along rubbing at Dawson's ankles as he walked into the house. He poured cat food and fresh water in the cat's dish, which temporarily mollified Max.

Reaching into the refrigerator, Dawson retrieved a bottle of beer, unscrewed the cap and took a pull. Just as he started for the den, the phone rang.

"Hello?"

"You busy Dawson?"

"Hey Dad. No, I just got in from the store."

"Walk out front,"

"Huh?"

"I'm pulling up out front. Come and see my new toy."

"You got the camping trailer?"

"Yes, it's a beauty."

"Great."

"Come see it."

"On my way."

He hung up and walked through the living room and out the front door with Max bringing up the rear. Dawson's father had pulled to a stop on the shoulder of the road in front of the house. He had purchased a new travel trailer, now hooked to the back of his truck. Mr. Lee was walking back to the trailer's door when he saw Dawson walking across the yard.

"Isn't it sharp looking?"

"It sure is Dad!"

When Mr. Lee opened the trailer door, Max shot up inside. He laughed.

"Well, I think Max is excited about it too!"

Dawson shook his head.

"Max is a trip."

They stepped up inside and Mr. Lee showed him the trailer's layout.

"This is a twenty-four footer. It can sleep up to eight, though I think it would be tough. It has a slide-out with a nice roomy bed."

"This is really nice Dad. I know you and Mom will enjoy getting away some."

Dawson noted that the trailer was loaded with amenities. It had a nice kitchen and a tub and shower combo in the surprisingly roomy bathroom. There was a 22-inch LED television mounted at the end of the upper kitchen cabinet. There were lots of drawers and cabinets as well as an astonishing number of storage compartments that made use of all available spaces.

Max sniffed around the nooks and crannies then made himself comfortable on the sofa. When they got ready to go, Dawson picked Max up and carried him out. Mr. Lee stood back and proudly looked at the trailer.

"This is wonderful. I have always wanted one of these Dawson. Rebecca and I plan to take it down to the Florida coast after you and Lianne get back from your honeymoon."

"Great idea Dad. The store is running great with Holly and the crew so we can both back off some and let it run itself. I plan to go up to D.C. at least once a month and stay four or five days at a time."

"Good. Just know that you and Lianne are welcomed to use this camper too. You should go ahead and get a towing package installed on your truck. I think you two would have a good time going camping in this."

"I'm sure we would Dad. I will check into getting the truck hitched up and take you up on it later in the summer or fall."

Mr. Lee said goodbye. Dawson and Max watched him drive away with his new toy in tow. The trailer was impressive looking as it disappeared around a curve in the road. Dawson thought about how much fun it would be for him and Lianne to go on a trip and staying in the trailer.

He chuckled to himself as he thought about the tub and shower combo.

"That would be a tight fit, but it would be mighty cozy with Lianne!" he said, grinning at the visual of it.

"Meow?"

"Sure Max. We could take you along with us.

"Meow."

CHAPTER 60

The wedding was fast approaching. On Thursday before the Saturday wedding Lianne and her parents arrived. They had decided to drive down instead of flying. Dawson and his parents had dinner with them that evening at the Calloway Inn. Over dinner they discussed the wedding plans and went through the checklist of details. Afterwards, Lianne walked Dawson and his parents out to his truck and said goodnight. She would stay with her parents until the wedding.

The bride's relatives began arriving on Friday morning. The Palmer's had rented three cottages at Callaway Gardens. Aunts, uncles, and cousins arrived. At 9:00 a.m. Dawson drove to the airport and picked up Lianne's two girlfriends who were to be in the wedding. They would be guests at his house until Sunday.

Feeling uncomfortable about having to take care of them per Lianne's request, he solicited Crucita to spend the entire weekend at the house. She would be able to tend to their needs.

A catered luncheon and pool party was planned at Dawson's house for Friday afternoon. Crucita would be in charge of the catering staff and keeping things under control. Two large canopy awnings had been rented and set up in the back yard with plenty of tables and chairs.

The plane landed with the two girlfriends of Lianne's onboard. Dawson had wondered how he would know them but Lianne assured him that they would recognize him. Minutes later two very attractive women came through the security station. They both smiled and waved when they saw Dawson staring at them.

"Hello ladies. I take it you are the bride's friends?"

"Yes we are Dawson. We are so pleased to meet you at last," said the brunette.

They both hugged and kissed him on the cheek.

"I'm Lisbeth Meadows," said the brunette, "and this is Jordon Simms."

"Nice to meet you both. I welcome you and hope you enjoy your stay."

"I am sure we will," said Jordan.

He took them over to baggage claim and collected their extensive array of luggage. Using a rental cart, he loaded all of their baggage and led them to the truck and loaded everything. He helped them up into the truck and got an embarrassing eyeful of Jordan's nether places as she climbed into the seat. She was wearing a short skirt that left little to the imagination. She and Lisbeth laughed at how red his face had gotten.

"Don't be shy around us Dawson. We're all friends here!" chirped Lisbeth.

He smiled and shook his head. It was going to be an interesting time until the wedding was over. On the ride home the two ladies chattered like magpies. They kidded and bantered with Dawson about his southern accent. By the time they got to his house he felt as though they were old friends. He readily found that he genuinely liked them.

Lisbeth and Jordan complimented Dawson on his home and both liked the bedrooms he assigned them. They were quite taken with Crucita who seemed to blossom in their company. Both Lisbeth and Jordan spoke fluent Spanish and enjoyed conversing with Crucita in her native tongue. This is going to go much better than I could have hoped for, said Dawson to himself.

The catering crew and wait staff arrived and set up for the wedding party. Lianne and her parents arrived. She proudly gave them a tour of the house. Soon more guests arrived, both Lianne's side and Dawson's. The house and backyard became a beehive of activity. Lisbeth and Jordan took it on their own to pitch in and be hosts and help Crucita manage the catering service. Whenever Dawson tried to help with something he was shooed away and told to enjoy himself. Confused by all of the proceedings, Max spent most of the afternoon hiding in the garage.

With everyone gathered out back, the wait staff began serving the food and drinks. During dessert Lianne and Dawson took turns introducing their family and friends. Dawson caused a stir of excitement among the crowd when he introduced Peyton and Cali Kinsley and their daughter, Lindsey. Lianne then called everyone's attention and said she had a special announcement to make.

"Dawson and I both want to thank all of you for being here for our special time. Needless to say, all of this is the happiest time of my life."

The crowd broke out in cheers and applause; she waited until it died down.

"For everyone who traveled the distance to attend this event, we salute you. It is wonderful to know you care that much to come down to see me get married tomorrow."

Several people spoke and thanked Lianne and Dawson for the invitation and wished them well. Lianne thanked them and smiled while holding her hands up again.

"Now, if everyone is comfortable I would like to tell you a little story and I have a surprise for Dawson."

She turned to him and then nodded at Lisbeth and Jordan.

"Now Dawson, if you would, have a seat while I give a little talk."

Lianne's two friends led Dawson to a chair in front of the crowd, but off to the side of Lianne. They sat him down then sat beside him both Lisbeth and Jordan held his hands.

CHAPTER 61

Lianne's face was alive and her eyes sparkled as she stood before the gathering. Dawson could see the professionalism in her stance and demeanor. She was in her element in front of an audience with a story to tell.

"Friends and family. Many of you know a little about how Dawson and I met and ended up together. Most of you do not know the entire story. So, if Dawson will allow me, I would like to share it with you."

All eyes fixed on Dawson. His face flushed hot with embarrassment. Jordan giggled.

"There he goes again."

Lisbeth leaned over and put her mouth close to his ear.

"Just nod yes Dawson."

He complied. Both ladies kissed him on the cheeks bringing a round of cheers. Lianne beamed with joy.

"Now, here goes. I met Dawson while I was on assignment in Afghanistan. My cameraman, Jim Baxter, and I were attached to the company of U.S. Army soldiers that Sergeant Dawson Lee was a member of. I met him and did an interview with him just as I did many of the soldiers. Anyway, Jim and I followed his company around for about a week as they went about their regular duties. Then they were given an assignment to go out and try to capture some Taliban terrorists that were hiding at a remote compound. Jim and I followed the company as they hiked into the mountains to where the Taliban hideout was located. They found the compound which was comprised of a small cluster of buildings on a large open field. Dawson's company met up with another unit and got into position and prepared for the assault on the compound.

As Lianne spoke, there was not a sound anywhere. All eyes were on her. She had everyone's full attention.

"Sergeant Lee's commander pulled him out of his squad and gave him the task of leading Jim and I along so we could film the units in action. We were placed toward the back of the company as the soldiers moved in for the attack."

She looked at Dawson and smiled.

"I might add Dawson was not happy to be given the assignment to babysit us while someone else led his team into battle. I was quite happy because I had taken a liking to him. But, he paid me no attention except on a professional basis."

There were some chuckles in the crowd.

"The order came down the line to move out for the attack on the compound. Like I said, we were toward the back of the company as they made their way across the wide open field. Not long after we were on our way toward the compound, we came under fire. It was horrific. There were bullets flying in all directions and explosions to our left and right. It was terrifying."

She swallowed her tears.

"Sergeant Lee immediately took charge and ordered us back to safety. While we were running back to cover, Jim and I got separated. Soldiers were being hit and falling all around. When I got back to the safety of an embankment I looked out on the field and saw Jim lying on the ground. He had been shot. I turned to Dawson and begged him to rescue Jim."

With tears in her eyes, Lianne walked over behind Dawson and put her hands on his shoulders. Embarrassed, Dawson stared down at his lap.

"Without a second thought, Dawson took off through a hail of bullets and RPG explosions. He fired his weapon on the run and made it to Jim. He grabbed Jim and started carrying him back to safety when an explosion went off near him. He was critically wounded. I must tell you folks, I lost it then. Jim was injured and I caused Dawson to be injured trying to save my friend."

Tears streamed down her face. She kissed Dawson on top of the head.

"The battle finally ended. The medics tended to Jim and Dawson and thank God they were still alive. The medics worked diligently on both men while they were waiting to be air lifted to the hospital. Dawson was barely conscious. I went to him and thanked him from the bottom of my heart. The helicopter came. He and Jim were loaded onboard and whisked away. I did not know if either would live to see another day. Thank goodness, both survived."

There were claps and cheers. Lianne held up her hands for silence.

"Jim was hit in the chest and side by three bullets. He has since recovered nicely. Dawson, as most of you know, almost lost his arms and legs. He was ultimately sent to Walter Reed Hospital in D.C. for treatment. After I got back to D.C. I looked him up. And ladies and gentlemen, from that, here we are today!"

There were more claps and cheers along with a standing ovation for Dawson. He shyly nodded his thanks to everyone. Lianne held her hands up again.

"I told all of you that story because I wanted you all to know how proud and lucky I am to have Dawson. I have thanked him many times for his bravery that day which brings me to my point of all of this."

She kissed Dawson on the cheek. Then, Jordan and Lisbeth pulled him up. Lianne looked up into his eyes.

"Dawson. I have some special guests who want to meet you and one in particular who wants to formally thank you for your service and your bravery."

She took his hand and turned toward the back of the house.

"Dawson, I would like for you to say hello to Jim Baxter and his family."

From out of the back door of the house Jim, his wife, and their two children came. Dawson's legs turned to rubber and almost gave way. Jordan and Lisbeth supported him as tears flooded his eyes.

CHAPTER 62

Dawson was touched deeply when he saw Jim Baxter and his family. The two men embraced one another while the gathering of friends and family stood and applauded. Jim then introduced Dawson to his wife, Kendal, and their children, Chelsea and Toby. Kendal put her arms around Dawson and thanked him over and over while lavishing him with kisses.

When the reunion died down, Lianne reported that as a wedding gift that Jim was going to video the wedding for them. She then added that Peyton had volunteered to photograph it. Dawson was pleased beyond measure.

As the afternoon progressed, the children in attendance were allowed to swim while the adults visited. At 4:30 p.m. the caterers served an early dinner and by 6:00 p.m. the guests were leaving. Lianne found Dawson and took him to the side so they could talk a few minutes.

"How did you like my surprise?" she asked.

"That was really special. I was embarrassed by your speech but seeing Jim and his lovely family made it all worthwhile."

"Well…" she grinned wickedly. "I have one more surprise for you."

"Uh-oh. I don't think I can take much more," he said, shaking his head in a moment of adoration for Lianne.

"Oh, but I think you will enjoy this one."

"Okay. Lay it on me." Eyeing her suspiciously.

"I have commissioned a little bachelor party for you tonight."

He looked at her curiously.

"How so?"

"This one is unusual. Other than Peyton, I have not met any of your men friends. So I did not know who to invite. So instead of guys, you will have gals to party with. You are going to have a dream night. Jordan, Lisbeth, and Cali are taking you out to a special club to party with you. This is my wedding present to you on your last night of being a single man."

"I don't know about this Lianne." He protested, giving her a concerned look.

She giggled and kissed him.

"I promise you will enjoy yourself. The girls assured me that they would take care of you and keep you out of trouble!"

He shook his head in amazement.

"I don't know what to say."

"Just shut up and kiss me."

"Yes ma'am."

While they were still embraced Cali, Lisbeth, and Jordan grabbed him and told Lianne they would take care of him. As they herded him into the garage, Lianne called out to Dawson.

"I will see you tomorrow if you survive tonight!"

When they got to Dawson's truck, Cali took his keys.

"I'm driving, you are ours now!"

"Yes ma'am."

Cali got in behind the wheel. Dawson got in on the passenger side after Lisbeth and Jordan climbed into the back seat.

"Where are we going?" he queried.

Lisbeth and Jordan giggled.

"You'll know when we get there. Sit back and enjoy the ride!" Cali said as she reached over and patted him on the cheek.

Fifteen minutes later they were on Victory Drive near the military base. Dawson knew then that they were taking him to a strip club. Cali pulled into the brightly lit night club called the Pink Pony. The parking lot was full so Cali pulled around back and through into a private fenced in area that was reserved for employees. After helping everyone out of the truck, Dawson followed the women to the back door.

Cali rang a doorbell and moments later a pretty young woman opened the door. She greeted Cali with a hug and said hello to Lisbeth and Jordan. She then turned to Dawson and smiled.

"I'm Amanda, the owner and manger here at the Pink Pony. Welcome. I have a special table ready for you. I hope you enjoy yourself tonight. We will do our best to make sure that you do."

"Nice to meet you Amanda. I am sure I will have a memorable time."

Amanda led them down a short hall past several dressing rooms, then out on to the club's main floor. It was dark except for multicolored lights and strobes flashing on the main stage and runway. The sound of heavy metal rock made it all but impossible to talk. A beautiful young woman was gyrating to the beat with little more on than a g-string.

The group was led to a condoned off corner that contained an L-shaped sofa with a small table. Amanda seated Dawson in the center portion of the sofa. Lisbeth and Jordan took places beside him. They were all smiles, enjoying the spectacle.

"You enjoy yourself!" Amanda said and kissed him on the cheek.

"Thank you."

Amanda took Cali by the hand and the two headed toward the hallway in the back.

CHAPTER 63

A waitress wearing a revealing outfit suddenly appeared in front of Dawson.

"What would you like to drink sir?"

"Ah, I would like a bourbon and coke please."

"Coming right up."

She took Lisbeth's and Jordan's drink orders and left. Moments later she returned with the drinks. Dawson reached for his credit card. The waitress smiled and kissed him on the cheek.

"You money is no good here. Drinks and entertainment are taken care of. Enjoy!"

Dawson took a sip of his drink and felt it burn his throat as it went down. A new dancer came out on the stage and began dancing. Settling back, Dawson sipped the bourbon and took in the show.

"This is awesome!" chortled Jordan. "I have always wanted to see what all strippers do."

"Me too!" chimed Lisbeth. "These girls surely are gorgeous. Look at the money that dancers are taking in."

Men were lined along the stage and runway holding up bills. The dancer swayed and moved to the music, collecting the money and giving each customer a peck and a close up moment when she hovered down in front of them.

Jordan leaned over to Dawson.

"Isn't she gorgeous?"

"Yeah, she sure is!" agreed Dawson.

"Cali said that if you see a girl you like that she will come and dance just for you."

"I'm not sure if my heart could take it," replied Dawson, dead pan.

She bopped him on the shoulder playfully and laughed.

"That's not what we hear from Lianne!" she crowed.

"Huh?" he simpered.

Lisbeth had joined in and both women propped their hands on his shoulders.

"Lianne and us are very close. You have made her the happiest girl in the world. She says you are the best there is!" Jordan cooed.

"Mm-hmm." He was at a loss for words.

"Pick one," Lisbeth said, pointing at the different dancers who were out on the floor working the customers for table dances and cocktails.

"They are all pretty. I don't know which I like best."

Jordan jumped up and walked over to one of the dancers and spoke to her. A moment later Jordan returned and sat down. Three dancers came over and introduced themselves to Dawson.

"Nice to meet you all."

The attractive redheaded dancer leaned over and put her arms around Dawson's neck and kissed him squarely on the lips.

"We hear you are getting married tomorrow. Congratulations. We are here to give you a lasting memory of your single days."

Dawson just sat there with a cheesy grin. Tina, the red head, spread his knees apart and stepped between them. The other two women sidled up to his side. He was surrounded by a beavy of beautiful women including Lisbeth and Jordan.

A new song began to play. It had a strong thumping beat and all three dancers began working their bodies, ever so close to him. Filled with a mixture of embarrassment and elation, Dawson willed himself to loosen up and enjoy the erotic titillation.

As the dancers worked their bodies to the music, they removed their tops and leaned in to tease and caress him with their bare breasts. When that song ended, the old Phil Collins classic, "In the Air Tonight," came on. Dawson's heart began to hammer in his chest as the three women slipped out of their bottoms and took turns dancing between his legs.

Each dancer was uniquely beautiful. Dawson was happily suffering stimulus overload and meltdown. He broke out in beads of sweat. He could not think or speak. He just sat there in a delicious sensual stupor.

The song ended. Each dancer sat on Dawson's lap, gave him a kiss and wished him a happy marriage. Lisbeth and Jordan slid back close beside him and put their arms around him.

"How ya doing?" asked Lisbeth.

"I don't know," he said, and really meant it.

"Aww. I think he needs three more dancers!" crowed Jordan.

"No, no. I don't' think I can take another round!" feigning a heart attack.

They laughed and both kissed him on the neck and shoulder. Cali and Amanda came back with drinks for everyone. They sat and talked for a time. Dawson felt like a king in the company of so many lovely women.

CHAPTER 64

Before Dawson and his dates left the Pink Pony, Amanda pulled him up on the stage and announced that he was getting married tomorrow. In the midst of cheers, whistles, and cat calls, all of the dancers paraded around him and planted kisses on his cheeks.

When the party got ready to leave, Amanda walked them out to the truck. She hugged Cali goodbye and promised to get together with her and Peyton soon. On the ride back to Dawson's, Cali told them the story about how she worked her way through college dancing at the Pink Pony.

"Amanda and I danced together there. Then I got my degree and opened the accounting business. Amanda ended up becoming the owner operator of the club. She's doing very well with it."

Lisbeth and Jordan were intrigued with her story and peppered her with questions all the way home. Dawson sat quietly enjoying the afterglow of the fantasy evening. When they got back to Dawson's house, Cali hugged them all goodnight and got in her car and left for home.

In the house, Dawson said goodnight to Lisbeth and Jordan and retired to his bedroom. He showered and climbed into bed. He lay there thinking about Lianne and was amazed at her arranging the evening for him.

"She must really trust me," he said softly. "I must never, never do anything to lose her trust."

Dawson drifted off into blissful sleep. He did not stir until 6:00 a.m. when he heard Crucita knocking on his door and calling his name.

"Breakfast is ready Dawson. Lisbeth and Jordan are getting dressed now."

"Okay, thank you," he said groggily. "Be there in five."

He quickly dressed, brushed his teeth and combed his hair. In the kitchen he found Lisbeth and Jordan already at the table eating. Max was busy crunching on his food. He looked up at Dawson, meowed once and returned to his eating.

"Good morning. How is the groom this fine morning?" asked Lisbeth.

"Oh, none the worse for wear."

"How did you sleep last night?" queried Jordan.

"I had a hard time getting to sleep but after that I slept fine."

Lisbeth let out a yell and Jordan guffawed. Dawson's face turned scarlet when he realized what he had said. Crucita looked at all of them, trying to figure out what was so funny. Dawson held his hands up in supplication.

"I didn't mean that literally. Forgive me."

"We were actually happy to hear that," said Jordan and grinned. "We wanted to make sure you are on 'point' tonight!"

She giggled and looked at Lisbeth who was snickering.

"Yeah, you know, on POINT!"

They laughed again. Crucita shook her head and went back to serving more coffee. The jokes and bantering continued until they finished eating and got ready to go. Dawson loaded them and their clothes and makeup kits for the wedding in the truck. He drove them to the Calloway Inn where Lianne and her family were staying.

Mrs. Palmer met them at the door and said hello while Lisbeth and Jordan went on in. Being traditional, Mrs. Palmer would not let Dawson see Lianne until she walked down the aisle. She stepped outside and pulled to door to.

"Dawson, things will be crazy for the rest of the day until you two get on the plane for your honeymoon. I just wanted to say that Richard and I both welcome you into the family. Lianne is a wonderful person. Take care of her Dawson. She lovers you deeply. You will never have to worry about her ever being unfaithful or uncaring. It will be a challenge with her career but with love and devoted hearts, you will make it."

"Thank you Mrs. Palmer. I will do my very best to be the man she deserves."

"I know you will. If I can ever help you in any way, don't hesitate to call on me or Richard. She is our heart. We want the best for her and you."

She paused.

"You know she can't have children. She has a deep hurt because she can't. I would like to ask you to consider one day adopting a child or two so she can have the pleasure of being a mother and raising a family."

Dawson smiled and nodded thoughtfully.

"I don't have a problem with that at all. My only concern is how much of a problem her career and being gone a lot would pose if we try to adopt."

"I really don't have an answer for that. But, I know if you really want it, things will work out for you."

"I will keep that in mind Mrs. Palmer."

CHAPTER 65

Saying goodbye to Lianne's mother, Dawson drove from Pine Mountain toward Tanner. He stopped at a convenience store in Cataula and filled the truck with gasoline. While inside he fixed a cup of coffee to go and paid for it and the gas with a debit card. When Dawson walked back out and climbed in the truck he noticed a folded piece of paper sticking under the windshield wiper blade.

Putting the hot coffee in the console cup holder, he opened the truck's door and leaned out and retrieved the piece of paper. When he opened it up and looked inside, his heart skipped a beat. It was a simple note that said:

I still love you. I always will.

It was Amydee's flourishing handwriting. Dawson looked around but saw no sign of her anywhere. Not realizing he had been holding his breath, he sucked in air and gasped.

"I don't need this," he muttered.

Visibly shaken, he buckled up and sought to compose himself as he drove on home. Pulling into the garage, he had an eerie feeling. Instead of punching the remote button to close the garage door, he got out of the truck and looked up and down the road in front of the house. Satisfied that no one was following him, he punched the remote button and closed the garage door. He then opened the kitchen door and went in.

"Crucita!" he called out.

She had cleaned the kitchen and he then saw the patio door ajar. He saw her sweeping the patio. He slid the glass door open and smiled.

"Hey there. I'm back." He said.

"Good morning again. Your father called and wants you to call him back."

"I will. Thank you."

She came into the kitchen and put the broom in the utility closet.

"Dawson, may I speak with you a moment?" she asked shyly.

"Sure Crucita. What's on your mind?"

"I would like to say how happy I am for you and Lianne. I wish you much happiness."

"Why thank you Crucita. I am a lucky man. I am also fortunate to have you and your father working for me, and I hope, for a long time to come."

"We appreciate you letting us work for you. I like working here and taking care of your beautiful home. I will take very good care of it while you and Lianne are away."

"Well, think of this as your home too. You and your dad are like family." He chuckled. "And you know Max is crazy about you!"

Crucita giggled. She clasped her hands together and looked down shyly. To Dawson's surprise, she wrapped her arms around him and hugged him. He hugged her back and kissed the top of her head. She looked up at him with tears in her eyes.

"What's the matter Crucita?"

"I'm so happy for you both. This is a good day."

"Yes it is a good day. Thank you."

"You make me so happy Dawson."

"I do?"

"Yes, you gave me and my father good jobs. You help us. Now we have a good life here. We thank you."

"You are very welcome," he said softly, and held her.

"Meow, meow."

Max was at their feet rubbing and rooting his way between their legs.

Crucita giggled nervously and backed away.

"Well, I guess he's jealous," said Dawson.

"Meow."

"He just wants more food," said Crucita.

Dawson laughed.

"I am going to take a shower and get organized Crucita. We have a wedding scheduled for later. I can't be late."

"Do you mind if I go ahead and take my shower and wash my hair? I want to look my best today."

"Why sure. The house looks great. I can't believe you have gotten it put back together after the big party yesterday."

"It was a very nice party Dawson. I had a good time."

"As hard as you were working, I was afraid it would be too much for you. I am proud of you Crucita. You did a professional job of handling things."

"Thank you."

Dawson excused himself and went into the bedroom. He found that Crucita had already laid out everything he would need for the day. She had also packed his bags for the honeymoon. His tuxedo was hanging on the door, pressed and ready to wear. He stopped and looked at it a long moment. Tears pooled in his eyes. He felt a wave of bittersweet emotions pass through him.

"In a little while Lianne will be mine forever."

Along with the warm thoughts of Lianne, uneasy feelings about Amydee filtered through his happiness. Forcing himself to shake them off, he headed for the shower.

CHAPTER 66

Sitting on the side of the bed, Dawson had on the tuxedo pants and shirt. He was putting on his socks when the phone rang.

"Hello?"

"Hi handsome. What are you doing?" asked Lianne.

"Oh, I'm getting dressed to go to a wedding."

"Anybody I know?"

"I'm not sure, but I think you would like her," he answered jokingly.

"That person had better be one Lianne Palmer, soon to be Lee."

"Hmm. That name has a familiar ring to it," he replied, deadpan.

"You rat you!"

He laughed.

"Well Dawson, are you ready?"

"Sure am."

"Last chance to back out."

"No way."

"You didn't find a better woman last night?"

"Umm. I saw some mighty beautiful women, but none of them can give me what you give me."

"And what is that?"

"Real love," he replied softly.

"Ever the romantic, Dawson Lee. I love you with all of my heart!"

"And I love you."

"See you at the altar."

"I will be there."

Dawson said goodbye and finished getting ready. He checked himself in the mirror. Satisfied, he nodded at his reflection. He closed his eyes.

"Lord, please let this all go as planned. Let it be a good day for everyone, especially Lianne."

He took one last look and turned the bedroom light off and walked into the den. Crucita was sitting on the sofa.

"Oh Dawson, you look so handsome."

"And look at you. You are absolutely lovely. If you were a little older and I was a little younger, and I had not met Lianne, I would be trying to marry you."

Crucita preened and beamed a beautiful smile.

"Shall we?" he asked.

"I'm ready."

"Meow."

Max stood starring at them flicking his tail.

"Sorry Max. You can't go. Too many people. We'll see you later. Hold the fort down," said Dawson as they walked out into the garage.

Dawson helped Crucita up into the truck then hopped in and soon they were motoring toward Calloway Gardens. The two went over the plans for the rest of the day. After the wedding ceremony Crucita would drive Dawson's truck to the reception at Callaway Inn, then to his house when it was over. Dawson and Lianne would be chauffeured from the Chapel to the reception, then to the house. There they would change clothes and load their bags in the truck. Crucita would ride with them to the airport and bring the truck back home. She would stay at Dawson's and watch after the house and take care of Max and pick them up at the airport on their return.

At the entrance to the gardens, the ticket booth agent presented Dawson with a special pass and he drove on to the Chapel. There were already a line of cars along the road and most of the parking spaces were filled. His father saw him and waved him to a reserved parking space.

"My goodness Crucita. You look marvelous!" said Mr. Lee as he helped Crucita from the truck.

"Thank you, Sir."

"Your father is already here and down at the Chapel."

Mr. Lee had closed the store early so the staff could attend the wedding. Dawson, his father, and Crucita walked down the gray slate steps that led across the little stone bridge over the stream and to the chapel by the lake. The entire scene was resplendent.

Surprised, Dawson saw that Jim Baxter had set up two large flat-screened televisions outside the Chapel. There were rows of seating for those who could not fit inside. The attendees would be able to see the ceremony on the monitors as it took place inside.

Dawson walked around and spoke to everyone that was there. He was pleased with all of the decorations and flowers around the Chapel. Peyton was standing by with his camera and took some candid shots of Dawson and his father as they waited for the ceremony to begin.

The wedding director informed everyone to take their seats. The organist began playing and then the procession began. The parents of the bride and groom were escorted in. Then Lisbeth and Jordan, the bridesmaids were walked in and took their places around the altar. Lindsey appeared at the entrance of the path and the wedding march began. Dawson took a deep breath and put on his best smile.

CHAPTER 67

Dawson's heart fluttered when the congregation rose. On the inside monitors near Jim's camera station, he could see Lianne and her father descending the winding steps and crossing the stone bridge. Even on the small screen he could clearly see how breath taking beautiful she was in her wedding gown.

The flower girl, a heart stopping micro-Cali, stepped off and began dropping flower petals until she reached the altar and took her place with Lisbeth and Jordan. Then came Lianne and her father. Her shiny jet black hair was a stark contrast to the pearl white dress and sheer veil she wore. Slowly they walked the short distance and Lianne took her place beside Dawson.

The exchange of vows became a blur to Dawson. His anxiety level was through the roof. When it came time to say the "I do's", Lianne looked up into his eyes. Dawson's knees felt as though they were filled with jelly. Two glistening tears of joy dripped from Lianne's vivid blue eyes. One tear splashed softly on her left cheek as if in a vain attempt to wash away the soft makeup she wore.

"You may kiss the bride," stated the minister.

Dawson faltered a moment. It was as if he had a lapse of memory, forgetting where he was. Lianne softly cleared her throat. It was enough to kick start his brain. He gently kissed her on the lips. And with that, it was all over. A done deal!

The bride and groom walked down the aisle and out into the sunshine by the lake. Well-wishers converged on them and gave them their approval and prayers. Soon the crowd dispersed and headed for the reception at the Inn. Peyton took pictures of the wedding party while Jim and his crew took down the video equipment. For a brief moment Dawson thought he caught a glimpse of Amydee up near the parking area above the Chapel.

Pictures over, Dawson and Lianne were loaded in the limousine and rode to the reception. On the ride over, Dawson discreetly watched for any sign of Amydee but did not see her. He willed her out of his mind.

The reception hall was crowded. The bride and groom were met with a boisterous round of cheers when they walked in. Handshakes, pats on the back, hugs and kisses were abundant. Soon everyone was eating, the cake was cut and served, toasts and speeches were given.

Finally it came time for the bride and groom's first dance. Dawson and Lianne stepped out on the dance floor. The band started off with the Leona Lewis' song, "Footprints in the Sand." The two newlyweds embraced one another and slowly danced around. After a couple of dances together they split up and danced with the guests. Dawson danced with Cali while Lianne danced with Peyton. She then danced with her father and Dawson with his mother. He danced with a host of beautiful women including Lisbeth, Jordan, Holly, and Amber. He sought out Crucita and danced with her.

"I have never seen such a beautiful wedding Dawson. I hope one day to have such a wedding!"

"You will Crucita. You are a fine young lady. Some guy will be exceptionally lucky to win your heart."

"My prayer is that he will be as kind and handsome as you are Dawson," she said softly.

Dawson smiled at her sweet naiveté' and held her close. The song ended and he kissed her cheek.

"Thank you for the wonderful dance."

She hugged him again.

"You and Lianne have a wonderful honeymoon. Your home and Max will be waiting for your return."

Time came for them to get to the airport for their flight. Dawson and Lianne said their goodbyes and piled into the limousine amid a barrage of cheers and well wishes. The chauffeur whisked them away and to the house. While they were changing, Crucita made it home and quickly changed into jeans. She and Dawson loaded the luggage into the truck.

Lianne picked Max up and kissed him on the head as they got into the truck. Moments later they were on their way to the airport. Lianne had not known where they were going for their honeymoon until Dawson announced it at the reception. They were to fly to San Francisco and would spend their first night there. The next day they would travel north of San Francisco to Sonoma and spend a couple of days in wine country touring the different wineries there in Napa Valley.

"Crucita, I left a list of phone numbers and address of the hotel in San Francisco and the cottage in Sonoma we will be staying at. Lianne and I will both have our cell phones too. Feel free to call if you have any problems or need to relay any messages. Mom and Dad will check in with you and call on them if you need to."

"Don't worry Mister and Mrs. Lee. I will take good care of everything."

Lianne smiled.

"I like that Mister and Mrs. Lee. You made it sound so special Crucita."

"You two are very special," confirmed Crucita.

Arriving at the airport, Dawson checked them in with the airline and turned in their luggage. Crucita hugged them both goodbye and watched them pass through security to board their plane.

CHAPTER 68

Dawson and Lianne hardly had time to unwind before the commuter plane landed in Atlanta. Their flight to San Francisco was already at the gate when they got to it. Minutes later they were onboard and streaking westward chasing the sun.

Traveling first class, the two newlyweds stretched out and sipped on champagne while still basking in the afterglow of the perfect wedding. They were both quiet, lost in their own thoughts. Time to time each would look at the other and smile in disbelief. For Dawson, it felt as though he was in a fairytale dream.

"Mister and Mrs. Lee, would you two like to eat dinner this evening?" asked the stewardess. "We have chicken fricassee with yellow rice and a fresh summer salad."

"Yes please," replied Lianne.

Dawson nodded his approval.

"I'm hungry" professed Lianne. "I really didn't eat much at the reception. I was too nervous."

"I know. I didn't eat much either."

While the two ate, a comfortable silence hung between them; they felt no need to fill in the spaces. They sipped their champagne and ate, passing an occasional comment, and smiled lovingly at each other.

After their meal, the stewardess brought them coffees. She struck up a conversation with Lianne.

"Aren't you Lianne Palmer from CNN?"

"Yes I am."

"I thought so. I wasn't sure when I saw the manifest having you listed as Lianne Lee."

Lianne smiled and said proudly, "My name just changed a few hours ago."

The stewardess clasped her hands and beamed with joy.

"Congratulations you guys. I am so happy for you!"

"Thank you," said Dawson and Lianne.

"I am a longtime fan of your news reporting Lianne."

"Why thank you again."

The stewardess gave Lianne a concerned look.

"Will you be changing your name to Lianne Lee on television?"

"Dawson and I have been discussing that. I will probably leave my professional name Palmer, but I may go with Palmer-Lee."

"I like Palmer-Lee," chirped the stewardess.

"It sounds very nice."

"You are right. It does sound nice. That is what my boss suggested."

"Mister Lee. What do you prefer?" asked the stewardess.

He smiled and said, "I really don't have a preference. I'm just glad I have her. I do think it would be better for her television persona to stick with Palmer in their somewhere. Seems like it would be less confusing to her fans. Palmer-Lee is not bad. It would be easier than just Lee."

The stewardess looked at Lianne and nodded appreciatively.

"You have a wonderful husband there. He is very thoughtful and respectful of your profession. Hang on to him. He's a special one!"

"I know. I'm lucky I found him. There are not many like him out there."

"Don't I know it!" she exclaimed and laughed. "Well, I'll leave you two alone. Enjoy the rest of the flight. I'll check back with you."

The stewardess left. Lianne turned to Dawson. She leaned over and kissed him, then lay back looking at him admiringly.

"I hope you will always be okay with me being recognized wherever we go. I don't want it to ever cause problems for us."

"Never, I'm so proud of you Lianne. I am honored to be by your side. I don't care what name they know you by as long as you are mine. I surely don't' mind at all being married to the famous news correspondent Lianne Palmer or Lianne Palmer-Lee or Lianne Lee."

Lianne shook her head and smiled.

"It's still hard to believe we are husband and wife now."

"Yep, it sure is!" I pray I never lose the feeling I have for you right now."

"Same here. I will do whatever it takes to keep our marriage the best there is."

"Me too."

She touched her fingers to her lips and then pressed them against his.

"Tell me I'm not dreaming," she said.

He shook his head.

"I can't. I'm wondering the same thing myself. This is just too good to be true."

Dawson reached over and caressed her cheek.

"Thank you for loving me."

"Don't' thank me. Show me."

"Here?" he queried, wiggling his eyebrows. "Hmm. Might not be a good idea. How long before we get to San Francisco?"

"Too long."

Lianne looked at him mischievously.

"The lavatory is right there. There is no one looking. I'm sure our friendly stewardess will look the other way for a few minutes."

And she did!

CHAPTER 69

It was shortly after ten when they landed in San Francisco and deplaned. Collecting their luggage and finding the Alamo Car rental center, they were soon motoring toward downtown in a new Mustang GT. The GPS map feature led them right to the entrance of the hotel. The car was put into the hotel's parking garage while the two checked into their room.

The suite was up on the twentieth floor and offered a commanding view of Fisherman's Wharf, the bay, and the majestic Golden Gate Bridge. Tired but hungry, Lianne ordered room service while Dawson took a quick shower. As soon as he got out, she got in while he waited on their food.

When the porter arrived with their meal, he set the two filet mignon dinners on the table along with Caesar salads, a bottle of wine, and a small vase of flowers. Dawson tipped him and bid him goodnight. Lianne came out of the bathroom wearing a thick white terry robe provided by the hotel. Her hair was wet. She wore no makeup and still looked refreshingly lovely.

"I'm sorry if I look like a drowned rat on our honeymoon," she said as she sat down at the table.

He smiled at her.

"Lianne, I don't think you could look bad if you tried."

She laughed.

"I think you need glasses!" she paused. "No, scratch that. Don't get glasses. You might get a real look at me then."

Dawson grinned and raised his eyebrows.

"My eyes are fine dear. I have seen you close up and personal. And, I must say, I like it!"

"You silver-tongued devil!"

"Thank you." he bowed. "Now eat. I have plans for dessert."

"You do?"

"Yep."

"What?"

"You."

"Me?"

"Yep, you."

"Little ol' me?"

"Uh-huh."

They both got tickled and it took several minutes before they could calm themselves to eat their food. Half way through their late dinner Lianne put her fork down. She picked up her wine glass and held it up.

"Dawson. I don't think I have ever been happier than I am right this moment."

He clinked his glass against hers.

"Nor I Lianne. If it took getting wounded in Afghanistan to end up with you, then it was worth it. Somehow I know deep down inside that we have a love and now a marriage that will last forever."

"I have the same feeling Dawson. I don't say it lightly either. I will be by your side from now on. I know that my work will keep us apart from time to time but I just know in my heart that we will persevere."

"I will keep the home fires burning no matter where your work takes you."

She sat back a moment, then looked at him with a serious expression.

"Dawson, promise me this. If my work ever causes you to want to walk away, please let me know. To keep from losing you I will gladly give it up. I mean that Dawson. I really do."

"That's a noble offer Lianne. I pray nothing like that ever happens. I knew what I was getting into when we decided to do this thing. I love you Lianne with all of my heart and soul. I have long since accepted your career and I will stand by you all the way. I will not make you decide between your job and me. Who you are and what you are and do makes me love you that much more. I am so proud of what you do. I am honored, as I've said before, that you have chosen me to be your husband. For that, I am going to be the best I can be for you."

She smiled, then loosened the tie on the robe and slipped it off of her shoulders. She was wearing a sheer nightgown that left little to the imagination. Dawson sucked in a breath and let it out slowly.

"I think I'm in love," he said softly.

"You better be!" she chided.

"Oh I am. I am!"

It was late when they fell asleep in each other's arms. Even though they had made love many times, this time it was different. It was as if their love making was anew. Dawson felt he had almost touched heaven.

CHAPTER 70

When Lianne awoke she saw Dawson standing at the window looking out across San Francisco. He sensed that she was awake and turned to her. They looked at each other for a long moment.

"Good morning, Mrs. Lee."

"Good morning, Mister Lee."

"Breakfast?" he asked.

"Yes please."

"I'll call and order room service."

"No, let's get dressed and go eat somewhere," she suggested.

"Fine by me."

Twenty minutes later they were riding the elevator down to the lobby and found the hotel's restaurant. They were seated quickly and ordered breakfast. Both ate a hearty meal and had refills on their coffees. Lianne leaned back in her chair and smiled at Dawson. He looked at her with curiosity.

"What's on your mind?"

"Oh, I was just admiring how handsome you are."

"Well, thank you for the compliment. You don't look so bad yourself."

She giggled.

"What are the plans for the day, my husband?"

"Hmm, I thought my sweet wife and I would take the car and head up to Sonoma and check out the wine country there."

"Sounds good to me. You know that wine makes me frisky."

"That's the point!"

She laughed, almost spilling her coffee.

"You are something else Dawson Lee. I am so happy with you."

"Care to show me?"

"Race you to the room!"

Two hours later they checked out and retrieved the rental car. The valet loaded their luggage in the trunk and wished them a safe trip. Minutes later they were on 101 north crossing the Golden Gate Bridge. Continuing north, Dawson caught Highway 37 then 128 North into Sonoma and Napa.

It was near noon when they reached Sonoma and picked up the key to their rental cottage. On East Napa Street, Dawson pulled into the Les Petites Maisons and found a quaint little cottage that was theirs for the next few days. Lianne was all smiles when she unlocked the door and walked in.

"This is so romantic!"

"Yep, that was the plan!" he beamed.

"You did good Dawson Lee!"

The cottage was like a small house. It had a nice large deck, gas grill, and an outdoor fireplace. Inside it had its own kitchenette, a small living room, and a bedroom with a lovely four-poster bed piled with over-stuffed pillows. The walls were decorated with warm landscape photos and the lighting was soft. The cottage even contained coffee-table books.

Lianne and Dawson unpacked and hung their clothes, then drove to Sonoma Plaza to shop. They went in the country store and purchased a variety of snacks, drinks, and supplies. After taking all they bought back to the cottage, they went for a drive to familiarize themselves with the area.

Sonoma is a small town with only about 10,000 residents. Dawson and Lianne were pleased to see that the town had a large number of world-class restaurants. They made plans to eat at a different one each day.

The surrounding countryside was dotted with several wineries, both small and large international operations. Plans were made to which ones they would visit and indulge in their wine tasting rooms.

Though Sonoma is known for some of the best chardonnays and pinot noirs in the world, Dawson and Lianne also learned that because of the diverse geographic range that is also produces a large array of grapes affording the wine connoisseur some unusual wine tasting opportunities.

Rather than eating lunch at a restaurant, the two chose to return to the cottage and have a late lunch there. Lianne made sandwiches of pita bread cut into a pocket and filled with prosciutto, romaine lettuce, and dressing. She opened a bottle of zinfandel and poured two glasses.

Sitting outside on the deck, the newlyweds relaxed and enjoyed the pleasant scenery and one another's company.

"This is great isn't it?" asked Dawson.

"It sure is. This was a wonderful idea Dawson."

"I had thought about Hawaii or Jamaica, but I decided that we might enjoy a slow paced atmosphere for our first week of marriage. We haven't spent much time just relaxing together."

"You are right about that. We have always had a full schedule of things to do. This is just what we need. You are the greatest, Dawson Lee!"

"I pray you will always think that."

"Me too. I plan on it."

CHAPTER 71

Later in the afternoon Dawson and Lianne took a leisurely walk. Just a short distance from the downtown area of Sonoma, they encountered acres of grapevines. Between the vineyards were areas of knee high grasses that were dried and whispered like wheat as the wind blew through.

The two worked up a sweat and an appetite by the time they returned to the cottage. Each took a shower and dressed for dinner. Instead of driving to a restaurant, they chose to walk west on Napa Street for a block and a half, then over to Spain Street. There they found an impressive French country-styled restaurant. The owner recognized Lianne and gave them the quietest table in a low-ceiling and beamed room. The tables were simply set with cloths the color of old tera-cotta frescoes. A Mediterranean-blue jug held a small bunch of white daises. Little table lamps cast intimate pools of light, and it felt as though they were alone.

The food, the wine, the atmosphere were sublime. The emotion of the moment was at times overpowering for Dawson. It was truly a dream come true to have and to hold Lianne forever more. At times the two would lock eyes and feel the electric sweetness pass between them.

Toward the end of the meal, the owner of the restaurant came by with a bottle of Schramsbert Champagne and two crystal flutes.

"Mister and Mrs. Lee. I would like to thank you for dining with us and say congratulations on your marriage."

He then poured the champagne and smiled at Lianne.

"My wife and I enjoy your news reports and specials. You do a wonderful job and you have such a beautiful voice."

"Thank you," Lianne said. "I appreciate the compliments. Dawson and I appreciate the champagne as well."

Dawson nodded.

"You have a wonderful place here. The food is superb."

By the time the two left, they had drank half the bottle of champagne. The owner insisted they take the remainder with them. They walked back to the cottage hand in hand enjoying the comfortable night air. There were few cars on the streets, making for a quiet and peaceful walk.

At the cottage, Lianne excused herself and went into the bathroom. A few minutes later she walked out wearing a royal blue nightgown that accentuated the deep blue of her eyes. Dawson was busy pouring glasses of champagne when he looked up and saw her.

"Oh my!" he gushed.

"You like?"

"Very much!"

Her blue eyes were depthless as he bent over and kissed her lips. It was a soft imperceptible touch, and Lianne held her breath at his sweetness. Her heart throbbed, her fingers tightened on his arms as she anticipated the next kiss.

"Ohhh!" she moaned as her body trembled with desire.

Dawson stroked his hand down her hair and on down her spine and let it rest on the small of her back. Lianne felt herself losing control with want.

With hands that all of a suddenly seemed unwieldy, she sought to unbutton his shirt. Dawson waited a moment then helped her. They kissed as though they were drowning and would find the breath of life in the others mouth.

In bed their initial frantic love making turned into something softer. Lianne wept as they made love; not from sadness, but from extreme joy. Later she explained that she felt as though she had left her body and felt an ultimate sense of peace.

While they made love, Dawson reached a plateau he had never climbed before. He was speechless with gratitude as he held her. Her breath against his throat, the graceful curve of her back under his right hand, and the sweet smell of her hair was poetry that words could not equal.

When it was all over, neither would relinquish the hold they had on the other. Through the night they dozed and awoke, only to pull the other closer as if the world was coming to an end.

The sun was well up in the sky when the two lovers stirred and rose. Lianne took a shower while Dawson made coffee. He then took a shower while she made fresh fruit bowls for their breakfast.

While they were having a relaxed breakfast, Lianne powered up her laptop and checked her messages and emailed her parents, letting them know how well things were going so far. When she finished, Dawson did the same with his parents.

It was late in the morning when they dressed and left out for a day of exploring and wine tasting of some of California's finest.

CHAPTER 72

Dawson walked out of the cottage and got into the Mustang while Lianne finished gathering her things and locking up. He cranked the engine and found pleasure in listening to the throaty rumble of the big V-8.

Lianne grinned as she bound down the steps and into the car.

"This car is so awesome. You look grand behind the wheel. It must be a wonderful feeling to be in control of such an amazing machine."

"It does feel good. You know, it's about time you learned how to drive."

"Yes, I would like to learn one day soon."

As Dawson backed the car into the road and drove to their first stop, he explained how to operate the automatic transmission, the gas and brake pedals. Within minutes they were pulling into Sebastini Vineyards and Winery, just off Fourth Street East.

Sebastini's had a vast parking lot and there were already several tour buses parked. As Lianne and Dawson walked to the tasting room they noticed that several visitors were lounging outside in chairs around fountain. In the tasting room they ordered the seven-wine tasting package that included some of California's best cabernet, sauvignon, merlot, and chardonnay. While they were at Sabastini's they learned that it is one of the oldest continually operating vineyards in the United States.

For lunch, Dawson and Lianne rode downtown to a bistro, and then afterwards drove out Gehricke Road to Ravenswood Winery, famous for its zinfandels. In the tasting room Dawson ordered a cheese plate to go along with the wines they tried. One of the cheeses that came with the order was from the Vella Cheese Company nearby and tasted great with the glass of rose' of zinfandel they were sampling.

Before leaving Ravenswood, the two had glasses of gewürztraminer while relaxing outside on the lawn, taking in the view of the vineyards. It was mid-afternoon when they walked out to the parking lot. Dawson stopped in front of the Mustang and looked at Lianne.

"How do you feel?" he asked.

"Great. Couldn't be better?"

"Good. Want to learn to drive?"

"Really?" she grinned.

"Yep. Hop in the driver's seat and I'll teach you. There's hardly any traffic so this is as good of a place as any."

He helped Lianne adjust the seat and the steering wheel so she could reach the pedals. She barely could see over the dash. There was a picnic blanket in the backseat so Dawson refolded it and she sat on it giving her a little more height. He had her start the engine and then went over all of the control features. With his instructions she backed out of the parking space and drove out onto Gehricke Road heading away from town. They drove out into the countryside with Lianne driving slowly but steadily. After several miles he had her turn around and drive back to town and to the cottage. She parked the car and turned the engine off.

"How about that? You did great Lianne!" he said. "You drive like a pro!"

"Oh Dawson. That was so much fun. I never knew it would be so easy. I love the way this car feels. Do they all drive as easy as this one?"

"Well, most vehicles operate about the same. But each one of them has a different feel. Some better than others."

"How about your truck? It looks hard to drive."

"You would be surprised at how easy it handles. It's just big and powerful. You keep that in mind and you would not have a problem. This Mustang is powerful and you handled it well so I know you could drive the truck."

They got out of the car. Lianne ran around and jumped into Dawson's arms.

"I love you so much. You are a fantastic driving instructor! If I were to get a driver's license it would sure make my boss happy. There are times when I am on assignment and need a car. We always have to hire a car and driver for me. That gets costly. My boss is gonna be thrilled to hear about this!"

After resting a while, the two got dressed for dinner. They went to another fine restaurant downtown Sonoma. They began their meal with a tropical cucumber and avocado salad which Lianne enjoyed so much that she had a second. Their main course was grilled chicken breasts with peach-blackberry salsa. Too full for dessert, they finished out the meal with fresh coffee.

Dawson paid the bill and the two stepped out into the night. The stars were out in all their glory.

"Is there anything you want to do before we go back to the cottage?" Dawson asked as he opened the passenger door of the mustang for Lianne.

Her face lit up with a big grin.

"You know that little dirt road I turned around on today?"

"Yeah?"

"Let's go there and park for a while."

"My, my. What's on your mind?"

"You."

By the time they had reached the secluded little trail of a dirt road, Lianne had taken her stockings and underwear off. Dawson parked the car and turned to her as she slipped her dress over her head. He grinned.

"This sure is a small car. How do you propose we do this?"

"You are a smart man. You figure it out," she said and giggled.

And he did.

CHAPTER 73

Over the next days, Dawson and Lianne toured more wineries in Sonoma including Buena Vista Carneros Winery and Bartholomen Park Winery. He took Lianne out several times and let her drive the Mustang. They took one day and drove over to Napa and visited two wineries there.

The couple spent some time shopping for souvenirs and gifts for their parents, Crucita, Dawson's store employees, and Lianne's girlfriends. They also purchased several special bottles of wine to be shipped home. The two decided that on each wedding anniversary for several years to come they would celebrate with a bottle of wine from their honeymoon adventure in Napa Valley.

On Friday they packed and drove back to San Francisco, turned in the rental car and boarded an early flight for home. The past week had surpassed their greatest expectations.

Well into the flight back toward Atlanta, Dawson fell asleep. When he awoke he saw Lianne's deep blue eyes looking at him.

"Hey," she said softly. "Did you have a good nap?"

"Yes I did. We should be rested up after being on vacation for a week, but to tell you the truth, I'm worn out!"

She giggled and said, "Me too."

He took her hand, then leaned over and gave her a quick kiss.

"Did you enjoy your honeymoon Mrs. Lee?"

"I sure did Mister Lee. How about you?"

"It was a dream come true. What was your favorite part?"

"Hmm. I think it was that hunter-green Mustang. I liked learning to drive it and I really enjoyed that night under the stars when you made love to me."

"That is a special memory, isn't it?" he said and kissed her again.

Their flight was a little behind schedule when they landed in Atlanta but were able to make their connecting flight to Tanner. Crucita was waiting for them when they arrived at the airport. She hugged and kissed them both and told them how much they had been missed.

When the luggage arrived, all three grabbed bags and headed to the parking lot.

"Where's the truck?" Dawson asked, looking around.

"I came in my car. I hope you don't mind. Your father put your truck in the shop and it is to be delivered this afternoon."

"Oh yeah, what's wrong with it?"

"Nothing. He is having something installed on it so you can pull his new camping trailer with it. He said it is a wedding gift to you."

Dawson smiled and shook his head. He knew his father had bought the travel trailer with him and Lianne in mind as much as for himself and Dawson's mother.

They piled the luggage into the trunk of Crucita's car and climbed in. Instead of going straight home, Crucita took them by the store. Dawson's father, Amber, and Roberto were working. Everyone was excited to see them. Dawson learned that the store had run fine while he was gone. Sales had also been great that week.

"Did you see your truck in the parking lot Dawson?" asked his father.

"No, I didn't notice. Crucita told me you were having the towing package installed for me."

"Yeah. I thought it would be good to get it done for you." He nodded. "Mine and your mom's wedding present for you two."

"Thanks Dad."

Lianne hugged him and kissed him on the cheek. His smile was priceless.

"Would you two be up to dinner at our house this evening? I know your mother would like to see you and we would like to hear about your trip."

"We would love to," said Lianne. Dawson nodded in agreement.

Since the truck was ready, Dawson drove it while Lianne rode with Crucita. He followed behind them all the way to the house. A feeling of sheer wonder overwhelmed Dawson as he watched the two women deep in animated conversation as they cruised along. He could see Lianne's delicate little hands busy gesturing and the bright smile on her face. Occasionally she would glance back at him and throw a kiss.

"How did I ever get so lucky?" he asked, his heart swelling with pride.

Crucita helped them unload their luggage, then packed her overnight bag and said goodnight. Max was ecstatic to see them and stayed underfoot while they unpacked. Lianne made a late lunch of soup and salad then they took a swim and lay by the pool for a time.

That evening they dressed and drove to Dawson's parents for dinner. It was an enjoyable evening sharing the tales of their honeymoon adventures. The Lee's were thrilled to hear that Lianne was learning to drive.

"You will be a southern gal before you know it!" said Dawson's father.

"I'm already catching myself saying 'ya'll' sometimes. I really have to watch what I say when I'm on camera!"

They laughed and bantered with her. After dinner Dawson's parents showed them a large cache of wedding gifts that had accumulated over the week from friends and relatives that missed the wedding. The Carter's, Amydee's parents, had even sent a gift.

The back seat of the truck was packed with assorted household gifts when Dawson and Lianne headed home. It was like Christmas as they sat in the den opening the multitude of wonderful presents.

CHAPTER 74

The two newlyweds spent Saturday sorting out and putting up wedding gifts. They made a large stack of items that would be used at the Georgetown house. That Dawson could ship to her later.

After eating lunch they sat down and wrote thank you notes to all of their friends and family that attended the wedding and or sent gifts. Late in the afternoon Lianne packed her bags. She would fly back to D.C. that night so she could have Sunday to organize and get ready to return to work on Monday morning.

Before taking Lianne to the airport, Dawson took her to Outback Steakhouse for dinner. Even though she was leaving, they were both upbeat and in good spirits. The goodbye at the airport was easier now that they were married, or so they believed. And, to a degree it would be because of the fact that they now were permanently bonded.

On Sunday morning Lianne called and the two talked for a while. They both marveled at the new level of comfort and peace they felt now that they were husband and wife. They said goodbye with plans for Dawson to call that night.

He then called his father who was packing and getting the travel trailer ready for a trip. Mister and Mrs. Lee were going to Florida and would spend a few days near the ocean. Dawson would watch over the store. His mother invited him over for lunch and asked if he would help his father finish packing so that they could be ready for an early start on Monday. Dawson readily agreed.

A few minutes after Dawson and his father hung up, the phone rang. It was Crucita. She asked if it would be all right if she brought two children she was babysitting for the day over for a swim.

"Sure Crucita. I will be gone for most of the afternoon. Make yourselves at home. Just keep a close eye on them in the pool. There are some life jackets for children in the pool shed."

"Thank you Dawson. I will take good care of them."

"All right then. I'll see you later if you're still here."

He got ready and drove over to his parent's house. After eating lunch with them, he and his father finished loading the trailer with food and supplies. They put some water in the trailer's tanks and some sanitizer in the toilet, checked the running lights and signals, and made sure everything was tied and in place so it wouldn't roll around. Satisfied that everything was ready to roll, they were through. Dawson then said goodbye and that he would see them when they got back home later in the week.

On the way back home he stopped and did some grocery shopping to restock the kitchen. When he pulled into the garage he saw that Crucita was still there. She and the two small children were playing in the pool. He walked out on the patio and said hello.

"Hi Dawson. Thank you for letting us swim."

"Sure thing, anytime. Would you and the kids like for me to grill some hotdogs or hamburgers? I would be happy to."

"Are you sure? I know they are hungry."

"No problem. I'm happy too."

The children were happy with the idea and called for hot dogs. Dawson lit the outdoor grill and brought in the groceries while it heated up. He placed a half dozen hotdogs on the grill while putting away the groceries and getting the buns, chips, and condiments ready.

While manning the grill, Dawson watched Crucita and the children playing in the pool. He took a moment to study Crucita. She was pretty, in an unusual way. Much like her father, she had a firm chin and an aquiline nose that created a sharp profile. However, hers was softened by her large brown eyes and full lips. She still had a bit of the coltish, gangly build of a young teen on the verge of womanhood. At seventeen years old, going on eighteen, he wondered how much more she would fill out. If she did, the boys would be like bees on honey, he thought, chuckling to himself.

Crucita tried several times to help Dawson with the food preparations but he would not let her citing that it was his treat. They ate in the shade on the patio and the two children, a boy of five, and a girl of three, ate surprisingly well. They appeared to be having a great time. Dawson enjoyed talking to them. He helped the boy change into his clothes when they were through swimming.

After both kids were dressed, Crucita had them watch cartoons while she helped Dawson clean the grill and the kitchen. As the two were washing dishes, Crucita looked up at Dawson with admiration in her eyes.

"You are very good with children. Do you and Lianne plan on starting a family soon?"

Dawson swallowed a lump that formed in his throat.

"Ah...Well. Lianne is unable to conceive."

"Oh but Dawson, all these bedrooms, the pool, the big yard. You must want children?"

"Yes I do, I did. It's just not in the cards now."

Tears welled up in Crucita's eyes and she put her arms around Dawson.

"I am very sad for you," she said, her head against his chest.

"Thank you Crucita. That's sweet of you. I pray that you will have a fine husband and children of your own when the time comes."

CHAPTER 75

A week after the wedding and honeymoon, Lianne left for a three week assignment in Haiti. She was to film a one hour special on the recovery and rebuilding progress of the Haitian people from the earthquake of a few years back. This would be the first extended period she and Dawson were apart. Dawson spent more time at the outdoor store when he and Lianne were apart. He loved the store and found comfort there.

Dawson's parents enjoyed their trip to Florida and staying in the travel trailer. With Dawson around the store more, Mr. Lee decided to take another trip. This time he and Dawson's mom would go up into the mountains of Virginia. They would be gone for two weeks.

It was Monday morning; Lianne had been gone to Haiti for a week now. His parents had left out over the weekend for their trip. Crucita arrived early and had breakfast ready. He sat at the table eating his eggs and bacon while reading the morning paper. Max was happily crunching away on his bowl of food. The phone rang. It was Holly. She was scheduled to be at the store at opening time. Her baby was sick and she was taking him to the doctor and called to say she would be in to work as soon as she could.

"Don't worry Holly. You know Monday's are slow in the morning time anyway. Just give me a call when you get a handle on what's going on with your little boy. Roberto will be in at noon so I can handle it until then just fine."

"I really appreciate your understanding Dawson. I do apologize for such short notice. I just don't want to ask Mom to take him. I feel like since I am his mother that I should be the one to take him."

"I understand completely. I don't blame you Holly. You worry about your boy. Let me know something when you can."

"I will call you just as soon as I get through at the doctor's office."

Dawson finished eating breakfast, said goodbye to Crucita and left for the store. Since he would be by himself, he wanted to get there early and make sure everything was in order when he unlocked the doors at opening time.

Being almost an hour early, the parking lot around the shopping center was practically empty of cars. Dawson unlocked the front door, let himself in and locked it back. He turned the lights on, put on a pot of coffee, and then unlocked the safe. He retrieved the till with the basic amount of operating cash in it and put it in the cash register, then powered up the computer system.

Pouring a cup of coffee, he added cream and sugar and took a sip as he walked to the front.

"Ahhh. Ready for the day!" he said while unlocking the front door.

Moments later a UPS truck pulled up out front. The delivery driver brought in a much needed shipment of freeze-dried trail foods. Since things were slow, Dawson decided to go ahead and put them on out for sale.

Busy stocking the shelf, he was down on his knees when he heard the front door open. He quickly put the packs of freeze-dried ice cream on its peg and stood up to greet the customer.

"Good morning. May I help …. Ohh."

Dawson froze as he stood looking into the face of Amydee. She laughed and shook her head.

"I wish you could see your face Dawson. Come on now, I'm not that frightening, am I?" she chided.

"Umm…" He could not think of what to say.

Amydee looked around a moment.

"I like your store here."

She walked to where the poster-sized photograph of him, Lianne and Cali posing in outdoor gear was hanging.

"My, my!" she said, shaking her head.

Dawson just stood where he was.

"You got a cute little wife there. It must be nice being married to someone so famous. Tell me Dawson, are you happy?"

"Un-huh."

"Is she better than me?" Amydee asked, sticking out one hip and puffing out her chest.

She was wearing a short pleated skirt reminiscent of a cheerleader that made her long legs appear even longer. Her spiked heels brought out the musculature of her shapely legs. The skin-tight top she wore barely contained her perfectly shaped breasts.

"What do you want Amydee?"

"Gee. You sure don't seem happy to see me. I came to do some business with you."

"What can I do for you?" he asked warily.

She looked at him and grinned.

"Come on Dawson. Cant' you be a little more enthusiastic than that? Surely you don't treat all of your customers as if they have the plague."

Determined to not let her get to him, Dawson forced himself to smile.

"Sorry Amydee. What can I help you with today?"

She looked around a moment.

"I would like to try on a pair of those Timberline hiking boots there," she said, pointing to a display.

"Size six, right?"

"You remembered!"

He grunted and said, "Be right back," feeling his face flash scarlet.

Dawson walked to the stockroom and got a pair of boots her size. Taking a deep breath, he steadied his nerves and went back out to face Amydee.

CHAPTER 76

Amydee was sitting down in the fitting chair in the shoe section when Dawson walked back out of the stockroom. He sat down on the foot stool in front of her. Miles of shapely legs were practically in his face. He busied himself with getting a boot out of the box so as not to stare. She raised one leg up and slowly slipped her high heel off.

"Here, you need to slip this boot sock on to make sure you get a snug fit," he said, handing her the sock.

"Sure. Whatever you say," she replied sweetly.

Partially lacing the boot he positioned it on the stools foot prop and Amydee slipped her foot into it. He then laced the boot up and tied it.

"How does that feel?"

"Great," she replied.

"Stand up and try it."

"Let's put the other one on and I will."

"Okay."

He got the other boot out of the box, slipped it on her foot and laced it up.

"All right, you can see how these feel now."

"Dawson," she said softly.

"Yes?"

"Look."

She spread her legs wide open. She had no panties on. Shocked, Dawson sat there a moment while his brain tried to figure out what to do.

"See anything you like?" she asked, coyly.

Dawson put his head in the palm of his left hand, positioning his face away from the bottom end of Amydee.

"Please Amydee. Don't do this."

"What's wrong Dawson? Don't you want me?"

She reached out and put her arms around him. He shrank inward into a tight ball. Amydee slid forward and tried to straddle him. He worked his way backward out of her clutches and stood up.

"Lock the front door Dawson. Let's go in the back for a while," she said in a soft sultry voice.

"No Amydee. Please go."

He turned and walked to the sales counter and got behind it. Amydee got up and sauntered over and went around the counter to where he was standing. She put her hands on her hips.

"I don't think I want these boots. You can take them off of me," she said, then hopped up on the counter and spread her legs.

Dawson backed up against the wall.

"You can take them off," he said, his voice unsteady.

"Awe come on Al Bundy. You are the shoe salesman. I am the customer. Make the customer happy."

"No Amydee," he said and closed his eyes.

In a flash she slid off the counter and pressed up against him. Her arms around his waist, she pushed her chest into his and lightly brushed his lips with hers, eyes searching his.

"I'm not going to force you to do something you don't want to do," she said. "If you want me to go, say so. Tell me to go."

She kissed him again, running her tongue across his clinched lips. She began breathing heavy as she caressed his body, pressing against him with her pelvis. Her perfume, that oh so familiar wonderful scent was intoxicating. She kissed his neck, his throat. She pulled her top down, exposing her breasts.

"Unh," Dawson groaned.

"Yes, yes. It's good, isn't it? We can be just like we used to be baby. Come on. Take me," she urged.

He reached up and pushed her back to arm's length. A flicker of fire lit his eyes.

"No Amydee! No! I can't do this. I won't do this! What we had is dead and gone."

She stood there staring at him. Her eyes flashed hurt and despair. Blinking away tears, she pulled her top back down.

"Well, I see now you really don't want me anymore."

She backed up a little.

"You still have to take these boots off Al Bundy," she spat sardonically.

"Keep them."

She laughed.

"You don't have the guts to take them off of me. Do you?"

"I am not going to argue with you Amydee. Either take them off yourself or take them with you with my compliments."

Amydee reached in the pocket of her skirt and pulled out her panties. She tucked them into Dawson's shirt pocket.

"Even trade Al!" she quipped and spun around.

She walked over and picked up her shoes and purse then walked out the door. Dawson walked to the bathroom and threw up. He pulled the panties out of his pocket and flushed them down the toilet.

Washing his face, Dawson worked to regain his composure. He walked back out to the sales floor and stood at the register. The store was quiet. He could still smell Amydee's perfume. He broke down and wept.

CHAPTER 77

"Dawson, are you all right?"

Jerking at the sound of a voice, Dawson crawled out of the deep void of futility he had fallen in. He had been standing by the cash register and didn't see or hear Holly when she walked in and greeted him.

"Umm. I'm sorry. My mind was off in space somewhere."

"Are you sure you're okay? You look a little pale."

"Yeah, I'm fine Holly." He shook off the tension in his gut. "How's Jason?"

"He has an ear infection. I got his prescriptions filled and dropped him off with Mom."

"Well, I'm glad it was something easily treatable."

"Yeah. Me too."

A customer came in and Dawson walked away from Holly to help them, happy for the diversion. Holly went about getting organized and into work mode.

The encounter with Amydee had shaken Dawson terribly. She was so incredibly beautiful, so tempting. Amydee knew his weaknesses and exactly how to push his buttons. Maybe this time she had gotten the message and would leave him alone, he hoped.

The rest of the day went much better for him. When he got home, Crucita had left him dinner. While eating, the phone rang. It was Lianne calling from Haiti. Hearing her voice brightened his spirits and he was able to put the incident with Amydee behind him. He was able to tell Lianne all was well without her detecting that he was not being totally truthful.

"Good save," he muttered when he got off the phone.

With Lianne off working in Haiti, Dawson did not want to worry her about his confrontation with Amydee. Somehow, he was feeling good about the encounter with her. He suddenly felt that she would leave him alone now.

The days and weeks began to move on. Dawson would visit Lianne at their home in Georgetown and she would come to Tanner when she could. Lianne's schedule was full and she was often on the road. On her visits to Tanner, Lianne continued learning to drive and had obtained her learner's permit. When it came time for her to take her driver's test, Dawson rented a car for her to use rather than have her try it in the truck. She passed without a problem and the two went out for special dinner to celebrate.

"Here I am twenty-seven years old and I finally have a driver's license. I feel like a sixteen year-old!" professed Lianne.

"I might say dear that you still look like you are sixteen…. Well, maybe eighteen!"

She laughed.

"Flattery will get you everywhere Mister Lee."

"Hope so!" he quipped.

Another weekend came to a close and another ride to the airport to see Lianne off. It was the middle of October and she had no other travel assignments until after Thanksgiving.

As usual, the airport was crowded with soldiers coming and going to the nearby army base. Unable to find a place to sit, Dawson and Lianne went into the lounge and had a drink while waiting for her flight. They went over again his plans to drive up to D.C. the next week. He would be bringing up an assortment of items they had received as wedding gifts to go in the Georgetown house. He would in turn take some of Lianne's things from Georgetown back to Tanner. Dawson was getting used to and actually enjoyed living in two homes.

"Why don't you invite Crucita to ride up with you? She has never been to Washington and it would be fun to show her around. She could help you drive too."

"Not a bad idea. You sure you want me to?"

"Yes, please do. I mentioned her coming up for a visit and she said she would love to."

"All right then, I'll check with her."

"Do you think Max would like to ride that far in the truck? I sure miss him, you know."

Dawson laughed.

"I don't know. He does pretty good riding around town. Let me think about it. If Crucita decides to come along; maybe then two of us could handle him okay.

"Great!" she said, beaming him her brilliant smile.

Time came for Lianne's flight to board. They kissed one another and she was off again. Their goodbyes now were for the most part pleasant. Their routine now was comfortable. They talked every night and generally went no longer than three weeks without seeing each other. Dawson was truly happy with his life.

CHAPTER 78

Crucita was thrilled with the idea of going to Washington D.C. when Dawson invited her. Roberto was pleased and thanked him for doing so. After packing the truck and piling Max in the backseat, they rolled out after Dawson left work on Wednesday evening. They would drive until late, sleep over in a motel, and then travel on to D.C. the next day. They expected to be in Washington D.C. by early Thursday afternoon.

Traveling north on I-185, they continued on I-85 north. Dawson stopped a couple of times to let Max out to stretch and take care of business. He had a litter box in the back floor board but developed a habit of waiting until they stopped somewhere to go.

Max took to lying on top of the backseat headrest and staring out the back window of the truck. He would occasionally get down and crawl up front, sometimes sitting on Crucita's or Dawson's lap. Max proved to be a better traveler than Dawson could have hoped for.

Late in the night the travelers arrived in Charlotte, North Caroline. Dawson pulled off the interstate and stopped at a motel. He rented rooms for him and Crucita. With Max in tow he said good night and crawled in bed. Six o'clock came quick and they were on the road again.

At noon they ate lunch in Fredericksburg, Virginia, and then rolled into Washington D.C. Crucita was in awe as they passed near the Mall of D.C. and she could see the monuments, the Capital, and the White House.

Dawson was able to find a parking spot near the front of the Georgetown house. He fed the parking meter and unlocked the house and put Max inside. Unloading the truck took several trips for him and Crucita. He showed Crucita around the house then left her and Max there while he took the truck to a parking garage nearby.

Max explored the two floors of the house and then took up residence on a spot near the top of the stairs and went to sleep. Dawson called Lianne and told her they had arrived. She was excited to hear from them and asked to talk to Crucita.

"I'm so happy you came, Crucita!"

"Me too. You have a nice home Mrs. Lianne. I have always wanted to see the capital of the United States. What of it I saw coming in was magnificent.

"Well, you will get to see it all. Dawson and I would like for you to come up here again. Think of this as your home too, just like at Dawson's.

"Thank you Mrs. Lianne."

"I will see you guys about five-thirty, okay?"

"Yes ma'am."

"While Crucita unpacked and got her things situated in the guest bedroom, Dawson set up the new litter box and bowl for Max that Lianne had bought ahead of time. He filled the litter box and poured food and water for the cat. Max came bounding down the stairs when he heard the cat food being poured.

Max was happily crunching away when Crucita came back into the kitchen. She looked around at the appliances and checked the cabinets and refrigerator.

"I would like to cook dinner for you and Mrs. Lianne. I don't see much to choose from. Do you have any suggestions?"

"There is a great market just a short walk away. Let's go take a look and we can decide there."

The walk to the market was pleasant. The cashier and the manager both said hello to Dawson when he and Crucita walked in. He was now a familiar face in the neighborhood. Dawson introduced Crucita to them and the two began looking around the store for something special for dinner.

To Dawson's surprise, Crucita lit up when she started looking around at the array of vegetables and meats. Smiling at her delight, Dawson backed up and let her pick everything. She was in her element. He made a mental note to let her start doing the shopping back in Tanner.

While Crucita shopped, Dawson picked out an assortment of wines along with a bouquet of flowers. With the grocery cart loaded, they checked out and Dawson paid the bill. Crucita looked at him curiously while they were waiting for his credit card receipt.

"How are we going to carry all of this?"

Dawson smiled.

"They deliver. We're not in Tanner anymore," he said and chuckled.

"Thank you for shopping with us Mister Lee. It's good to see you back. Vinnie will deliver this within the hour," said the casher.

"I appreciate it Marie. We'll see you soon."

The two walked out onto the sidewalk and headed back toward the house.

"I like this!" exclaimed Crucita.

"I do too. It's actually fun having two houses and two different lifestyles."

"You are a lucky man."

"Don't I know it!"

CHAPTER 79

Lianne was due home around 5:30 p.m. By five o'clock the house was filled with a wonderful aroma. Crucita was well on the way of having dinner ready. She had done a superb job preparing a Texas Brisket with spicy coconut corn and glazed sweet potato chunks.

While Crucita was cooking, Dawson sat outside on the patio enjoying the cool October air and letting Max explore the vegetation and sniff new smells. At 5:15 p.m. they went in and Dawson helped set the table for the three of them. Crucita looked at Dawson, her eyebrows furled. He knew she was wondering if they were expecting company.

"Crucita, Lianne and I want you to sit with us and eat. There is no need for you to feel you have to eat in the kitchen."

"But Dawson, I am your employee," she protested.

"Yes, that is true. But you are family too. When it is just us or just me and Lianne, you will eat with us. If we have dinner guests, then I will let you decide what is comfortable for you. You can choose to sit with us or eat separate. It will be up to you. How's that?"

"I am honored," she said shyly.

"Don't be honored, be family. We mean that Crucita. We love you and your dad. I see us all as more than friends. We are all family."

Crucita's eyes misted over. She looked down, embarrassed and quickly wiped her eyes. Then she slowly looked up at Dawson and into his eyes. He could feel new level of understanding pass between them. Crucita had finally reached a point where she felt a part of the Lee family and not just an employee. The corners of her lips turned up and gave him a quick shy smile and she returned to preparing dinner.

With the table set, fresh flowers in a vase, and the wine uncorked and ready, Dawson looked at the clock.

"She should arrive any second now," he said.

A moment later the front door opened and Lianne walked in, all smiles.

"Whoo hoo! Something smells good and two of my favorite people are here."

She sat her purse and laptop bag down, and then fell into Dawson's arms. Max raced up and rubbed against her legs. Lianne squealed when she saw him.

"And look! You brought my baby."

She picked Max up and cuddled him.

"Did you enjoy the ride up buddy?"

"Meow."

After cuddling him another moment, she put him down and hugged Crucita. Lianne told her again how happy she was to have her there.

"Thank you for inviting me."

"You are so very welcome. We want you to come up as often as you would like. I can't wait for you to see the sights here. Dawson will take you to see some tomorrow. I know you're gonna love D.C.!"

"I already do."

"Yeah," said Dawson with a chuckle. "She fell in love with Dino's Market."

"It is nice, isn't it?" agreed Lianne.

While Lianne washed up, Crucita set the food on the table and Dawson poured wine for him and Lianne. When Lianne came back in, they all sat down to eat.

"I'm so happy you are sitting with us Crucita. This is more like it!"

She then looked at the food before her. Her face lit up.

"Oh my God, Cructia! You made me a cucumber and avocado salad. It's my favorite since Dawson and I discovered it in Sonoma."

Crucita giggled.

"Dawson looked the recipe up on the internet and we got everything needed to make it from the market."

Lianne took a bite and groaned in ecstasy.

"Fabulous! Great job Crucita. And thank you my favorite husband."

Dawson raised his eyebrow and feigned shock.

"You mean you have more than one husband?'

She laughed.

"No, I don't think I could handle another. But, if I did, you would absolutely for sure be my favorite!"

Crucita giggled at Dawson and Lianne's antics. She began to relax and enjoy being a part of the family as Dawson kept saying she was.

When dinner was over, Lianne went to take a shower and put comfortable clothes on. Dawson helped Crucita clear the table, clean the kitchen, and load the dishwasher. Crucita tried to get him to sit down and watch television but he refused.

"Nope. We are all going to have coffee in the den and catch up on all the latest, you included."

"Oh Dawson. You two are so special to me. You treat me too good."

"Well, I for one think that is impossible to do. When you came up here to D.C. with us, you are a guest. I did not bring you up here to just work. Here we all pitch in on whatever needs to be done."

She shook her head and smiled.

"Thank you," she said softly.

CHAPTER 80

"Meow. Meow!"

"Umm. Max. What are you doing? It's still dark."

"Meow!"

Dawson rolled over and sat up. The cat rubbed his head against Dawson's chest and purred.

"Meow, meow, meow."

"Hmm. I guess you're hungry, huh?"

"Meow."

He checked the time. It was 6:15 a.m. The alarm was set for six-thirty. Lianne had to be at work at eight. Yawning, Dawson cradled Max in his arms and started easing out of bed. A small hand reached over and grabbed him.

"Where are you going?" asked Lianne, groggily.

"I have a hungry cat here."

Max slid out of his arms and nudged Lianne on her cheek with his cool, moist nose.

"Eeeuuuuh! Too early for kisses Max."

The cat placed his front legs on her chest. Purring, he started kneading her with his paws with one, then the other. Lianne started giggling.

"He's making biscuits!"

Dawson shook his head and laughed.

"All right boy. Come on."

He picked Max up and the two got out of bed. Dawson turned as he started out of the bedroom and glimpsed back at Lianne. He never tired of looking at her. They locked eyes. She smiled at him.

"Good morning pretty lady."

"Morning to you, kind sir."

"Max and I will have coffee ready shortly. I think I will walk down the street and pick up bagels for everyone."

"That will be good. Thanks."

Dawson fed Max, put the coffee on to brew, and got dressed. He walked over to the breakfast café and picked up an assortment of bagels and a cup of coffee to go. He sipped on the fresh brew on the walk back to the townhouse. Lianne had just come downstairs and was pouring two cups of coffee when he walked in. She was dressed for work and as always, looked immaculate. Smiling, she handed him one of the cups and kissed him.

"I haven't heard a peep out of Crucita. Should we wake her?" she asked.

"No. Let's let her sleep a while longer. I know she was tired from all of the traveling."

They sat at the table and ate. Lianne got tickled when she watched Max walk over to the door to Crucita's room and tried to push it open.

"Let her sleep, Max."

"Meow."

He looked at Lianne then at the door and lay down in front of it.

"That cat is something else!" she professed.

"He is at that," confirmed Dawson.

"Want another cup of coffee?" asked Lianne as she got up from the table.

"No more for me. I've had enough for now."

She poured another cup for herself and sat back down.

"Have you decided where all you want to take Crucita today?"

"No, not really. We'll do the White House, Capital, and Washington Monument, then I'll leave it up to her."

"Sounds like a good start."

Finished with her coffee, she and Dawson sat on the sofa for a few minutes before time for her to go to work. Lianne laid her head against his shoulder while they talked.

"I enjoyed last night with you," she said.

"I did too Lianne. I always look forward to our times together."

"It feels good having you, Crucita, and Max here together. It's like you brought our other home here."

"You know, you're right! I never would have thought that all this would work out as well as it has."

"I agree. We have a good marriage Dawson. Both have great parents. We have our own careers that so far have not caused difficulties, and we have two great homes."

"We have the best of both worlds," he said, pulling her closer to him.

Lianne looked up at him and their lips came together. The kiss was long and meaningful. When they separated, she let out a sigh.

"All of a sudden I don't want to go to work."

Dawson laughed.

"What's on your mind?"

She grinned coyly and said, "You."

"Hmm. How long we got till you have to leave?"

"Half hour."

"Long enough?"

"Yep. Let's go!"

CHAPTER 81

Lianne had just left for work when Crucita got up. Dawson drank a glass of orange juice while she ate a bagel. Then they set out for a day of sightseeing.

Boarding the Metro, the two rode a short distance and got off at the mall near the Capital. Rather than join the throngs of people being led around by a tour guide, Dawson showed Crucita the highlights and they moved on.

They were lucky and arrived at the Washington Monument and entered a short line of waiting visitors. Within twenty minutes they were riding the elevator to the top for a scenic view of D.C.

Dawson and Crucita then walked the short distance over to the White House and took the guided tour. It was past lunch by the time they finished so Dawson found a café near the White House and he and Crucita had lunch.

After a brief walk down to the Lincoln Memorial, the Viet Nam Memorial, and the Korean War Memorial, Crucita was worn out, as was Dawson.

"That sure is a lot of walking!" exclaimed Crucita.

"Yeah. You need to be in good shape here."

Hopping back on the Metro, they rode the few blocks to Georgetown and were home by three-thirty.

"Put your swimsuit on and I'll meet you in the hot tub," Dawson said as he headed upstairs.

"Umm. That's a great idea."

Dawson changed into his swim trunks, went back downstairs and poured glasses of tea for them. He had just gotten in the warm water when Crucita joined him. Easing down in the water, giving a sigh of relief, she lay back and smiled.

"I had a wonderful time today. Thank you."

"I'm glad you enjoyed it. There is so much history to see here. We are just hitting the high points this trip. When you come back up we'll spend more time at the ones you like the most."

"All right. What will we do tomorrow with Mrs. Lianne?"

"I know she wants you to see the Smithsonian Museums. You could spend weeks covering all there is to see. Lianne knows the most interesting exhibits so we'll let her be the guide."

Neither Dawson nor Crucita stayed in the hot tub for long. Crucita retired to her room to rest a while before Lianne came home. They had plans to go out for dinner that evening. Dawson dressed and relaxed in the den. He switched the television on and watched for Lianne on CNN.

After Lianne came in from work, they all caught a taxi and rode to Chinatown and had dinner. It was Crucita's first experience at eating Chinese cuisine and she thoroughly enjoyed the meal.

On Saturday they rose, ate breakfast near the Capitol mall, and then began touring the museums. Along the way they took a side trip to Ford's Theatre where Lincoln was shot. Later that evening Lianne asked Crucita what she enjoyed the most that day? Her favorite was the museum of American History. She especially enjoyed the display of all of the first ladies inaugural ball gowns. They had all of them on exhibit, beginning with Martha Washington's to this present first ladies gown.

Lianne cooked dinner and the threesome along with Max spent a relaxing Saturday night watching a movie and talking. Before going to bed, Dawson and Crucita packed for the trip back to Tanner. Dawson had gotten the truck out of the parking garage and had it parked right outside the front door.

They rose early, had breakfast, and by 6:00 a.m. were on the road for home. They planned to drive straight through. Max took his usual perch on the backseat headrest, taking in the scenery as they rolled southward.

Dawson stopped every few hours so they could take a break. He and Crucita changed out driving whenever they stopped. Just after dark they pulled into the house at Tanner. The outside lights were on and the house never looked so good to the three tired travelers.

Max ate then curled up and went to sleep. Too tired to drive home, Crucita called her father and told him she would stay there for the night. She would see him the next evening after work. She and Dawson ate a quick meal of soup and salad, took showers, and Crucita went to bed. Dawson called Lianne and talked to her a few minutes then went on to bed himself.

It had been a nice trip. Crucita had enjoyed herself. Dawson had enjoyed having her traveling with him. She had relaxed a lot and was more at ease around him and Lianne. They had come to view her as their adopted daughter.

"I already miss you terribly Dawson."

"Same here."

Lianne would be working steady until Thanksgiving. They had decided to alternate holidays with their parents. This year they would have Thanksgiving with her parents and spend Christmas with his. Dawson would dive back into working at the store and count off the days until he could be with Lianne again.

CHAPTER 82

As Christmas drew near, sales at Lee Outdoor Sports increased dramatically. Holly and Dawson were steadily ordering new merchandise to replenish the inventory. Dawson hired two high school students to work part time during the holiday season.

Lianne was busy as well. They had not had time to be together since Thanksgiving. But, she would be in on Christmas Eve and would be there through the first of the New Year.

Dawson was at the store every day. Often he worked from opening to closing. His father was working more hours and his mother even came in during the afternoons and all day on Saturdays.

With business doing so well Dawson decided to give all of his employees a bonus. He had planned on giving each a one hundred dollar gift. Instead he gave the full timers five hundred each and the part timers two hundred each.

Spending so much time at the store, Dawson depended heavily on Crucita to get the house in order for the holiday. He had strung all of the outside Christmas lights and decorations and he had brought home a large Christmas tree. Crucita decorated for him and put the inside decorations out. One evening he took her with him to shop for gifts for his family and Lianne's. He bought gifts for all of his employees. On his lunch hour one day he went and purchased some gifts for Crucita and took care of ordering a very special present for Lianne.

He had wanted to have a Christmas party and dinner at the house but just did not have the time. Besides, Lianne could not be there. The Kinsley's invited him and Lianne to their Christmas party but he declined citing his work load and the fact that Lianne would not be there.

During the days before Christmas the store was busier than Dawson could have imagined. Mountain bikes were a big seller for the store. This kept him and his father busy in the back assembling them. Hiking boots were popular with school kids. Sales were brisk. The store was running out of all size. Luckily a large shipment came in and saved the day.

On Christmas Eve Dawson closed the store at one o'clock and let all of the staff go for the holiday celebration. He thanked them all and gave them their gift and bonus check. After dropping the store deposit off at the bank, he headed for Atlanta. With the heavy holiday air traffic he made plans to pick Lianne up in Atlanta instead of her taking a chance on making her Tanner connection on time.

Finding a place in short term parking at Hartsfield airport was a challenge for Dawson. Circling the parking decks for several minutes, he finally caught a break when he spotted someone just pulling out of a parking spot. As luck would have it, Lianne's flight was forty-five minutes late. Dawson certainly thankful he had made the right decision in picking her up there in Atlanta.

After getting a cup of coffee, Dawson settled in by baggage claim to wait for Lianne to arrive. When he saw her his heart leapt for joy. All smiles, she was lugging two large shipping bags filled with wrapped presents. She wore a lively red dress and had on a Santa hat. When she saw him, Lianne squealed and ran into his arms.

"Oh my goodness. I have missed you so much. Merry Christmas Darling!" she crowed.

"Merry Christmas to you." Squeezing her tightly.

He retrieved her luggage and the two made their way to the truck. Moments later they were on I-85 South heading toward Tanner.

"How was your flight down?"

"Oh it was crazy! It's snowing heavy in D.C. Flights were backed up. We got a very late start. I'm so happy you wanted to pick me up here. You are so thoughtful Dawson. That's why I married you."

He feigned surprise.

"And I thought you married me for my body!"

She playfully socked him on the shoulder.

"You cad you. You know better than that. I married you because no one else would have you!" She chirped brightly.

He laughed.

"You know you are so right!"

A look of shock spread across Lianne's face. Her eyes flew open wide. Her mouth formed an 'O'.

"Oh my God Dawson! I'm so sorry I said that. I was just joking," she said apologetically. Her face bore a pained expression.

"Huh?" Looking at her confused.

"I wasn't making sport of Amydee leaving you. Honest. I was poking fun at you being such a bear at Walter Reed."

Dawson laughed again. He patted her leg and gave it a squeeze.

"Well, you are right on both accounts. No one else would have me and I was a grumpy bear at the hospital."

"You are wrong to think nobody would want you. But, thinking like that might keep you loving me."

"Whoa Lianne! I am very lucky to have you. You are the best thing that had ever happened to me."

"Keep talking like that and you will have to pull over somewhere."

He grinned and kissed her hand.

CHAPTER 83

Traffic on the interstate was light. Dawson made good time on I-85 to Tanner. It was just after dark when they came into view of the house lit up with the holiday decorations.

"Oh my. How pretty!" expressed Lianne.

"Wait till you see the decorations inside, and the tree."

Crucita's car was parked in the driveway blocking Dawson's access to the garage. He pulled to the right of it and parked on the grass near the front door.

"Why did Crucita park there?" asked Lianne.

Dawson shrugged his shoulders.

"I don't know. It's no big deal. She'll only be here for a little while. I asked her to stay long enough so we could give her gifts to her."

"Good thinking."

While they were getting out of the truck and gathering Lianne's bags, Crucita opened the front door and came out to help. She hugged Lianne and grabbed a bag.

"Dinner is ready. It's been ready for a little while. Come on in and eat while it's still warm."

"Sure thing. I'm hungry," said Dawson as he walked by Crucita and winked at her.

Max met Lianne at the door. She sat her two bags down and picked him up. Lavishing him with love and kisses, she walked over and looked at the nicely decorated Christmas tree. She marveled at the huge assortment of gifts under it.

"This is a wonderful job Crucita. Dawson had told me how good of a job you had done!"

"Thank you Mrs. Lianne. Come on now. Let's eat."

The table was set and the food was ready and waiting on the sideboard. Crucita had baked a ham and had an assortment of holiday desserts on the counter. The three sat down and enjoyed the feast and one another's company.

Once finished with the meal they took fresh cups of coffee into the living room and gathered around the Christmas tree. Dawson pulled out several gifts for Crucita and handed them to her. Lianne gave her three gifts from her bag. Crucita then handed each their gifts from her.

"All right ladies. Let's do it!" said Dawson.

Paper and ribbons began to heap up around them, much to Max's delight. He attacked and rolled in the flotsam of gift wrapping. Lots of ooh's and ah's, and thank you's ensued.

Between Lianne and Dawson, Crucita received a nice assortment of clothes, shoes, and jewelry. Tears came to her eyes when she opened a gift of diamond earrings from Lianne and Dawson together.

"While you are here Crucita, let's give Dawson the present you and I picked out when you were up visiting."

"Okay!" Crucita said with a grin.

"Hmm. Must be something special!" Dawson said, smiling with delight.

"It sure is my dear husband!"

Lianne handed him a small box and he began taking the ribbon and gift wrapping off of it. When he peeled the last of the paper away and saw the brand name on the box he was stunned. He looked at Lianne with a shock of surprise.

"Open it!" she urged.

Dawson flipped open the top of the presentation box and stared in amazement. It was a Rolex Submariner watch. His hands trembled and tears leaked from his eyes. Lianne and Crucita both went to him and wrapped their arms around him.

"I don't know what to say," he said with sobs of joy.

"Just say you love us," said Lianne as she kissed his cheek.

"I love you both!"

Lianne kissed him again and Crucita gave him a tight hug and kissed his cheek. He was trembling so badly that he could not remove the watch from its display mount in the box. Lianne took it and got it out and placed it on his wrist.

"That's a fortune right there!" he quaked.

"You are worth it, Dawson. You deserve it. Enjoy it. Think of Crucita and me when you look at it."

"I sure didn't expect a gift like this. Everything I got you pales to this," he said, shaking his head.

Crucita put her hand over her mouth trying to suppress the big grin on her face.

"You look like the cat that ate the canary. What's up?" asked Lianne, looking at Crucita.

"Oh, I am just happy. This is such a wonderful time. This is the best Christmas I have ever had."

"Well then, we are happy to be a part of it," said Dawson.

After giving Max his presents of cat toys, Crucita and Dawson cleared the table and put the leftover food away. Dawson had packed enough food for her father to eat and helped her load her gifts and things into her car. Lianne had changed clothes and then she and Dawson said goodnight to Crucita. The two then settled in the den with a bottle of wine.

"It has been a great time so far, hasn't it?" asked Dawson.

"Yes it has. And, it's just started too. We have Christmas at your parents tomorrow. What time do they want us over?"

"Mom said to call when we got ready. Anytime is good, but they do expect us to have lunch with them."

"That's fine. I like your mother's cooking. I hope she makes that wonderful dressing again."

"Oh she will. She knows you like it so she will always make it especially for you."

CHAPTER 84

Before going to bed Lianne called her parents. She and Dawson wished them a Merry Christmas. By 10:30 pm both were fast asleep. On Christmas morning Lianne was the first to wake up. She was brewing coffee when Dawson woke and came into the kitchen.

"Merry Christmas!" Lianne said brightly.

"And a very Merry Christmas to you."

"Meow."

"You too Max!"

Dawson poured cat food for Max while Lianne fixed their coffee.

"Ready to open the rest of our gifts?" she asked.

"Yep!"

They sat by the tree and opened small presents they had gotten for one another. Also both had gifts that Lianne's parents had sent along with her. When they were done the two sat on the sofa in each other's arms.

"Breakfast?" Lianne asked.

"Waffles?"

"Sounds good."

Lianne prepared the waffle batter while Dawson set up the waffle iron. He made the waffles while she set the table. They sat and ate while looking out across the backyard. It was lightly raining. The soft rain pattered against the bay window of the dining room. As they finished eating, Dawson sat back and looked at Lianne.

"I'll do the dishes," he said. "Would you mind going and pulling the truck into the garage?"

Her eyebrows furrowed into a question mark as a strange look of irritation spread across her face.

"It's raining Dawson. All I have on is this flimsy nightgown."

"It won't take but a second. It's just sprinkling. It won't hurt you. You won't melt!"

"Why can't you do it? You have your sweatshirt on?"

He looked at her, his expression unreadable.

"Because I am your husband and I want you to pull the truck into the garage out of the rain," he said dead panned.

Her nostrils flared with anger at his command.

"Dawson Lee, you have never ordered me around before. I am your wife, not your slave!"

He grunted and said, "Just do it, Lianne. I'm doing the dishes. That's only fair. Isn't it?"

She let out a loud sigh.

"All right Dawson. I will do it. Don't you ever order me around again, ever!" she groused.

Jumping up from her chair, Lianne stomped through the kitchen and into the garage. Dawson grinned and shook his head.

"Boy will she be sorry," he muttered.

There was a loud scream coming from the garage. Max had been standing in the open doorway to the garage but scrambled in fear and ran for cover.

Laughing, Dawson got up and walked to the kitchen door leading into the garage. Lianne was standing in the middle of the garage screaming and crying at the sight before her. It was a brand new dark green Ford Mustang GT.

Dawson walked out to her. Lianne was shaking so bad that she collapsed in his arms as her knees gave way. Her sobs of joy were in uncontrollable waves.

"I cannot believe this!" she blurted out breathlessly.

"Merry Christmas sweetheart."

"I feel so ashamed. I was mad at you for bossing me around."

Dawson laughed.

"That's okay. I had to get you out here some way."

"Well you could have told me you had the car out here!"

"That would have spoiled the moment."

He lifted her up and opened the driver's door, then helped her into the seat.

"This is so incredibly unbelievable!"

"Believe it Lianne. This is yours. I love you with all of my heart. I said it before and I say it again, I will spend the rest of my life trying to show you."

She squealed with delight and patted his leg vigorously.

"This is what Crucita was smiling about last night!"

"Yep, she wants you to take her for a ride in it later today."

"My very own car!" she exclaimed with joy.

Lianne took several deep breaths to calm herself down. She wiped the tears from her eyes. Turning to Dawson, she reached up and cradled his face in her hands.

"Let's make a memory," she said softly.

"It's too wet to take this thing out on a dirt road."

"Right here is just fine."

"I like the way you think."

And with that, Lianne climbed over the console to his side of the car.

CHAPTER 85

At 10:00 am the garage overhead door opened slowly. The low throaty rumble of the powerful Mustang could be heard. Sitting on a specially made cushion that Dawson had an upholstery shop make, Lianne put the transmission into drive and rolled out of the garage and onto Jones Road. Soon she and Dawson were cruising toward his parent's house. The rain had stopped; the sky was still a leaden gray.

Beside herself with wonder, Lianne was all smiles as she drove her new car. The look of elation in her face was priceless and warmed Dawson's heart. His mother and father were standing on their porch as Lianne pulled into the driveway and flashed the headlights.

"You look good behind the wheel Lianne!" called Mr. Lee.

"Isn't it awesome!" crooned Lianne.

Dawson gathered the gifts from the back of the car while Lianne hugged the Lee's and proudly showed them the car.

"That's a mighty powerful machine Lianne, you be very careful with it," cautioned Mr. Lee in a concerned tone of voice.

"Oh I will Mister Lee. I am a careful driver. Your wonderful son taught me well!"

Dawson grinned with pride.

In the house, the Lee's poured up mugs of hot spiced apple cider as the group sat by the Christmas tree to exchange gifts and talk. Lianne told them the story of how Dawson tricked her to go into the garage to discover the car.

"I almost beaned him. I thought he was being such a jerk. Goodness, did he ever get one over on me!"

"Dawson had a hard time trying not to tell you about it when he picked it up at the dealer last week," said Mrs. Lee.

"I was afraid Crucita would slip up and tell her. She was excited as I was about it."

"I'll have to get her for that!" chided Lianne, and then laughed.

"Well, you will get your chance shortly. We have invited her and Roberto over for lunch. They have no other family here so we got them to come for a while."

"That's great Mom. I know they appreciate it."

Along with gifts from the Lee's, Dawson had left a few there for Lianne. He had picked out an assortment of CD's for her car, a pair of sunglasses, and a Ford Mustang logo cap. She laughed and squealed with delight when she put the hat on and looked in the mirror.

"I feel southern!" she crowed.

"That's my girl!" cried Dawson.

The doorbell rang. It was the Garcia's. Crucita and Lianne hugged then went out to the Mustang with the CD's. They listened to a little music while the two looked the Mustang over. They made plans to go for a drive after lunch.

The Lee's had gifts for Crucita and Roberto. They opened them, then the group had lunch. Mrs. Lee had baked a turkey, ham, dressing, and all of the usual holiday dishes along with a fine selection of desserts. Everyone was in good spirits and enjoyed themselves.

During dinner Mr. Lee opened a bottle of Champagne. Glasses were passed around. Roberto allowed Crucita to have a glass for the celebration. Mr. Lee then stood up and announced he wanted to make a little speech. Everyone sat back and smiled.

"First, I would like to say to you all how happy Rebecca and I are to have all of you, our family, here today. This past year has been quite a year, especially for you, Dawson. Your mom and I thought we were going to lose you there in the beginning. But then thanks to Walter Reed, and especially to our fine daughter in law here, we have you back. And, I might add, even better than when you left for Afghanistan."

"Here, here," collectively from everyone.

He then turned to Lianne and held up his glass.

"Lianne," his eyes glistened. "What can I say? You are the greatest gift Rebecca and I could ever hope for in a daughter in law. We are so proud of you and who you are, especially for the fact that you are in the family now. We truly love your parents as well. They are fine people."

Pausing a moment, he took a sip of champagne. He looked at Crucita and Roberto and smiled.

"I must say, you two are a godsend to the Lee family. Roberto, that was some luck that I picked you up on the corner that day to help us set up the store. You are one of the finest men I have ever known. You are a great asset to the store. With you there, I have little to do. You and Dawson are a good team. I salute you."

He smiled at Crucita and nodded appreciatively.

"You, young lady, are an angel. You have been a blessing to us all, especially to Dawson. He and Lianne see you as their surrogate daughter. And, Rebecca and I claim Roberto as our second son. We love you both."

He paused again, and then nodded thoughtfully.

"I can say without a doubt that I am the happiest man in the world. I have a great wife, a wonderful son, a fantastic daughter in law, and two adopted family members. All of you make for a better life. If this were the last day of my life, I could not be happier than I am right now. I am truly, truly blessed."

There was a moment of silence, and then everyone thanked Mr. Lee for the fine speech. Dawson felt a strange sense of unease in his gut. That was a weird speech he gave. He had never talked like that before, Dawson thought to himself. He then felt a twinge of shame for thinking that way. He shook it off. His father had never been known to be so melancholy, but he did say some very nice things. Dawson smiled.

CHAPTER 86

After lunch the women ran the men out of the dining room and kitchen while they cleaned up. Dawson, his dad, and Roberto sat in the den by the hearth and relaxed. A short time later Mrs. Lee served them fresh cups of coffee. Lianne and Crucita left to take the Mustang for a drive. When they returned an hour later, the Garcia's said goodbye and left for home. Dawson and Lianne then loaded their gifts in the car and said their goodbyes.

Back at the house Dawson took several digital photographs of Lianne and the Mustang. She then emailed them to her parents and her girlfriends, Lisbeth and Jordan. For want of somewhere to go so Lianne could drive, Dawson suggested they take in a movie at the theatre. A short time later they were sitting in the theater munching on buttered popcorn and eating chocolate.

That night near bedtime, Dawson found Lianne in the kitchen looking into the garage at the Mustang. He smiled and put his arms around her from behind.

"There you are. I was wondering where you had gotten off too."

"I was just looking at the car again. My car! I just can't believe it. I never dreamed I would ever learn to drive, much less own my own car. I was content with living in D.C., riding the Metro or taking a taxi. Then I met you!"

She turned around in his arms and put hers around him.

"Any regrets?" he asked softly.

"Not a one."

"That's music to my ears."

Wanting to finish off the day in a special way, Dawson built a fire in the hearth. He had inflated a large air mattress and Lianne had made it up with sheets and a comforter. The two settled on it in front of the warm fire. With all of the lights off and with only the soft glow from the fireplace, they made more memories. Later the pair of lovers slept curled together with Max at their feet. It was a perfect ending to a glorious Christmas Day. Then, it all came crashing down.

It was early in the morning the day after Christmas, still dark. In the fireplace was a pile of glowing embers giving off a faint light. The phone began to ring. Dawson sat up, coming out of a deep sleep. Confused for a moment, he then realized they were in the den. Lianne began to come awake and she too looked to see where she was. She looked at Dawson questioningly.

"Who would be calling this time of the morning?" she asked her voice raspy from sleep.

"I don't know. I'll get it honey. Lay back down," Dawson said as he disentangled himself from Lianne, the covers, and Max.

The phone was in the kitchen. In the dark he made for it as quickly as he could without crashing into anything. He finally reached it and clicked in on.

"Hello?"

"Dawson."

"Mom?"

"Dawson. It's your Dad. He's real sick. He woke up complaining of severe heartburn. He then said he thought it was a heart attack. I called an ambulance. They just left with him and they are taking him to the Medical Center. Will you meet me there? I'm leaving now."

"Mom, why don't I pick you up and take you?"

"No Dawson. I'm dressed and heading out the door. It would take too long. I'm sure he will be all right. I'm just very concerned. I will see you there."

"Okay, Mom. I'll be there in a few."

Lianne had heard enough of the conversation to know it was an emergency. She was already heading for the bedroom to get dressed. Dawson told her what his mother had said while he was scrambling to dress himself.

"He's never had any serious health problems, just a little high blood pressure from time to time. Surely he will be fine."

Moments later they were ready and walking into the garage. Lianne took the lead.

"I'll drive Dawson."

"I'm fine."

She stopped and held her hand to his chest.

"No Dawson. I will drive," she said firmly.

He nodded in agreement.

"You're right Lianne. I am too stressed to safely drive. Thanks."

Fifteen minutes later they pulled into the parking lot near the emergency room. Parked and out of the car quickly, they hurried in the hospital and looked for Dawson's mother.

She was not in the emergency waiting room. A receptionist told Dawson and Lianne that she was down the hall in a small waiting room on the left.

Following the directions, the two rushed down a long hallway by several trauma and treatment rooms. They found her sitting in a chair; a doctor was standing in front of her.

"Mom!"

She looked up at Dawson and Lianne, tears streaming from her eyes.

"He's gone. Thomas died," she said, her voice quaking.

"Mister Lee. I am Doctor Anderson. You father had a massive stroke. We could not save him. I am sorry for your loss."

CHAPTER 87

The reality of his father's death hit Dawson instantly. He felt as though he had stepped into a watery haze. Though his eyes could see vivid colors and bright whites, he could not focus not discern anything around him.

The saving grace of the moment was Lianne. With both Dawson and his mother in shattered pieces, she stepped forward and took charge. Lianne spoke to the doctor and got all of the details she could, then spoke to the hospital officials about the procedure to transfer Mr. Lee's remains to the funeral home. She gathered Dawson and Rebecca and led them to the car and drove to the Lee's home.

Rebecca appeared to be in better shape than Dawson. She and Lianne made coffee and sat at the table while Dawson sat in the den staring blankly at the cold ashes in the fire place.

Lianne took a pad and began making notes on what needed to be done. She questioned Rebecca and got what funeral home she wanted to use and where the insurance policies were and what they covered. Then she retrieved Rebecca's address book and made a list of who all needed to be called. She would begin making calls as soon as things settled down. For the moment she just sat with Rebecca and helped her pull together. She checked regularly on Dawson and coaxed him to the table to drink a cup of coffee.

Whenever Lianne would try to engage Dawson into talking, he would break down. Rebecca bravely tried to console him, but she teetered on the edge of her coping abilities herself. Lianne excused herself from the table and took the phone into the bathroom and called Crucita. She asked her if she would help out. Crucita graciously accepted. Lianne had her stop by the pharmacy where a prescription for a sedative for both Dawson and Rebecca had been called in by Doctor Anderson.

An hour later Crucita arrived. Lianne had her take Dawson home and stay with him while she and Rebecca called the funeral home to make an appointment. She began calling relatives while Rebecca changed clothes. Lianne called her parents with the news and they said they would catch the next available flight out and would be there as soon as they could.

Crucita drove Dawson home. She gave him a sedative and got him to lie on the sofa in the den. She sat and held his hand as he cried himself to sleep. Once he was asleep she busied herself with getting the house in order for the coming days of mourning.

Lianne drove Mrs. Lee to the funeral home and helped with making the arrangements. She stayed with her at the house until her parents arrived at the airport late in the afternoon.

Soliciting the help of a neighbor, Lianne got her to sit with Rebecca while she went to pick her parents up. They drove from the airport back to Mrs. Lee's. The Palmer's decided it would be best to stay with Mrs. Lee and help her.

Leaving Lianne's mother with Rebecca, she and her father went to check on Dawson. Crucita met them at the door and told them that Dawson had not roused since he had taken the sedative.

The next days were trying for everyone, especially Dawson. He and his father had been so close. Dawson could not seem to wrap his mind around the fact that his father was now gone forever.

The viewings at the funeral home were difficult for Dawson. The funeral itself was the hardest, especially the service at the chapel. He thought the worst was over until at the graveside service it ended with a military honor guard taking their place before the flag, draped coffin of Mr. Lee. He had been a soldier and had served in Viet Nam. The twenty-one gun salute and the mournful taps from the bugler were too much for Dawson to bear. So distraught, he was not aware of the last words spoken by the priest, the presentation of the flag to his mother, nor the ride to his parent's home.

Family and friends came by to offer their condolences to the Lee's. Peyton and Cali came by. Everyone from the store came by. Holly and Roberto had taken the lead and were handling the store operations. They closed the store for the day to attend the funeral.

The Carter's came by, including Amydee. Lianne had already noticed her at the funeral. Amydee walked up to her and offered her condolences.

"I'm Amydee Carter. You are Lianne, Dawson's wife, right?"

"Yes I am."

"I did not come here to cause any problems. I just wanted to pay my respects. The Lee's were always very kind to me. I won't speak to Dawson, but do tell him how sorry I am for his loss, okay?"

"I will. And, thank you for coming."

Amydee stood there a moment, hesitating, and then mustered up the courage to speak again.

"You know I tried to get Dawson to come back to me after you two got together."

"I know, he told me about it."

Amydee's eyes widened with surprise. Her cheeks reddened with embarrassment.

"Anyway, I won't try anything like that again. I know he really loves you and I am happy for him. I do still love him and miss him. I regret what I did to lose him. I can't change that. You are lucky to have him. I wish you two all the happiness."

"That's very kind of you Amydee. I wish you well too. I hope you find happiness one day."

To Amydee's surprise, Lianne hugged her, when she said goodbye and walked away. Amydee knew she had met someone of a caliber and class far beyond anything she ever hoped to be.

CHAPTER 88

The days and weeks following the funeral passed quickly for Dawson. Later he could recall little of them. He had gone back to the store and robotically worked trying to put some normalcy in his life. Lianne was flying back and forth to D.C. as her schedule permitted.

Crucita steadfastly kept the house in order. She always seemed ready and available to Dawson and Lianne. The store staff put forth extra effort to keep the business running smoothly.

Dawson's spirits remained low, even when Lianne was down he was not much better. He functioned on autopilot. As time went by he buried himself in his work at the store. There were times when Holly or Amber would force him to leave and take a break. He did visit his mother frequently. She came over to his house regularly as well. Often she had dinner with him and Crucita. Sometimes after she cooked, Crucita would quietly ease out of the house and leave them two to talk. She often felt helpless, but stood by silently waiting to do what she could for Dawson. His mother continually encouraged him to let his grieving go and move on.

Over the next months he finally started back visiting Lianne in Georgetown. However, the zest of happiness in Dawson's life remained lackluster. There was always an underlying current of sadness just below the surface. Lianne often found him lost in thought and withdrawn. He struggled to put up a faux front of being okay, but he was a poor actor at hiding his true feelings.

If things were not hard enough for his fragile soul, another heavy blow came. Lianne was given a two month assignment in which she would again cover the war in Afghanistan. This struck a chord of fear in Dawson. He knew well the daily unexpected dangers that lurked on every corner for Westerners there. In spite of her assurances that she would be well taken care of, the concern for her safety was almost more than Dawson could handle.

Prior to her assignment for the trip to Afghanistan, Dawson had been accepting of her going to somewhat dangerous places. However, this one, he knew too well the danger. This revelation caused their first rift, leaving both terribly hurt and unsettled.

When Lianne had told him of the assignment he had been up in Georgetown with her. When he flew back to Tanner they had not resolved the chasm that was between them. It was the first time they had ever been in a serious disagreement and had not settled it before the sun went down.

When the two would talk on the phone they said little of importance, both avoided the issue that was driving them apart. They still said they loved each other when they got ready to hang up, but as time went by those words began to ring hollow. Out of desperation, Lianne called Mrs. Lee and confided in her.

"You know Dawson loves you more than life itself. He will come around before you leave. Lianne, he loves you too much to stay mad. He is afraid of losing you. I know it is because he's still not over losing his father. He does not want to lose you too. Right now you are the main focus of his life and that has been shaken."

"What can I do Rebecca? I love him so much. This assignment is my job. It is what I do. Surely he understands that. It is no different than when he was a soldier and was ordered to go."

"My dear, please be patient. He knows that. He will come around. But, please do this. Do not leave until you have tried all you can to make peace with him. I know my son. He will accept it. He may not like it, but he loves you so much he will come around and accept it. You need to talk to him. Don't do it over the phone. Come down here if you have to, but do talk to him face to face.

"I leave in two weeks. I will try to find a way to get there. You are right. And, I certainly don't want to leave with us like this."

"If you two can work this out and get through it, then I believe you can make it through anything life throws at you."

Lianne thanked her for the advice and said goodbye. That night when she talked to Dawson she tried to be upbeat and cheerful. He was amenable but when they said goodnight nothing had been accomplished toward reconciliation. Lianne sat there at the kitchen table for a long while thinking of what to do. It was Tuesday night. She decided that on Wednesday that she would not call him as she was supposed to. Instead, she would see if he would call her back.

Wednesday at 10:00 p.m. she did not call. Dawson was irritated and concerned but would not call her to see what happened. So upset, Lianne decided on Thursday to make reservations to fly to Tanner on Friday evening. If he were to call her on Thursday night, his turn to call, she would tell him. If he did not call, she would show up at the house on Friday night and they would settle the issue, one way or another.

Thursday night at 10:00 p.m., Dawson did not call her.

CHAPTER 89

11:30 p.m. Wednesday night.

"She's not going to call," Dawson groused.

Frustrated, he turned the lights out and lay down. He was beginning to realize that his crass behavior lately had pushed Lianne away. His heart started to soften, and then he got angry again.

"I won't call her tomorrow night. I'll see how she likes it. She can call me or else…."

It was hours before he finally fell asleep in frustration. When he got up and went to work, he was exhausted. At the store he was withdrawn and quiet most of the morning. After lunch Holly talked him into going home and getting some rest. He was too tired to argue with her and drove on home.

On a whim he took two of the sedatives he had and went to sleep. He slept long and hard. He woke feeling sluggish and disoriented. When he looked at the clock he was surprised to see it was 4:00 a.m., Friday morning. He scrambled to check the phone messages. Lianne had not tried to call.

Dawson got up, took a shower, which helped wake him up and erase the cobwebs from his fuddled brain. Not wanting to sleep anymore, he dressed and brewed a pot of coffee. After feeding Max he sat in the den watching CNN. His heart tripped in his chest when he saw a taped report by Lianne.

Watching her closely, Dawson could see the strain in her eyes and hear it in her voice. He was hurting her. He had to accept that she needed to go to Afghanistan. It was her job. He had accepted that fact when he fell in love with her. She had a job to do and wherever it took her, he should support her. Surely she would be all right.

With tears in his eyes, he finally opened the floodgates. He let out the months of agony and pain that had built up from the loss of his father. Dawson realized he had been clinging on to Lianne too hard. He had to let her go to do her work. He would be there for her, waiting for her when she came back home.

At 6:00 a.m. Crucita let herself into the kitchen. She was surprised to find Dawson already up and dressed. He smiled at her, the first smile she had seen in a long while.

"Good morning Dawson. Have you had breakfast?"

"No, and I'm hungry!" he replied cheerfully.

"Wow! Are you okay?"

"I'm going to be Crucita. I know I have been a total butt lately. I want to apologize to you and ask for forgiveness."

She looked at him a moment then walked over to him.

"It is not me that you need to apologize to, it is Lianne. She is the one who is suffering."

"You are so right. I am going to see if I can straighten out everything with her today. I'm going to catch a flight to D.C. and be waiting for her when she gets in from work. I have a lot of making up to do."

Crucita smiled and put her arms around him.

"I'm so proud of you Dawson. Lianne loves you so much. You know she is just doing her job."

"I do now. I understand she's doing what she is called to do. I was blind and stupid. I can't hold her back from doing the work she loves. I have been such a fool."

"Yes, you have!" she said and kissed him on the cheek. "Now, I will cook you a big breakfast before you go."

After he ate, Dawson tried to call Lianne. He got no answer.

"Must have already left for work," he muttered.

After saying goodbye to Crucita, Dawson drove to the store. When Amber and Paul arrived he already had coffee made and the store ready to open. He told them that he was taking the weekend off and left some instructions for Holly when she came in.

From the store he drove to the airport. He went straight to the Delta ticket counter and asked for the earliest flight to Washington D.C. Much to his chagrin there were no available flights to Atlanta until late that night.

Undeterred, he jumped back in the truck and drove to Atlanta's Hartsfield airport. Putting the truck in long term parking, he went in to buy a plane ticket. The earliest ticket he found landed at Dulles International, some thirty or so miles out from D.C., it was mid-afternoon. He then caught a taxi and walked into the Georgetown house at three-thirty.

Having not taken the time to eat since breakfast with Crucita, he made a salad and a sandwich. He sat down at the table to eat. Smiling, he pushed aside a stack of mail and bills that Lianne had apparently been working on last night. There was a legal pad that she had been making little notes on. He was smiling at the heart she had drawn with their initials in it. His heart lurched as his focus locked on a flight reservation schedule she had jotted down on a piece of paper.

"Oh man!" he sputtered, spitting out chunks of lettuce and tomato.

Pulse racing, his throat constricted and he choked out a cry.

"Oh my goodness!"

There on the scrap of paper was the flight number for a booking to Tanner via Atlanta. The departure time from National was at 4:30 p.m. It was now almost four. He snatched up the phone and called her cell phone. No answer.

In a flash he was out the door hailing a cab. Moments later he flagged one down.

"National Airport as quick as you can. Here's a fifty to do it!"

"You go it Bud!"

CHAPTER 90

The taxi driver was fast and efficient. At twenty after four Dawson was dropped off at the terminal. He ran inside to the Delta counter. Knowing he could not get past security without a ticket, he quickly explained his emergency to an agent. She knew who Lianne Palmer-Lee was and picked up a phone and placed a call to Lianne's departure gate. She smiled when she hung up.

"If you will wait right over there Mister Lee, someone will bring her to you shortly."

"Thank you so much Ms. Delaney."

Moments later a Delta representative brought a confused Lianne through security. Her face lit up with surprise when she saw Dawson. She thanked her escort and walked over and stood in front of her husband. Her eyes pooled with tears, she put her arms around him. He kissed her on top of the head.

"Here or Tanner?" he asked softly.

"Here."

"Let's find a cab and go home."

He took her shoulder bag and the two walked out and found a taxi. They said little to one another until they reached the house. Lianne poured them each a glass of wine and they sat down to talk. Dawson started off by apologizing for his behavior and promised to support her in her work, regardless of where it takes her. She thanked him and apologized to him for her part.

They laughed and cried as he told her about the obstacles he encountered trying to get to D.C. to talk to her. They made love. The flame of love and devotion for one another was once again rekindled and burned even brighter.

Late into the night they fell asleep snuggled closely together. Dawson awoke to Lianne bringing a tray to the bedroom.

"Breakfast in bed for the man I love."

"Oh my goodness. What did I do to deserve this?"

"You came to me. You came home," she said softly.

A lump formed in his throat. His eyes watered.

"Lianne, what can I do to make up to you for the way I have treated you since Dad died?"

"You're off to a good start. But, I am not the only one you hurt. Think about your mom, Crucita, Holly, Amber, Paul, and Roberto, just to name a few."

"Oh my. Looks like I have a lot of apologies to make."

Lianne helped him situate the tray of food. She then got hers and settled in beside him.

"Now Dawson, I want you to listen to me. I have something I want you to do. This is for your own good, and really for all of us who love you."

"I will do whatever you want for you forgiving me."

She put her hand on his arm and gently squeezed it.

"Hear me out. I have been talking to your Mom and we came up with this wonderful idea."

He looked at her curiously.

"Oh yeah?"

"Yes now, hush and listen. You know your Dad talked about taking the camper trailer on a long trip out west."

"Yeah?"

"I said hush and listen!" she quipped and playfully popped him on the arm.

"Yes ma'am."

"Shush!"

She giggled.

"Come on now, I'm serious."

"Okay, okay. I'll behave and listen."

"Now, your mom and I want you to take the trailer and make that trip in his memory. Do it for your dad and do it for you. You need a break Dawson. You need to get away. Do it while I'm gone. We can still stay in touch. I will call you every day or two while I'm in Afghanistan."

She took a sip of coffee.

"The store will be fine while you are gone. Holly can manage it. Your mom will keep an eye on it. Take the trailer and go somewhere, like to say, California and back. See the states, enjoy yourself, think of your dad and live for him."

Dawson sat quietly listening and thinking about what she was saying. He took a bite of bacon and chewed it for a moment, then swallowed. He picked up his cup of coffee and held it in salute.

"Sounds like a good idea. Let me think about it."

"Oh no Buster! All of us are ready to burn you on the stake if you don't back off, relax, and regroup."

He shook his head and chuckled.

"Mom is fine with this idea?"

"It was her suggestion silly!" she said and gently bumped him on the shoulder with her head a couple of times.

Dawson held up his hand.

"Okay, if I do this, how long of a trip do I take? A week, a month?"

"Ever how long it takes to find the old Dawson and bring him back home," she said, then added, "Just as long as you are here when I get back. I'm taking a long vacation then."

He sighed.

"Okay then, I'll do it."

Lianne grinned.

"Good!" she kissed him. "That' settled. Eat, and then do some more of what you did last night."

"Gladly."

CHAPTER 91

Dawson and Lianne emerged from the house after spending the morning in bed. It was near noon. They walked to a bistro for lunch. The air was chilly but the sun was out and made for a pleasant walk. The two continued to reconcile their differences and discussed further the idea of Dawson taking the road trip and exploring the west. While out, they stopped by a small bookstore and he purchased a couple of travel guides for the western states.

At first Dawson had thought about saying he would go to make Lianne happy, then after she was gone to Afghanistan he would just not go. The more he thought about it, the more he began to understand the significance of getting away. The idea took hold and slowly began to appeal to him and he felt a stir of excitement.

That night the two of them went out to dinner and dancing. They did not stay out late as they usually did. By 10:30 p.m. they were back home and relaxing in the hot tub with a fresh bottle of wine.

On Sunday, Dawson spent the day helping Lianne get the household finances in order. She prepaid the utilities and other monthly bills for the time of her absence. During the remaining time before Dawson's flight back to Tanner, he and Lianne held each other and said their goodbyes. She would be leaving for Afghanistan later that week.

Because of the emotional turmoil of their impending separation, Dawson elected for them to say goodbye at the house rather than at the airport. He would take a taxi without Lianne accompanying him. This would be the first time they said goodbye that way.

As expected, the closer it came to the time for him to leave, the harder it was for them to control their emotions. Lianne was the first to break. She laid her head against his chest; tears flowed down her cheeks and dropped onto his shirt.

"Dawson, I know this is lame to say, but please try not to worry too much about me. I will be fine. I will not take any unnecessary risks. I will not go out on any kind of missions with the troops. I will draw the line there. I will stay as safe as I can. I'll be back before you know it."

He exhaled slowly and pulled her closer.

"I'll do my best not to worry, but you know I will anyway. I could not stand to lose you too. I will take the trip for you, Mom and for Dad. I will be waiting for your calls and I will be waiting right here when you come home."

"Have the hot tub ready."

"Will do."

It was time to go. Lianne had called a taxi for him. They stood on the front steps and kissed goodbye. Dawson got in the taxi and looked back at Lianne standing on the steps until he could no longer see her.

"Please Lord, watch over her," he whispered as the taxi sped toward the airport.

Forty-five minutes later the cab pulled into Dulles International. Dawson choked as he paid the exorbitant fare, but was thankful for the time of solitude during the ride. He took a deep breath and walked into the terminal and onto the plane outbound for Atlanta.

The flight was uneventful. He landed on time, retrieved his truck from long-term parking and drove back to Tanner. It was half past ten when he pulled into the garage. He got out of the truck and stood beside Lianne's Mustang. Running his hand across the smooth surface of the hood, a smile came to him. He thought about the look on her face when she first saw the car.

Unlocking the kitchen door, he turned the light on inside and smiled again. He could smell food. Crucita had come by and made dinner for him. Max was sitting by his bowl crunching on a fresh serving of cat food. Evidently Crucita had just left.

"Meow."

"Hello little fellow. Miss me?"

"Meow."

Dawson pulled the warm plate of food out of the oven and sat it on the table. He poured a glass of tea and sat down. While eating he called Lianne to let her know he was home and said goodnight.

"Dawson, you showed me how much you really love me this weekend. I will never forget this time we shared. I will be back soon and we will have a lifetime of happy moments like we had this weekend."

She paused.

"I have been thinking a great deal and I have decided that when this assignment is over I am going to make some changes. My contract is coming up for renewal. I am going to request less extended out of town and country assignments. I want to spend more time here with you."

Dawson was speechless. All he could squeak out was an "I love you."

CHAPTER 92

"Good morning Dawson. I thought I might have to wake you," greeted Crucita as she walked into the kitchen, are you still tired from the weekend trip to D.C.?"

"I am feeling a touch of jetlag this morning."

She handed him a cup of coffee and had him sit at the table while she finished cooking breakfast. He shared with her his reconciliation story with Lianne. When he told her about Lianne's desire for him to take an extended vacation, she smiled.

"Are you going to do it?"

"I promised her that I would. I was all for it but the more I think about it the less I want to do it."

She gave him a concerned look.

"Do not go back on your word to her!" she said tersely.

"You are right," he simpered, feeling a rush of shame.

It was at that moment that Dawson decided that he would definitely go. When he got to work he was happy to see that Holly was already there. She was busy running sales and inventory reports for the accounts. He told her of his plans to take some time off.

"I'm so pleased to hear this," she said with a warm smile. "You have not been yourself since your father passed away. This is just what you need, a nice long trip. I sure wish that I could go with you!" She giggled. "But, I don't think your wife would be too happy about that. And besides, somebody has to hold the fort down. I'm very happy to do it. Take all the time you need Dawson. Don't worry at all about here. The store will be just fine."

"I don't doubt it whatsoever Holly. I know how capable you are. In fact, this gives me a good opportunity to let you know I am giving you a raise."

She grinned.

"You won't get any complaints from me about that. I do appreciate your confidence in me. I really enjoy working for you. I love this store. I love my job."

"Happy to hear that."

"When do you plan to start your vacation?"

"I thought I would leave this weekend. I want to make sure I am home to talk to Lianne each night until she leaves for Afghanistan. I know I should be in cell range anywhere I go. I just don't want to take a chance and miss saying goodbye."

"I wish my husband had been as thoughtful, maybe we would still be married."

"You will find a good one next time."

"I hope so."

Over the next couple days Dawson got everything ready for his trip. He picked up the travel trailer from his mother's house and pulled it home and parked it beside the garage. He began packing it provisions, clothes and personal items.

Crucita was a great help in getting things organized and stored in the various compartments of the camper. Dawson' mother came over and showed him some of the features that he was not aware of. She was very pleased that he was going to make the trip.

"Dawson, I want you to enjoy yourself. See America for your father. He was so looking forward to it."

"I will Mom. Is there any place in particular that Dad wanted to see?"

"He wanted to travel all the way to California and back. Just head west and see where your heart takes you. Wherever you go and whatever you do, your father would be proud of you. You know he will be watching over you."

Dawson felt a pang of grief in his heart.

"Mom, would you like to go with me?"

"Oh Dawson, goodness no. This will be your adventure. I was just going along for Thomas. It's not something I really wanted to do. I do wish you didn't have to go alone. I wish Lianne could do this with you."

"So do I Mom. I would much rather her be going with me than back to the war zone."

"Me too Dawson. You have to try not to worry too much about her. Given who she is, I feel like she will be well watched after."

"I hope so Mom. Hopefully she won't have to go back there again. America's part is supposed to end soon."

They finished up in the camper and walked into the house. To Dawson's surprise, His mother presented him with the title to the travel trailer. She had already had the insurance for it transferred to his name. There was not much else left for Dawson to do now but strike out on his great adventure.

CHAPTER 93

When Dawson and Lianne talked on Tuesday night she told him that on Wednesday he would get a special delivery package. It would contain something for him to take on the trip and could be used at home as well. He asked what it was but she would not say. She would explain all about it after he received it. This left him curious and perplexed as to what it could be.

At work on Wednesday a Federal Express truck delivered a box to him containing a new laptop computer. After opening it up, he Amber and Roberto looked over the computer with interest. Dawson was puzzled by it.

"I have a good laptop already. I wonder why she sent me a new one."

"Ahh, look!" said Amber. "It has a built in video camera. You will be able to have video communications with Lianne. Isn't that wonderful? You will be able to see and talk to one another in real time, half way around the world!"

"I tell you, Lianne is really something!" he professed, and meant it.

"You are so lucky to be married to someone so famous. It's awesome knowing someone like her."

"Sometimes, I still can't believe my luck."

That night when he and Lianne talked, she had him power up the laptop and took him through the procedure to connect with her. Moments later they were looking at one another.

"Have I told you lately how beautiful you are on camera?" he asked with a cheesy grin.

"Not enough cowboy. I like to hear your sweet words. Isn't this great that we can see and talk to each other now?"

"Yes, I like this set up. I can see you like this while you are in Afghanistan?"

"Yep. Jim Baxter set yours and mine up to do it. He said occasionally we may have a bad connection. It sounds kind of like a cell phone deal. Anyway, let's plan on each night at ten that we try to contact each other with this. If something happens and we can't, then go to the cell phone."

"All right."

"Oh, once I get situated in Afghanistan we'll figure out an appropriate time to link up because of the time difference."

"No problem. I will work around your schedule."

The two talked for a while longer then signed off. Thursday night they were able to connect without a problem. Lianne was due to leave out the next day. For the next few days she would be traveling to Afghanistan and getting situated. Tentative plans were to connect on Sunday night. If it was a no go, then Monday night.

It was difficult for Dawson to look at Lianne on real-time video and say goodbye. He tried not to show the pain that was hammering in his chest. It was readily evident that Lianne was doing the same.

"What time are you leaving tomorrow?" he asked, changing the subject.

"We're leaving at noon. What time do you plan to head out on your adventure?"

"I thought I would leave out early on Saturday morning."

"Have you decided if you are going to take Max with you?"

I'm still debating that. That is a lot of traveling for him. He did well on the trip to D.C. I want to take him but I'm unsure of how so many days of riding will affect him."

"Crucita will watch him if you leave him. You know he'll be well cared for."

"I know," he chuckled. "She loves him and he surely loves her. He stays right with her whenever she is here."

"You know Dawson, I'm not so sure if it would be a good idea to take him. There are a lot of parks and places that don't allow pets."

"I haven't thought about that. Guess that settles the issue."

"Awe! Now I feel bad that he can't go and be company for you."

Dawson smiled and touched the screen of the laptop with his finger.

"I'll be okay. If we can talk and see each other like this regularly, then I will be just fine."

"You know, I'm happy to hear you say that!"

There was a pregnant pause.

"Well..." she said. "I guess it's time we sign off and say goodbye and good night. Don't want to start blubbering on the screen."

Her eyes misted over. She wiped away the tears. Dawson tried to speak but got choked up. Through tears, Lianne smiled at him.

"Dawson, know that I love you with all of my heart. You will be on my mind every moment I'm away. I will be careful and I will be back in your arms soon."

"I'll miss you terribly, Darling. I love you so very much."

With that they ended the video feed. Dawson's shoulders slouched. He exhaled like a deflating balloon. His heart ached. A surge of loneliness engulfed him. He collected Max up into his arms and carried him to bed with him.

"Sleep with me tonight Buddy. I'm lonesome for your mom."

"Meow."

CHAPTER 94

Dawson spent most of Friday at the sports store. He and Holly went over the books and placed orders for new merchandise. They would stay in contact regularly and Dawson's mother would help out as needed.

On the way home he stopped by the grocery store and bought a few more items to take along on the trip. When he got home Crucita was waiting on him. She had prepared a large dinner for his last night at home.

"Wow! What a spread. This is very sweet of you Crucita."

"I wanted you to have a good meal before you go. It was Max's idea," she said with a shy smile.

Dawson laughed.

"I really appreciate you Crucita, and Max too. I am sure going to miss you both."

Crucita gave him an uneasy smile. Dawson looked at her and read her discomfort.

"Is everything okay?"

"Yes, I am happy that you are going on vacation but I am going to miss you too. I enjoy cooking for you and talking care of your needs."

"I won't be gone long Crucita. Maybe two weeks. I think that will be long enough to satisfy Lianne and Mom. I'm mainly doing this for them and in memory for Dad."

She nodded thoughtfully. They sat down and ate. Dawson went over several things for her to do while he was gone.

"There is plenty of cash in the house account. Use the debit card to get whatever you need. It's about time for Max's vet checkup. If you get a notice in the mail and are up to it, call and make an appointment and take him."

She giggled and said, "Only in America!"

Dawson laughed and shook his head. It took him a moment to realize what she meant. Roberto had told him that he had been so poor in Mexico that he could not afford for them to go to a doctor when they were sick. Rather than say anything, he changed the subject.

"Crucita, while I'm gone, take the Mustang for a drive occasionally to keep the battery charged."

She grinned.

"Are you sure."

"Yep. Lianne wanted me to ask you to do that for her."

"I will be happy to!"

Though she objected, Dawson helped Crucita with the dishes. He then wiped the table while she cleaned the counters.

When Crucita was finished with all she needed to do, she gathered her things to leave. Dawson walked her outside to her car.

"I'll call you late tomorrow to say hello and let you know where I am at."

"Okay, I will keep my cell phone near at all times. Call if you need anything."

"I will."

They stood there an awkward moment.

"Well goodbye Dawson," she said, looking down at the ground. "Have a safe trip."

"Take care Crucita."

She then looked up into his face and broke out in tears. Dawson put his arms around her and pulled her close.

"Now, now. I'm not leaving forever. I promise to keep in touch regularly. Call me anytime too."

"I'm sorry. I am worried for your safety and I am afraid for Mrs. Lianne going to that awful war. I do not want anything to happen to you or her. I love you both."

"We love you too. If you feel the need to worry, then worry about Lianne. I will be fine. This is no big deal compared to where she's going."

Crucita laid her head against his chest. Dawson kissed her on top of the head.

"I'll be back soon."

"Okay."

He helped her in her car and waved as she drove away.

"What a wonderful heart."

While he was standing in the front yard, Dawson decided to hook the travel trailer to the truck while it was still light enough to see. Once it was attached and the wires connected, he checked the brake and running lights.

Satisfied that everything was in order, he loaded the last of the supplies and got ready to turn in for the night. Tomorrow would be a full day of driving.

"Come on Max. Let's go to bed."

"Meow."

CHAPTER 95

The tocsin of the clock reverberated through Dawson's skull as he groped in the dark to shut the alarm off.

"Ugh!" he groaned, sitting up and yawning.

He looked at the clock, 4:00 a.m. He shook his head.

"Time to begin Dawson's great adventure!" he bemused.

Reaching around in the dark, he felt for Max but could not find him. Strange, he thought. Max was usually curled up on the bed with him. He got up, thinking little of it went in the bathroom and showered and shaved.

As he dressed, Dawson wondered again where Max was off to. He would usually be under foot mewling to be fed. Shrugging his shoulders, he walked into the kitchen and flipped the light switch on. Max was sitting at his food bowl crunching on fresh cat food.

"Huh?"

Confused, Dawson looked around.

"Crucita?" he called out.

"Meow."

"Not you Max. Is Crucita here?"

Max began to purr and rubbed up against his legs. Dawson then noticed the coffee was ready and there was a warm plate of food on the table. He walked over and sat down at the table. Tears came to his eyes when he saw a framed photograph of Crucita, Lianne, and Max together. Next to it was a note. He sucked in a sob when he read it.

Dear Dawson,

Take this picture along with you to keep you company. It is to remind you that we love you and we will be waiting for your return.

Love
Lianne, Crucita, and Max

Composing himself, Dawson got up and poured a cup of coffee, then sat back down and ate the plate of eggs, bacon, and grits. It was apparent that Crucita had cooked it at her house and brought it over just before he awoke.

Before leaving, Dawson washed the plate, cup and silverware and sat them in the dish drainer. He held Max while he wrote a thank you note to Crucita and let himself out of the house. He stood in the front yard a few minutes and stared at the house and smiled. He loved this place, his and Lianne's.

"See you soon."

He climbed into the truck, cranked the engine and warmed it up. Putting the transmission into drive he eased down on the gas pedal of the Ford 150 and pulled the Jay Feather twenty-four foot travel trailer out onto the road.

From Jones Road he turned onto Veteran's Parkway then took I-185 North until it connected to I-85 south which actually led him westward to Alabama. He set the cruise control at 55 mph and switched on the satellite radio. He smiled when he heard the song "Ride Like the Wind," an old Christopher Cross classic.

"Well, for better or worse, I'm on my way."

In the middle of the morning Dawson pulled into a truck stop in front of a dog track just off of I-85 in Shorter, Alabama. He used the restroom, topped off the gas tank, and got a cup of coffee to go, then rolled back onto the interstate.

Traffic began to thicken as he neared Montgomery. Minutes later he cruised right on through the Alabama Capital on to Selma. Soon he crossed over into Mississippi. He stopped in Meridian for lunch, and then caught I-20 which would take him well into Texas.

Pushing on, Dawson passed through Jackson, then on to Louisiana. When he reached Shreveport it was late in the evening. Too tired to search for a RV park, he pulled into a motel for the night.

After a hot shower and a change of clothes, Dawson walked next door to a buffet restaurant and had dinner. Back in the room he undressed and got ready for bed. Before turning the lights out he called Crucita.

"Hello?"

"How is my favorite girl?"

"Dawson! I am so happy to hear from you. How is it going so far?"

"Fine."

"Where are you now?"

"Shreveport, Louisiana."

"Sounds like you had a good day of traveling."

"Yes I did. Pulling the trailer is a breeze. It's a lot easier than I thought it would be."

"I am happy to hear that."

"How are things going there?"

"Good. I have decided to stay at your house while you are gone. My father has two of his friends staying with him for a time. They just arrived here from Mexico and they are looking for work."

"No problem. I'm happy you are staying there. I know Max is pleased. By the way, how is he?"

She laughed.

"He is just fine. He's sitting in my lap right now."

"Great. I miss you guys."

"We miss you too. We are fine. You have a good time. We'll be waiting to hear from you."

"Wish you two were with me."

"Us too."

A large lump formed in Dawson's throat. It took him a moment to compose himself.

"I'll call you tomorrow. Meantime, if you need me, call."

"Good night Dawson. I love you."

"I love you too, Crucita."

CHAPTER 96

On I-20, the Sunday traffic was light until Dawson got closer to Dallas. He had slept later than he had planned that morning and did not reach Dallas until well after lunch. He had seen signs for a Camping World campground in Fort Worth so he punched the coordinates into the GPS and followed the map and arrived there at two-thirty. He would spend his first night in the travel trailer there.

After registering and finding his campsite, Dawson set up the trailer for camping by leveling it, then plugging in the water and power. He then went inside and extended the rear-wall slide out bed. Since he had full-hookup, there was no need to rely on the small water tank. In minutes the air conditioner had the inside of the camper nice and cool. Once the hot water heated he took a quick shower and slipped into shorts and a t-shirt.

Turning the 22-inch LED television on, Dawson automatically flipped the channels till he found CNN. Laughing and shaking his head at what he had done, he then slowly clicked through the other channels. He settled on music channel and began putting a late lunch together. Opening a package of sliced ham, he made two sandwiches. Then he pulled out a bag of chips and a coke. He settled back on the sofa to watch television and eat.

While lounging and eating, he gazed around the efficient and well apportioned camper. Thoughts of his father swirled around in his mind. He almost choked on a bite of sandwich as he remembered how excited his father was when he first bought the camper and brought it by to show Dawson. He could still visualize the twinkle in his father's eyes while he proudly showed the camper's features. Sighing heavily with the shadow of grief still hanging around, Dawson refocused on the television and tried to think about other things.

Finishing up with his lunch, Dawson got up and washed the utensils and plate he had used. He was surprised at how big the sink was for such a compact camper. After towel drying everything, he put everything away.

Wanting to stretch his legs from the last two days of driving, he walked to the Camping World store and looked around. It was filled with everything imaginable for the RV or camper. He looked at the outside furniture and purchased a folding table, lawn chairs, and a welcome mat to place at the entrance to the trailer.

Back at the camper he opened up the liquor cabinet and made a spicy Bloody Mary and sat outside enjoying the fresh air. As he sat there he got on the cell phone and called his mother and Crucita. His mother was pleased to learn that he was in Dallas-Fort Worth and enjoying himself.

After his calls, Dawson went back inside and mixed him another Bloody Mary, and fired up the camper's oven. He broiled a nice thick steak and put a baking potato in the microwave. When it was soft he split it open and slathered it with butter and sour cream. Along with a small salad he ate the hearty meal while watching CNN.

By 10:00 p.m. he had the laptop setup and waiting for Lianne to connect. As if on cue, she appeared and smiling broadly. Dawson's heart surged with a dizzying array of wonderful feelings of love and longing.

"I can see you Dawson!"

"And I can see you too. I must say, you are a sight for sore eyes! Have I told you how beautiful you truly are?"

She laughed.

"Never enough. I can never tire of hearing you say that!"

"Well, how are things there?"

"I'm in Kabul. It's much the same as when I last saw it. I will be visiting one of the U.S. bases tomorrow to do my usual meet and greet with the soldiers. I hope to get a pulse on the mood of the times for the troops."

"Have you had any difficulties?"

"None so far. It looks like this will be a fairly easy tour."

"I hope so. Come back to me safe and in one piece."

"Oh, I intend to. Anyway, enough about me. How are you? I can see you are in the camper. Where are you?"

"I'm at a campground in Fort Worth. The drive has been pleasant so far. I haven't done anything but travel. Now I plan to start doing some of the touristy things that strike my fancy as I come to them."

"Great. I talked to Crucita. She misses you terribly."

"I know. I miss her too. If she was my real daughter, I couldn't love her more."

"You know, I feel the same way. I can see that she looks at me as a mother figure."

"Yes, I have noticed that too. I'm sure she needs someone to look up to since her mother is gone. You are a great role model and inspiration to her."

Lianne grinned and clucked.

"Make my head spin Mister Silver Tongue!"

"It's true you know, you are."

"I know Dawson. I am flattered. I see how she tries to copy some of the things I do. She wants to rise above and be somebody. I think we should help her be the best she can be."

"Any ideas?"

"Why don't we put her through college?"

"Hmm. Sounds like a good start. We'll talk more about it and when you get back we will both sit down with her and go from there."

"Okay."

They talked a while longer with plans to connect on Tuesday at the same time. The two kissed their fingers and touched the screen before logging off.

CHAPTER 97

After talking to Lianne, Dawson went on to bed. When he turned the covers back he discovered two cards tucked under the pillow. One was from Lianne and the other from Crucita and Max. They were both thinking of you cards. He smiled through tear filled eyes as he read them.

The slide-out bed was large and roomy. In spite of it having a thin mattress, it was fairly comfortable. He slept well, waking up to the five o'clock alarm, refreshed and ready to roll. After a quick but filling breakfast he cleaned up and secured all of the loose items. He was on the road by six o'clock. Staying on I-20, he made for Abilene.

I-20 connected to 84 and he took it, heading north to Lubbock. There he found a small RV park and set up for the night. Sleeping a little later than normal, he pulled out of the park at 8:00 a.m. He stopped and had breakfast at a small old-fashioned café. He left there and got on MLK Jr. Boulevard and then on East Thirty-First, where he found the city of Lubbock Cemetery. Parking near the entrance, he climbed down out of the truck and walked along the gravesites until he found Buddy Holly's grave.

Other than the song, "That'll Be the Day", Dawson could recall very little of Buddy's music. He knew the tragic story of his death when the airplane he was riding in crashed. After paying his respects, Dawson quietly walked back to the truck and got back on 84 and drove to Littlefield.

The home of country music singer, Waylon Jennings is in Littlefield. Following Waylon Jennings Boulevard into town then taking Hall Avenue, Dawson found the famous Waymore's Liquor Store that was run by family members of Waylon's. Inside the store was a museum dedicated to Waylon. On display were his first guitar and several pieces of memorabilia. After checking out the artifacts, Dawson bought a fifth of Vodka and two bottles of Bloody Mary mix and said goodbye. When he stopped for lunch, he was in Clovis, New Mexico.

A short break at a convenience store and Dawson drove onward to Albuquerque and found another Camping World campground. This time he unhooked the trailer then set it up and connected to the power and water. He had planned to spend a few days touring the area. Too tired to do anything else, he cooked dinner and relaxed in front of the television watching CNN.

While lounging he called his mother and told her where he was at. She told him that she had spent the afternoon at the store and that everything was fine there.

Crucita was happy to hear from him. She told him that she and Max missed him.

"I miss both of you too. I've been gone four days now. It seems much longer."

"Have you checked your emails?"

"No."

"I sent pictures of me and Max."

"That's great! I'll check them out after we hang up. That reminds me, I have got my digital camera and I have not even thought about using it."

"Send lots of pictures of you and the places you visit. Don't forget to send them to Mrs. Lianne too."

"All right. I'll do that tomorrow."

They said goodbye. He powered up the laptop and read his emails and looked at the pictures she had sent. They were several photos of her holding Max and smiling at the camera. It warmed his heart to see them.

At ten o'clock the connection to Lianne came through. She was wearing a bullet proof vest and military fatigues. He knew she was following the soldiers around now. She broke into a big smile when she saw him.

"Hey my handsome husband. Whatcha doing?"

"Watching CNN for my favorite reporter."

"My goodness. I think you are a CNN junkie!"

"Yep. All because of you my dear."

She giggled.

"Happy to hear that. Now, tell me all about what you have been up to and where you are."

He told her about the stops in Texas and his plans to explore New Mexico tomorrow. Much to his dismay, Dawson learned that Lianne was near some heavy fighting and had seen an army vehicle get blown up by a mine. He did his best not to say much though he wanted to remind her to be careful.

"I know you are worrying, Dawson. I can see it in your face. Please know that I am not going to accept any more assignments here until the fighting is over. There are plenty of other reporters who would be happy to do this."

"That's nice to hear. I want you safe and out of harm's way."

CHAPTER 98

As the sun came up over the nearby mountains lighting up the desert. Dawson was sipping on a cup of coffee. He had slept well but woke early. It took a while before he realized he was restless. He was actually anxious to go exploring.

Since he was up early and ready to go, Dawson decided to spend the day visiting Santa Fe, some distance away from Albuquerque. With a thermos of coffee, he left the campground and drove north. Traffic was heavy but the drive was pleasant.

In Santa Fe he explored the Indian craft shops and toured the San Miguel Mission that was originally built in 1610. After eating lunch in town he drove to the nearby Bandelien National Monument Park to see the Indian cliff dwellings there. They had been built by the Anasazi people, descendants, of Pueblo Indians. The living spaces had been built on the protected ledges of the cliffs around 1000-1300 A.D. and were in remarkably good condition from Dawson's perspective.

It was getting late in the afternoon when Dawson made it back to Albuquerque. He found a Mexican restaurant and had dinner before retiring to the camper. Once there he showered and changed into shorts. What was becoming a ritual, he mixed a Bloody Mary and sat outside the camper and took in the sunset. There were other campers around him. However, he made no attempts to socialize. He was enjoying the solitude and chance to spend time in contemplation and thoughts of his father and his life.

Dawson's childhood had been great. He went fishing and hunting with his father. His dad taught him to swim, to camp, to play ball, and a million other things. He had instilled in Dawson good morals and work ethics. They rarely had a disagreement and if they did, it was usually over something trivial. Dawson had always idolized his father. Looking back, he and his father were like best friends when Dawson became an adult.

"I miss you Dad. I hope you are watching down on me. At first I did not want to take this trip. Now, I'm glad I did. I can see that it is doing me a lot of good. I do miss home, Mom, Lianne, Crucita and Max. I miss our outdoor store and everyone there. You know Dad; this trip is helping me appreciate more and more what I have. I am so very, very lucky. Thanks to you and Mom, I have turned out okay. I know you did a good job with me because look what I have for a wife. She is absolutely the greatest, Dad. We don't have the ideal marriage because of our careers, but it is working out nicely. You know I sure did not want her to go on this trip to Afghanistan, but I am doing my best to be okay with it. I have to trust in God that she will be safe and will come back to me soon."

A lump formed in his throat. A tear dripped to his cheek.

"Dad. If you can, watch over Lianne. I just can't lose her. Losing you was hard enough. I can't lose her too."

ONCE UPON A MIDNIGHT DESERT

If felt good to verbalize his thoughts. Finished with his catharsis and holding an empty glass, he went in and mixed another drink. He set up the laptop and checked and responded to emails. He then left the computer on and waited for the 10:00 p.m. connection with Lianne.

A little after nine o'clock his cell phone rang. It was his mother. She had gotten his email and the pictures he had taken and enjoyed seeing them. He promised that he would take and send more during his expedition. She reported that everything was fine back in Tanner. An "I love you" and a "goodnight" she said goodbye.

Lianne did not log in at ten. Dawson waited until eleven-thirty before shutting the computer down. In the meantime he had tried her cell phone but it would not go through either. Rationally he could surmise that she was somewhere with no cell service, but still, he worried.

Somewhat disheartened, he went on to bed. Hopefully tomorrow would be better and she could get through. Sleep did not come easy. He kept drifting off only to wake up and check the time. Finally at 3:00 a.m. he got up. First he tried her cell phone, but no luck. Then he got online and sent Lianne an email. He did it before he happened to check the incoming box. A burst of relief coursed through his veins when he saw one from her. She was in an area where service was poor, just as he had suspected. She said she should be able to be back to where she could connect with him tomorrow night.

So relieved with hearing from her, he went back to bed and slept until eight-thirty. Feeling sluggish when he did get up, Dawson made a pot of coffee and drank three cups before he was alert enough to cook and eat a light breakfast.

His plan's for the day was to explore Albuquerque. After a shower and getting dressed, he left out for a day of checking out the sights in the city.

CHAPTER 99

In an odd mood and unable to figure out what was going on in his fuddled brain, Dawson rode aimlessly around Albuquerque. No desirable destination would come to mind. He eventually ended up at the city's museum and walked through it without being engaged and enjoying it. Once back on the road, he could hardly recall what he had seen. While he was there, he did pick up a selection of brochures. One caught his eye. It was a brochure on the atomic bomb museum located at the nearby Kirkland Air force Base. Interest piqued, he drove to it.

The first thing he noticed when he passed through the post security checkpoint was how immaculately groomed and pristine clean the streets and grounds were. That was one thing he had always admired about military installations. They were always well maintained.

The building the museum was housed in was unassuming and innocuous for what it contained. He went in and first saw a video of America's efforts to develop and utilize the atomic bomb during World War II.

While watching the video, Dawson looked around and was surprised to see quite a few Japanese visitors. He felt a sense of sadness for the people of Japan and what they must have endured when the two bombs were dropped on them. From a soldier's standpoint he understood the necessity of why the bombs were used, but he still felt and empty hole in his gut.

The museum displays were impressive. It was fascinating to see and touch the two full scale replicas of "Fat Man" and Little Boy" that were dropped on Hiroshima and Nagasaki.

Finished with the museum tour, Dawson started back to the base entrance when he noticed the Post Exchange and commissary. He had his veteran's ID card so he decided to stop in and look around. He bought a few items for the camper then shopped for some groceries to restock the refrigerator. From there he drove on back to the campground.

It was still early in the afternoon but he was out of the mood to do anything. He started to hook the travel trailer up and head out westward but decided that by the time he got ready and going that it would be late. Instead, he had a sandwich and pulled out his collection of roadmaps and spread them out. Tomorrow he would make for Arizona, he resolved with a nod.

With a couple of hours before dark, Dawson decided to have the oil changed in the truck. He had seen a lube service center near the campground. He drove over and got into the short line and waited his turn. Minutes later he was directed into a service bay. He pulled the truck into place and went into the waiting room and sat down. A few minutes later an attendant came in and called his name.

"Mister Lee?"

"Yes?"

"Your air filter needs changing. Do you want us to replace it for you?"

"Sure thing."

"We checked your fluid levels and your coolant was almost a half-gallon low. We could not spot a leak anywhere but you might want to keep an eye on it."

"I will, thank you."

Dawson had noticed the engine water temperature gauge was running higher than it had normally been reading at. He had attributed it to pulling the travel trailer and been in a hotter climate. He made a mental note to keep a close check.

Since he was out, Dawson decided to eat at a restaurant rather than cook. When he got back to the campground it was an hour before dark. He turned the television on CNN, mixed a Bloody Mary, and sat at the dinette table and powered up the laptop.

Checking the emails he opened one from the store. Holly asked his advice on giving a discount price on six canoes that a customer wanted. She added that the store was running smoothly ad asked how he was doing. He sent a message back with a suggested discount for the canoes and filled her in on the trip thus far. Along with the message, he attached several photos he had taken.

Crucita had also emailed him and included pictures of Max and her. Instead of emailing her back, he picked up the cell phone and punched in her number. She answered on the first ring and was excited to hear from him.

"I had lunch with your mother today. We had a nice visit. She is so sweet."

"She is a great lady."

"So Dawson, how are you?"

"Doing good. I am going to leave out for Arizona tomorrow. I'm thinking of going to the Grand Canyon first. I know Dad wanted to go there and then I will probably go to Orgon Pipe Cactus National Monument. He always talked about wanting to go there. It's all the way down on the Mexican border, kind of out of the way."

"You should do that for him."

"I know. It just appears so out of the way of everything else."

"I know nothing of the places but it must have something special to offer for him to want to go there. You should do it."

"Well, he has always had a thing about cacti. The park is supposed to have some of the oldest and prettiest kinds."

"There you go then. You must go!"

"I will Crucita. Thanks for the advice."

CHAPTER 100

Nervous with anticipation to hear from Lianne, Dawson was sitting by the laptop at ten o'clock. Suddenly there was a flurry of noise and the video snapped on. At first Lianne's face faded in and out without audio. The image was lost moments later then popped back perfectly clear.

"Dawson, can you hear me?"

"Loud and clear!" he gushed with a sigh of relief.

"You're clear now on my end. Anyway, how is it going?"

"Fine, but I want to know about you?"

"It's going well. We have lots of reports filmed and filed. We got caught up in a skirmish but it only lasted a few minutes. Thank goodness none of our people were injured. I am doing humanitarian type stuff now on the conditions of some of the villages and people caught in the middle of this mess."

"Good to hear things are not too bad for you. I am still here in Albuquerque but I plan to get back on the road tomorrow. I will be in Arizona by noon if there are no difficulties. Things are going good for me. I am enjoying the trip so far. Did you get the pictures I emailed you?"

"Yes I did. Santa Fe is gorgeous. We'll have to go there together for a look one day."

"That's a deal!"

"One thing about it, you will know where some great places to go are when we get bored and want to travel."

He chuckled.

"With our schedules, I don't think we will get a chance to get bored."

Lianne beamed a beautiful smile. Her eyes teared up and she sniffed.

"I really do miss you. I have never been homesick before when I've gone on an overseas assignment."

"No offense, but I am happy to hear that!" he said with a big grin.

She giggled.

"Just wait until I get back home to you Buster!"

"Oooo, I can't wait."

Lianne was smiling again and cheered up. They said their goodbyes and logged off, both feeling better. Happy, Dawson went on to bed and rose at 6:00 a.m. Having already hooked the trailer to the truck, he was on his way in a short time. Toward noon he rolled in to Gallup and had an early lunch.

Rolling along on I-40, Dawson crossed over into Arizona. He wanted to make it to Flagstaff and spend the night before heading north to the Grand Canyon. On into the afternoon he was nearing Holbrook and saw signs for the Petrified Forrest National Park and the Painted Desert.

"Sounds like it might be a nice place to visit."

He took the north entrance Exit 311 to the park and stopped at the Painted Desert Visitor Center. He looked at the displays and gathered guides and information of the park. According to the park map he was at the northern start of a 28-mile scenic drive that first went north through the Painted Desert, then south to the parks southern terminus.

As soon as he started on the drive through the park he was surrounded by astonishing panoramic views of the Painted Desert's multicolored rock layers. Along the section of the desert there were several pull offs with stunning views.

After a time he crossed over I-40 and headed south on the scenic drive. He stopped at Puerco Pueblo and saw a Kiva, an underground chamber that the native people had once used as a ceremonial spot. Near it was Newspaper Rock that was covered with ancient designs made by Native Americans.

Continuing on he stopped and took pictures of "The Teepee's" which were cone-shaped hills that were standing off in the distance. A short distance from there Dawson took a side road that looped around through Blue Mesa, a mountain overlooking the surrounding badlands and petrified woods.

He drove for some time through magnificent forests of petrified wood. Soon he reached the southern end of the drive and stopped at the Rainbow Forrest Museum before leaving the park. There he saw displays of skeletons of the animals that once lived in the area. There were also many samples of the various petrified wood found in the park.

At the southern entrance to the park, Dawson got on Highway 180, drove north and connected back on to I-40 in Holbrook. He drove for a half hour and stopped in Winslow to spend the night. Smiling, Dawson chuckled when he remembered reading that one of Winslow's claims to fame was that the Eagles said in their song "Take It Easy" the words, "Well I'm standing on a corner in Winslow, Arizona..." Winslow is also on the famed old Route 66.

Too tired to find a campground, he checked into a motel for the night. He had dinner at a nearby restaurant then took a long hot shower and settled in for the night.

CHAPTER 101

A good night's rest, Dawson was back on I-40, nearing Flagstaff. Thirty-six miles out he saw the signs for Exit 233 and Meteor Crater.

"Hmm. Sounds interesting. Might as well," he said taking the exit ramp.

Six miles later he was looking down into the world's best preserved impact crater caused by a nickel-iron meteor that smashed into the Earth about 49,000 years ago. The impact measures 4, 100 feet across and 560 feet deep. The park guide said it would hold 20 football fields.

The museum there turned out to be quite interesting to Dawson. On exhibit was a 1,450 pound meteorite. There were space exhibits that honored astronauts and told the story of the first manned flights through the trips to the moon.

Pleased that he had stopped, Dawson climbed back into the truck and headed on to Flagstaff. When he drove into town he stopped and had lunch. While eating he had taken a travel guide in with him to look at. His plans were to head north and visit the Grand Canyon. Suddenly the desire to drive south struck him. He could see the southern part of Arizona first then come back through the Grand Canyon sites when he started back from California.

He shook his head at the realization that he was arguing with himself on where to go. It did not really matter, did it? He had no set schedule or itinerary. He was just looking to see what was around the next corner, or bend in the road, musing to himself.

Dawson finished eating and paid for his meal and walked back to the truck. He drove to a service station, filled the tank with gas, and checked the oil and coolant. The coolant was once again a little low. He bought a gallon of antifreeze and poured half of it in the over flow tank and got it back to level.

Soon he was traveling south on I-17. Late in the afternoon he rolled into Phoenix and stayed there for the night. Early the next morning he picked up Highway 85 South just off of I-10, went through Gila Bend, the small towns of Ajo, Why, and entered Pipe Organ National Cactus Monument. This park was one of the main places Dawson's father had wanted to visit. He had always been intrigued by the desert climate and especially fascinated with the various types of cactus plants.

"For you, Dad," he said as he pulled into the parks visitor center.

Just before shutting the truck's engine off he noticed the water temperature gauge was running hot again. He raised the hood and noticed that the coolant reservoir was empty again. He closed the hood and walked into the center. He would let the engine cool then check over the coolant system.

In the visitor center he gathered brochures and guides. He talked to a ranger about the RV campground in the park. He was disappointed to learn that the 208-campsite Park had no electrical or water hookups for RV's or travel trailers. It had restrooms, showers, and access to drinking water. The park also did not have shade trees, but worst of all for Dawson was that it had no cell or internet service. Dawson had planned on setting up camp for a while and spend time exploring the park his father so wanted to see.

The park attendant suggested to Dawson that he drive back to Why or Ajo and check out their RV parks. Both had more amenities and had cell service. He recommended Belly Acres RV Resort in Ajo. It had full hookups and was near gas stations, grocery stores, and restaurants. Dawson thanked him and said goodbye.

Back at the truck again, he raised the hood and looked as best he could for coolant leaks. He found a small amount of residue on the bottom of the engine but could not find where it had come from. Pouring the rest of the container of antifreeze into the coolant tank, he cranked the engine and watched the temperature gauge for a moment. It remained in the normal range so he drove on back to Ajo.

Belly Acres was surprisingly nice. It boasted 47 landscaped lots. The one Dawson rented was a pull-through lot. It was located at the end of a lone street so he was secluded and away from the crowd.

After unhooking the trailer from the truck, he then leveled it and extended the rear slide out. He hooked up the water and power. Hot and tired, he took a shower, changed clothes, and made two sandwiches and opened a bag of chips. He sat back, relaxing in the air conditioning, ate and watched television. Rested and refreshed, he walked to the NAPA auto parts store that was adjacent to the campground and purchased another gallon of coolant.

Too late to ride back to Organ Pipe to look around, Dawson rode around the little town of Ajo and checked it out. There were a few restaurants and stores. He stopped at a grocery store and bought fresh fruit and vegetables, then drove back to camp.

After putting the groceries away, Dawson gathered up all of his dirty clothes and walked to the laundry and washed and dried them. With plans to stay for a while, he cooked a big dinner and left the dishes in the sink. He would clean up his mess tomorrow.

The wireless internet service and cell service was great so he checked in with his mother and Crucita. At 10:00 p.m. he was waiting by the laptop when Lianne logged in. They caught one another up on their days and said goodbye with plans to contact again soon.

CHAPTER 102

Just after daybreak Dawson was up and had made coffee. He cooked eggs, bacon, and a small pan of canned biscuits. There were only a few RV's and campers near him. It was quiet and peaceful. The early morning temperature was mild and pleasant. Setting up the portable table of the parking pad, he had breakfast outside and watched the sun come up over the desert.

The campsite he was parked at was surrounded by clusters of paloverde, mesquite, and several mature ironwood trees that offered some shade during the day. There were several species of cacti nearby including the prickly pear, hedgehog, and several large saguaros that dotted the landscape.

Dawson smiled when he thought about being in the middle of the Sonoran Desert. The primal beauty that long before him had an appeal he could not describe. Whatever it was that held interest to his father had drawn him in too. The desert held a lot more color than he thought possible. There were numerous flowering plants that brought a vivid touch to the desert palette.

The sun was well up when he walked into the camper to get his third cup of coffee. When he walked back out he went to collect the breakfast dishes from the table and froze. The pan with the biscuits that he had not eaten was empty.

"That's odd," he said looking around.

Something had gotten them in the minute he had gone in and poured a cup of coffee and walked back out. He looked under the camper and around the parking pad but saw no signs of an animal or fowl. In the trees were cactus wrens chirping. They were way too small to have gotten the biscuits and flew off with them.

"Oh well!" he mused, shrugged his shoulders and went inside.

He washed last night's dishes plus the breakfast ones then got ready to ride to Organ Pipe Park and look around. Having read over the brochures and guides, he brought along plenty of water to drink as per their recommendations. He had a full canteen and a six pack of 10-ounce bottles in a cooler in the back seat of the truck. Also, he brought along a day pack with a first aid kit, sunscreen, and snacks for the day. He planned to hike some of the nature trails in the park.

He stopped back in at the Kris Eggle Visitor Center just inside the park. He watched a short video presentation of several sites of the Monument Park. He then looked in the exhibit room and took a leisurely walk on the nature trail behind the center.

After he left the center, Dawson took the 21-mile driving tour, Ajo Mountain Scenic Loop. He drove through impressive stands of organ pipe, saguaro and other cacti. He saw tall cliffs and volcanic mountainsides. His drive was on a graded dirt road but it was relatively easy going for the truck.

At noon he drove to Lukeville, located in the southern part of the Monument. It is the port of entry on the U.S.-Mexican border. He looked around the small semi-desolate town. Stopping at the gas station he bought a coke and a bag of chips and drove back into the Monument Park interior. He rode through the Twin Peaks Campground in the park. It was nice but crowded.

Just outside the entrance to the campground he stopped and walked the 1.2 mile Desert View Nature Trail. He saw his first roadrunner bird. Chuckling to himself, Dawson thought of the roadrunner cartoons he enjoyed as a child.

Late in the afternoon he drove back to Ajo to the trailer, turned the air conditioner on and took a shower. Looking in the refrigerator, he decided to have a nice steak for dinner. In one of the outer storage compartments Dawson pulled out a small grill and set it up by the door. He added charcoal and got it going. While in Texas he had bought a six pack of Lonestar beer and it had been on ice all day. He drank on while preparing the salad and baked potato.

The coals were ready. Dawson placed the steak on the grill and was greeted by a sizzle of searing meat and a mouth-watering aroma that made his stomach growl. Back inside he began nuking the potato in the microwave. The evening air was comfortable enough that he turned the air conditioner off and propped the trailer door open. While the steak was grilling, he sat outside eating chips and salsa and sipping on a beer.

The evening sun was low on the horizon and cast long shadows among the desert flora. The moisture free air felt good to Dawson after spending his life in the humid Deep South.

When the steak was ready, he went in and got his salad and baked potato and took it outside to the table. He went back in for steak sauce and a fresh beer. Setting them on the table he took the tongs and picked the steak up off the grill and placed it on the plate. It was then that he noticed the chips that were in the bowl had disappeared. He stared at it in disbelief.

"Now I know that bowl was half full a minute ago. He looked around in the evening shadows but saw nothing. Shaking his head in wonder, he sat down and ate.

CHAPTER 103

The steak tasted exceptionally good. The butter soaked the potato equally delicious. Dawson nodded his approval. It must be the Arizona desert air that makes thing taste better.

Finished eating, he stepped back inside to get the bowl of fresh fruit he had cut up and chilled for dessert. When he stepped back outside again, he froze. The peeling and remnants of the baked potato were gone from the plate. Puzzled, he looked around but it was dark now. Other than the area that the single outside light fixture of the camper lit up, he could see nothing.

He walked to the truck and retrieved the flashlight from the dash pocket and switched it on. As he walked back to the patio area he shined it around looking for the food bandit. He stopped short when he reached the table.

"What the....?"

Stymied, Dawson saw that the bowl of fruit he had just sat down was gone. There was not a single chuck of cantaloupe or honeydew melon left. He shined the light under and around the camper over and over, to no avail. Then for a brief moment, in the underbrush of mesquite a short distance away, a pair of eyes glowed eerily green from his light. Then in an instant, they were gone.

"I guess you are the culprit, whatever you are!"

Dawson chuckled as he cleared the table and took everything inside. He washed the dishes and settled back to watch CNN. Lianne was to give a report from Kabul on the conditions there. When she came on, Lianne was radiant. Dawson was glued to the television noting every nuance of her facial expression and intonation of her speech. His heart ached with loneliness when the report ended and the commercial came on. It was bittersweet seeing her there on television and knowing she was a world away.

Still having a taste for fruit, Dawson cut up some more and ate his fill. He took the rinds and scraps and put them in a bowl. Then he sat the bowl on the steps of the camper. He turned the television off and listened for a few minutes, but heard nothing. Wondering if the creature had moved on, he opened the screen door and looked out. He broke out in laughter when he discovered that the bowl was already empty.

"I'm going to find out who you are Mister Critter. I know you're out there and I know you can hear me!"

He shined the flashlight around but saw nothing.

"Oh well, goodnight little fellow. See you tomorrow." He paused. "If I'm lucky."

Before going to bed, Dawson pulled out the Organ Pipe brochures and looked at the trails he had yet to explore. He had taken some beautiful pictures of the desert so far and planned to take many more. Looking at the brochures reminded him of the camera so he powered up the computer and transferred the pictures in the camera to the hard drive.

Rising early, Dawson had breakfast, packed his day pack with lunch, and locked the camper. In the truck, he cranked the engine and sat there a moment warming it up. The windshield was dusty so he switched on the windshield washer and let it do its work. Before heading on to Organ Pipe Cactus National Monument he stopped and bought a cup of coffee at a convenience store, then rolled south.

Just a few miles out of town he happened to notice that the water temperature gauge was climbing steadily. Before he could pull off on the side of the road, the gauge was reading in the red.

Unlatching the hood, he raised it and saw that the coolant reservoir was empty again. He got the container of antifreeze and ended up pouring the entire gallon in before it was visible in the bottom of the coolant tank. It was then that he noticed a steady drip of antifreeze coming from the bottom of the radiator and the front of the motor.

"Oh crap!"

Wherever the leak was, he knew now it was serious. Shaking his head with concern, Dawson climbed back in the truck, turned around and drove back to town. He pulled into a service station. A mechanic put the truck on a service rack and checked for the problem while Dawson waited outside. A few minutes later the man came out wiping his hands on a rag.

"Mister Lee. You have a cracked radiator. This is a new truck. It should still be under warranty. I hate to tell you but the nearest Ford service center in in Phoenix or Tucson."

Dawson absorbed the bad news a moment.

"What would it cost to fix the radiator?"

"It would be expensive. We don't have a radiator shop anywhere around here. The main problem is that all I could do is replace it. That could take several days just to get one in here. I would recommend you contact the Ford dealership and have them come get it."

Dazed and dismayed, Dawson thanked him. The mechanic topped off the radiator with water so Dawson could get it to the campground and park it at the trailer. By the time he got there it was running hot again. He quickly backed the truck into the parking spot before shutting it down.

"Looks like I might be here longer than I planned," he muttered as he unlocked the camper and went in. "At least I have my home on wheels."

CHAPTER 104

After brewing a pot of coffee and setting up the laptop, Dawson sat down and went online and looked up the nearest Ford Service Centers. He called and spoke to the service department of the one in Phoenix. Explaining his dilemma, the representative kindly arranged to have a tow truck come and pick his truck up. They would also bring a rental vehicle to him to use while his was being repaired. The representative could not give Dawson an estimate of time for the repairs until they had a chance to check the truck out.

"Well, nothing to do but wait," he said with a sigh.

Anxiety welled up in him as he pondered his quandary. He was not mad or particularly alarmed. It was just that he found that he did not like the idea of being out of control or helpless. This situation reminded him of when he was first in Walter Reed Hospital without the ability to get around on his own. He chuckled to himself and shook his head.

"I got through that. I can do this little inconvenience blind folded."

With nothing to do but wait for the tow truck. Dawson cleaned out his truck and then surveyed the cabinets and storage compartments of the camper. He ran across things that he had forgotten that he had brought along.

In one of the large outside entry storage compartment Dawson looked at the fishing gear, camping, and backpacking gear that he had brought and not used. There was nowhere to fish here but he had wondered what it would be like to hike out into the back country of the desert and camp. He looked out across the wide open expanse of desert before him and at the rough-hewn mountains and hills in the distance and thought of the possibility. It would be an adventure to do that, he surmised.

It was near noon when the tow truck operator called from the entrance to the campground. Dawson directed him to the campsite and stood in the road to watch for him. The tow truck was a roll-back type and on it sat a Ford SUV that Dawson would drive until his truck was repaired.

The driver unloaded the SUV, then loaded Dawson's truck and was soon gone. Dawson got in the SUV, looked it over and drove it to the grocery store. He filled the shopping list he had made earlier and drove back to the camper. After putting up the groceries and supplies he made a sandwich and a salad for lunch and sat down to eat. While eating he emailed his mother, Crucita, and Lianne with the news of his truck problems. He also sent several photos he had taken at Organ Pipe Cactus Monument.

Finished eating, Dawson put the scraps of bread in the bowl that had little salad left and sat it outside on the steps. From inside he watched for a while to see if the animal would come and get it. Nothing happened so he finally gave up and busied himself.

Later, Dawson decided to go for a drive and discovered the bowl he had placed outside was empty. He chuckled and put it back inside on the counter. He would try again later to catch a glimpse of the food bandit.

He loaded up the SUV and drove on to Organ Pipe Park. Since it was not too hot, he walked the 4.2 mile Victoria Mine Trail. It led to an old silver mine and back. When he reached the mine he took a break and sat under the shade of a fifteen foot tall organ pipe cactus that was estimated to be 80 years old.

Early evening had arrived when he made it back to Ajo. Instead of cooking, he opted to stop by a restaurant for dinner. When he got back to the camper, Dawson made a Bloody Mary and sat outside. He had bought a large bag of dry roasted peanuts at the store and ate on them as he sipped his cocktail.

The setting sun brought out beautiful shades of red, orange, and purple on and around the mountains off to the west. Dawson longed to trek to them and stand on top of one.

"Might just do that since I'm stuck here for a while."

He stepped back into the trailer to mix another drink. Out of the corner of his eye he caught a glimpse of brown fur at the table, and then in a flash it was gone. He looked out and around but saw no sign of the animal. The handful of peanuts that were lying on the table were gone.

Dawson laughed.

"Well my friend. Somehow we got to meet."

He sat out on the little patio area until well after dark but saw no more of the furry brown creature. It had disappeared so quickly that he did not have any opportunity to see what it might be.

At ten o'clock he had the laptop ready and waiting but received no login from Lianne. She had not answered his email either. He went to sleep praying she was all right.

CHAPTER 105

When morning came, Dawson had little desire to go exploring. His futile fretting about Lianne had made for a bad night of sleep. He had awakened off and on so many times that he lost count.

He got up, put the coffee on and took a shower. Dressed, he poured a cup of coffee and opened the front door. When he did, he saw a flash of fur scurry behind a large cluster of cholla cactus.

"Well now, good morning to you fellow! Let's see if we can get a look at you."

After propping the front door open, Dawson sat on the sofa and tossed several peanuts still in the shell out on the patio. By and by a creature with a light brown body a long white snout crept slowly toward the concrete pad. It had a long tail that bore faint rings, much like a raccoon's.

Dawson sat very still and watched as the animal quietly reached the pad. It quickly snatched the peanuts up in its mouth and retreated behind some ocotillo. He could see enough of the animal through the foliage that he could tell it was busy eating the nuts.

Tossing a few more peanuts out, the process was repeated. Dawson then eased onto the floor close to the open doorway. He tossed more nuts and sat still. The creature watched him a moment then eased up for another quick grab and withdraw to safety of cover.

Amazed, Dawson was quite taken by the animal. He had never seen anything like it. It distantly favored a raccoon but also reminded him of a ferret; a fat one at that. The animal was about the size of a large house cat. It was young and looked to weigh about ten pounds. Its face and nose looked longer and larger than a raccoon. Dawson was also able to see that along with the white nose it had a whitish colored belly.

"Got to get a better look," he whispered.

Slowly, not to spook the creature, Dawson got up and went inside. He cut pieces of honey dew melon and put them in a bowl. He also filled a bowl with water. Slowly, he descended the steps and sat the two bowls on the concrete pad a short distance from the steps. Careful not to make any sudden movements, Dawson sat back just inside the doorway.

All of a sudden the animal was at the bowl as if it had magically appeared. Dawson had been looking for it in the underbrush. Evidently it had been under the trailer. Warily it looked up at Dawson, crouched and ready to run at the first sign of danger.

Sitting as still as possible, Dawson watched the furry creature, rapt with fascination. Finally the critter sidled up by the bowl of melon chunks sniffing the sweet aroma. It then sat back on its haunches and began to eat. Dawson studied it intently.

From the side, the animal's nose reminded him of an aardvark he had seen, only in pictures. Its black feet were much the same as a raccoon's.

The odd looking animal finished the melon chunks, drank some water, licked its front paws with its tongue and stared at Dawson expectantly.

"Did you enjoy your meal?" Dawson asked softly.

The creature flinched at the sound of his voice but did not run. It continued to stare at him with intense intelligent eyes. Then, slowly it moved away and sauntered into the thicket of mesquite and disappeared.

"See you later fellow," Dawson called softly.

He collected the empty fruit bowl but slid the water bowl in the shade of the steps and closed the door. Ten minutes later he was frying up a pair of eggs and had bacon strips in the microwave. While eating he thought about the fascinating creature he had befriended.

"Oh man. I should have taken a picture of it!" he gushed.

Nodding his head, he made up his mind to do so when he saw it again.

"I'll take a picture of it and show it to the park ranger at Organ Pipe. I'm sure he can tell me what it is."

Later in the morning he called the Ford dealership in Phoenix. He learned that the truck had a defective radiator and leaking water pump. It would take a couple of days to fix it. He was told to call back in three days.

For some reason he was not all that thrilled to do anything other than stay around the camp. He finally took a walk around the campground while a pot of beef stew was warming up for lunch.

The nearest neighbor he had was three lots away, which suited Dawson fine. He encountered several adults and children who were staying in the campground. Most said hello and he spoke to them all as he walked. He stopped by the camp office and told the lady at the desk that he would be staying for at least another three or four days. She was friendly and told him to stay as long as he liked.

CHAPTER 106

The afternoon passed off without fanfare. Dawson spent the time sorting through the camping gear he had brought along. He packed and organized the large internal-frame backpack he had never used before. He had made up his mind to spend at least one night out in the desert far away from it all. It would be quite an experience to get a taste of what his ancestors experienced when they traveled through this barren landscape.

Not in the mood to cook he decided to go out for dinner. He showered, put on clean clothes and drove around looking for somewhere different to eat. He found a small restaurant with a bar that boasted great steaks. It was early so there were few people eating. Instead of taking up a table, he sat at the bar. He ordered a beer, a thick steak, potato logs and a salad.

He had just finished his salad and started on his steak when a woman sat on a stool beside him. She greeted the barkeeper by name and ordered a beer. Dawson looked up and nodded a hello. She smiled at him and nodded. He at first thought she was Hispanic, but the move he looked at her and listened to her talk to her friend, the bartender, he realized she was Native American. Her nose was broad but with her oval face, made her attractive. She had dark eyes that sparkled with cheerfulness. Her silken black hair hung to her waist. She was stout of build but still feminine and pleasing to the male eye. She wore little jewelry other than earrings and a wedding band. Dawson smiled when he noticed she was wearing cowboy boots, jeans, and a white western-style button-down shirt. Not the stereo-type of an Indian, he mused. She turned and smiled at him again.

"How's the steak?" she asked.

"Great!"

"Mind if I eat with you?"

"Of course not. It would be my pleasure!"

She turned to the barkeep.

"Judy, would you order me a steak like his?"

"Medium rare?" asked Judy.

"Yes."

"Coming right up."

The lady sat back and took a pull from her beer. She smiled at Dawson again and stuck out her hand.

"I'm Kay."

Dawson took her hand and introduced himself and said, "Nice to meet you."

"Same here. So, Dawson, where are you from?"

"You mean I don't look like I'm from here?" Feigning surprise.

She laughed.

"No you don't."

He groaned and held up his hands in supplication.

"Guess you're right."

"I know I am," she giggled. "I also know that you are staying in a nice new travel trailer at Belly Acres."

He looked at her curiously. She laughed.

"It's a small town. No secrets. Besides my friend Linda works at the campground office."

"Ah, I see," nodding appreciatively.

"So, what's your story Dawson Lee. What are you doing all by yourself and as far from everybody as you can get."

He shook his head and grinned.

"I'm very transparent, aren't I?"

She giggled.

"I'm Indian. We know these things. I can see a lot of sadness in you. You are either running to or away from something."

"Hmm. Not bad," he said, then took a bite of steak and thoughtfully chewed on it.

Kay's meal arrived and she began to eat. Dawson told her about the death of his father and that it had been his wish to visit Organ Pipe Cactus Monument. He talked about his wife and her work that currently had her in Afghanistan. A look of surprise lit up Kay's face.

"Your wife is in Afghanistan! My husband is stationed there right now. He is in the Army."

"My wife is reporting out of Kabul at the present time."

"How wild is this!" she exclaimed.

They laughed and talked about their lives as they ate. Dawson found Kay to be warm and outgoing. He felt comfortable around her and was certainly happy for the company.

Kay, whose name was Kayenta, was born and raised on the nearby Tohono O'odham reservation. She and her husband have two grown children. Dawson was surprised at this because he had guessed her to be in her mid to late twenties. Instead, she was closer to forty. Her husband was a reservist and had done one tour in Iraq and now had been almost a year in Afghanistan.

Dawson finished his meal and sat with Kay as she finished hers. They had another beer then he said he was going back to the campground.

"Would you mind if I come by for a visit with you? I have enjoyed talking to you Dawson. It's nice to find someone with their spouses in the same war."

"That would be great. Do you work?"

"No."

"How about coming over for breakfast? I know you're familiar with the land. I want to take an overnight hike out into the desert. Maybe you could give me some pointers and direct me to a good place to go."

She laughed and said, "Think twice about going. This land is unforgiving. Consider using a guide. We'll talk more about it tomorrow. I think I can make a good suggestion for you."

"Great then, thanks."

CHAPTER 107

There was still plenty of daylight when Dawson got back to the camper. He cut up more fruit and got the camera out. Sitting in the doorway, he tossed our chunks of fruit. After a few moments the wary furry creature skulked from under a creosote bush just off from the patio. It slowly crept up and ate the chunks of fruit.

When Dawson would toss more chunks, the animal would flinch, but did not run away. Dawson took several pictures of the creature then laid the camera down. He marveled at the unusual animal that stood only a few feet from him. Maybe Kay would know what it is, he thought to himself.

Slowly, Dawson eased his feet down on the first step. The creature stopped eating and stared at him. Dawson slid forward and eased down on the step and sat down. The animal backed up a ways. Its tail was raised and the end of it twitched, much like a cat.

Sliding down to the second and last step, Dawson got tickled when the furry critter started chirping and twitching its tail faster.

"Calm down fellow. I am a friend. I want to get to know you. I have lots of sweet fruit for you."

He laid the fruit in a pile less than two feet from where he sat, and then got still. The animal sniffed the air and watched Dawson for a moment. Grunting softly, it lowered its head and slowly crept toward the pile of fruit. When it climbed up onto the concrete pad the animal sat back on its haunches and looked at Dawson again. Sensing that maybe it was okay, the creature cautiously crawled over to the fruit and took a tentative bite.

Satisfied that no harm would come to it, the furry animal began to eat in earnest. After eating all of the fruit it sat back and licked its paws.

"You sure are the most outrageous and finest looking thing that I have ever seen, whatever you are." Dawson said softly.

To his surprise, the animal lowered its nose to the ground and placed it between its front paws. It stayed that way for a moment then backed up and sauntered back to the cover of the mesquite.

"Goodnight Buddy. I'll see you tomorrow."

Dawson set up the laptop and transferred the pictures of the animal from the camera to the hard drive. He was pleased with the photo of his new found creature.

"What are you my friend?" he asked again.

While waiting, with hopes that Lianne would come through, he thought about how good the day had turned out. He met a very pleasant lady and had a wonderful time talking to her. And, he had met his unusual little furry friend. Maybe tomorrow he could get even closer to it. He wondered if it would let him pet it, or maybe eat out of his hand.

A flood of relief washed over him when Lianne came online. He saw her wonderful smile.

"Hey Sweetie! How are you?" she asked, brightly.

"I am fine now that I'm with you. You look great."

"I'm happy to see you Dawson. I could not get through to you yesterday. The cell phone would not go through either. But anyway, here we are at last. So, tell me what you have been doing? Oh yeah, I got the desert photograph from Organ Pipe National Cactus Monument. They are absolutely lovely, postcard perfect. You will have to take me there one day."

"Gladly."

Dawson told her about the strange animal he was getting to know. He told her about meeting and dining with Kay. He also told her that Kay's husband was stationed there in Kabul.

"Get his name and unit. I will try to locate him. Maybe I can arrange a call to Kay for him."

"I'm sure she would appreciate that. I am supposed to get with her tomorrow. She is going to help me arrange an overnight trek to the desert backcountry. She mentioned helping me get a guide."

"That sounds a little dangerous, traipsing off into the desert. Promise me that you will be very careful."

Dawson laughed.

"This is nothing compared to where you are right now."

"It's not so bad. Not like it was when you were over here."

"I'm happy to hear that. I want you back home safe and sound as soon as possible."

"Looking forward to that day. When I do come back I am taking a vacation. I plan to stay right under you so long that you will want to sign me up for an assignment far off just so you can get some rest."

"Hmm. Fat chance for that, but, it sounds like you miss me!"

"You bet I do! Its times like this that I really do realize just what we have and how much I love you."

"I like the way you talk."

"That's my line Dawson Lee!"

CHAPTER 108

Expecting Kay at 7:30 a.m., Dawson was up at seven and had just finished brewing a pot of coffee. He poured a cup and was sitting on the patio when she drove up. He walked to her truck to greet her.

"Good morning Dawson. Lovely day, isn't it?"

"It sure is. Come on in."

He showed Kay around the travel trailer and poured her some coffee.

"This certainly is a nice little home on wheels you have here. Looks like you have everything you need."

"Yep, pretty much. My dad did a great job when he chose this one. It's actually more than I need."

The two quickly fell into a comfortable sync while cooking breakfast together. Dawson set the dinette table as Kay began loading their plates with eggs, sausages, hash browns, and biscuits.

They enjoyed chatting while eating. Dawson had the television on low and turned to CNN. During the meal he glanced up and saw Lianne giving a report.

"There she is!" he said, pointing to the television.

"Who?" asked Kay.

She stared at the news report a second and let out a gasp of surprise. "That's Lianne Palmer-Lee!" Her eyes flew wide opened. "For gosh sakes, I didn't connect you two. I can't believe I am having breakfast with her husband. I have been a fan of hers for a long time. She is such a wonderful reporter."

"I agree with you there. She is quite a lady!'

"How did you get so lucky to find her? I don't think it has been that long ago that she changed to Palmer-Lee."

"We've been married about a year now. We happened to meet in Afghanistan, of all places. I was stationed there then."

Kay sat back with her mouth open in amazement.

"We all sure have a lot in common, don't we?"

"Yes we do, and I certainly am happy we met."

"Me too. I can't wait to write Walter about meeting you."

"Oh yeah. I talked to Lianne last night. She said if I will email her your husband's name and unit, she will try to contact him and say hello for you."

"That would be great. He will be surprised and honored to meet Lianne."

"All right then. After breakfast we'll email her. You can send him a message too."

They finished eating then Kay helped him wash the dishes. He went online and emailed Lianne and let Kay type in a message for her husband. Dawson started to shut the computer down when he finished, but a thought came to him. He snapped his finger.

"Oh, while I've got the computer on, let me show you a picture of an animal that's been coming around. I have been feeding it and I am mystified by what it is."

When Dawson brought the photograph up, Kay started laughing.

"Why that's a coati!"

"Huh?"

"A coati. It's in the raccoon family. You don't see many of them around here. They are just a varmint, nothing special."

"Well, I like this one. It's neat."

She giggled.

"You can't find anything better for a pet?" she chided, grinning.

"I've got a great cat at home!"

"So, you are an animal lover?"

"Yep, I am."

"Me too. Where is the little beggar now?"

"It's usually nearby. Let's see if we can get it to come for a visit."

Dawson reached in the refrigerator and pulled out a bag of seedless white grapes and put them in a bowl. He and Kay went out on the patio and sat down. Dawson tossed a few grapes near the mesquite thicket. Soon the coati appeared and started eating. Each time he tossed a grape, Dawson threw it shorter so to bring the animal closer to them.

The coati got within six feet of them and stopped. It sat back and stared at them. It then lowered its snout and stuck it between its paws.

"I wonder why it's doing that." Dawson asked in a whisper. "It did that yesterday."

"That's a submissive posture. She's being friendly to you."

Dawson looked at Kay askance.

"She?" he queried.

"Yes, the females have a smaller nose and teeth. Males are usually much larger than this one, so I'm sure it's a female."

The coati rose up again and looked at them expectantly. It chirped and held its nose to the ground and its tail aloft.

Kay turned to Dawson and whispered, "Let me have the grapes."

He handed her the bowl. To his surprise, Kay got out of the chair and eased down on her knees.

"Watch this," she whispered.

CHAPTER 109

The coati stepped back when Kay eased off the concrete pad by the camper. Remaining on her knees, she began to make soft clucking sounds and whispering something in a language that Dawson did not recognize. The animal started moving toward her, its tail up and nose lowered.

It only took a few seconds for the coati to cover the short distance to Kay's outstretched hand, then she stuck out the other. It first sniffed one palm up hand, then the other. Kay gingerly reached into the bowl between her legs and pulled out some grapes. The coati sniffed then began eating them out of her hand.

Dawson was further amazed when Kay started rubbing the coati's head and back. Kay soon settled down cross-legged and the coati eased up into her lap. Continuing to softly woo the animal, Kay coddled and petted it as if the coati were a baby.

She turned and smiled at Dawson. Slowly, Kay stood up, still cradling the coati in her arms and walked to him.

"Would you like to hold her?"

"Yes, what do I do?" he asked softly.

"Let me ease her down into your lap first."

She did.

"Now, rub her head. Scratch behind her head and under her chin. She likes that. Don'cha girl?"

The coati responded to his fingers with gratifying grunts. Dawson caressed her fur. The upper part of her back coat was a little stiff compared to her sides and belly. She was silky soft there.

Rotating around in Dawson's lap, the coati then rolled over on to her back so he could scratch her belly. She laid her head in the crook of his arm and looked up at him, her eyes glazed over with ecstasy. Dawson was completely in awe.

"Tsk, tsk. What a sight!" chortled Kay.

"Isn't she something?"

Kay giggled.

"You are a strange one Mister Lee. I think the desert sun has baked your brain. You are in love with a trash eater!" she chirped playfully.

Dawson laughed.

"But, you have to admit, she is a little darling."

She shook her head and smiled.

"You are a trip!"

Dawson fed the coati the rest of the grapes and held her a while longer. He gently put her down and stood up. The creature looked up at him with an expectant expression.

"I guess you're still a hungry girl. Let me see what we can find."

He stepped up into the trailer where Kay had already gone to find more fruit. The coati climbed to the top of the steps and peeked in. She then gingerly climbed up into the camper and hunkered down just inside the doorway.

"Well, well. Look at that!" Dawson said. When he happened to look down.

"Looks like you have a permanent friend now. You know I think she must have been someone's pet. Females usually travel in groups. Males are the ones who are solitaire. You're not going to be able to get rid of her. It's like feeding a stray dog. She will keep coming back."

"That's fine with me. I'd like to keep her if I can figure out how to take her with me."

Kay laughed and shook her head.

"Here pretty girl," Dawson cooed as he sat a bowl of cut up apples and bananas down on the floor.

While his furry friend ate, Dawson and Kay sat at the dinette with fresh cups of coffee. They talked more about his desire to venture into the back country of the desert and camp for a night or two. She warned him again about the dangers of going alone since he had no experience in desert survival other than limited training he had in the military.

"Kay, you mentioned that you could help me find a guide. Would you mind doing that? I would really like to do this."

"Not at all. How long do you want to stay out there?"

"A day and a night should be enough to get a good feel for it. But, if a guide has something longer in mind, I'm game for it."

"Okay then. Sounds good. When would you like to do it?"

"The sooner, the better. I'm stranded here while my truck is being repaired. So, I could go on short notice if needed."

"Let me make some calls and I'll get back with you. I'll try to call you back later today if I can."

"Sure thing Kay. I really appreciate your help with this."

They exchanged phone numbers. Kay said she needed to go. While the two had been talking, the coati ate the fruit then began exploring the camper. She slinked around nervously, carefully and occasionally looked back at the doorway for a quick exit if necessary.

Dawson walked Kay out to her truck and thanked her again and said goodbye.

Walking back to the camper, he slowly went in and sat down on the sofa. He watched the coati as she sniffed and peered around and under everything. Dawson laughed when she hopped up on the counter and almost slid off the slick surface. The coati looked at Dawson a moment as if she were checking to see if it was okay for her to be there.

Sensing that things were all right, the coati then hopped to the top bunk nearby. After looking around a moment she lay down and peeked over the edge of the mattress. She looked at Dawson then let out a soft sigh, making herself comfortable. Dawson shook his head and smiled.

While the coati watched from on high, Dawson went online and looked up the animal he was intrigued with. He learned indeed that the coati was in the raccoon family. Their habitat ranged from Central America to Southern Arizona. The diurnal mammals like to eat fruit and small vertebrate prey. Dawson also learned that in South and Central America they were commonly kept as pets. They could be litter trained but the article warned that they could be difficult to control or train. He looked up at the Coati on the bunk and smiled. She was apparently asleep.

"I think you are an exception to the rule girl. I wonder how you would like living in Georgia?" he whispered.

The wheels were turning in his head. He wondered how the coati would do traveling in the truck.

CHAPTER 110

"Well, well. I see you peeking at me pretty girl!" Dawson said, standing at the counter making two salads.

The coati had been asleep on the top bunk at the front of the camper. She sat up and cocked her head from side to side watching him with curiosity.

"I guess you're hungry too, huh?"

She stood up and stuck her snout over the side of the bunks sniffing.

"I thought you might like to have a fresh garden salad with me. It has tomatoes, cucumbers, and green onions in it. I'll leave the Italian dressing off of yours, okay?"

The coati looked at him, gave a little chirp and crouched to make a jump for the counter.

"Whoa girl. Let me help you. We don't want salad all over the place."

He reached up and eased her into his arms. After hugging and petting the coati, he sat it down on the vinyl floor. He washed his hands and went back to preparing the salads. His little friend stood up on her hind legs and sniffed.

"Hang on just a second longer and I'll have yours ready girl."

After sprinkling some croutons on top, Dawson sat the bowl down along with another filled with water. She went to work on it immediately. The coati would eat a few bites then look up at Dawson with bright cheery eyes that seemed to radiate trust and adoration for him. He chuckled at himself for thinking he could read her emotions.

Along with his salad, Dawson made himself a ham sandwich and cut it into four pieces, put them on a saucer and placed them beside her salad bowl. She sniffed the sandwich then wolfed it down. Dawson laughed as he watched her licking mayonnaise off of her front paws.

"I guess Kay is right. You'll eat just about anything!"

The coati looked up at him and let out a series of chirps and grunts. He wondered if she was laughing along with him.

She ate all of her food and drank from the water bowl, then sat back and stared at Dawson while he ate. He finished and gathered all of the dishes and sat them on the counter to be washed.

"We might need to go outside now girl. I'm sure you could probably use a restroom break."

He opened the door and stepped down to the patio. The coati followed him obediently. She looked up at him when he sat down on the lounge chair.

"Go ahead girl. Take a potty break."

She turned and strolled out a short distance to a patch of sand. The coati looked back at Dawson then started scratching out a hole. She squatted and stared back at him. He could not help but laugh at her. She had her long mouth hanging open as if she was grinning with relief.

"You know girl, I have a feeling that you would easily take to a litter box. I'll have to see about finding one for you. I need to go to the grocery store and buy more fruit and stuff for you to eat."

Dawson went back in and got a pad and pen. He started making a grocery list of items that he thought the coati might like. When he finished, he went back to the door and looked out. She was nowhere to be seen. He pulled the door to and stepped into the bathroom to use the toilet. There was a noise coming from outside. It took Dawson a moment to realize the coati was scratching at the door. He started laughing when he heard her chirping and snorting.

As soon as he opened the door she hopped up into the camper, looked around, then sat down and looked at him.

"Girl, what am I going to do with you?"

He chuckled and picked her up. Cuddling her, he sat down and held her like a baby.

"I need to go to the store girl. I don't think it would be a good idea to take you with me this time. I'm not sure if I should leave you here inside while I am gone either. We'll try it after I get you a litter box."

He put her down and got ready to go. Opening the door, she followed him out again. He had a handful of peanuts and laid them on the concrete pad. She sniffed them and started eating on one. Dawson walked to the SUV and opened the door and got in. When he cranked the engine the coati looked up at him and then scampered to the vehicle. She sat up on her hind legs mewing and keening.

"Oh my goodness!"

Dawson felt like his heart was going to break. Shaking his head, he opened the driver's door. The coati came over and looked up into the vehicle. When he reached for her she backed away. He looked at her for a moment, unsure what to do.

Closing the car door, he put the SUV in reverse and eased back and out into the road. The coati sat watching him, her tail aloft and twitching nervously. Putting the vehicle in drive, he slowly rolled down the street. She sat at the end of the driveway staring at him forlornly. Dawson felt like he was abandoning her as he drove away. He was amazed at how much she had come to mean to him in such a short time.

CHAPTER 111

At the grocery store Dawson picked out a variety of fruit for the coati. He found the pet supply section and chose two pet dishes and litter pan, plus a large bag of cat litter. He then looked at the pet food and decided to try a bag of Meow Mix cat food. If the coati would eat cat food, it would be a plus when he got back home. He chuckled at the thought of seeing Max and the coati together.

"Looks like somebody has a new cat!" said Kay from behind him.

Dawson spun around, saw her and smiled.

"Yeah, something like that."

She laughed.

"That four-legged garbage disposal has got you hooked!"

"Yep, she does. She cried when I left her sitting in the driveway a minute ago."

"Awe, she'll be fine. You can't get rid of her now. Like I said, she's like a stray dog. Feed them once and they won't leave."

"I hope so."

She giggled.

"Say, what are you doing after you leave here?"

"I guess I'll head back to the campground."

"How about meeting me over at the bar for a drink? We can talk about your camping trip."

"You found a guide for me?"

"Yes I did. I'll tell you all about it if you'll buy me a beer."

"You got it. But first I'll need to drop these groceries off at the camper. Some of this needs to be refrigerated."

"Don't worry about that. Tell the cashier to bag all of that separate and Judy will put it in the cooler while we visit."

"Sure, if you think she won't mind."

"She won't mind at all."

Both finished their shopping, checked out, and Dawson followed Kay to the little restaurant and bar. Kay took his bag of fruit and meat inside. Judy, the bartender, put them in the beer cooler.

Dawson ordered beers for both of them and they relaxed at the bar and chatted with Judy for a few minutes. She then left them to talk while she waited on some other customers. The chilled air of the bar and the ice cold beer felt good as Dawson took a long pull from the bottle.

"Okay, what have you got for me as a trek and a guide?" he asked.

"All right. Here's a plan for a two night desert adventure. Your guide would take you out into the back country in the late afternoon when it starts to cool down some. It's too hot to do much hiking in the middle of the day. Anyway, you would hike a couple of miles and set up camp before dark at the base of a mountain. There at camp there will be a small water source to replenish your supply. Also, there is a cave there to explore. It was used for Indian ceremonies in ancient times. Then, the next morning you would trek up into the mountains and spend the night on top of one. The next morning you would hike back out and get in before it gets too hot. How does that sound?"

Dawson nodded thoughtfully.

"Sounds good to me. How much will it cost and who will be my guide?"

She grinned.

"You won't find a better deal. All it will cost is the food for the guide."

"Wow! That is a good deal. Who will take me?"

"You're looking at her!" she said, holding her hands up in the air.

Dawson's eyes squinted with delight. He grinned at her.

"Are you serious?" he asked.

"Yes I am. I know this country as good as anybody. I want to see that you get your wish to experience a real desert, and it will be one that you will surely remember. This land is unforgiving, but there is a beauty that takes a special eye to see. I know that you are one who will appreciate it."

"Well now. I thank you for your vote of confidence in me. When do you want to do this?"

"How about tomorrow afternoon? The hike I propose will take about three hours to get to where we will camp."

"Okay then, I'll have everything ready."

They went over what all equipment and trail foods he had. Kay indicated that she had her own backpacking gear so the two had everything covered that they would need.

Dawson drove back to the campground feeling good and with a smile on his face. He was looking forward to the trip. As knowledgeable as Kay was, he knew it would be a wonderful learning experience.

When he pulled onto the driveway and parked, the coati came rambling out of the mesquite thicket and met him at the door. She traipsed in as if she owned the place. Dawson filled her new pet dishes, one with water and the other with cat food. She sniffed the Meow Mix then began eating it with a look of satisfaction.

Dawson put up the groceries, took a shower, and slipped on shorts and a t-shirt. When he came out of the bathroom the coati had climbed back up to the top bunk and laid down. She watched him as he opened a beer and popped a bag of microwave popcorn. He then settled down on the sofa and watched CNN, hoping to catch a glimpse of Lianne.

CHAPTER 112

Captivated by the coati, Dawson sat at the dinette table watching it sleep. He had taken a picture of it curled up on the top bunk asleep, one of its front legs hanging over the side.

While he still had the laptop on, he emailed his mother, Crucita, and Lianne with pictures of his new furry friend. Still excited, he decided to call Crucita and talk to her. She answered on the first ring and was happy to hear from him. He told her to turn the home computer on and take a look at the pictures he had sent.

They talked while she booted up the computer and went online. She was telling him about Max catching a bird and bringing it into the house and letting it go. Dawson laughed as she described her antics of trying to catch the bird and getting it out of the house without Max getting to it first.

"Okay, I'm opening the attachments now," she said.

"Good, what do you see?"

"Some kind of animal. What is it?"

"A coati. It's kind of like a raccoon."

"Oh yes. I have seen some from a distance where we lived in Mexico, but never up close."

"This one is friendly. I can pet it and hold it."

"Oh wow! I see the picture where it is on your bed in the camper. My goodness, what a strange looking thing!"

"Yeah, but it's really neat."

"What are you going to do with it?"

"I'm thinking of trying to bring it home."

"Do you think that's a good idea?"

"I don't know but I sure am taken with it. She is so sweet. How do you think Max would like having her for a playmate?"

She laughed.

"I don't think Max would be happy with competition in the house."

"Yeah, you're probably right, but I think he would get over it, don't you?"

"I guess so. What about Mrs. Lianne? Do you think she would go for it?"

I don't know. I just sent her the pictures of it when I sent yours. I'll spring it on her the next time we talk, which hopefully will be tonight."

"How are you going to get that thing home?"

"I haven't figured that out yet. Maybe I can get a pet carrier and keep her in it."

"Is it legal to have a wild animal like that?"

"You know, I have no idea. I'll worry about that when and if I get it home."

She snickered.

"You are a big hearted man, Dawson."

"Yeah, I know. I'm an old softie for a pretty face."

She laughed again.

"You call that pretty?" She chirped brightly.

"How dare you talk about my pretty little coati girl!" he chided merrily.

"I'm surprised you don't have a name for the little runt yet."

"I'm working on it. And, she's not a runt. She's a little princess."

"Dawson Lee, I think you have been out in the sun too long. The desert heat can do strange things to you."

"Well, if I can get her home, I will guarantee that you will fall in love with her too."

"Hmm, we shall see. But, I don't think Max will approve."

"There is enough room there for two pets. He'll just have to get over it."

"Lord help us! I can't wait to hear what Mrs. Lianne has to say about it," she chortled.

"My goodness, you're right. I better work on my sales pitch. If she's harder to sell than you, then I'm in trouble."

Crucita laughed a moment, and then fell silent.

"You know Dawson. This is the happiest I have known you to be since your father passed away. If making a pet out of that furry thing makes you happy, then bring her home. We all love you Dawson. We want you to be happy because you make us happy with your love. You are my second Dad and I love you very much."

Dawson's eyes misted over. It took a moment for him to find his voice.

"I love you too, Crucita. Lianne and I think of you as our daughter too. Since we can't have children, we want to be a part of your children's lives, either as extra grandparents or as godparents. It doesn't matter as long as we can spend time with them and spoil them rotten, and then send them home to you."

She laughed.

"Now who says I'm getting married and having children? What if I want to work for you and Lianne from now on?"

"Oh but Crucita, you are so beautiful. Mister Right is just around the corner. You will meet him one day and you will get to feel and know what I feel with Lianne."

"That's so sweet Dawson. I just hope whoever I find is just like you!"

"You mean you want a guy with a pet coati?"

She giggled.

"No coati."

CHAPTER 113

Sitting at the dinette table going over the list of backpacking supplies and equipment for the hiking trip, Dawson heard a soft plop. The coati had dropped to the floor from the top bunk. She stretched and yawned, then sidled up to him.

"Hey girl, have a good nap? Now that you are awake, let me set the litter box up for you and see if you will take to it."

He opened the bag of cat litter and poured half of it in the litter pan. The coati watched on with interest. She then sniffed the litter, stepped over into the pan with her front paws. After scratching around a moment she then climbed on into the pan and squatted. She did her business, covered it up and hopped out.

"Good girl! Excellent job. Now I won't have to worry about you staying inside."

Putting the remaining cat litter in the cabinet, he then went outside and retrieved the tent and sleeping bag from the street side storage compartment. The coati followed him, watching every move he made. He stopped and smiled at her.

"I tell you what, let's you and I go for a walk around the park. We'll work up an appetite for dinner."

The sun was getting low on the horizon. The air was cooling and comfortable as they walked along the campground streets. The coati trotted and loped along beside him or would lag behind then scurry to catch up with him. When they would pass other campers, the two would get curious stares and several, "What it the world is that?" questions. Most would come out to have a look at the coati. She took if all with self-assurance, but staying right beside her master.

When they made it back to camp, Dawson decided to try to acclimate the coati to riding in a vehicle. He opened the driver's side door and sat inside without cranking the engine. The coati reared up and poked her head inside, sniffed around then hopped up onto the floorboard. He watched her as she climbed over, under, and around throughout the front and back of the vehicle. She then stretched out on the passenger seat, looking at Dawson with curious eyes.

Seeing that she appeared comfortable, he rolled the driver's side window down and pulled the door to, under his arm. She flinched when the door clicked shut but stayed put. He then cranked the engine. The coati stood for a moment then hunkered down, looking warily around.

"Come on over here girl. It's okay," he said in a soothing voice.

She cautiously crept across the console and onto his lap.

"See there," he said, petting her. "Everything is all right girl, nothing to be afraid of."

Putting the SUV into gear, he backed out into the road and slowly drove around the campground. The coati looked around nervously but remained in his lap. He made a loop around the campground and parked.

"Good girl," he said softly.

Dawson sat a few minutes soothing and petting the coati. They then got out and went inside the camper. He made dinner and the two ate then settled in for the night. Excited about the coati and the upcoming hiking trip, he hoped Lianne would log in at ten so he could show her his furry friend and let her know he would be gone for a few days.

Kay called and went over her list of things needed for the hike. After comparing notes it was clear that they would be well prepared for the desert adventure.

"Where will we leave from?" he asked.

"Since you thought Organ Pipe was so nice, I thought I would take you to a place that touches on Organ Pipe and the reservation. It will almost be into Mexico too. The hills and mountains there are splendid. Other than Mexicans slipping across the border through there, very few outsiders have ever been there. If you were not with me, you would not be allowed to go into this sacred area."

"Wow! I feel honored to get to do this with you. I really appreciate it."

"I think you will get a lot out of this Dawson. The land is so special and beautiful in a rugged way."

"Good deal. I hope that Lianne will contact me tonight so I can talk to her before being gone for two days. I worry about her."

"I understand perfectly. I worry about Walter. Each day I look for a letter from him. When I see that envelope, I know he is okay."

"Maybe Lianne will get a chance to visit him soon. If she gets in touch with him and can do a video visit, would you mind coming over at ten o'clock to talk to him?"

"Of course not. I'm usually up to at least eleven or twelve."

"All right then. When we can get it worked out I'll let you know. Oh yes, before I forget. Why don't you plan on coming over for a late lunch before we start out for the trip?"

"Can do. I'll be happy to."

She paused.

"By the way, how's the critter doing?"

"She's great. She took to the litter box and loves Meow Mix. We went for a nice walk around the campground together. I even took her for a ride in the SUV. She's not crazy about it but she did okay."

"You're amazing Dawson. You are hard up for company!"

He laughed.

"Maybe so, but she's a great gal."

"What do you plan to do with her while you're gone?"

"Well, I thought she might tag along."

Kay broke out in laughter.

"You know, I figured as much. You are sure enough in love with that garbage gobbler!"

"Now, now. That's my baby you're talking about!"

"How do you think she'll do?"

"I think she'll stay right with us."

"Let's hope so. If she gets lost, we'll never find her."

She laughed.

"You're probably right."

CHAPTER 114

Sitting at the table in front of the laptop, he watched the program as it loaded in and got ready to receive Lianne's login if she was able to get through. Feeling anxious to hear from her, Dawson was drinking a Bloody Mary to calm his nerves. He made a series of wet rings on the table with the condensation dripping down the sides of the icy cold glass. It was ten after ten and his anxiety level was rising.

Sensing his unease, the coati climbed up onto Dawson's lap and laid her head against his chest. He smiled and scooped her up into his arms as one would a small child. Scratching around her neck, she made small grunts of ecstasy that made him laugh and eased his tension.

Finally, the computer program alerted him that Lianne had logged in. He felt relief tumble over him like a tidal wave. Then, in a flash, there she was, all smiles and as beautiful as ever.

"Thank goodness I got through to you," she gushed, with relief in her voice.

"Yeah, I was beginning to get worried that we would not connect tonight. I tried your cell phone and could not get the call to go through."

"I tried too. But, thankfully were together now. I'm so happy to see you Dawson. I sure miss you."

"Same here."

"Now, tell me about this weird looking creature you found."

"Well, let me introduce you." He held up the coati. "Say hello to your new mom."

Dawson took the coati's leg and waggled it at Lianne.

"Eeeuuuuh! That thing looks like an ant eater!"

"Well, I think she's a distant cousin to them."

Lianne laughed.

"What in the world are you going to do with that thing?"

"Umm, well... I kind of been thinking about bringing her home with me so Max will have a playmate."

She squealed and guffawed.

"That ugly thing will scare Max to death!"

Dawson put his hands over the coati's ears.

"Don't call her ugly. You'll hurt her feelings."

"Oh my word. You've been out in the desert too long!"

"Harrumph! That's that same thing Crucita and Mom said."

"Well duh! You should listen to them," she said and laughed.

"Seriously Lianne. What do you think about me bringing this little sweet thing home? She's litter trained already and eats cat food. And, anything else you give her. One thing for sure, she would be one of a kind back home."

"Goodness, I hope so!"

"Is that a yes?" he asked, a pleading look on his face.

Lianne giggled and smiled at Dawson.

"What am I going to do with you, Dawson Lee?"

He looked at her with eyes of hope and said, "Never let me go."

"Hmm. That's a given."

"I like that answer."

"So, have you named that thing yet?"

"No, I guess I need to. Any suggestions?"

"How about Ugly Betty?"

"Nope!"

"Thing?"

"No way."

"Cousin It?"

"Nuh-unh!"

"Oh, I got the perfect name. How about Amydee?"

Dawson's eyebrows puckered his eye wide open with mock surprise.

"Why Lianne Palmer-Lee. I cannot believe you said that!" he said tartly, trying not to laugh.

She snickered.

"I can't either. It just came out. I'm sorry."

"Sure you are!" grinning. "You very well see that this little doll here is much too pretty to be compared with Amydee."

Lianne giggled.

"Remind me to never let you go to the eye doctor."

"You've said that before. Anyway, my vision is just fine, thank you very much. I see how beautiful you are, especially your red hair and green eyes.

"Dawson Lee, just wait until I get my hands on you."

"I can't wait."

Her voice quaked for a second. She cleared her throat and wiped a tear.

"I really, really miss you, Dawson."

"Me too, you."

"I am happy you found your strange little pet. If she makes you happy then I'm all for you bringing it home."

"You'll love her too when you get to meet her."

She smiled at Dawson with pure love in her heart.

"All jokes aside, I'm sure I will too. I'm not sure how Max will feel, but it will all work out."

Dawson went on to ask about Kay's husband. Lianne said she had not gotten to locate him yet, promising to do so in the next day or two. He then told her about the two day back country trek with Kay as his guide.

"I'm happy to hear she's going to guide you. I did not care for the idea of you roaming around in the desert alone."

"Kay really is an interesting lady. She grew up on the Indian reservation near here and knows all about the country around here. I am looking forward to this trip."

"Well, be very careful. I'll check off and on with my cell phone and see if I can get through. Maybe by chance you will be in cell range sometimes. If not, I will try to contact you online in three nights. Regardless, I will email you. If I meet up with Kay's husband I will email you. I'll try to video a message from him and send it to you for her."

"Thank you. Anything you can do will be appreciated."

"Dawson."

"Yes."

"Don't find anymore weird creatures to bring home."

"I'll try not to."

CHAPTER 115

Just after dawn the quietude of the little travel trailer was broken by a dull thump, lapping noises, and then crunching sounds. In the semidarkness Dawson could make out the coati at the food bowl.

"Good morning sweetie. Sleep good?"

She turned and looked at him and made a series of chirpy greetings, then resumed eating. Dawson got tickled listening to the crunching. When he would breakout in laughter the coati would stop and stare at him, then go back to eating when he stopped.

Wide awake now, Dawson got on up and started the coffee brewing. He started for the bathroom to take a shower when his cell phone rang. Very unusual to get a call so early, he quickly grabbed it and clicked it on.

"Hello?"

"Dawson."

"Lianne! Everything all right?" he asked, with alarm in his voice.

"I'm fine. Everything is okay. Sorry to worry you. I need for you to see if you can get Kay to be there at the computer with you in, say, about an hour. I'm going to log on and I will have Sergeant Benecome with me so they can visit. How's that?"

"Great! Let me call her now. If you don't get a call right back from me then you will know she is on her way here."

"Okay, great. We're heading to the base now. He knows I'm coming and is waiting. I'll get back with you shortly."

"All right. I love you so much."

"I love you too."

He said good bye, filled with excitement. It was a nice surprise to hear Lianne's voice again. Kay answered and he could tell she had still been asleep.

"Kay, this is Dawson. I am sorry to call so early but if you would like to talk to your husband on the video cam program, Lianne will have him online in about an hour."

"Whoo hoo! I'll be there in thirty, bye."

Dawson laughed when he clicked off. It felt good to be able to do something special for her and her husband. He could truly relate to the heartache of miles of separation, especially when one was in a war zone.

"Well girl, we've got company coming."

The coati looked up and chirped. She looked back at her food dish then up to him hopefully.

"All right," he chuckled. "A little more. We have a big day ahead of us."

He poured more cat food for the coati, then took a quick shower and dressed. In the middle of pouring his first cup of coffee he heard Kay pull up. He set out another cup, filled it and opened the door for her. The coati stuck her head out and chirped repeatedly when she saw it was Kay.

"For gosh sakes! I guess you've moved in to stay," said Kay as she walked up to the door and picked up the coati.

"Come on in," called Dawson while booting up the laptop. "I have you a fresh cup of coffee ready."

Kay stepped in, still cradling the coati. She kissed Dawson on the cheek.

"I'm so excited to get to see and talk to Walter. I can't thank you and Lianne enough for this!"

She put the coati down and sat at the table and sipped her coffee. The coati let out a few grunts then went outside. Dawson watched her disappear into the scrub brush. He felt confident that she would return soon, but then again, he wondered why he felt a twinge of anxiety.

He and Kay sipped coffee and waited for Lianne to log in. Kay was trembling with excitement.

"Here it comes!" exclaimed Dawson, as the program began to click and beep. The connection was made and Lianne's face and lovely smile filled the screen.

"Hey Dawson, is she there?"

"Yes she is."

Dawson turned the laptop to the camera was on Kay.

"Hello Kay Benecome. How are you?" asked Lianne.

Kay was speechless for a second, but quickly recovered and replied, "I am fine, thank you. I'm so pleased to meet you Lianne. I am a big fan of yours."

"Why thank you! Now, I have a big fan of yours who wants to say hello."

Lianne moved aside and Kay's husband sat down in front of the camera. He was a handsome man with dark obsidian eyes and a warm smile.

"Hello Kayenta," he said, his voice cracking with emotion.

"Walter, my Walter…."

Kay broke down in tears of joy. She struggled to check her emotions. It took a moment for the two to settle down before they could talk. Dawson eased outside and sat in the shade so Kay could have some privacy. Several minutes went by before she appeared at the door.

"Lianne wants to speak to you before she ends the visit."

Dawson went in and talked to her a few minutes. They said goodbye with plans to connect in three days.

When he shut the computer down, the coati came bounding in the camper and headed to the water dish. Kay thanked Dawson over and over for the special visit with her husband. She hugged him then went back home to get ready for the hiking trip.

"I'll see you for lunch."

CHAPTER 116

During the morning after Kay left and before she returned to have lunch with him, Dawson worked on getting the coati used to riding in the Explorer. He took her on several short rides around town. She did so well on the last ride that he stopped at a service station and filled the SUV while she watched from the car's window.

For lunch Dawson had prepared a hearty lasagna and salad. He, Kay, and the coati ate their fill then left out for the Tohono O'odham Indian Reservation. Since Kay knew the territory, Dawson had her drive. He had planned to have the coati sit in his lap, but shortly after they got underway she made herself comfortable in the back seat, spending her time staring out the window.

Kay drove from Ajo to Why then picked up high way 86, taking them on to the reservation. After several miles she turned south and they passed through the small reservation town of Gu Vo. They continued on until reaching a remote, desolate area near the Mexican border, adjacent to Organ Pipe Cactus National Monument.

When they parked, Kay placed a reservation placard and a note on the dash of the Explorer explaining their purpose for parking there. She told Dawson that many illegals and drug smugglers crossed the border near where they were. She said they could possibly encounter the border patrol at any time while they were out.

"A border patrol helicopter or plane may spot us and check us out.   Nothing to worry about. The best thing we can do if we see illegal's is to stay clear of them. But, I will tell you now, I would help someone in distress as long as they are not drug smugglers. Many of them are dangerous and unpredictable."

"I understand. I know me and if I can help someone in need, I will."

Kay laughed.

"That's an understatement for you! Look at what you took in." Pointing at the coati.

"Hey now, I think it was the other way around. She took me in."

"Hmm. You have a point there." She put a wide-brimmed hat on. "All right. Let's get started."

Both donned their backpacks and started out across a pristine landscape that seemed foreboding and enticing at the same time. Kay led the way following what appeared to be old trails either made by animals or humans. Dawson could not tell which it was. The coati trotted right along beside him. At times she would pause, sniff the air, then scamper off into the mesquite or paloverde thickets and disappear. She was never gone for more than a few minutes before she would reappear, often times in unexpected places.

At first appearance, the desert landscape was gently rolling and stark. However, Dawson quickly found that looks were deceiving. There were numerous arroyos, or dry washes, that they had to negotiate around or through.

Dotting the desert were large numbers of saguaro cacti, many of them as much as thirty or forth feet tall. Kay told Dawson that a saguaro only an inch tall might be ten years old. The forty or so feet tall ones were as much a two hundred years old.

Many of the cacti they saw were in bloom, adding splashes of color to the otherwise muted land. Kay stopped at a large organ pipe cactus which she said is a relative of the saguaro. She pointed out several nodules on the cactus that were flowering buds that opened at night and closed early in the morning she promised to show him some in bloom that night.

"Below the flower buds at the base is its fruit. It is said to taste like your watermelon you have in the south. Our people sometimes harvest them to make medicines."

Kay's knowledge of the land was impressive. She taught Dawson many things about the harsh desert life and how plants and animals survived and thrived in the wildness there. The nature lessons she gave as they walked helped pass the time on the trail.

They slowly began an upward ascent on the gajada, or rocky slopes of the mountains where they would soon make camp. Often stopping for short breaks, they took refuge in the shade of large cacti or the desert trees. Dawson and Kay frequently sipped water in order to stay hydrated. He had brought a large plastic cup that he poured water in for the coati to drink.

For Dawson, the coati was a joy to have along on the trek. He never tired of watching her scamper about, sniffing and exploring. She was in her element. He was impressed at how agile she was at maneuvering around the multitude of thorny obstacles that lay in all directions.

By early evening they had arrived at the campsite. It was a spot that had been well used. Kay was appalled at the sight of numerous plastic gallon jugs and trash scattered about.

"I had heard that a lot of illegals were passing through this area. I'm so sad by the ecological mess they were making, more so than they themselves. Most of this rubbish will not decompose in this climate.

Dawson slipped out of his pack propped it against a large rock. He looked around.

"Where shall I set the tent up?" he asked.

"Wait before you unpack. Let me check on a better spot to camp. If no one has discovered it, this place will be much better."

Kay dropped her pack and quickly disappeared through a maze of scrub and rocks.

CHAPTER 117

When Kay left Dawson at the campsite and disappeared into the thick stand of mesquite and huge rocks, the coati took off after her. Dawson suddenly felt awkward and alone. It was eerily quiet. The air was still. There was not a cloud in the sky. Sweat dripped into his eyes and stung. Off in the distance, giant cacti looked like tortured humans, arms twisted up and down. Some stood tall as telephone poles. Everything looked dream like. The desert was dead still as though the world had stopped turning.

Dawson drank a few swigs of tepid water from the canteen. He backed into the shade of a boulder and sat down. Scanning the thorny bushes and endless cacti, he caught movement. Twenty feet away a tortoise crawled into its burrow. He then saw a tarantula making haste across the trail, a scorpion disappearing under a rock. Amazed, Dawson realized that there was more life here than he first imagined.

After what seemed an eternity, the coati came loping out of the underbrush. She scurried up to Dawson and let out a long series of chirps and grunts. It appeared she was excited about something. He then noticed was wet from head to toe.

"Looks like you found the water source that Kay talked about."

Moments later Kay emerged. She sat down by him and pulled out her canteen and drank heavily from it.

"It's a bit rough going but let's make camp in the cave. Thank goodness it has not been discovered and ruined like this spot."

"When we start back out day after tomorrow, why don't we bag up as much as we can carry of this and take it with us?"

Kay looked at Dawson along moment, her face filled with admiration.

"My people would be very proud of you. I think I may christen you as an honorary O'odham. You have a heart of gold Dawson Lee."

"Well, thank you. I'm not really anyone special. I was just brought up to respect the world we live in."

"You were brought up well. That says a lot about your heritage."

"Well, thank you again."

The two hoisted their packs and put them back on their tired backs. Dawson followed Kay through a thorny scrub and loose rocky footing. Everything around them bristled with needles, reaching out to draw blood. Progress was slow in the beginning but the way eased as they made their way upward and along the base of a cliff. The evening sun was beginning to cast a dull glow on the flats of the reservation below them.

Working their way around some large boulders, then squeezing between two, suddenly they were at a cave opening. Dawson stood staring at it in amazement. It seemed as if it had just appeared by magic.

On the strenuous path up, Dawson's cheeks were burning, as well as his ears and eyelids. His scalp was drenched with sweat. When he stepped into the entrance of the cave it was if he had walked into an air conditioned building.

"Oh my. What a relief!" he proclaimed.

"This is nice, isn't it?" Asked Kay as she walked a short distance in and dropped her pack.

The cave proper was roomy but not large by most standards. The ceiling height was fifteen feet at the highest point and twenty at the widest, with a depth into the mountain of less than fifty feet. There were remnants of a fire ring and ashes that Kay said dated back to ancient times of her people. With a flashlight she showed Dawson a mosaic of primitive drawings and symbols on both walls.

A short distance further back from the fire ring was a small shallow pool of water. Its source flowed from a crack in the wall. The pool ran off and traveled a few feet along a narrow channel in the floor then dropped through several small holes and disappeared. The coati was already wading out into the water, gleefully wallowing in its coolness.

"This is an awesome place Kay. It's like an oasis secreted away for the privileged few."

"You don't know how privileged you are. You are the first white man that I have known to ever be in here."

Kay then showed Dawson an area near the old fire ring to set up camp. She suggested they set up the tent because of snakes and other creatures often seeking water and respite from the heat. While he put the tent up, Kay filtered fresh water from the pool to replenish their supply and for cooking their evening meal.

The tent up and ready, Dawson then put the sleeping mats in it along with both sleeping bags. He then got the cook stove set up and lit, then organize the cookware.

"What are we having tonight." asked Kay.

"A special treat. I froze two nice steaks and had them wrapped and insulated. They should be thawed out by now."

"Good thinking. They will taste even better out here. I'm famished."

CHAPTER 118

The mouthwatering aroma of steaks on the grill filled the cavern as Dawson cooked their dinner. While he had been cooking, Kay and the coati went out for a few minutes "foraging for dessert" as she put it. She came back in with several little pulpy fruit balls. Kay called them "pitahaya dolce" which she said was the Spanish name for the fruit of the organ pipe cactus.

Dawson has brought along a supply of cat food and some apples for the coati. He quartered two apples and poured some cat food into a plastic bowl. She happily crunched and smacked while he finished cooking his and Kay's food. The steaks and fried potato slices tasted as good as they smelled. Kay complimented his outdoor gourmet skills.

"You did a fine job with dinner Dawson. Now, let me give you a sweet reward, compliments of the Sonoran Desert."

When she started slicing the red, sugary pulp balls with black seeds, the coati scrambled to her side.

"She already knows what this is. Look at her!"

Dawson laughed.

The coati was trying to climb onto Kay's lap, begging for the fruit.

"Hang on girl. I've got enough for you. Let Dawson have some first. He's never had any."

The fruit's appearance reminded Dawson of the inside of a kiwi fruit, except that it was a reddish-purple instead of green.

"I like this stuff. It's amazing what delicacies one can find in such unusual places."

"There are more than most people realize."

Dawson had made cups of coffee for them and the two sat by the lantern and watched the coati finish off the cactus fruit and scraps.

"She's a fine garbage disposal. There is not much edible that's safe around her," said Kay.

"I had wondered how she could survive in this environment but I can see that she can do well."

Kay looked at Dawson.

"How come you haven't named her yet?"

"I have been waiting for a good name to come to mind and I think you just gave it to me a few minutes ago."

"What's that?"

"I like the name Sonoran. I was thinking of calling her Sonora."

Kay's face lit up with a big smile.

"Excellent name Dawson. It fits her!"

"Well then that settles it. Sonora it is!"

"Mm-hmm, Sonora Lee. I like it."

Both laughed. The coati looked up at them and chirped a few times then snorted.

"I guess she approves," offered Kay.

As the evening progressed and they began to settle down, Sonora found a rocky niche in the wall of the cave. She rooted around a moment, then lay down and watched Dawson and Kay from her high perch.

With fresh cups of coffee, Dawson and Kay went to the entrance of the cave and looked out on the night time desert and the star filled sky. The tall cacti took on a ghostly appearance in the moonlight. Dawson thought they looked like zombies standing in a vast graveyard.

It was the night sky that struck him the most. The stars appeared brilliant and white hot again at the indigo sky. The stars seemed closer, as if you could reach out and touch them. Dawson was astonished as Kay pointed out various groups of stars and constellations.

"I'm impressed Kay. You are one smart lady."

"Why thank you. We have several telescopes and observatories on the reservation. I've spent a lot of time there. You might want to check them out at Kitt Peak while you are here."

She went on to tell him that she knew how to navigate through the desert by using the sun or stars. Intrigued by her knowledge and skills, Dawson got her to talking about her heritage. She told him that their name, the O'odham translates to the "People" but that it really is more complex than that. The People are "Those Who Emerged from the Earth" meaning the sand, or dry earth; endowed with human quality. Kay went on to tell him that there are presently about 25,000 members of the Tohono O'odham Nation. Most of the reservations income comes from its three casinos.

Getting late, the two went back in and prepared for bed. They took turns taking a sponge bath at the little pool. Kay secured the food stash for the night then she and Dawson climbed into their sleeping bags inside the tent.

It had been a good day of hiking and learning new things. The trip for Dawson had already been immensely rewarding. Tomorrow they would ascend the mountain and sleep on the summit. Dawson would be sleeping in the clouds high above the desert.

CHAPTER 119

Well into the night several thunderous reports echoed across the desert. The sound woke both Dawson and Kay.

"What was that?" Dawson asked, sitting up.

"Gun shots!"

"Huh?"

"Somebody fired some shots. Not a good sign," replied Kay.

Sonora appeared at the mesh screen door of the tent chirping to get in, obviously frightened. Dawson unzipped the door and she hopped in, climbing into his arms. She was trembling with fear.

"It's okay girl," he said in a soothing voice, rubbing her gently.

Kay slid out of the tent after putting her boots on. She switched a small penlight on for a moment and eased quietly to the entrance of the cave squatted down. Dawson slipped his boots on and he and Sonora crept out and sat down beside her. The night air was cool and still.

"Anything?" he whispered.

"No. Sound carries long distances out here. It's hard to tell how far away it is. I would suspect its drug smugglers. Often times they enlist or coerce illegal's trying to go north as mules to carry their drugs. Sometimes the unsuspecting mules are murdered when they have no further use for them."

"That's awful."

"With that campsite over there being so heavily used, I am sure it's a stop for illegal's and drug smugglers before they cross the mountains. There is a small pass that cuts through to the other side. It's relatively easy to negotiate and saves miles of traveling through the desert or following the road we came in on. If they take the road, it's too easy to be spotted by the border patrol or by the reservation police."

Dawson and Kay sat for a long time without hearing or seeing any movement across the vast expanse of desert that displayed spooky shades of black and grey.

"I'm wide awake now. How about some coffee?" asked Dawson.

"Sure, don't light the lantern. Use your flashlight but keep it low to the ground and cover most of it with your hand. Don't' want anyone to spot us."

"All right," he replied and quietly eased back inside.

He lit the gas burner and switched off the flash light, using the faint blue glow of the flame for a light source. Sonora was by his side and nudged his leg until he understood that she was hungry. He poured a small amount of cat food and quartered an apple for her.

With two hot cups of coffee, Dawson shuffled back to the cave entrance and sat down beside Kay. He was amazed at how much light filtered into the cave from the stars. The world below him seemed to give off a soft glow.

Soft crunching sounds emanated from back inside the cave. Kay giggled.

"Sonora's a pig," she whispered.

"Yeah, but you have to admit, she is a real sweetie."

"You need your head checked."

Suddenly the faint sound of voices floated across the plains. Kay held her hand up, signaling for silence.

"What do you think?" Dawson whispered after a time.

"This time of night, whoever it is, not good."

An hour passed and they neither heard nor saw anything.

"Should we try to get some sleep?" asked Dawson.

"You go lay down. I'm not sleepy. I'll just sit out here a while longer."

"I'm really too keyed up to lie down too."

Then, from just to the right of the cave about where the campsite lay they heard what sounded like the cry of a child. A voice, indiscernible, spoke, and then silence. A few minutes passed then they heard childlike whimpering, then again silence. Kay motioned to Dawson and the two retreated back into the cave. They made their way to the tent and squatted beside it. Kay leaned in close to him.

"Listen Dawson," she whispered. "I'm going to ease down and check out who that is. I want you to keep your coati here. Don't let her follow me."

"Are you sure about going down there?"

"Yes, I need to know what is going on. If it is drug smugglers using the camp as a stop then I will report it when we get back."

"Please be careful, Kay."

"Oh, believe me. I will."

Kay had Dawson take Sonora and sit inside that tent with the doorway zipped closed. The coati grunted and paced by the mesh door, obviously wanting to go with her. Kay quietly made her way to the cave entrance and disappeared from view.

"Settle down Sonora. Kay doesn't need you rambling along with her. She's on a dangerous mission. Let's you and me sit here and be quiet and wait for her to return."

CHAPTER 120

Time passed excruciatingly slow while Kay was gone. Dawson's nerves were on end as he sat holding Sonora trying to keep her quiet and calm.

After what seemed an eternity he heard her, then saw her at the entrance coming up from the rocky ledge. To his surprise she was carrying a small child.

"Here," she whispered, holding out the child. "Take the little one. Keep her quiet while I go get the others."

He took the little girl and Kay disappeared without any further explanation. The child in his arms was small and frail. She was either asleep or in a state of shock, for she made no sound and she was as limp as a dishrag. Dawson took her into the tent and gently laid her on his sleeping bag.

A short time later Kay reappeared, this time with a larger child, a boy. At the entrance, she let him down out of her arms and then led him into the tent. In Spanish she told him to lie down beside his sister. She put her hand on Dawson's shoulder.

"Keep them quiet. I've got one more to go."

She disappeared into the darkness again. Later she returned leading a man who was obviously in distress. Kay had him sit down by the tent. She told Dawson to light the stove. While he was doing that she lit the lantern and turned it down to a faint glow and sat it behind the tent to diffuse the light even more. The area around them glowed blue from the light filtering through the fabric of the tent.

Kay softly spoke to the man in Spanish as she boiled a pan of water. From her canteen she gave the man a cup of cool water and he drank it quickly. They talked in low voices for several minutes. She then turned to Dawson.

"While I tend to him, try to get the children to drink a little water. Don't give them too much."

Dawson got his canteen and sat down at the entrance of the tent. The boy was sitting up staring at him. Dawson then saw that he had Sonora in his arms. She had her head resting on his shoulders. Dawson reached out and rubbed Sonora's back.

"Good girl," he whispered.

Unscrewing the cap on the canteen, Dawson held the spout to the little boy's mouth. He took several swigs. The girl child sat up and took some too. Dawson spoke to them softly to try to keep them calm. It was readily apparent that they were quite shaken and disoriented. Both were disheveled and wreaked of sweat and fear.

After drinking the water, the little girl laid her head against the coati, which was still in the boy's arms. Dawson eased out of the tent to check on Kay. She had the man's shirt off and was treating a wound on his side.

"What's happened to these people?" he whispered.

"Victor here and the children were part of a small group of illegals trying to slip across the border and go north. A band of drug smugglers found them and forced them to carry drugs for them. When they stopped to rest the children's mother refused their advances and they killed her. Last night this man took the children and escaped when they stopped for a rest break. The smugglers chased them and Victor was wounded but managed to elude them and save the children. The bullet just grazed his ribs and probably cracked one. He is in pain but he will be all right."

"Is he the children's father?"

"No. He knew their mother. They were from the same village. The children's father died some time ago. They have no family except for a poor elderly aunt. They are orphans now."

"How heartbreaking."

Dawson looked back at the two small children, and then looked back at Kay.

"What do we do now?"

"We need to get these people out to safety. We'll get them to the border patrol or to the reservation police so they can be helped."

"What will happen to them?"

"They will be shipped back across the border."

"What about the kids?"

Kay sat quietly for a moment and looked off into the darkness."

"I guess they will be a ward of the state of Mexico. They'll go to an orphanage."

Dawson swallowed a huge lump that had formed on his throat. He eased back over to the tent and peered in. The two children were curled up asleep. Sonora lay between them. She looked up at Dawson and made a snuffing sound then laid her head across the little girl's chest.

The night sky began to give way to dawn. Kay stood at the entrance and carefully scanned the desert below them. She was sure that the drug smugglers were long gone now. She came back in and suggested they cook breakfast.

Volunteering to cook, Dawson soon had scrambled eggs and bacon ready. They fed Victor and he and Kay ate. The children were still asleep. Kay had crawled in and checked on the two kids. She saw they were terribly scratched up and filthy.

"We'll let them sleep a little then feed them. They need to be cleaned up and their scratches tended to."

CHAPTER 121

As dawn spread a soft orange radiance across the desert, the quietude of the early morning came to a sudden end. Every bird in the desert, it seemed, began to sing at the same time. Kay patiently scanned the desert again but saw no signs of human activity. She finally came back in.

"Dawson, will you cook breakfast for the children while I clean them up."

"Sure thing."

Victor had settled down near the entrance. He sat with his back against the wall. He had fallen asleep and leaned to one side against his pack.

Kay got the little boy and led him back to the pool of water. With a rag, she washed the grime off and cleaned his scratches and cuts from his encounters with thorns and splinter.

The little girl woke up, whimpered, and then started to cry. Dawson gathered her up in his arms and held her while he cooked.

"Bring her on back here to me," called Kay.

He took the little girl to her and led the boy back and set him in the doorway of the tent. He was shivering from the cold bath so Dawson took his sleeping bag and wrapped it around him. Sonora crawled up onto his lap and the little boy held her in his arms, murmuring softly in Spanish to her. He then looked up at Dawson. His large brown eyes pooled with tears.

"Mi Madre," he sobbed.

Dawson sat the boiling pot of oatmeal to the side and put his arms around the broken hearted child and kissed him on the forehead.

"I'm so sorry my little friend," he said softly.

He held the boy a few moments and then handed him a bowl of strawberries and cream flavored oatmeal. Sonora tried to stick her nose into the bowl.

"No Sonora, that's his. You've already eaten."

The child looked at Dawson quizzically.

"Sonora?" he asked.

"Yes, Si. That is her name," Dawson said, pointing to the coati.

"Sonora," the boy said softly.

Kay brought the girl back and sat her beside her brother. He wrapped some of his sleeping bag around her. Dawson handed her a bowl of oatmeal. The two ate mechanically without seeming to enjoy their food. It was obvious the two sad little children were traumatized.

"Where is Victor?" asked Mary.

Dawson looked up and saw that Victor was no longer sleeping by the entrance. His pack was gone as well. Dawson gave Kay a puzzled look.

"He was asleep over there a moment ago, I think. I really didn't pay much attention to him" he replied.

"I think Victor has given us the slip. I could go after him but it's not worth it. He probably won't make it too far without getting picked up. His injury will slow him down. We'll alert the border patrol and reservation police to be on the lookout for him."

The sun was now well up and the cave bright with light. Dawson and Kay fed the children again and tended to their multitude of cuts and scratches. Kay deftly pulled out several thorns from both children. They let out a few whimpers, but otherwise, both were stoic as she quickly treated their wounds.

After the children were fed and doctored, Kay had them lay back down and rest. Both fell asleep with Sonora cuddled between them. Kay and Dawson sat down for a break with cups of coffee. From time to time she would peer in on the kids, and then sit back down by Dawson. She smiled at him and squeezed his arm.

"I have gained a whole new perspective for Sonora. She is a saint. She senses their distress and vulnerability. See how she offers herself to them for comfort."

"Yeah I see. I knew there was something special about her when I first saw her. I didn't realize how much until just now. I surely am happy she's with us."

Kay patted Dawson's arm and said, "I am too. I really am. I can fully understand now why you are so taken with her."

Dawson sat back, took a sip of coffee and sat it down beside him.

"So, what do we do now? What's the plan?"

"Let's just stay here until later in the afternoon then head back to the car. The children are exhausted. We'll let them rest, feed them another good meal, then head out. If we don't run into a border patrol officer, we'll take them to the reservation police."

Dawson let out a sigh.

"Somehow, I don't feel good about it."

"I know what you mean. I hate to see them go back to Mexico and end up in an orphanage."

"What are their names?"

"You know, I didn't even ask. I was so concerned with their physical welfare that I did not think to ask. Let's see what's in the pack the boy had on."

Kay picked up the well-worn pack and opened it. There were some small packages of food, extra underwear for the boy and girl, including some women's, and a padded envelope. Inside the envelope she found birth certificates for the children and a Mexican passport for the mother.

"Oh my," said Kay, looking up at Dawson. "The children are half O'odham and Mexican. There are many of our people living across the border. We used to travel back and forth freely but not now because of the fencing and border restrictions."

"Does that mean the reservation will help the kids?"

"Not necessarily. They are still considered illegal's. Therefore they will be deported."

Dawson's hopes for their welfare were quickly dashed.

CHAPTER 122

Sitting near the entrance of the cave where the light was the brightest, Kay studied the birth certificates and documents that belonged to the children. The boy's name was Miguel Rivera, six years old. The girl, Saray, was four. Their now deceased mother was Mari and had recently turned twenty-five. Mari was from the O'odham tribe. The father of the children was Mexican. Both children had been born in Sonoya, just across the border from Lukeville.

While Kay and Dawson were sitting by the entrance and talking, Sonora came out of the tent, stopped and chirped at Dawson then disappeared down the narrow path to the cave.

"I guess she's taking a break," said Kay, giggling.

"That's my nurse Sonora!"

They heard a shuffling and Miguel crawled out of the tent and came and sat down by them. Dawson put his arm around the sad looking little boy and studied him. He was thin but healthy looking. His short hair was sandy brown from spending time in the sun. His large brown eyes signaled utter despair. Kay engaged him in conversation. She would interpret what he said to Dawson as they talked.

From Miguel, Kay learned that he, Saray, and their mother had lived in a village near Sonoya. Their father had died some time ago for Miguel could recall little of him. His mother was taking them north so she could find a job and a better life for them all.

They heard a small whimper and Saray came out of the tent. She came to where they were and climbed onto Kay's lap. She had a thick head of disheveled hair that stopped at her shoulders. She had large brown eyes and dark circles underneath them that highlighted her unease. Kay said that she had more of the O'odham people features than her brother. Saray sensing that they were talking about her stuck her thumb in her mouth and stared at Dawson as he talked to Kay.

"Such beautiful children," commented Dawson.

Kay looked at him for several seconds.

"Don't get attached to these children. We will have to turn them in."

"I already am," he said softly, looking away.

"What am I going to do with you," she said, shaking her head. "Let's feed them a hearty meal. They will need their strength for the long walk ahead."

"Let me do the cooking," he said. "I have a good wholesome meal in mind."

"No complaints from me."

While Dawson cooked, Kay treated the children's cuts and scratches again with Neosporin. Dawson had chosen a hearty meal of beef stroganoff to cook for them. He also served instant potatoes and peas and carrots with it. Neither child ate much, but he was pleased that they did get some down. He took a one-liter bottle of water and mixed Gatorade powder in it which both children seemed to enjoy.

Sonora came rambling back in. She walked up to the children, sniffed and checked to see if they were okay and let out a satisfied snort. Miguel picked her up and petted her tenderly.

"Sonora," he said softly, kissing her on the head.

Kay's eyes misted over at the show of affection for the coati. Her heart grew heavy with concern for the children's future.

During the early afternoon Dawson took down the tent and packed it. He and Kay prepared everything for the long hike back to the vehicle, this time with two small children to worry about. The temperature was hovering in the mid-nineties. While getting the children ready Dawson noticed that neither one had socks and their feet were covered with blisters. Their shoes were old and ill fitting. To rectify the problem he cut down his extra socks and fitted them both with a pair.

Before heading down from the cave and out into the desert, Kay fed both children some high calorie trail snacks and more Gatorade. Seeing the children eat, Sonora grunted and whined until Dawson gave her a cup of cat food.

With canteens and bottles filled with fresh cool, filtered water, the group slowly made their way down from the secret cliff side cave and made their way southward back to where the Explorer was parked. Within minutes everyone was dripping with sweat. Progress was slow with the children in tow. Neither Kay nor Dawson wanted to push them. They took their time and paced themselves and took frequent breaks.

Less than an hour underway and Saray's energy flagged. Dawson picked her up and began carrying her. Though awkward with her and wearing his backpack, he rallied his strength and persevered. Kay took the lead with Miguel in the middle and Dawson bringing up the rear.

Sonora trotted along beside Miguel, often chirping as if encouraging his friend to keep going. They continued to take frequent breaks, more so for Dawson's benefit than anything. Kay offered to carry Saray or Dawson's pack, but he refused.

By the time they finally made it to the SUV, it was almost dark. The three hour trek took them more than five hours with the children. Dawson almost burst into tears of relief when he saw the Explorer. It was a most welcomed sight.

CHAPTER 123

"Whew! Your Ford never looked so good," proclaimed Kay as she reached it and dropped her pack.

Miguel worked his way around the patches of brittle bush and hedgehog cactus and stepped out on the road. He collapsed by the Explorer. Three minutes later Dawson and Saray arrived. He gently sat her down, then with great relief, slipped out of his backpack.

Kay took her canteen and poured the remaining water on the children's heads and cleaned as much of the dust and grim off of them as she could. Dawson gave Sonora a cup of water then unlocked the SUV and opened the doors and the hatch. He loaded the gear then put the children in the back seats and slipped off their shoes and socks.

Sonora drank her water and hopped in the SUV and climbed onto Miguel's lap. Kay chose to drive and she and Dawson piled in and they got underway. She tried her cell phone while they headed north but could get no service. It was totally dark by the time they were nearing the little reservation town of Gu Vo. Dawson checked on the kids and both were asleep.

"Are you going to take them to the police now?"

Kay put her hand on his.

"We really need to Dawson."

"I know," he said softly, looking out the window, his heart heavy with sadness.

They arrived at Gu Vo. Kay slowed when she saw a police car coming out of a side street and turning toward them in the oncoming lane. She started to flash her headlights to signal the policeman to stop, but looked over at Dawson and kept going. He looked at her curiously.

"Against my better judgment I am going to let them spend the night with you. We'll clean them up and let them get a good night's rest. I will go to the police in the morning and we'll turn them over then."

Dawson expelled a long breath of air.

"Thank you Kay. These kids have been through hell. A good bath, some hot food, and a good night's sleep will be great for them."

Kay reached over and put her hand on Dawson's arm.

"I know you feel sorry for them Dawson. They are not stray animals like the coati. They are a major responsibility. They are illegal's too. By law they must go back to Mexico."

"How are the orphanages down there?"

"Well, from what I have heard, not all that great. They won't starve is about all I can assure you of."

"Maybe I could find out where they end up and help them."

She looked over at him and squeezed his arm. A heavy silence hung for a moment.

"Kay. Those kids need a good home and a family to love them."

"You're telling me something I already know Dawson. I surely couldn't take them in."

"I could," he said softly.

"Dawson," Kay admonished. "How could you? That's a major decision to make and should be made with your wife. She's in Afghanistan and you can't even get in touch with her right now. Think about what you are saying. You can't even speak their language and they can't speak yours."

"I could learn. I have a built in interpreter at the house right now."

She looked at him incredulously.

"Whatever are you talking about?"

He told her about Crucita.

"Well, that's fine and well Dawson. But let me ask you this. What happens when you and Lianne start having kids of your own? Are you going to push these two aside? What would happen to them then?"

Dawson sat silently for a moment.

"We can't have kids," he replied softly.

Kay put her hand over her mouth in embarrassment.

"Oh, I'm so sorry!"

They rode in silence. They did not speak anymore until they reached the campground. Kay helped him get the children inside and offered to help him bath and feed them.

"I know you are tired Kay. I'll take care of them. You go on home and rest. I will see you in the morning. I'll get them up and have them fed and ready for you to turn them over to the authorities."

Kay looked in his sad eyes, trying not to show her own sadness and said, "okay, well. I will call you when I get ready to go to the police department."

He nodded that he understood. Kay put her arms around him.

"I feel as bad as you do about this Dawson. We must do the right thing. These are human beings for gosh sakes. These are not animals. The coati is one thing, two children lost in the desert with no mother or father is an entirely different matter."

"I know Kay. You are right. My heart is just telling me otherwise."

"Mine is not feeling all that great about this either. Those two little desert angels are pulling on my heart too."

Kay kissed him on the cheek and gave him a squeeze before she let go. She then picked Sonora up and hugged her.

"You help Dawson watch after the children. I will see you guys in the morning."

Sonora looked up at Kay and grunted as if she were saying yes."

CHAPTER 124

Miguel and Saray sat on the sofa of the camper watching Dawson and furtively took in their surroundings. Their sweat stained faces mirrored their fragile and labile emotions. Neither spoke but watched every movement Dawson made as he fed and watered Sonora.

He then poured two glasses of orange juice and handed them to the kids. While they sipped the cool juice he turned the television on and found a cartoon channel. They stared at it with blank faces. He ran a tub of warm water and motioned for them both to undress and get in. Silently they complied.

Dawson gently washed Miguel's hair and rinsed it off with a plastic cup. He then shampooed and rinsed Saray's hair. With a wash cloth he helped each child scrub off the desert grime. He then got them out and helped them dry off. In Miguel's pack he dug out a pair of underwear for each. Since they had no other clothes, Dawson put a t-shirt of his on each child. He then brushed Miguel's short hair and Saray's thick mop of luxurious curls.

Motioning them to sit at the dinette, Dawson refilled their juice glasses and heated a bowl of soup for each of them. He then made them sandwiches. Miguel ate all of his. Saray ate only half. Both children were notably fatigued so Dawson put them in the bottom bunk together and covered them up. Sonora climbed to the top bunk and peered down at them. To Dawson's surprise, Saray giggled at the coati staring down at her. Dawson smiled and gave each one a pat.

"I'm going to be right here if you need me. Call me Dawson if you need me," he said, pointing to himself.

"Dawson," repeated Miguel, pointing at him.

Dawson then leaned over and kissed each child on the forehead. He left the television on but turned the volume down low. The two children watched the cartoons through drooping eyelids and soon drifted off the sleep. Dawson turned the television and the lights off except for one night light over the stove.

After eating a sandwich and taking a shower, Dawson climbed on his bed with the laptop. He checked his emails and found one from Lianne. She informed him that she had been given an assignment that would take her to the southwestern part of Afghanistan to the Helmand providence. She was to report on the transition from the control by the U.S. Marines at Camp Leatherneck to Afghan Security Forces. To Dawson's dismay Lianne indicated that she would be out of contact with him for the time being.

So dismayed by her news, Dawson did not bother to email her back. Instead, he shut the computer down and pushed it aside. Easing out of bed he quickly padded over and checked on the children.

"Desert angels," he whispered, thinking about Kay's name for them.

Looking at the small sleeping forms, he wondered what tomorrow would bring for them. Where would they sleep tomorrow night? Would they be well taken care of? Would someone adopt them and love them? He choked up and shuddered with dread for them. They had been through so much over the last few days. What more traumas lay ahead for them?

Tired and frustrated, he lay down but could not fall asleep. He quietly got back up, mixed a Bloody Mary, and sat outside on the patio. Looking up at the stars, he took little pleasure in their beauty.

"Oh Lianne," he groaned, as a sob caught in his throat. "I really need to talk to you right now!"

Dawson felt so alone with his heart filled with concern and love for the sleeping children inside. He fantasized about hooking the travel trailer to the truck and taking off with them. Would Kay turn him into the authorities if he did? How could legally keep them once he got home? What would Lianne think?

It was almost midnight. Still unable to unwind from his anxiety, Dawson slipped inside, got the cell phone and sat back out on the patio. He called home.

"Hello?" answered a sleepy Crucita.

"Hey Crucita. I know it's late but I would like to talk to you. Do you mind?"

"Of course not. What's wrong?"

He told her the entire story about finding Miguel and Saray. She listened intently and let him talk out his emotional turmoil.

"And you say that Kay plans to turn them over to immigration in the morning?"

"Yeah. I know it's what we are supposed to do but I sure feel bad about it. I don't see any way around the legalities. I am sure you well know how hard it is for illegal's here."

Crucita was silent for a moment.

"I don't want to say much on the phone. There are ways to get the proper paperwork. Dad knows who and how. Do you understand?"

"Yes I do. Thank you. Unfortunately this may be out of my hands in the morning. I am going to try to find out from the police and immigration about how to adopt them."

"Well, let me know if either me or Dad can help."

"Will do. Thank you, Crucita. Goodnight."

CHAPTER 125

Sleeping very little, Dawson was up at dawn. He fed Sonora and made coffee. The two went outside. Dawson sat on the patio and watched dawn break while Sonora went exploring.

In just a few hours the kids would be turned over to the authorities. Would he ever see them again? What would it take to adopt them from Mexico? Surely he and Lianne could qualify. His main worry was Lianne's work schedule and being gone often.

"What to do," he said with a sigh.

He drank his coffee and sat for a long while worrying over the situation. He got up and was starting to go back in for another cup when he heard a truck approaching. Kay pulled in behind the Explorer and parked. She got out and walked to where Dawson was standing. Sonora came bounding out of the scrub brush and Kay picked her up and hugged her. Kay looked at Dawson, her eyes were red and her eyelids were puffy. She appeared to be very tired.

"You got a cup of coffee for a friend?"

"Sure, I was just going in for a refill. I'll get you one. Have a seat."

He eased into the camper and returned moments later with two cups of coffee. Kay was sitting in the lounge chair with Sonora lying in her lap.

"How are the kids?"

"Okay, they are still asleep. Neither woke during the night. I'm sure they are totally spent."

"It's good they slept so well. How did you do with them after I left?"

He told her about bathing them and washing their hair, how he fed them and let them fall asleep watching cartoons.

"That's great Dawson. You will certainly make a wonderful father one day." She immediately put her hand over her mouth. "Oops, I'm sorry. I forgot you said you and Lianne can't have kids."

"That's okay," he said softly.

She looked away and sat silently a moment. She took a sip of coffee and looked at him.

"Listen Dawson. I had a terrible night. I have just about worried myself sick over these kids. I stopped by the reservation police department on my way here."

"What did they say?" he asked with a startled look.

She looked at him a moment.

"I could not make myself get out of the truck. I decided to come talk to you first so we can decide what to do."

"Kay, I'm torn to pieces over this. I don't think I can be of much help to you."

She picked Sonora up from her lap and cradled her like a baby and slowly began to rock.

"Last night while I lay in bed thinking about those kids, an old story came to me. Want to hear it?"

"Sure Kay."

"There once was a little girl that kept every doll that her family and friends had given her. Over the years they had become tattered and worn. Some had missing eyes and ears and a few had lost some or most of their hair."

She paused and took a sip of coffee, then readjusted Sonora in her arms.

"One day a friend of her mother's came for a visit. With pride the little girl invited the guest to visit her bedroom and meet her dolls. All of her dolls were carefully displayed on her bed. She told her guest that she loved all of her dolls."

Kay kissed Sonora on the top of her head.

"Picking up a doll with a button missing from an eye, part of the thread missing from its lips, and a face that had become worn from being held so much, the little girl told the guest that she loved this doll the most. When asked why, the girl said because if she didn't, probably nobody would."

She fell silent, tears streamed down her cheeks. Dawson stared curiously at her for a long moment before he spoke.

"What are you saying Kay?"

"Convince me that you really want those kids and that you will take them and give them all the love you can."

A huge smile spread across his face.

"Last night I talked to Crucita. I found out we have a source that can get us documentation for the kids. I don't know how good it is or much more than, it can be done for a price. I do have good faith in my source."

Kay nodded she understood.

"What does Lianne think about this?"

"I can't get through to her. She's away from Kabul. I know Lianne. I know she will be pleased."

"Are you sure?"

"Yes I am Kay. I am sure."

"How are you going to communicate with the kids? You can't speak Spanish."

"I can get on the phone right now and have Crucita fly out tonight or in the morning. She can help us until we can speak each other's language. My truck should be ready the first of the week and we can head out for home then."

"If we do this, you will have to keep these kids hidden until you leave from here. It would be suspicious for you to be seen alone with them. It will help when Crucita is here and seen with them.

"I understand. The only problem at the moment is that I need to buy clothes for them. They have nothing. The clothes they were wearing are too tattered to put back on them."

"We can deal with that."

"Are you saying I can keep them?"

"How can I not, Dawson. I know you have a good heart. Those kids have a chance of a lifetime with a father like you and a famous news correspondent for a mother."

Dawson trembled with happiness.

"Would you talk to Miguel and Saray? Explain everything and see if they are okay with it."

"Yes, let's cook breakfast and have a talk with them."

CHAPTER 126

Kay volunteered to cook breakfast while Dawson drove to the grocery store for milk and fresh fruit. When he returned, the children were up and sitting at the dinette table. Kay was serving up pancakes for them. Dawson poured the glasses of milk while Kay filled their plates and set them in front of the two wide-eyed kids. Kay put a pancake with syrup in a bowl for Sonora and set it on the floor, and then she and Dawson joined in the eating with Miguel and Saray.

When everyone finished eating, Kay told Miguel and Saray that they needed to have a serious talk. As she explained the situation to them she translated Miguel's answers and questions. Saray sat looking on but said nothing. After a few minutes of talking with Miguel she turned to Dawson.

"He understands as much as a six year-old can that his mother is dead and won't be coming back. He also understands that he had no other family that can take him and his sister. He said he would like to live with you if his sister can come too."

A tear dropped from Dawson's eye and he choked back a sob.

"Oh course his sister can come. I would not have it any other way."

Dawson got up and hugged and kissed both children, then Kay.

"Let me call Crucita and see if I can get her on out here."

He took the cell phone and walked out to the patio and sat down. She was happy to hear from him. He explained what was taking place. She agreed to fly out on the next available flight and help him with the kids and getting them safely back to Georgia.

"I will get online and make flight arrangements for you. I will get back with you right away. Thank you, Crucita."

Off the phone, he went online and arranged a flight from Tanner to Phoenix. She would arrive at 6:00 p.m. that evening. Dawson called Crucita back gave her the flight information. While he had been online, Dawson sent a quick email to Lianne that he really needed to talk to her.

Dawson washed the breakfast dishes while Kay checked out the kids and treated a few of their deeper cuts and scratches, least they get infected. Many of their little wounds had already scabbed over. Kay then brushed Saray's hair and braided it.

With nothing but Dawson's t-shirts on, they loaded up in the Explorer and along with Sonora drove to Gila Bend. There, Kay went in a department store and bought the kids a pair of shorts, pants, and two shirts apiece. She also got them some new sneakers, socks, and underwear.

Back at the camper, Dawson and Kay made lunch for everyone. After they ate, Kay stayed for a little while then said goodbye. She had some errands to run and planned to ride with Dawson and the kids to pick Crucita up in Phoenix.

While Kay was gone, Dawson ran a tub of water and let the children take another bath. He then helped them put on their new clothes and shoes. He had planned to put shorts on them but with their legs so scratched up, he thought it best they wear long pants. He certainly did not want to call any attention to them. Once Crucita was with them they would not look so out of place. Crucita could pass for the kid's mother.

Having made fruit salads for everyone, including Sonora, Dawson and the kids sat on the patio under the shade and ate. Sonora ate her fruit then disappeared into the brush. Kay arrived and they got ready to leave for Phoenix. Dawson called for Sonora but she did not return.

"Surely she will be all right while we are gone," assured Kay to a worried Dawson.

Not knowing what else to do, he left two bowls of water and one of cat food by the camper's steps. Everyone piled into the Explorer and Dawson set out for Phoenix.

At 5:15 p.m. they pulled into Sky Harbor International Airport and found a place to park. By the time they got inside and the kids went to the restroom, it was time for Crucita's plane to arrive.

Crucita was a beautiful sight when she walked through security. It was then that Dawson realized that he was homesick for his life back in Tanner. A touch of home rushed into his arms that made his heart swell with joy.

Dawson introduced Crucita to Kay then presented her to the children. She got down on her knees and introduced herself in Spanish to Miguel and then to Saray. To everyone's surprise, Saray immediately took to Crucita and stayed right with her while they retrieved her luggage and walked to the SUV. Dawson wondered if Crucita reminded Saray of her mother.

Before heading back to Ajo, Dawson took them to a restaurant for dinner. Miguel and Saray were wide-eyed with wonder as they took in the sights and sounds of festive the atmosphere. Dawson figured that this was probably the first time they had ever been in an establishment as extravagant as this one. His heart felt a tug as he looked at their faces agog with curiosity. He said a quick prayer for their mother and promised her that he would always care for them and would make sure they knew her name and that she loved them. It was sad that the only picture he had of Mari was of her passport photo.

CHAPTER 127

Dinner over, Dawson was pleased that Crucita was able to coax the children into eating better, especially Saray. As they piled into the Explorer, Dawson spied a Target store nearby.

"Kay, you think it would be safe to take the kids shipping over there?" he asked, pointing to the store.

"I don't see why not. Miguel and Saray look like they belong to Crucita, especially Saray. Just look at her. She has latched on to that young lady like glue!"

Dawson smiled and shook his head, filled with happiness.

"Let's do it!"

At Target, Crucita put Saray in a shopping cart and the group headed in. Dawson had Kay go along with her to shop for Saray. He took Miguel and went to the boys section to outfit him with a small wardrobe.

Once both kids were loaded up with clothes, Dawson then took them to the toy department and let them pick out a few things. Crucita helped her pick out a doll and a set of toy jewelry. Miguel found a G.I. Joe he liked and a large set of plastic road construction vehicles and men.

While they were in the toy section looking around, Dawson wandered over to the pet section and picked out a bright red pet collar and lease for Sonora. Before they let the store he went to the front where the vending machines were located. There was one that made name tags for pets. He picked one out and watched as the machine engraved Sonora's name on it.

On the ride back to Ajo, Crucita sat between Saray and Miguel. They seemed to be enamored with her. Saray cuddled up to her. She laid her head against Crucita's chest and held her hand.

When they reached the campground and pulled into the campsite, Sonora came loping up to the Explorer. Dawson felt a rush of relief. He had been worried about his little friend.

Crucita was initially wary of the coati, but Sonora quickly won her over. She was surprised at how well Sonora was with the children.

Kay stayed a few minutes then bid them goodnight. Dawson walked her out to her truck. She put her arms around him and kissed him on the cheek.

"I feel like we have made the right decision. With Crucita's help, you will do fine with the children. I just know Lianne will fall in love with them."

"I feel good about this Kay. Those are beautiful kids. I'm looking forward to doing all the things that dads do. I can't wait to get started."

Kay grinned at him.

"Looking forward to it, huh? Looks to me like you have already started. I saw the joy in your face at the restaurant and at Target."

Dawson chuckled.

"Yeah, I guess you are right. It is fun. I like to see them smile. I want to give them the best life I can."

She kissed him on the cheek again.

"I'll check on you tomorrow. Call me if you need me."

"Will do Kay."

He watched her drive away and went back in. Crucita had changed the kids into their pajamas and was helping Miguel organize his toys in a storage drawer.

"Crucita, I have been sleeping in the big bed and Miguel and Saray slept together on the bottom bunk. The top bunk belongs to Sonora."

She looked at him and shook her head. He grinned at her and threw his hands up.

"Anyway, I thought if you don't mind sleeping with them I will take the bottom bunk and you guys take the big bed."

Crucita looked at the big bed a moment and said, "I can sleep on the sofa. I hate for you to give up your bed. The kids will be fine where they have been."

Miguel had been watching and listening to them. He evidently understood what the conversation was about and asked Crucita if she would sleep with him and his sister. She looked at Dawson and said, "How can I say no?"

With the sleeping arrangements settled, Dawson and Crucita put the little ones to bed. She then took a shower and changed into her night clothes. Dawson had turned the lights off except for the kitchen night light. He had powered up the laptop and checked to see if Lianne had left a message. She had not.

Leaving the computer on, Dawson and Crucita sat at the dinette table and waited until ten o'clock in case Lianne was where she could get through to them. At 10:30 p.m. Dawson shut the computer down. Crucita told him goodnight and crawled in bed with the children.

Not sleepy, Dawson sat on the bunk and tried to call Lianne's cell phone but could not get through. He then called his mother and talked to her and updated her on Miguel and Saray. His mother's biggest concern with the children was the legal issue.

"Dawson, you know you could jeopardize Lianne's career if it came to light you were keeping illegal aliens?"

"I know Mom. I have seriously thought about it. Somehow I have to believe that we can get documentation that will take care of that issue."

"Let's hope so. I am thrilled with the notion that I have grandchildren. I just don't want to get attached to them, and then something happens and lose them."

"Me too, Mom."

CHAPTER 128

The camper was quiet, save the soft sounds emanating from the big bed full of sleepers. Sonora had even opted to join them. Unable to fall asleep, Dawson quietly got up, mixed a Bloody Mary, and eased out to the patio and sat down.

When he went out, Dawson had not turned on any lights inside or outside the camper. He left the door ajar in case Sonora wanted out. Sure enough, moments later she stuck her head out the door.

"Hey girl," he whispered.

She came on out and hopped up onto his lap.

"I think you love those kids as much as I do. Help me watch after them. I can't wait until we all get back home and settle down. I think you will like living there. I hope you and Max get to be the best of friends."

Sonora snorted and chirped, touching Dawson's chin with her wet nose. Dawson gave her a hug.

"Since we are up, I have a present for you. Let's see if you will like it."

With her in his arms, Dawson quietly slipped back into the camper and got the pet collar and a banana. He took Sonora back to the patio and fed her the banana pieces while he put the collar on her and adjusted it to fit.

When the entire banana was gone, Sonora sat up and shook her head. Dawson sat her down on the patio. Sonora tried to back out of the contraption that was around her neck. He picked her up and cuddled and soothed her disquiet.

"You need to get used to wearing this collar girl. I want to make sure that when someone sees you that they will know you are a pet and not just a wild animal."

Sonora finally settled down and seemed to accept the collar. He took the laptop back outside with him and booted it up. Checking the email account, he again found no message from Lianne which he did not really expect. Sitting there a moment, he decided he needed to give her a heads up on what he had done. He took a deep breath, flexed his fingers, and began typing.

Dearest Lianne,

You remember you told me not to bring anything else home besides the coati. Well, guess what? I am not sure how to put this, but I have found two of the most divine creatures in the desert you could ever imagine. I want to add them to my treasures to bring home. I know I'm coming across as being nuts so let me explain.

First let me tell you a little story:
Once upon a midnight desert there were two people and a coati who took a hike and ...

Typing furiously, Dawson told Lianne the entire story. He then cryptically alluded to the documentation hurdle and that it would be accomplished in some form or fashion. That subject he did not want to discuss freely least someone read the email other than Lianne.

Finished with the message, he sent it on its way then shut the laptop down. Still not sleepy, he gathered the dirty laundry and he and Sonora walked to the Laundromat and washed clothes.

No one was at the Laundromat at such a late hour so Sonora had the run of the place. She explored around, under, and behind the washers and dryers. Dawson bought a bag of corn chips from the vending machine and fed them to her. He could not help but smile and chuckle with her bright red collar with the golden name tag dangling from it.

It was 2:30 a.m. when they walked back from the Laundromat and got ready for bed. Sonora climbed to the top bunk and settled in for the night. Crucita had awakened when they came back in. She went to the bathroom. When she came out she sat on the edge of the bunk with Dawson. Both sat looking over toward the sleeping children.

"They are so precious Dawson. I am so thankful that they were found by you and Kay. Anybody else and they may not have been so lucky."

"It was divine luck that we were there it the right place and time."

"You are a wonderful man, Dawson. You were good to me and my dad from the moment you met us. Because of being Mexican and coming to this country to make a new start, there are many who frown on us and shun us. But you, you Dawson, you are an exception to the rule. You and Lianne have been so gracious to me and my father. You have given me more than I could have ever dreamed of."

Crucita wrapped her arms around Dawson. He embraced her and kissed her cheek.

"Lianne and I love you so much. We want you to live the American dream to the fullest. We plan to do all we can to see you reach your full potential. You and your dad are two of the finest people I have ever met. Both of you are like family to us and you will always be."

"I love you Dawson. Goodnight and thank you."

"I love you too. Sweet dreams."

CHAPTER 129

The smell of brewing coffee and an odd sensation of a presence brought Dawson out of a deep slumber. When he opened his eyes, Miguel and Saray were at the bedside staring at him. Saray had her hand on his arm, gently patting it. Dawson smiled at them.

"Well now, good morning Miguel, Saray."

"Eat," said Saray in perfect English.

"Breakfast, eat," said Miguel.

"Ahh, Crucita has started the English lessons. Muy Bueno!"

Saray giggled and crawled up into his arms. Dawson planted a sloppy kiss on her cheek. She giggled and put her arms around his neck and kissed his cheek.

"Well, my goodness!" exclaimed Dawson, looking at Crucita who was watching and grinning from the kitchen stove where she was cooking breakfast.

She smiled at him then spoke to Miguel in Spanish. He beamed a big smile then climbed up and joined Saray and Dawson.

"I have been explaining to them that you will be their father from now on and I am their big sister. I told them about their home and that they will have their own room and their own bed. I also told them about their new mom and that she is a very famous lady and will love them very much."

"That's good. I so want them to be happy and be able to have all the good things that life has to offer."

"I know they will. You and Lianne will make sure they do. They will be happy and they will make you proud."

"I already am."

Dawson got up and cleaned up for breakfast then they all sat and ate together. While they were eating the phone rang. It was the Ford dealership service department in Phoenix. The truck was almost ready and it could be picked up on Monday morning. Dawson thanked the man and said he would be there. When he hung up he smiled at Crucita.

"All right! We can pick up the truck on Monday morning. I think we'll get it, come back and hook up and start for home. I will feel much better when we get these kids far away from here. Call me paranoid but I don't want to take a chance of them being discovered and taken, now that we have them bouncing back so well."

Crucita nodded in agreement.

"I feel the same way."

The phone rang again. It was Kay calling. She asked how things were going. She and Dawson talked for several minutes. He invited her over for lunch.

"I have got some things I want to do today. I still have the children's birth certificates. I am going to do a little exploring and see what other information I can find out about them without drawing any suspicion. I am going to make some inquiries and try to confirm whether or not they have any other family besides the elderly aunt."

"Oh, okay," Dawson replied, trying to hide his apprehension in his voice. "Do you need my help?"

"No, no. You take it easy and lay low with the kids and Crucita. I would not advise taking them to the stores or restaurants here in town. If you want to do something like that, go to Gila Bend or Phoenix."

"I will. I just mainly want to let them rest and get their strength back up, as well as get used to me. I'm getting my truck back on Monday, so I think we'll head for home after I get it."

"Good idea. I hate to see you go but it would be best. I don't want anyone around to get wind of the kids. We don't know what has become of Victor. I have not heard if he has been picked up or not. I'm going to try to find out without raising any red flags."

"That would be good. I hope Victor is long gone by now. If he gets picked up, surely he would be afraid to mention being a witness to a murder and abandoning two little kids in the desert."

"Yeah, you're probably right. At least he did save their lives and left them in good hands."

"I agree."

They said goodbye with plans to have dinner together that evening. While the morning was still cool and comfortable, Dawson, Crucita and the children sat outside. Sonora scampered about and played with Saray. Miguel brought his toy road construction set and played in the sand. Crucita looked at Dawson and smiled with admiration.

"You are something else Dawson Lee. You go on vacation and end up with a ready-made family. I am sure you are going to throw Mrs. Lianne into shock!"

He raised his eyebrows and looked at her with uncertainty.

"How do you think she will handle all of this?"

"I don't know for sure when she learns of this. But, I do know that once she meets them that she will fall in love with them."

"I sure hope so," Dawson expressed with a tinge of trepidation.

His confidence had waned some as the reality of what he was doing sank in. He had made a major life changing decision concerning their marriage without consulting Lianne, albeit she was unavailable and the decision could not be put off. He hoped that Lianne would be acceptable with taking on two children without any warning, much less proper planning. Would everything work out? Will Lianne be happy with this?

CHAPTER 130

As the day slipped by, Dawson got the jitters and worried about the children. Kay had made him somewhat uneasy with her talk of checking into the children's background. He was afraid that the immigration service or police would get wind of it and take the children away.

After lunch Dawson went online and checked his emails. None from Lianne. There were two from Holly at the store and one from his mother. He answered them and sent Lianne an update on the kids.

Crucita spent the afternoon giving the children English lessons. Miguel was a quick study and picked up words and phrases like a sponge. Saray was bashful but seemed to understand more English than she would speak.

While working with the kids, Crucita translated their names into English. Miguel was Michael and Saray was Sarah. Crucita told Dawson that they both liked the English version of their names. He readily agreed they would use the English ones.

Crucita taught Miguel how to print the name "Michael" and she worked with Saray to write "Sarah". She checked with Dawson and they agreed to shorten "Sarah" to "Sara to make it easier for Saray to spell.

Not long after the name issue was settled, Kay called. She asked how the kids were doing. Dawson told her about their English lessons and their choice to use the English version of their names.

"How do you plan to spell their names?" she queried.

"You must be psychic! We were just working on that. We will do Michaels the regular way, M-I-C-H-A-E-L, but we decided to spell Sarah; S-A-R-A."

"That's great. I think using English names will be even better."

"Well, tell me. What have you found out about our children here?"

"Not a whole lot. I still have some digging to do. Why don't you meet me at our favorite watering hole at six? We can have a drink and dinner and I will fill you in on all I know."

"Okay then. I'll meet you there."

They said goodbye. Whatever Kay was up to and had learned, he felt must not be too bad because there seemed to be no sense of urgency in her voice. He felt a dose of relief because he felt that now the kids were in no danger of being picked up.

"Crucita, I am going to meet Kay this evening for dinner. She will tell me then what information she has learned about the children. Why don't you take the Explorer and drive to the grocery store and get something special to cook for you and the kids while I'm gone. I'm sure you could use a break from being cooped up here in the camper."

"Are you sure? I don't mind staying and letting you go shopping."

"No, no. You get out for a few minutes I wish we could all go but it's best to not let the kids be seen around here."

"Well, okay then."

She spoke to the kids about what they might like to eat and decided to make them an American style pizza. Dawson sat on the sofa with Michael on one side and Sara on the other while they watched cartoon network together. He was not particularly interested in cartoons, but it felt good to be doing something with them.

While they watched television, Sara sucked her thumb and occasionally cut her eyes up at Dawson, studying him. She finally eased one hand into his. His eyes teared up from the incredible show of trust and love from his new little daughter.

The children began to nod off while sitting with Dawson. He turned the television off and took them to the bed and had them lie down. They both looked at him expectantly so he climbed in bed by them and lay down. Soon Michael dozed off. Lying there facing them, he watched Sara look at him with her big brown eyes. She whispered, "Sara, Sara, Sara."

Dawson grinned and kissed her little hands.

"Yes Sara, my Sara."

"My Sara," she repeated.

A while later the door to the camper opened and Dawson opened his eyes. He had not realized he had fallen asleep. Crucita quietly eased in and sat a bag down and went back to the SUV for more. When she came back Dawson was putting the groceries away.

"I'm sorry I woke you," she whispered.

"Oh, no problem. I didn't mean to fall asleep. The kids got sleepy watching television. I laid down with them for a few minutes and fell asleep unintentionally."

Sonora shot in the door from outside. Dawson fed her and made himself a cup of coffee while Crucita finished putting the groceries up.

ONCE UPON A MIDNIGHT DESERT

CHAPTER 131

Crucita was making a homemade Mexican style pizza when Dawson left out at a quarter of six to meet Kay for dinner. Michael and Sara both kissed him goodbye and said, "I love you" as he got ready to leave. He was still feeling the tingling effects of the lingering smile on his lips when he pulled into the restaurant and bar.

Arriving before Kay he went to the bar and ordered a beer from Judy, the bartender. She told him that Kay had called and said she would be a few minutes late but to please relax and wait.

"No problem, Judy. I'm early anyway."

He and Judy talked between her serving other customers. She quizzed him about Lianne. She too was a fan. It was thrilling for her to get to know Lianne's husband.

"Looks like Judy has been talking your head off!" greeted Kay as she walked up to the bar.

She kissed Dawson on the cheek and sat down beside him.

"Well Kay, it's not every day we get somebody so special in here."

Kay laughed.

"All right Dawson. Let's me and you get a table and let Judy work for a change. Judy, will you get me a beer, and a fresh one for Mister Special."

Judy giggled.

"Sure thing. Coming right up."

The two got a table and ordered steak dinners. Judy brought their beers. Kay took a long pull on hers and sighed with relief.

"I have been a busy girl and I have a lot of things to share with you."

"I pray its good news."

"Oh yes, for the most part. First, I drove down south of the border to Sonoya and tracked down the children's elderly aunt. She had already found out about the death of Mari. The murder took place near the Mexican side of the border. She and two others were killed. The Aunt's worried about how she will pay for Mari's burial."

Dawson held his hand up.

"I'll take care of that."

Kay patted his hand.

"You know, I had a feeling you would. I have the information on who to get in touch with concerning that. Anyway, the aunt is the only surviving relative that was involved in the kid's life and is indeed very poor. Her health is bad too."

"Anything I can do?"

"I seriously doubt it, Dawson. She's old and frail. It's just a matter of time."

"Sorry to hear that."

"I had a long talk with her and told her about you and the kids. She is pleased to hear that we found them and that you are willing to take them as your own. She even signed them over to you."

"That sounds promising."

"It gets better. Hang on."

Their steaks arrived. Kay stopped talking while the waitress arranged their meals and filled their water glasses then left.

"Now, I took the liberty of doing something special for you. I have some connections and I called on them. I know some people in the right places that can do things that usually can't be done easily."

She reached in her purse and pulled out a thick envelope.

"I know I'm not making any sense so let me lay it all out. I have ninety-nine-point-nine percent pure adoptions papers giving Michael and Sara Rivera to you and Lianne. Locally, these might be questionable, but five states away they should suffice nicely. So, take these with my blessing and officially raise those kids as your own. Like I say, it's official now – sort of, kind of, but don't show them around here."

Dawson was speechless. His hands trembled as he took the adoption papers and read them. He also found new, official looking birth certificates showing that the children had been born in the United States. He looked up at Kay, tears leaked from his eyes. He quickly wiped them away.

"I don't know what to say, Kay."

"Don't say anything. Just take those little angels home and love them. I would like to stay in touch with you and hear how they are doing."

"That I will certainly do. If you and Walter ever want to come for a visit either in Georgia or our D.C. home, you would be very welcomed."

"Same here."

"Lianne wants to come out and see Organ Pipe Cactus Monument one day. We will surely visit you when we do. I want Lianne to meet you."

"That would be wonderful. I would really appreciate the opportunity to get to know her."

There was a quiet pause as the two ate and enjoyed the moment. Dawson was so excited that he could hardly eat or even taste the food he did eat. Over their after dinner coffee, Dawson recovered enough from the shock of news to thank her again. She laughed and leaned over and kissed him on the cheek.

"You are truly a good caring man Dawson. I have met two such men now. I married one of them."

Dawson shook his head and smiled.

"You are the finest Tohono O'odham woman I have ever known."

She grinned and said, "And the only one you have ever known!"

Dinner over, Dawson and Kay said goodnight to Judy. He walked Kay out to her truck. He gave her a hug and thanked her again.

"Would you like to come over and visit a while?"

"No, not tonight. I'm kind of worn out. It has been a busy but productive day."

"I believe that!" Dawson agreed, shaking his head. "You pulled off an amazing feat and I can't thank you enough."

"You can thank me by having a good life with your fantastic wife and those two darlings. And, your other little desert angel, the one and only Sonora."

"She is special, isn't she?"

"Yep, I think you are a regular Doctor Doolittle!"

The two hugged again.

"I can tell you this Kay. I have had quite an experience here in southern Arizona. I only came here because my father had always wanted to and I wanted to fulfill his dream."

"Well Dawson. Take it from an old wise medicine woman, it was meant to be. The great spirits brought you here. Your father is one of those great spirits among the stars now. He had a hand in all of this."

Dawson nodded sagely. A huge lump rolled down his throat, tears slid down his cheeks.

Kay put her hands on his cheeks and looked into his eyes.

"Your father was a special man Dawson Lee. He has passed that legacy on to you. Now you can pass that on to your two children."

"That, I will proudly do," he said, and meant it.

CHAPTER 132

Pulling into the parking space at the campsite and shutting the engine off, Dawson smiled when Michael, Sara, and Sonora came running out to greet him. When he got out of the truck both children grabbed him by the arm.

"Come, ice cream, eat." Urged Michael.

"I would love some!"

Crucita was sitting on the patio scooping ice cream into bowls. She smiled at Dawson as he walked up carrying Sara in his arms.

"Hey Daddy Dawson," she greeted.

"Hello to you my eldest daughter."

"How do you like being a dad?"

"I love it. Couldn't be happier." He paused. "Well, I could be if Lianne was here to celebrate with us tonight."

"Sounds like Kay had some good news for you."

"Yep. Our dearest friend Kay worked some magic. We now have official adoptions papers for the kids. She says that they should be good enough to get Social Security cards for the two U.S. born orphans."

Crucita nodded understanding and appreciating.

"Let's celebrate then. Here's a bowl of ice cream Daddy Dawson!"

She handed everyone a bowl full of ice cream and even had one for Sonora. It was dark now and the stars were out in all of their magnificence. Dawson looked up at them and smiled at his father.

While they all sat outside enjoying the cool night air, Dawson got out two chemical break and shake lights for the kids. Michael and Sara were amazed by their green glow. They ran around looking like two-legged fireflies as they chased Sonora.

It was after nine o'clock when the happy campers wound down and went inside. Crucita gave the kids a bath and put them to bed, each still holding on to their chemical light sticks. Dawson helped tuck them in and kissed them goodnight. Both said again in English that they loved him.

After Crucita took a shower, Dawson took his. By then the kids were sound asleep. Dawson set up the laptop and emailed Lianne. He gave her an update and told her about the adoption papers. He also informed her of their plans to start for home on Monday, reminding her to contact him as soon as she could. That done, he sent the email and shut the computer off. He and Crucita sat on the sofa in the dark and quietly talked for a short while. Sonora had climbed onto Crucita's lap and she was petting her.

"You know Dawson. I don't think Mrs. Lianne will ever let you go on vacation by yourself again. If you did, you would have to buy a bigger house with the kind of souvenirs you bring home."

He grinned.

"I did well, didn't I?"

"Yes you did Dawson. You did real well!"

Crucita kissed Dawson goodnight and climbed in bed with Michael and Sara. Sonora took her perch on the top bank and settled in for the night. Dawson eased into his bunk and lay there thinking about how lucky he was. He drifted off to sleep wondering about Lianne and if she was safe and well.

He was awake before anyone. As soon as he got up Sonora plopped down and went to the door and stared back at him. He let her out and made a pot of coffee. After cutting up a bowl full of cantaloupe, he took it and his coffee and sat outside. Sonora strolled back from exploring and ate her fruit.

Since it was early Dawson decided to gather up the dirty clothes and take them to be washed. He and Sonora walked along the quiet campground streets and to the Laundromat. He loaded two washers and sat down to wait. Sonora climbed onto his lap.

A car pulled up outside and Dawson heard a door open and close. An older lady came in with a basket of laundry. She saw Sonora and took a step back.

"What is that?"

"This is Sonora. She's a coati. She is in the raccoon family."

"Does she bite?"

"No ma'am. She's quite friendly."

The lady got her clothes to washing then came and sat down beside them. She tentatively patted Sonora and soon warmed up to her. She and Dawson chatted while they waited on their wash. He learned that she and her husband were from Canada and enjoyed traveling several months out of each year.

By the time Dawson dried and folded his laundry, he and Mrs. Lemieux were like old friends. Before he and Sonora left she got her camera and had him take a picture of her holding Sonora.

He and Sonora then said goodbye and walked back toward their campsite. Sonora trotted along, occasionally stopping to explore a new scent. When they got back to the camper, Crucita and the children were up and breakfast was almost ready.

"Good morning everyone," he greeted.

"Good morning Daddy Dawson," greeted Michael, followed by Sara.

Dawson looked at Crucita who wore a big grin. He smiled at her and the children.

"Well, a big good morning to both of you my lovely children."

CHAPTER 133

Crucita washed and dried the breakfast dishes while Michael and Sara stood on the patio and watched Sonora eat a banana. Dawson was drinking another cup of coffee and wiping down the dinette table.

"What do you have planned for the day?" asked Crucita.

"I was just thinking about that. Since today is Sunday and we can pick the truck up in the morning, I thought we could spend the rest of today and tonight in Phoenix. I think maybe we could find a motel with a pool. The kids could swim and play in the water and have a good time. We have a long haul ahead of us. I think it would be good for us all to do some fun things today."

"Shall I pack for us?"

"Yes, get them a change of clothes. I'll pack me something. We'll pick them up some swim suits when we get there."

"I'll need one too. I didn't think to pack one."

"No problem."

"What about Sonora?"

"She's going with us."

Crucita laughed.

"You really love her don't you?"

"Yep. I really do! I'll pack her litter box and food."

They got busy packing and soon were on their way. Dawson had called Kay and told her their plans. He promised that they would have lunch with her before they left for home on Monday.

As they neared the outskirts of Phoenix, Dawson pulled into a motel with a pool. They were in Avondale on the western side of Phoenix. He found out the motel allowed pets so he checked them into a room with two beds. After getting settled in, they left Sonora in the room eating a bowl of fruit and drove to a nearby Walmart. They found bathing suits for Crucita and the kids. While Michael and Sara picked out a few pool toys, Dawson grabbed an assortment of snacks and soft drinks to have in the motel room. When they checked out at Walmart it was lunch time but the kids were too excited about going swimming. Within minutes everyone was in their swim suits and heading for the pool.

Carrying Sonora in his arms, Dawson brought along a bowl of chips for her to the pool. He sat down on a deck chair and fed her chips while Crucita got in the pool with Michael and Sara. While watching and enjoying themselves, Dawson snapped the leash to Sonora's collar and tried walking her around the pool area. She was confused with the leash and its limiting her roaming ability. Thankfully the other people at the pool did not seem to mind her being there. There were some curious questions and a few wanted to pet her as she learned to handle being leashed.

When Dawson sat back down, Sonora settled by the chair and watched the kids playing. Dawson took a chance and attached the leash to the chair and then eased off into the pool. Sonora watching him, cocking her head from one side to the other. After chirping a few times she settled in the shade of the chair and watched him swim around and play with the children.

An hour in the pool and everyone was ready to get out. They showered, ate a late lunch snack, and got ready to go out. Dawson had picked up a newspaper and found a movie theater close by and took everyone to see a new Disney release. When they left, Sonora was peering out at them between the curtains.

It was Michael and Sara's first time going to a movie theater. They were in awe of the big screen, the buckets of popcorn, candy, and soft drinks that they were enjoying. The movie was in English, neither one seemed to mind and appeared to be having a wonderful time.

The movie over, they went back to the motel to check on Sonora. She was curled up on the bed when Dawson opened the door. The coati was beside herself when they came in. She was happy to see them and enjoyed the praise she received from everyone.

Before taking the crew out to dinner, Dawson took Sonora for a walk. He was learning that like Max, she preferred to do her business in the real dirt rather than a litter pan. This trip she handled the leash even better. He was afraid to let her go without it for fear that she would wander off and get lost or ran over.

For dinner, Dawson took them to a traditional Mexican restaurant. The children brightened in the more familiar setting and food. Dawson made a mental note to have Crucita cook a traditional Mexican meal for them regularly or he would take them out to a Mexican restaurant often.

When they got ready for bed, Michael surprised Dawson by asking if he could sleep with him while Sara slept with Crucita. He looked at Crucita and smiled.

"I know they can say I love you but now I am beginning to feel that they do indeed love me."

CHAPTER 134

On Monday morning, Dawson took Crucita and the children to breakfast then dropped them back off at the motel. He left them getting ready to go to the pool and drove into Phoenix to the Ford dealership. The truck was indeed ready so he turned in the rental, thanked the service department manager and said goodbye.

It felt strange but good to be back in his beloved truck. Now he could get his little family and head for home. He was whirling with excitement to get back and settle in to a new life with a four and six year old. He missed the store, the house and his life there. Also, he missed the Georgetown home, the flights back and forth, and he especially missed Lianne.

"Maybe soon I'll hear from her," he mumbled.

At the hotel, Crucita had everything packed and ready to go. Dawson walked down to the office and paid the bill while she loaded everything and everybody in the truck.

On the way back to Ajo, he called Kay. Since it was mid-morning, he opted to go ahead and get the travel trailer ready for hauling and check out of the campground. They would leave there and eat lunch at her house before heading east.

As soon as he reached the campsite, Dawson left Crucita, the kids and Sonora there while he rode back to the office and settled his account. Crucita had already began getting things in the camper secured for traveling when he got back. He hooked the trailer to the truck and plugged in the running light harness. After retracting the rear slide-out, he finished stowing and securing all of the loose items.

By the time he had everything ready Dawson was sweating profusely. While everyone piled in the truck he was plucking the front of his light-blue cotton shirt, tugging it away from his moistening chest. Little rivulets of sweat were snaking down his skin and pooling at his belt line in the small of his back, making it hard for him to keep still. He wished he had not unhooked the water supply so he could take a quick shower.

"Oh well," he bemoaned and climbed behind the wheel and cranked the engine.

He slowly eased the camper off of the parking pad and onto the road and drove through the campground that had become like a second, make that a third home for him, he thought to himself. Sonora climbed onto his lap and looked up at him. She grunted as if sensing something in her world was changing. Michael and Sara kept staring back at the camper in amazement that it was connected to truck and rolling along behind them.

In a rapid burst of Spanish, Michael asked Crucita something and she burst out in laughter then rattled of an answer to him. She was still giggling when she explained to Dawson what Michael had asked.

"Michael wanted to know if the house on wheels back there will be the same one we will live in when we get to Georgia. He is confused because you said he and Sara would have their own rooms."

Dawson laughed.

"No wonder he keeps looking back at the trailer. Did you explain that we have a bigger house with no wheels?"

"Yes I did. I explained that the trailer was just to stay in when you go on trips."

Per Kay's directions, Dawson found her house and parked in the street in front of it. She met them in the driveway as they were getting out of the truck. Dawson asked if she would mind if he used her shower. She readily said yes. He got a change of clothes and showered while Crucita helped her finish making lunch.

They ate then Dawson and Crucita helped her with the dishes. Kay and Dawson exchanged addresses, phone numbers and email addresses. They promised to keep in touch. Kay looked at Dawson with tears in her eyes.

"I am sure going to miss you Dawson. I have really enjoyed getting to know you."

"Same here Kay. I am so thankful that we met. I am also thankful for your help with the children."

"You are very welcome. I know that they are in good hands and will have a much better life then what the alternative would have been."

"Yep, I agree."

Time to go. Kay walked them out. Before leaving, Dawson got out his camera and took pictures of Kay standing with Crucita, Michael, Sara and Sonora. Kay then took some of Dawson and everyone together. He promised to send her a set of the prints. He also promised to send her an autographed picture of Lianne when she got back home.

Kay cried as she hugged everyone and said goodbye. She and Dawson had talked in private and she had agreed to attend the children's mother's funeral when the body was released for burial and the arrangements were made. With that on her mind she cried even more when she hugged and kissed Michael and Sara.

"I love you Dawson Lee," she said, giving him a final hug and kiss goodbye.

"I love you too Kay Benecome, my O'odham friend."

She smiled through her tears.

"Maybe next time you come we can make you an honorary member of the O'odham tribe."

"I would like that. When the kids get a little older I would like for you to teach them about their O'odham heritage."

"I will be happy to."

CHAPTER 135

Leaving out of Ajo with the travel trailer smoothly rolling along behind them, Dawson and family made for Tucson. He had decided to avoid getting on the interstate until he crossed over into New Mexico. Aware of the inspection stations at the border, he was wary about encountering them. It was not that he was worried so much about the kids. He was more worried about Sonora. He was not sure how the inspection agents would react to his transporting a wild animal out of the state.

Sonora settled in for the ride. She often rode on Michael's lap or beside him. The two had developed a notable bond and Sonora sought to be near him wherever they went. Michael frequently coddled and talked to her. Sara appeared to be more of an observer of everything Sonora did. Sara had grown attached to the Cabbage Patch doll that she picked out the first time Dawson took her shopping.

Late in the afternoon they crossed over into New Mexico. Dawson worked his way on the back roads until he connected onto I-10 East. After putting some miles behind them on I-10 he stopped at a motel just off of the interstate for the night. He opted to not use the camper or stay at campgrounds while heading east. Since he had Crucita to help drive, Dawson wanted to cover as many miles as they could each day. He was ready to get the kids and Sonora home.

Whenever they stopped for gas or to take a break, Dawson did much like he did with Max when they traveled. He would put Sonora on her leash and let her take care of her needs in the grass or dirt. He did keep a litter pan in the truck but she usually waited until they stopped to go outside. He also let her ride sometimes in the camper so she would have some room to move around. Whenever they stopped to eat, Dawson would put her in the camper and turn the air conditioner on. Either he or Crucita would fill her bowl with fruit or cat food so she could eat while they did. At times she became restless with the long hours of riding, but for the most part she did surprisingly well.

Two days of persistent driving and they crossed over into Mississippi and stopped for their last night on the road. They went to bed late but rose early and got back on the road. Soon they crossed over into Alabama. Selma, Montgomery, Auburn, Valley rolled by and then into Georgia as they crossed the Chattahoochee River. South on I-185 off of I-85, a short while later they pulled into the driveway and home. It was just getting dark; the outside lights had come on. The house was a wonderful sight to Dawson. His mother was there waiting for them. When she came out the front door to greet them, Max was by her side. He ran to the truck when Dawson shut the engine off and opened the driver's door.

"Hello there Max! Long time, no see," Dawson said, greeting the cat as he picked him up and hugged him. "I have a surprise for you."

He put Max down and helped Michael out while Crucita got Sara out of the truck's backseat. Crucita was the first to reach Mrs. Lee and gave her a hug. Dawson hugged her then presented the children.

"Mom, this is your, grandson Michael, and this little beauty is your granddaughter, Sara."

"Oh my, what beautiful children!"

In Spanish, Crucita explained to the children who Mrs. Lee was. Michael asked something and Crucita turned to Mrs. Lee.

"Michael wants to know what to call you?"

"Oh well, my goodness. Umm, they can call me anything they would like, even Rebecca would be fine."

Crucita spoke to Michael and he tried to say Rebecca which came out to be "Becca." Sara smiled and repeated the name, "Becca".

Dawson chuckled and kissed his mother on the cheek.

"Well Mom, I guess Becca it is!"

She smiled and stuck out her hands for the children to take.

"Come children. Let Becca show you around your new home."

"Wait Mom. Let me introduce you to your other grandchild," Dawson said with a grin.

Mrs. Lee looked at him curiously, not sure if she understood him.

"Another one?" she said confused.

"Yeah, she's in the trailer."

Mrs. Lee put her hand over her mouth and giggled, "Oh, I almost forgot your little coati friend."

"Yep."

He opened the camper door and Sonora stuck her head out. Max had wandered up and started to hop in the trailer. Sonora dropped to the ground and sniffed at Max. He saw her, hissed, bowed up, and then bolted off around the side of the house.

"Well, Dawson said flatly, "I guess Max is duly surprised."

He scooped Sonora up and followed everyone into the house. His mother and Crucita led the children around, showing them each room.

Mrs. Lee had a surprise for Michael and Sara. She had gone out and bought decorative comforters, curtains, rugs and accessories for their bedrooms. Sara's was done in a little princess fashion and Michael's was done in Spiderman style. Both kids were awestruck by the size and splendor. Dawson figured it was like a fairy tale come true for them.

Crucita took the kids out back and let them see the swimming pool and big backyard. Dawson had already promised them that he would put a gym set and a playhouse out there for them very soon.

Sonora wandered around in the house then found Max's food and water dish in the kitchen and began eating his cat food. Max came in with Crucita and the children. When he saw Sonora eating his food, he growled and hissed. Sonora looked at him curiously for a moment then resumed eating, ignoring him. Dawson laughed and shook his head.

"Mmm, I'm not sure how to go about getting them to accept each other."

"You're on your own on that one!" said Mrs. Lee, then laughed.

CHAPTER 136

Michael and Sara were overwhelmed by their new home. Both stood in their bedrooms and stared, not knowing what to do. Sonora seemed to have no difficulty making herself at home. She roamed all over the house checking out the nooks, crannies, and new smells. She occasionally stopped and stared at Max who kept watch from a safe distance and shadowed her as she went from room to room.

"That sure is a strange looking creature Dawson," remarked his mother as she watched Sonora and Max warily eyeing one another.

"She's great though, Mom. You'll see."

Mrs. Lee had already started dinner for them before they arrived. She busied herself getting everything ready. Crucita tried to help but she shooed her away.

"No, no dear. You rest. I know you have got to be tired from all of the traveling."

"I'm okay Mrs. Lee. I don't mind at all. I'd like to help."

"Well then, you set the table while I dish everything up."

"Yes ma'am."

While they were getting the food ready, Dawson showed Sonora how to go in and out of the cat door. He took her out in the backyard and walked around with her. The kids had followed them out. They were still amazed to see the swimming pool lit up by the night lights. Both stood at the edge and stared down in the water.

"Pretty water," said Michael.

"Yes it is," said Dawson. "It is yours to swim in anytime you would like, just as long as one of us adults are with you."

He looked at Dawson, his brows furrowed as he tried to decipher what he had said. Dawson patted him on the head.

"I'll get Crucita to explain the safety rules about the pool to you and Sara."

Mrs. Lee opened the back door and called all of them to dinner. Dawson picked Sonora up and carried her back in. He was not comfortable letting her stay outside without someone watching her until she got used to where she was at. He decided that at bed time he would lock the cat door so she could not go out.

"Max won't be happy about that," he muttered as they went in the house.

Dinner was pork chops, mashed potatoes, and early June peas, plus homemade rolls, Michael and Sara ate well enough but it was apparent that fatigue had set in. After dinner Crucita got them both ready for bed. Dawson and his mother were sitting in the den when she brought them in to say goodnight.

"Shall we try them in their own beds tonight?" asked Dawson, looking at his mother and Crucita.

"Let's give it a try. First we'll put Michael to bed and let Sara watch, then we'll take her to her room," suggested Mrs. Lee. "Crucita, tell them that if they need anything to call out. It might be a good idea to leave their doors open too."

They all took Michael to his room. He climbed into bed and Dawson covered him up, and then kissed him. Everyone followed suit, even Sonora and she hopped up and lay down beside him. Michael wrapped his arms around her and gazed sleepily at the group as they retreated from the room. Mrs. Lee had put night lights in both rooms which left them in a soft green glow, reminding Dawson of the night he gave the kids glow stick lights to play with.

The same scenario was played out for Sara in her room. She snuggled up with her doll and accepted goodnight kissed from everyone, her huge brown eyes heavy with fatigue. When everyone started backing out of her room, Sara said "Kitty?"

"Ahh, I noticed you seemed to like Max," said Dawson.

He went and got Max and sat him on the bed by Sara. She rubbed his fur and patted him on the back. He lay down beside her and stared at Dawson, his tail twitching. Dawson chuckled and patted his head.

"I think Max is not too happy with me right now. I've brought an intruder home and upset his kingdom."

Easing out of Sara's room Dawson, his mother and Crucita sat down in the den. They talked quietly while waiting to see if the children would be all right alone in their rooms.

"Crucita, are you staying here tonight or are you going to your dads?" asked Dawson.

"I called him. He still has a couple of guys staying with him. I feel more comfortable here, if you don't mind."

"You won't get any complaints from me. This is your home too."

Mrs. Lee and Crucita finished cleaning the kitchen then she left for home. Dawson invited Crucita to join him in the Jacuzzi. He made himself a cup of coffee and poured her a coke while she changed into her bathing suit.

The two relaxed in the tub and made plans for the rest of the week. Dawson wanted to spend the next day at the store. Crucita said she and the kids would work on cleaning the travel trailer and let them swim in the pool some.

At ten o'clock Dawson was online and waiting for Lianne to connect if she could. It did not happen. He had gotten a short email from her CNN reporting station that said she was fine and would be in contact in the next day or two. Disappointed, Dawson shut the computer down. Checked in on the sleeping children, and then went to bed.

He lay there in the dark enjoying the comfort of his bed and thinking of Lianne. He sorely missed her. A soft clump and swishing sounds interrupted his musings. It was Sonora. She settled in by him. He then felt another soft plop and Max eased up toward the foot of the bed and lay down. Dawson smiled as he slowly drifted off to sleep.

CHAPTER 137

It was a little past six in the morning when he became cognizant. The sun was just showing in on another wise clear, blue sky over Georgia. Dawson was still feeling a bit road weary, but wide awake now, he sat up and looked out of the bedroom window.

Stiff and sore, he slowly got out of bed and stepped into the shower. Adjusting the water to as hot as he could stand it, he stood under the spray and let it rain down on his back and shoulders. When he immerged, dried off and dressed, he felt much better.

When he walked into the kitchen he was surprised to find Crucita cooking breakfast for him. She was fussing at Max and Sonora.

"What's going on?"

"I was just getting on to them. They are going to have to get along. The sooner they quit hissing and spitting at each other, the better."

She had placed Sonora's food and water dishes on the opposite side of the kitchen from Max's. Both animals were eating and eying each other, Max making occasional growling sounds while Sonora grunted and snorted.

"All right you two. That's enough!" scolded Dawson.

Max and Sonora looked up at him for a moment, then went back to staring at each other, but made no noises. The children were still asleep. Crucita had decided to let them sleep until they were ready to get up.

While she finished cooking, Dawson took a cup of coffee and stepped out back onto the patio. He watched the pine trees slowly ripple and frill in the early morning breeze. The swoosh and whisper of the wind through them brought a familiar comforting feel to his soul.

"Home," he mumbles. "Good to be home."

He had everything he could possible want now. The only drawback was that Lianne was still so far away. Maybe soon he would have her home.

"Come in and eat," called Crucita.

Dawson turned and smiled at her then went in and sat down. The two ate together. Crucita made notes as they ate and talked. Her main objective of the day was to empty the camper of food then scrub the refrigerator and stove. She would unload all of the clothing and wash those that were dirty. She would also make an inventory of what clothing the children now had and what they needed.

"I thought that maybe later today the children and I would stop by the store and let them meet whoever is there and see what their dad does for a living."

"Great idea. Holly and your dad should be there. I think I'll head on in now and sort through the mail and paperwork while it's quiet. Once the doors are open for business it gets a little hectic at times."

"I figured you would. That's why I got on up early."

"Am I that predictable?"

"Yep, you are," she declared, and smiled.

Instead of unhooking the trailer so he could drive the truck to work, Dawson left it where he had parked it and fired up the Mustang. He sat there as the engine warmed and breathed in Lianne's perfume that lingered in the car's interior. He shuddered and his eyes filled with tears; he missed her so much.

Swallowing his loneliness, Dawson backed the car out into the road and drove into town. It felt like he had been gone forever when he saw the store, parked and went in. He walked around the sales floor for a few minutes looking at everything. The store was in picture perfect shape. He stopped and stared at the poster of him, Lianne, and Cali, Kinsley modeling outdoor clothing. He studied the one of Lianne sitting in the kayak wearing a bikini. He longed to hold her in his arms.

"Whoa! Gotta get my act together."

He walked in the back room and got a pot of coffee brewing. While waiting for the coffee to make, he sat down at his desk. It was clean and neat, Holly's immaculate touch. The store was a magical place for him. He really loved it. It reminded him of his father.

"All right now Dawson. Get it together," he admonished, then got up and went to get coffee.

He poured a cup, added cream and sugar, and then walked back to the front sales area. He heard the front door lock click open and looked up to see Holly coming in.

She squealed with delight and ran into his arms.

"I am so happy you are back. My goodness, you look so good. I love your tan."

Overwhelmed, Dawson squeezed her with one arm trying to balance the full cup of coffee in the other and not spill it.

Holly was bubbling with excitement as she filled him in on some of the large sales they had made. She also showed him some of the new equipment that had come in.

A short time later Roberto came in and greeted him warmly. It was good to be back, Dawson kept saying to himself as he settled into a working mode.

Toward mid-morning Amber and Paul popped in to welcome Dawson back. Paul had brought a box of fresh pastries for the mini celebration. Everyone stood around drinking coffee and listening to Dawson's account of his adventures. Occasionally they stopped and helped customers then returned to the informal gathering. They were all thrilled to hear about his adopting two children and a coati. Since they were all there and business was still slow, Dawson called Crucita and had her bring the kids in to meet everyone.

"Oh Crucita, if you don't mind, bring Sonora along."

"Okay, we'll be there in a few minutes."

CHAPTER 138

When Crucita arrived with Michael, Sara and Sonora, the store's employees were excited and received them cordially. Amber was smitten with Sonora and coddled her like a baby. Holly took over Sara and lavished her with hugs and kisses. She knew enough Spanish to have a simple conversation with her. Michael wandered around the store, intrigued with the outdoor gear displays. He walked around and carefully looked at everything.

Customers came and went but the festive atmosphere remained. The only disappointment for Dawson was the question from everyone about what Lianne thought about the children. All he could say was that they had not talked and he felt she would be happy.

Before Crucita left with the kids and Sonora, Dawson fitted Michael and Sara with pairs of Timberland hiking boots. Both kids were quite happy with them. They said goodbye and Dawson helped them get Sonora safely into the car.

"I'll see you shortly after five," he said as they were leaving.

The afternoon went by quickly at the store for Dawson. When he got home, dinner was ready and they all ate together. Afterwards he and Crucita took the kids for a swim. When they got tired of the pool all of them ended up in the Jacuzzi.

At bed time Crucita got them into their pajamas, then said goodnight. He was pleased that they had adapted to their rooms and sleeping alone so easily.

Max and Sonora slowly began to calm down and tolerate one another. Crucita had placed the feeding dishes closer together. The two soon ate side by side without growling or bothering the other.

Crucita left to go visit her father and said she would be in late. When she left, Dawson made a Bloody Mary and powered up the computer. No email from Lianne. He looked at the time. It was a quarter of nine.

"Maybe," he said hoping that she would connect at ten.

He took the portable phone and walked out back and sat by the pool. Looking up at the moon, he wondered where Lianne was and what she was doing. He took a sip of Bloody Mary and sat it down. The phone began to ring. He picked it up and pushed the button.

"Hello?"

"I'm looking for a tall, dark handsome man who has lost his mind," came a familiar voice.

Dawson was so taken aback that he dropped the phone. It hit the deck chair and clattered onto the concrete apron of the pool. He caught it just in time before it skittered off into the pool.

"Lianne!" he shouted.

"Yep. It's me, my favorite husband."

"Favorite, I hope I'm the only one!"

"For the time being. You never know how things go. If he gets any crazier I may have to trade him in."

"Oh my goodness Lianne. It is so good to hear your voice."

"Not as happy as I am to hear yours."

"Oh honey, so much has happened since we last talked."

"You can say that again! I just got back to my room here in Kabul. I've been reading these wild emails from you. I'm still in shock Dawson. I really don't know what to say or think. This is all so monumental. I'll totally flabbergasted."

"I know Lianne. I understand. I am sorry for laying all of this on you so sudden and without warning. It all came down so quick. But wait until you see Michael and Sara, you will understand why I did what I did."

"I sure hope so Dawson."

Her statement set off alarm bells in his brain. He did not know what to say.

There was an excruciatingly long silent pause.

"So, did you bring that ugly fuzz ball of a creature home too?"

"Yes, I brought Sonora home too," he said with no joy.

"Hmm. What does Max think?"

"He's not real pleased but they tolerate on another."

"Dawson, I just don't know about all of this," she castigated.

"I'm sorry," he said softly.

"Tell me this. Is everything you did about those children on the up and up? You know the legal aspects?"

"Yes," he said uneasily. At least he hoped so.

"You do know that if anything ever came to light that was not above board, it would wreck my career? You understand that, don't you?"

"Yes, Lianne. I do. I would never intentionally do anything to hurt your career."

More silence.

"Well, I just got in. I want to unpack, eat and take a long hot bath. I will try to get on the video uplink with you-say, ten-thirty."

"Okay."

"Sure Lianne. I'll be standing by."

"Okay then. Love you...."

She clicked off without waiting for his response. Dawson sat there feeling queasy and troubled. He slowly got up and walked into the kitchen and poured his drink down the drain.

CHAPTER 139

Disheartened by the way Lianne talked on the phone, he was suddenly not all that excited about the real-time video connection with her that was to come. Dawson stood in the den and looked at the computer. Finally, he punched the power button. Once the system was up he called up the video program and left it on ready.

Feeling down, Dawson walked down the hall to Michael's room and eased in and stood by the bed. The precious boy had his new hiking boots in the bed beside him. Sonora was curled by his back. Dawson's heart soared with love for his son.

Quietly, he left Michael's room and went in Sara's. Thumb in her mouth, she was sleeping crossways on the bed, her covers kicked off and hanging off to the side. She looked so peaceful. It was hard to imagine that looking at them now, that just days ago their mother was murdered as they tried to cross the desert to freedom and a better life.

He walked back to the kitchen then stepped out on the patio and looked up at the stars and moon.

"Lord, what do I do? I love those kids in there, and I love Lianne. I could not give them up now. I don't want to lose Lianne either. Please Lord, I don't want to be forced to choose between them.

His breath caught and he shuddered with agony as he walked back inside. Picking up the phone, Dawson started to call Kay but thought better of it. He did not want to worry her. In fact, he did not want to tell her if Lianne rejected the kids.

It was almost ten-forty-five when Lianne came online. She was cheerful, but not her usual self. Dawson did his best to not let his hurt show. He did not bring up or volunteer anything else about the children. He did answer when she asked anything concerning them, which was very little. When they signed off on the video program he felt empty inside confused and hurt, he retreated to his room and sat in the dark when he heard Crucita drive into the garage and park.

His sleep was troubled and at 5:00 a.m. he got up, dressed and eased out of the house. He unhooked the trailer and drove the truck into town and pulled up to the Waffle House. Ordering coffee and an order of hash browns, he sat staring at empty air and ate with no joy.

He arrived at the store two and a half hours before time to open. Sitting in the office, he stared at the stack of paperwork in the inbox waiting to be done. He just could not focus nor bring himself to begin. After a few minutes he went in the stock room. He swept and mopped it even thought it was not really in need of cleaning.

The day went terribly slow. He hid his frustration by busying himself helping put up stock on the sales room shelves, ordering inventory and waiting on customers.

At 5:00 p.m. Amber shoved him out the door. He reluctantly drove home. No one was there when he got there. Crucita had left a message that she had taken the kids to Chuckie Cheese's and that they would eat while they were there. She had made him a light dinner and had it warming in the oven.

Unable to eat, he raked the plate of food into the disposal and got rid of it. He washed the plate and set it in the dish drainer.

At eight o'clock Crucita and the children made it home. Michael and Sara were excited as they showed Dawson the prizes they had won while playing the games at Chuckie Cheese's. Crucita then herded them in for their bathes. She and Dawson then put them to bed. Crucita said she was going to take a shower. Dawson used the opportunity to retreat to his bedroom.

A long while later the house was quiet. Dawson checked on both kids then went back to his room. He left the door ajar so he could listen out for the kids if they called out. He had not bothered to go online at ten to see if Lianne would connect. He did not expect her to anyway. And, he was not up to talking to her.

He quietly went to the kitchen and stood in the dark for a moment, not sure what he wanted. He then went to the bar and poured and downed a stiff drink of Jack Daniels. Taking a deep breath to quell the burning in his gut, he knocked back and swallowed a second shot of the fiery brew. His throat burned then went numb. He poured another two fingers and swallowed it. The infusion of alcohol hit him like a runaway train.

"Maybe I can sleep now," he muttered and made his way back to his bedroom.

Before lying down, he opened the drapes and let the moonlight in. The room took on a soft white hue. He slipped out of his sweat pants and climbed on the bed. He sat back against the headboard and looked out the window.

So focused on his misery, Dawson did not hear the soft shuffle coming across the carpet toward the bed.

CHAPTER 140

"Dawson."

He jerked when he heard his name. Dawson spun around to see Crucita standing there. She was wearing an outsized t-shirt nightgown. Her long dark hair had an electric blue sheen to it in the moonlight coming through the windows.

"Oh, I'm sorry. I didn't hear you come in."

"Do you mind if I sit with you for a few minutes?"

"No of course not Crucita. Everything okay?"

She got on the bed on her knees and scooted across until she was in front of him.

"No. Everything is not okay. I'm okay and the kids are okay, but you are not."

In an instant they were locked in an embrace. The dam burst and Dawson was crying his head buried in her shoulder. Between racking sobs he told Crucita about how things had gone with Lianne concerning the children. She held him and let him cry and talk about his pent up hurt and sorrow. He shuddered as she held him and rubbed her hands up and down his back.

"Hang on a moment. I'll be right back," she said and slid off the bed.

She left the room and moments later returned with another shot of Jack Daniels. She had him drink it all down and crawled back into his arms. She laid her head against his chest.

"I knew something was wrong when you were not up when I got in last night. Then you left before I got up and didn't call to check on us all day."

"I am sorry Crucita. I don't want to worry you with my problems."

"Dawson. You can always come to me. I love you more than you could ever imagine. I have never been treated as kind in all of my life as I have been with you. There is nothing that I would not do for you."

"You are a blessing Crucita. I love you very too. Without you I would be in a mess with these kids. I love them so much. I would not be able to communicate with them without you. I feel like I may have to choose between the kids and Lianne. I don't think I can do that. I do know I cannot and will not abandon Michael and Sara."

"No matter what happens Dawson, I am on your side. I will say this. If Lianne does not want the children, I will take them and raise them for you. If you will help me get a place and let me keep working for you, I can do it."

Tears came to Dawson's eyes.

"You are a champion, Crucita."

They lay in one another's arms and Dawson fell into an alcohol induced sleep with his face buried in her hair. When he awoke, sunlight was streaming in the window. He looked around for Crucita but she was gone. Sitting up, he noticed a note on the pillow beside him. It was from Crucita telling him that she had called the store and told them that he would be in later. Confused, he then looked at the clock. It was 9:30 a.m.

"Whoa!" he groaned as he got up.

His head was throbbing from the too many, too fast, doses of Jack Daniels. He slid to the end of the bed and sat there a few minutes getting his head in balance, then went straight for a shower.

It was well after ten o'clock when he emerged from his room. Dawson walked into the kitchen and found the coffee maker burbling its last bit of water as it finished its brewing process. In the dining room he could see Curcita at the table with Michael and Sara. While pouring a cup of coffee he listened as she worked with them on their English.

When the kids noticed him they came bounding into the kitchen. Sara wrapped her arms around his leg in a bear hug.

"Good Morning Daddy," said Michael. "My sister and me play in the yard."

"Very good Michael. Well spoken."

Sara looked up at Dawson and said, "Good Morning Daddy. My sister – ah my brother and me play in the …."

She paused trying to remember the word.

"Yard?" said Dawson.

Her face lit up.

"Si - yes in the yard. Play?"

"Oh, you two want to play in the yard."

"Yes Daddy," replied Michael.

"Sure thing."

Michael and Sara bolted out the back door with Max and Sonora right behind them.

Dawson took a sip of coffee and stood leaning against at the kitchen counter. Crucita came in and stood in front of him, shyly glancing up at him, unable to look him in the eyes.

"Would you like breakfast, or an early lunch?"

"No, nothing for me. My stomach is doing flip flops. Thank you for asking."

An awkward silence hung between them. Crucita looked down at the floor, wringing her hands nervously.

She finally leaned forward and laid her head against his chest.

"I am sorry about the troubles you have with Mrs. Lianne," she said softly.

Dawson set his cup down and wrapped his arms around her.

"Thank you for caring Crucita. I don't know what I would do without you right now. I would surely be lost, especially with the kids."

He kissed the top of her head. She looked up into his eyes. It felt as though she was reaching into his soul. An odd sensation caused the lower part of his stomach to tingle.

"Ah, Crucita. I don't remember a lot about last night. Did I do anything improper to you? You know, ah…?"

The corners of her lips formed a small smile as they curled upwards.

"No, you did not. You were a perfect gentleman. I probably would not have stopped you if you had tried something, but you didn't."

"Whew!" he said, letting out a rush of air.

Crucita laughed and kissed him on the cheek. She then made herself a cup of coffee. Dawson shook his head, feeling giddy with relief.

"You are something else Crucita!"

CHAPTER 141

Over the next days the Lee household began to settle into a comfortable routine. Dawson worked each day from nine to five. On weekends he took the children to movies, baseball games, the park, and the nearby recreational places such as Calloway gardens and Warm Springs. Occasionally Crucita went along, but most often it was just him and the kids. It was time when Dawson and the children learned to communicate with each other better.

Crucita steadily worked teaching Michael and Sara English and the weekend outings with Dawson proved great times for them to practice. School was fast approaching for the kids. Dawson had indeed gotten Social Security cards for them. They were now certified U.S. citizens.

Lianne contacted Dawson every other night. She was always warm and friendly. However, there was an unspoken wedge between them, both avoiding anything pertaining to the children. Dawson would answer questions about their welfare but volunteered little. He was dismayed that she had yet asked to see pictures of them.

The palpable void between Dawson and Lianne seemed to widen as her time neared for her to come back to the states. She did share some good news in that she had been offered the Washington D.C. bureau desk. It would take her off the road and she would spend much of her time monitoring and reporting governmental activities of the White House.

In early August Michael entered the first grade and Sara began pre-K. Crucita had planned to take them to school and pick them up but they wanted to ride the big yellow school bus with their friends. Their English improved in leaps and bounds as they immersed themselves into Americana.

Crucita had been wanting to go to college so Dawson helped her enroll in the local community college. She surprised him when she chose to study pre-law. Her goal was to become an immigration lawyer.

The outdoor gear store continued to be profitable and a joy for Dawson. He felt alive and happy while there in spite of the gnawing fear of what would happen when Lianne got back. He had resigned himself to letting her go for the sake of the children. They needed him. They had a home and lots of love. He wanted to keep it that way. He could not and would not forsake them.

Max and Sonora finally became friends. They even chased and played with one another, though would not share their food bowls. Dawson took Sonora to the veterinarian for a check-up. She was in good health and received a round of dog and cat vaccines, much to her consternation.

Lianne's two month stint in Afghanistan turned into three. Though Dawson loved and missed her, he did not protest the extension of time. She certainly did not appear to be troubled by it. When time neared for her to come back she informed him that she planned to spend a few days at the

Georgetown house before coming to Tanner. It did not surprise Dawson that she would, but what surprised him was that she did not invite him to come up. For the time being he shook it off and focused on work and the children.

Crucita began her classes at the community college. Luckily she was able to arrange her class schedule so that it did not interfere with being able to help get the kids off to school and being there when they got home. Her father's guests finally had gotten their own place to live so she began staying with him most of the time at night.

In Michael's first grade class they had show and tell each Friday. He had told their teacher about Sonora and she invited Dawson to bring her to class for show and tell. Michael's class was enthralled with Sonora. They all wanted to touch and pet her. She took it all in stride. Dawson smiled as he saw Michael's popularity scale shoot up several notches.

The weekend before Lianne was due back in the states, Dawson and Crucita threw a back to school party. It would be the last time the pool would be used before Dawson shut it down for the winter.

Dawson was pleased to see that many of Michael's and Sara's schoolmates made it to the party. And, to his surprise, Crucita had a special guest as well. He was a nice young man, a classmate of hers who was notably enamored with her. Dawson's heart took a leap backwards. He knew that one day Crucita would be gone and with a family of her own.

His musings were interrupted when Sara came running up, dripping wet from the pool, calling his name.

"Daddy, Daddy. That boy over there keeps staring at me with his face!"

Dawson chuckled. A little tow-headed, freckled faced boy sat on the side of the pool smiling at her, apparently smitten.

"Sara. I believe he thinks you are very pretty and wants to be friends with you."

"What does pretty mean?" she asked, giving him a serious look.

"Ahh. You know, ah-bella. Yes that's it bella. He thinks you are beautiful!"

"Oh!" she gushed, then ran back to the pool.

The two jumped off into the shallow water and began to play.

CHAPTER 142

The back to school pool party had been a great success. Michael and Sara had enjoyed every moment of it. Dawson had gotten to know several of the parents, which many lived nearby. Plans were made for their children to visit one another so they could play together.

Crucita and her friend left at five o'clock to go to dinner and a movie. Dawson's mother had come to help with the party and the two of them cleaned up before she left for home. Both worn out, Michael and Sara were in bed before eight-thirty.

Dawson cranked up the Jacuzzi, made a Bloody Mary, and slid into the tub and relaxed. It had been a good day. He so wished Lianne could see how much fun it was with the kids and share his joy. His heart grew heavy as he thought about her returning next weekend.

"Well, to her house anyway, "he muttered, still hurt that she was in no hurry to see him or the children."

A ten o'clock he was sitting in front of the computer when Lianne logged on.

"Hey Dawson."

"Hello Lianne. You look nice."

"Thank you. So do you."

"How are things going there?"

"Pretty good. We are wrapping our reports up. We'll start packing and midweek we will begin the trip back. We should be back in the states on Thursday. I'll call you when I get home. I think I will rest over the weekend and get caught up on things here. I have a meeting to attend to on Monday then I will try to come down later in the week."

"Sure," he said, feeling slighted. "Is there anything you need me to do?"

"No. You just stay there and take care of your family. I'll be fine. I'll see you later on."

Her words stung him. He felt a surge of pain shoot through every nerve fiber in his body. It was a struggle to not fall apart as he felt as if he were a drowning man. Taking a deep breath, he mustered up enough courage to keep his emotions in check and hold back the tears that were threating to spill forth.

"I could come up there and help you unpack and get squared away," he squeaked out nervously, his heart slamming like a jack hammer against his rib cage.

"No, Dawson. You need to stay there. I will be all right. I said I would be down later in the week."

"But I miss you Lianne. It's been almost three months since we have been together."

She looked at him and planted a faux smile on her face.

"A few more days won't hurt you Dawson," she said dryly.

He nodded jerkily, defeated. His heart had shattered and in pieces at this feet. He looked dolefully at the screen, wanting to end the session. He felt the urge to run and hide. Lianne sighed and rubbed her forehead.

"Look Dawson. I love you. I really do. But, things have changed since I left. You made some major decisions that have drastically affected our lives. I am overwhelmed by it all. My work is important to me, Dawson. I don't want anything to jeopardize it. I can't afford any scandal or black mark against my professional image. Surely you understand?"

"Yes Lianne, I do. I am very sorry for putting you in a tight spot."

She sat looking at him for a moment.

"No Dawson. I don't think you do understand me," she said, shaking her head. "I love you anyway. We'll work something out when I see you, okay?"

"Sure Lianne. I'll be here – we'll be here when you can come down."

She sighed, her eyes telegraphing frustration.

"I'll call you when I get home."

"Okay," he replied, blinking away hot tears.

"Take care Lianne."

"You too Dawson," she said softly. "I love you. I'll see you soon."

She logged off. Dawson sat staring at the computer screen for several minutes before he shut the system down. He felt so alone and lost. A wave of panic hit him. He desperately wanted someone to hold him, to love him, to take the hurt away.

"Crucita," he whispered.

He started to call her then remembered she was on a date. If he called, he knew she would be there. He needed her, but then he shook his head in disbelief at what he was thinking.

"No stupid. You can't cross that line. You are married to Lianne. You can't go to someone else. If you do, then it's over," he said, chastising himself.

He continued to berate himself for wanting Crucita to fill a foolish need and jeopardize all he stood for. Then as stupidly, he thought of Amydee. He knew that if he called her she would probably come running just to take pleasure in wrecking his marriage.

"Meow!"

He looked down. Max was standing in the doorway staring at him. Dawson picked him up and held him close.

"Come on boy. Let's go to bed. I need a friend to hang out with and talk to."

"Meow!"

CHAPTER 143

She slipped out of her clothes and slid in bed next to him. Slowly she ran her hands over his chest and softly kissed his neck and ears. A need rose in him greater than he had ever known. She pulled at his t-shirt. He helped her get it off and she kissed him on the chest. He ran his fingers through her long soft hair, crying out in need. She kissed his lips, first gently then in a desperate way as if she wanted to crawl inside of him. Slowly she straddled him. He moaned with the hunger of a starving lion.

"Daddy, Daddy!" cried Sara.

Snatched from his dream, Dawson sat up, eyes flying wild as he reeled in his senses and looked around. Sara was tugging at his comforter.

"Daddy, Sonora ate my cereal and won't give it back!" she whined, sticking out her bottom lip.

He smiled and pulled her up and into his arms.

"Well sweetheart. What do you think we should do about it?"

"Umm. I could eat ice cream instead."

"Aha. But, that's not a breakfast food."

"Could be," she dead panned.

Dawson got up and with her in his arms; he nuzzled her neck with day old whiskers. She giggled and laughed. He shook off the shameful dream he had left behind and began a new day with his wonderful children.

They had breakfast, dressed and went to church. Afterwards they stopped by the home building supply and picked up an angel statue Dawson had on order and had arrived. Loading it and several more decorative building blocks in the truck, they left and stopped by McDonald's and ate lunch before going home.

After changing clothes, Dawson went to work on the project in the back yard. He had built a raised flower bed and placed the ornate angel statue in the middle of it. Michael and Sara sat on the park bench he had already put in place. With the angel statue firmly in place, he sat down beside his kids.

"When spring comes we will plant some pretty flowers for your mother. I don't want you to ever forget your mother Mari. I know she loved you so much. She's in heaven now and is an angel much like this statue of one you see here. Anytime you want, come out here and visit her and talk to her."

With Michael and Sara sitting on either side of him, Dawson then pulled them to him. He told them how great their mother was and how much she loved them. He then told them that next summer he planned to take them to Mexico to visit her grave and say hello to their Aunt Mia.

On Monday, Crucita was there early. She cooked breakfast and got the kids ready for school. She and Dawson stood out by the road until they were on the bus and had gone out of sight. That evening when he got in from work Crucita had dinner ready and stayed until they put the kids to bed. She turned and looked at Dawson while collecting her things to leave for home.

"Dawson. Let's talk for a moment."

"Okay Crucita. What's on your mind?"

"You."

"What do you mean?" he asked as they sat down at the dining room table.

She reached over and took his hand.

"Dawson, I love you. I can't stand to see you hurt and miserable. You have been trying to put on a good face but I know your heart. I know you are hurting. Why don't you go to Georgetown and be at the house when she gets there. Try to work things out with her. I know how much you love Lianne. I know that she loves you. Like I said, I will stand behind you on whatever you decide to do. Go on up there. I will take care of Michael and Sara. Don't worry about them. Go now! Stay as long as it takes. And remember, if need be I will take the kids and raise them if it will save your marriage. You can be a part of their lives in any way you want or can."

Tears streamed down his face.

"Thank you Crucita. I love you so much. Whoever marries you is certainly going to be one lucky man."

The two talked things out and with her encouragement he agreed to go to Georgetown. He flew out on Tuesday evening for Washington D.C.

The Georgetown house had been closed up for three months now. On Wednesday Dawson went to the grocery store and bought everything needed to restock the cabinets and refrigerator. He vacuumed, dusted and aired out the house. The windows were washed he bought fresh flowers and had the place looking immaculate for Lianne's arrival.

He had worked so hard that by late Wednesday afternoon there was nothing else to do. He called Lianne's parents and took a taxi to their house and had dinner with them. While there, Dawson had planned to talk to them about the problem with Lianne accepting the kids. They might be able to provide him with some useful advice on how to deal with her. Try as he might, Dawson could not find a way to broach the subject with them.

Before leaving the Palmer's to go back to the house he did learn Lianne's flight schedule for her return. She was to arrive at Kennedy International on Thursday at two o'clock then fly out from there at three and arrive in Washington D.C. at three-forty five. This gave him an idea. When he got back to Georgetown, he got on the computer.

CHAPTER 144

At noon on Thursday Dawson walked down to the Metro stop and rode to Reagan National Airport. He boarded a flight and a short time later landed and walked into Kennedy International Airport. With plenty of time to spare he ate lunch at one of the airport restaurants then walked until he found the departure gate that would be the one where Lianne would come to for her flight to D.C.

It was now two o'clock, time for Lianne's overseas flight to land. By luck there was a bar across from the departure gate. Dawson went in and sat where he could watch for her and ordered a drink. He had bought a bouquet of flowers and planned to surprise her. While sipping the whiskey sour, Dawson thought of another time he did this same thing. He had slipped on the same flight she was on, surprised her and proposed to her. Smiling to himself, he took a sip and thought of better days.

At two-thirty he looked up and saw Lianne walking toward the gate. To his chagrin she was with a man. He had his arm around her shoulders. Dawson did not recognize him. He was tall, wearing a light-blue, long-sleeved oxford cloth shirt and a red-striped regimental tie. He had a blue sport coat slung over his shoulder. He was talking and laughing with Lianne as if they were the best of friends. She laughed and hugged him as they stood in front of the departure gate agent's counter.

Lianne checked in with the agent then the two walked over and sat down beside each other, still talking and laughing.

Dawson felt as if his entire being was suddenly devoid of air. He struggled to catch his breath.

"Sir, are you okay?" asked the barkeep.

He nodded. "Yeah, sure," gesturing as he sucked in air. He then turned so the man could not see the agony on his face.

It seemed an eternity before the boarding call for the D.C. flight was made. Dawson sat there on the bar stool unable to fathom seeing Lianne and the man together.

The man finally stood and pulled Lianne into his arms. They embraced warmly. He gave her a friendly kiss. To Dawson's surprise he lifted her up and spun her around, her squealing and laughing. He put her down, kissed her again then Lianne headed for the jet way, smiling and waving back at him. Just before disappearing from view she blew his a kiss. The man then headed off along the concourse and out of Dawson's field of vision.

Stunned beyond reason, he just sat there in a stoic state of disbelief. The last call was made to board the D.C. flight. A few minutes later he could see the jet way rolled back and the jet being backed away from the gate. Slowly, he got off the bar stool and walked out of the lounge, dropping the bouquet of flowers in a trash receptacle as he passed by it.

He walked around for a time then went to the airline ticket counter and told them he had missed his flight. They put him on the next flight that left an hour later. On the flight to D.C. he decided he would not go to Lianne's but would catch the next available flight back to Atlanta and home. There was no need to go to Lianne's.

Visions of the encounter with Amydee and her lover when he was at Walter Reed rambled through his brain. His heart was stricken and he fought to maintain his composure while sitting between two strangers on his flight.

When he got off the plane at National airport, Dawson walked aimlessly for a time. He was not worried about running into Lianne. Her flight had landed well over an hour ago and she would surely be home by now.

He eventually ended up at the Delta ticket counter and purchased a ticket to Tanner via Atlanta. It would be three hours before his flight left so he wandered around awhile, had a drink, then found his departure gate and sat down for the long wait.

Sitting near the large expansive windows looking out over the tarmac, Dawson watched the big jets rolling in and out of the gates heading for destinations unknown. He sat away from everyone thankful for the little space of solitude. He was in no mood to be around anyone. From time to time tears pooled in his eyes and he quickly wiped them away. His heart seemed to break over and over again.

Resting his elbows on his knees, Dawson propped his head in his hands and stared down at the floor. He wished he were anywhere but where he was at that moment. In the midst of his agony he felt a tiny bit of relief in now he would not have to decide between Lianne and the children. She had done that for him. He would go home now and spend his life being the best father that he could to Michael and Sara. But, having to do it alone had little appeal to him at the moment.

Tears blurred his eyes and tried to blink them away. When he vision began to clear he saw a little set of pretty feet encased in a pair of sandals. He stared blankly at the pink of the polished toenails as recognition slowly pulled his brain back into the moment. Dawson looked up and into the face of Lianne.

The two looked at each other, time seemed to stand still. Here expression was unreadable but her eyes were full of tears. They continued to stare at each other for a long while. Finally, Lianne reached out and cupped his chin.

"Let's go home Dawson."

He looked at her blankly, his brain misfiring.

"I have a plane to catch."

"There will be others. Come on. Let's go home."

As if a zombie, he let her lead him out and into a taxi. They rode in silence to the house, Lianne holding his hand. She led him in the house to the den and had him sit down. She sat down across from him and took a deep breath.

"I can explain," she said.

"What is there to explain?" he questioned.

CHAPTER 145

Lianne slid out of her seat and dropped to her knees in front of Dawson. She took his hands and looked up at him.

"When I got home I found that the house had been cleaned and stocked and decorated with fresh flowers. I thought Mom and Dad had done it. I called Mom and she told me about you having dinner with them last night. I called Tanner and got no answer at the house, or your cell. I called the store and Paul said you were supposed to be here. I looked around and found your reservation sheet for the flight to New York. It was then I realized that you must have been there and saw me, didn't you?"

"Yes. I saw you," he answered, his lips quivering.

Lianne began to smile even though there were tears in her eyes.

"Oh Dawson, I can just imagine what it looked like to you when you saw me with Harold."

She shook her head and smiled again.

"Harold is my favorite uncle. He lives in London. We happened to be on the same flight to the states. He's come home for a visit. That is the truth Dawson. It is not at all what you think. Please believe me."

Dawson stared at her, not knowing what to think. Lianne stood up and put her arms around him and kissed him. He reflexively kissed her back but without any real feelings. She took him by the hand and led him upstairs. The next few hours were roller coaster of emotions. They loved, they cried, they talked in circles. Lianne was punch drunk from jetlag and too many time zone changes. She fell asleep in his arms from exhaustion, both mentally and physically.

It was near noon on Friday before she half came alive. She and Dawson walked to a café for lunch and then spent a while in the hot tub. They made love. She fell asleep again and did not wake up until Saturday morning.

"I am sorry I have been so out of it Dawson. The trip back took a lot out of me."

"I understand. I'm just happy to be near you."

They had just finished breakfast and were sitting in the den watching the news. Lianne switched the television off and turned her attention to Dawson.

"Okay. Time to talk. I want you to tell me from the beginning about finding those two children and what all you have done with them so far."

And so he did. He told her all about finding them, Kay getting the adoption papers for him, bringing them home and their life now with him. Though she had not asked, he showed her pictures of Michael and Sara. He also expressed as best he could his love for them and that he wanted Lianne to fall in love with them too.

"They are wonderful kids. They need a mother. They need you."

There was a moment of silence as Lianne collected her thoughts and began to talk. She explained how she had felt left out and upset with what he had done. She did understand the urgency of the situation but never the less was still unhappy about it. She told him that she felt betrayed which greatly confused him.

When all was said and done, Dawson was left not knowing where he stood with Lianne. On Sunday he flew back to Tanner. Lianne had promised to come later in the week and meet the children and see how things went.

Before leaving for the airport he tried to talk to Lianne but the differences just seemed to get more muddled. On the flight home Dawson steeled himself to hold his head up and be the best father to the kids with or without Lianne. He would not let the outcome with Lianne deter his dedication to Michael and Sara.

Crucita and the kids were waiting for him at the airport. Sara ran and jumped up into his arms and kissed him several times. Michael then hugged him and told him how much he had missed him.

That evening after dinner Dawson and Crucita talked while Michael and Sara took their baths. He talked of Lianne's indecision and that he had no idea what would happen. Crucita then helped him put the kids to bed then he walked her out to her car. She put her arms around him and they held on to each other.

"It will be all right Dawson. You will get through this. You will be a stronger and better person for it too."

"I just don't know what to think or feel right now Crucita. I will be glad when it's over one way or the other. I don't like hanging on the fence like this."

They said goodnight and Crucita drive away. Dawson went back in and sat playing with Max and Sonora while watching television. He was tired, in more ways than one. He was more than ready to come down off of the emotional tidal wave and get on with his life. He needed to do it, especially for the sake of the children, for they needed him and depended on him.

Before going to bed he checked in on them and gently kissed each sleepy child then went to bed. Tomorrow he would do better, he promised to himself.

CHAPTER 146

Monday morning and the regular weekly routine began. Crucita had breakfast ready when he got up and dressed. Everyone ate, and then the kids headed out for the bus. Dawson went in to work at the store and Crucita off to classes.

The day at the store went well. A new selection of cold weather gear and clothing came in. Dawson helped tag it and put it out for sales. Then came a large shipment of boots. After lunch he and Amber put them out.

AT five o'clock he drove home. When he pulled up into the garage, Michael and Sara came running out to meet him. They both had notes from school reminding parents of the PTA meeting for Tuesday night. Michael wanted him to go because his class would be on stage and would sing several songs. Dawson promised that they would attend.

Crucita had dinner ready but did not stay to eat with them. She had plans to meet with a couple of friends and study for an upcoming exam. She kissed everyone goodbye and left.

After they ate, Michael helped Dawson clear the table and load the dishwasher while Sara fed Max and Sonora. They ate in the den where they had begun a ritual of Dawson looking at their school papers that were brought home each day. Michael often had homework but had usually completed it by the time Dawson got home.

At eight o'clock the children took their baths. Dawson helped them pick out their clothes for the next day if Crucita had not already done so. He had started another ritual in which he read to them before they went to bed.

On Tuesday evening after dinner, Dawson and the kids rode to their elementary school for the PTA meeting. Dawson had taken his camera and took several pictures of him on stage. When the meeting ended in the gym, Dawson then went to Sara's classroom and met with her teacher and got an update on her progress, and then he did the same with Michael. Both kids were doing well in spite of still having some minor language difficulties.

Happy with the kids progress, they celebrated by stopping at Sonic's for ice cream. Some of the other children and their parents were doing the same. Dawson met and talked to some of Michael's and Sara's friend's moms and dads.

Michael and Sara were late getting to bed but it had been a grand evening. Dawson felt good when he kissed them both goodnight and went to his bedroom. He started to call Lianne and share his joy for they had not talked since he left D.C. on Sunday. He sat staring at the phone and even picked it up before he changed his mind. It had been too good of an evening and he did not want to spoil the joyful feelings so he went on to bed.

Wednesday was another day of off and running to school and work. AT the store Dawson spent the morning with a merchandise salesman who showed him a new line of outdoor clothing. At noon he met Cali Kinsley for lunch and went over the financial reports for the business. He stayed busy right up until he left for home at five o'clock.

The garage door was already rolled up when he pulled in. Crucita was parked in her usual spot in the yard by the camper. Dawson gathered up the pile of mail he had brought home, and then got out of the truck. When he walked around the front of the truck heading for the kitchen door, he stopped in his tracks. His mouth dropped open and his heart skipped a beat. Lianne was standing there. She and Sara, who almost looked to be as big as Lianne, in her arms. Michael was standing beside them with a big toothy grin.

"Hey Daddy. This is the lady on the television!" gushed Michael.

Dawson nodded but could not speak. Sara slid out of Lianne's arms and jumped into his.

"Daddy, her name is Lianne. She says she wants to be our mommy like you are our daddy. Is that okay?"

"Yes Sara. It's fine with me if it is with you and your brother."

"Michael likes her. He wants to take her to show and tell!"

"He does? Well now, that's a fine idea," he said and kissed Sara on the forehead.

Dawson's lips quivered when he looked into Lianne's eyes.

"Hey," was all he could manage to day.

"Hey yourself." She smiled.

"I'm glad you are here."

"I am too." She paused. "Crucita has dinner on the table. Hungry?"

"I am now."

Dawson put Sara down and she grabbed Lianne's hand and led her into the dining room. Crucita met Dawson on the way to the table and kissed him on the cheek.

"I told you it would work out."

"That you did!"

Dinner was great though Dawson was so overcome with happiness that he had no idea what he had eaten. Toward the end of the meal Lianne announced that she had a month off and planned to spend every moment of it learning to do the "Mommy thing."

Late that night after the kids were asleep, Lianne and Dawson were snuggled in bed and she apologized for her crass behavior.

"I am so very sorry. I was thinking selfishly and not with my heart. Those are absolutely fabulous kids. Mom and Dad are going to really fall in love with their new grandchildren. I'm not sure how to do this but we will work all of this out. We made our marriage work without children so we can surely make it work with them."

"I like the sound of that."

They kissed one another.

"Dawson?"

"Yes?"

"No more trips alone for you."

He laughed.

"Crucita said you would say that."

"This is all too good to be true Dawson. I am a Mom now! I love it. I love to hear Sara call me Mommy."

"I'm very happy to hear that."

There was a soft whoop. Sonora had jumped on the bed. She sidled up to Lianne and nuzzled against her. Sonora rooted back up to her. Laughing, Lianne scooped her up and cradled her.

"This is one strange cat – I mean coati."

She is so ugly she's cute!" said Lianne as she lay against Dawson's shoulder. "You are something else my fine husband. I am so happy I married you!"

"I definitely like the sound of that!"

About the Author

John Evans spent many years as a psychotherapist and college instructor. He has graduate degrees from Troy University, Auburn University, and Calvary Christian College and Seminary. He is the author of a nonfiction work, *In the Shadow of Cotton*, a childhood memoir about coming of age in the 1950s and 1960s in a cotton mill village in the Deep South. He also has a nonfiction Christian guide, *Forgiveness: Seeking and Receiving*, that is an approach of both the biblical and contemporary psychological point of view. His fiction novels are in two series, Shannon and Thunder. Each can be read as a stand alone or in order.

Shannon Series: Thunder Series:

STORMS OF LIFE   *THREE OF HEARTS* (2019 release)

THE PROMISE KEPT

QUIET GRACE

ONCE UPON A MIDNIGHT DESERT

Visit the author at www.johnevans-author.com or FaceBook: John Evans

Made in the USA
San Bernardino, CA
20 December 2018